More praise ,

THE LIBRARY AT MOUNT CHAR

"One of the most original and inventive books I've read in a long time."

—*SF Signal*

"A terrific book, full of dark mystery and genuine beauty."

—Richard Kadrey, *New York Times* bestselling author of *Sandman Slim*

"Hawkins has created something magical here . . . works to tremendous effect."

—*Fredericksburg Free Lance-Star*

"Incredibly original and fresh and just a stunning debut."

—*Fantasy Faction*

"Brilliantly crafted . . . a new voice among the ranks of contemporary fantasy greats."

—*Dread Central*

"Funny, horrifying, and original. The kind of story that keeps yanking you off in ridiculous new directions every time you think you know what's coming next."

—David Wong, *New York Times* bestselling author of *John Dies at the End*

"Flawless . . . an intricately layered, tightly-constructed work that almost demands rereading. Easily one of the best books I've read so far this year."

—*Fantasy Literature*

"Mashes together fantasy and thriller, love story and dark comedy, into a wild trip at once unpredictable and unforgettable."

—Keith Donohue, *New York Times* bestselling author of *The Stolen Child*

"The most genuinely original fantasy I've ever read. Hawkins plays with . . . big ideas and does it with superb invention, deeply affecting characters, and a smashing climax."

> —Nancy Kress, Hugo and Nebula Award–winning author of
> *Beggars in Spain*

"Powerful writing, encompassing characters, and an exceptional story line . . . had me both shocked and laughing out loud on the same page."

> —*Book Riot*

"Funny, bizarre, moving, frightening, and surreal. The most original work I've read in ages."

> —Walter Jon Williams, *New York Times* bestselling author of
> *Destiny's Way*

"A pyrotechnic debut . . . the most terrifyingly psychopathic depiction of a family of gods and their abusive father since Genesis."

> —Charles Stross, Hugo and Locus Award–winning
> author of *Accelerando*

THE LIBRARY AT
MOUNT CHAR

THE LIBRARY AT
MOUNT CHAR

SCOTT HAWKINS

B \ D \ W \ Y
BROADWAY BOOKS
NEW YORK

Copyright © 2015 by Scott Hawkins

All rights reserved.
Published in the United States by Broadway Books,
an imprint of the Crown Publishing Group,
a division of Penguin Random House LLC, New York.
www.crownpublishing.com

Broadway Books and its logo, B \ D \ W \ Y, are
trademarks of Penguin Random House LLC.

Originally published in hardcover in the United States by Crown
Publishers, an imprint of the Crown Publishing Group, a division
of Penguin Random House LLC, New York, in 2015.

Library of Congress Cataloging-in-Publication Data is available upon request.

ISBN 978-0-553-41862-0
eBook ISBN 978-0-553-41861-3

Printed in the United States of America

Cover design by Christopher Brand
Cover photographs: (burned book) Mark Hooper/Gallery
Stock; (house) Mathias Clamer/Getty Images

18 20 19 17

For my sweet-natured and extremely patient wife,
Heather, with much love and many thanks

PART I

THE LIBRARY AT
GARRISON OAKS

Chapter 1

Sunrise

I

Carolyn, blood-drenched and barefoot, walked alone down the two-lane stretch of blacktop that the Americans called Highway 78. Most of the librarians, Carolyn included, had come to think of this road as the Path of Tacos, so-called in honor of a Mexican joint they snuck out to sometimes. *The guacamole*, she remembered, *is really good*. Her stomach rumbled. Oak leaves, reddish-orange and delightfully crunchy, crackled underfoot as she walked. Her breath puffed white in the predawn air. The obsidian knife she had used to murder Detective Miner lay nestled in the small of her back, sharp and secret.

She was smiling.

Cars were scarce but not unheard-of on this road. Over the course of her night's walk she had seen five of them. The one braking to a halt now, a battered Ford F-250, was the third that had stopped to take a closer look. The driver pulled to the opposite shoulder, gravel crunching, and idled there. When the window came down she smelled chewing tobacco, old grease, and hay. A white-haired man sat behind the wheel. Next to him, a German shepherd eyed her suspiciously from the passenger seat.

Ahhh, crap. She didn't want to hurt them.

"Jesus," he said. "Was there an accident?" His voice was warm with concern—the real kind, not the predator's fake that the last man had tried. She heard this and knew the old man was seeing her as a father might see his daughter. She relaxed a little.

"Nope," she said, eyeing the dog. "Nothing like that. Just a mess at the barn. One of the horses." There was no barn, no horse. But she knew from the smell of the man that he would be sympathetic to animals, and that he would understand their business could be bloody. "Rough delivery, for me and for her." She smiled ruefully and held her hands to frame her torso, the green silk now black and stiff with Detective Miner's blood. "I ruined my dress."

"Try a little club sody," the man said dryly. The dog growled a little. "Hush up, Buddy."

She wasn't clear on what "club sody" was, but she could tell from his tone that this was a joke. *Not the laugh-out-loud sort, the commiserating sort.* She snorted. "I'll do that."

"The horse OK?" Real concern again.

"Yeah, she's fine. The colt, too. Long night, though. Just taking a walk to clear my head."

"Barefoot?"

She shrugged. "They grow 'em tough around here." This part was true.

"You want a lift?"

"Nah. Thanks, though. My Father's place is over that way, not far." That was true too.

"Which, over by the post office?"

"It's in Garrison Oaks."

The old man's eyes went distant for a moment, trying to remember how he knew that name. He thought about it for a while, then gave up. Carolyn might have told him that he could drive by Garrison Oaks four times a day every day for a thousand years and still not remember it, but she didn't.

"Ohhh . . ." the old guy said vaguely. "Right." He glanced at her legs in a way that wasn't particularly fatherly. "Sure you don't want a lift? Buddy don't mind, do ya?" He patted the fat dog in the seat next to him. Buddy only watched, his brown eyes feral and suspicious.

"I'm good. Still clearing my head. Thanks, though." She stretched her face into something like a smile.

"Sure thing."

The old man put his truck into gear and drove on, bathing her in a warm cloud of diesel fumes.

She stood watching until his taillights disappeared around a curve. *That's enough socializing for one night, I think.* She scrambled up the bluff and slipped into the woods. The moon was still up, still full. Americans called this time of year "October" or, sometimes, "Autumn," but the librarians reckoned time by the heavens. Tonight was the seventh moon, which is the moon of black lament. Under its light the shadows of bare branches flashed across her scars.

A mile or so later she came to the hollow tree where she had stashed her robe. She shook the bark out of it and picked it clean as best she could. She saved a scrap of the bloody dress for David and tossed the rest, then wrapped herself in the robe, pulling the hood over her head. She had been fond of the dress—silk felt good—but the rough cotton of the robe comforted her. It was familiar, and all she really cared to know of clothing.

She set out deeper into the forest. The stones under the leaves and pine straw felt right against the soles of her feet, scratching an itch she hadn't known she felt. *Just around the next ridge*, she thought. *Garrison Oaks*. She wanted to burn the whole place to ashes but, at the same time, it would be kind of nice to see it again.

Home.

II

Carolyn and the rest were not born librarians. Once upon a time—it seemed long ago—they had been very American indeed. She remembered that, a little—there was something called *The Bionic Woman* and another something called Reese's Peanut Butter Cups. But one summer day when Carolyn was about eight, Father's enemies moved against him. Father survived, as did Carolyn and a handful of other children. Their parents did not.

She remembered the way Father's voice came to her through black smoke that smelled like melting asphalt, how the deep crater where their houses had been glowed dull orange behind him as he spoke.

"You are Pelapi now," Father said. "It is an old word. It means something like 'librarian' and something like 'pupil.' I will take you into my house. I will raise you in the old ways, as I myself was raised. I will teach you the things I have learned."

He did not ask what they wanted.

Carolyn, not ungrateful, did her best at first. Her mom and dad were gone, gone. She understood that. Father was all that she had now, and at first it seemed that he didn't ask so much. Father's home was different, though. Instead of candy and television there were shadows and ancient books, handwritten on thick parchment. They came to understand that Father had lived for a very long time. More, over the course of this long life, he had mastered the crafting of wonders. He could call down lightning, or stop time. Stones spoke to him by name. The theory and practice of these crafts were organized into twelve catalogs—one for each child, as it happened. All he asked was that they be diligent about their studies.

Carolyn's first clue as to what this actually meant came a few weeks later. She was studying at one of the lamplit kiosks scattered here and there around the jade floor of the Library. Margaret, then aged about nine, sprinted out from the towering, shadowy shelves of the gray catalog. She was shrieking. Blind with terror, she tripped over an end table and skidded to a stop almost at Carolyn's feet. Carolyn motioned her under her desk to hide.

Margaret trembled in the shadows for ten minutes or so. Carolyn hissed questions at her, but she wouldn't speak, perhaps could not. But Margaret's tears were streaked with blood, and when Father pulled her back into the stacks she wet herself. That was answer enough. Carolyn sometimes thought of how the hot ammonia of Margaret's urine blended with the dusty smell of old books, how her screams echoed down the stacks. It was in that moment that she first began to understand.

Carolyn's own catalog was more dull than terrifying. Father assigned her to the study of languages, and for almost a year she waded through her primers faithfully. But the routine bored her. In the first summer of her training, when she was nine years old, she went to Father and stamped her foot. "No more!" she said. "I have read enough books. I know enough words. I want to be outside."

The other children cringed back from the look on Father's face. As promised, he was raising them as he himself had been raised. Most of them—Carolyn included—already had a few scars.

But even though his face clouded, this time he did not hit her. Instead, after a moment, he said, "Oh? Very well."

Father unlocked the front door of the Library and led her out into the sunshine and blue sky for the first time in months. Carolyn was delighted, all the more so when Father walked out of the neighborhood and down to the woods. On the way she saw David, whose catalog was murder and war, swinging a knife around in the field at the end of the road. Michael, who was training to be Father's ambassador to beasts, balanced on a branch in a tree nearby, conferring with a family of squirrels. Carolyn waved at them both. Father stopped at the shore of the small lake behind the neighborhood. Carolyn, fairly quivering with delight, splashed barefoot in the shallows and snatched at tadpoles.

From the shore Father called out the doe Isha, who had recently given birth. Isha and her fawn, called Asha, came as commanded, of course. They began their audience by swearing loyalty to Father with great sincerity and at some length. Carolyn ignored that part. By now she was thoroughly bored with people groveling to Father. Anyway, deer talk was hard.

When the formalities were out of the way Father commanded Isha to instruct Carolyn alongside her own fawn. He was careful to use small words so that Carolyn would understand.

Isha was reluctant at first. Red deer have a dozen words for grace, and none of them applied to Carolyn's human feet, so large and clumsy when seen next to the delicate hooves of Asha and the other fawns. But Isha was loyal to Nobununga, who was Emperor of these forests, and thus loyal in turn to Father. Also she wasn't stupid. She voiced no objection.

All that summer Carolyn studied with the red deer of the valley. It was the last gentle time of her life, and perhaps the happiest as well. Under Isha's instruction she ran with increasing skill through the footpaths of the lower forest, bounded over the fallen moss oak, knelt to nibble sweet clover and sip morning dew. Carolyn's own mom had been dead about a year at that point. Her only friend was banished. Father was many things, none of them gentle. So when, on the first frosty night of the year, Isha called Carolyn over to lie with her and her child for warmth, something broke open inside her. She did not weep or otherwise show weakness—that was not in her nature—but she took Isha into her heart wholly and completely.

Not long after, winter announced itself with a terrible thunderstorm. Carolyn was not afraid of such things, but with each flash of lightning Isha and Asha trembled. The three of them were a family now. They took shelter together beneath a stand of beech, where Carolyn and Isha held Asha between them, cuddling to keep her warm. They lay together all that night. Carolyn felt their slight bodies tremble, felt them jerk with each crack of thunder. She tried to comfort them with caresses, but they flinched at her touch. As the night wore on she searched her memory of Father's lessons for words that might comfort them—"don't worry" would be enough, or "it will be over soon" or "there will be clover in the morning."

But Carolyn had been a poor student. Try as she might, she could find no words.

Shortly before dawn Carolyn felt Isha jerk and drum her hooves against the earth, kicking away the fallen leaves to expose the black loam below. A moment later the rain flowing over Carolyn's body ran warm, and the taste of it was salty in her mouth.

The lightning cracked then, and Carolyn saw David. He was above her, standing on a branch some thirty feet away, grinning. From his left hand dangled the weighted end of a fine silver chain. Not wanting to, Carolyn used the last light of the moon to trace the length of that chain. When lightning flashed again, Carolyn stared into the lifeless eye of Isha, spitted with her fawn at the end of David's spear. Carolyn stretched her hand out to touch the bronze handle protruding from the deer's torso. The metal was warm. It trembled slightly under her fingertips, magnifying the faint, fading vibrations of Isha's gentle heart.

"Father said to watch and listen," David said. "If you had found the words, I was supposed to let them live." He jerked the chain back to himself then, unpinning them. "Father says it's time to come home," he said, coiling the chain with deft, practiced motions. "It's time for your real studies to begin." He disappeared back into the storm.

Carolyn rose and stood alone in the dark, both in that moment and ever after.

III

Now, a quarter century later, Carolyn knelt on all fours behind the base of a fallen pine, peeping through a thick stand of holly. If she angled her head just so, she had an unobstructed view down the hill to the clearing of the bull. It was twenty yards or so wide and mostly empty. The only features of note were the bull itself and the granite cairn of Margaret's grave. The bull, a hollow bronze cast slightly larger than life, stood in the clearing's precise center. It shone mellow and golden in the summer sun.

The clearing was bounded on the near side by the stand of wild cedar in which Carolyn now hid. On the far side, David and Michael stood at the edge of a sheer drop-off cut into the hill to make a little more room for Highway 78. Across the road, twenty feet or so below, the weathered wooden sign marking the entrance to Garrison Oaks hung from a rusty chain. When the breeze caught it right you could hear the creak all the way up here.

Carolyn had snuck in very close indeed, close enough to count the shaggy, twining braids of Michael's blond dreadlocks, close enough to hear the buzz of flies around David's head. David was amusing himself by quizzing Michael about his travels. Seeing this, Carolyn winced. Michael's catalog was animals, and he had learned it perhaps a bit too well. Human speech was difficult for him now, even painful—especially when he was fresh out of the woods. Worse, he lacked guile.

Emily had visited the librarians' dreams the night before, saying that David required them to assemble at the bull "before sundown." That was different from "as soon as possible," a distinction that no one but Michael would overlook. Still, it might be for the best. Jennifer had been stuck alone with David for weeks, the two of them waiting on news of Father. Now, as David tormented Michael, Jennifer—the smallest and slightest of the librarians—worked at tearing down Margaret's grave. She trudged back and forth across the clearing, stooped over from the weight of head-sized chunks of granite, her strawberry-blond hair drenched in sweat. Still, after weeks alone with David, lugging granite in the hot sun was probably a relief.

Mentally, Carolyn sighed. *I suppose I should go down there and help them.* If nothing else, this would encourage David to divide his attentions among three victims rather than two.

But Carolyn did not lack guile. She would listen first.

David and Michael stood looking down over Garrison Oaks. Michael, like his cougars around him, was naked. David wore an Israeli Army flak jacket and a lavender tutu, crusty with blood. The flak jacket was his. The tutu was from the closet of Mrs. McGillicutty's son. This was at least partly Carolyn's fault.

When it became clear that they could not return to the Library, at least not in the near term, Carolyn had explained to the others that they would need to wear American clothes in order to blend in. They nodded, not really understanding, and set about rummaging through Mrs. McGillicutty's closets. David chose the tutu because it was the closest thing he could find to his usual loin cloth. Carolyn thought about explaining why this was not "blending in," then decided against it. She had learned to take her giggles where she could find them.

Her nose wrinkled. The wind smelled of rot. *Is Margaret back as well?* But no, she realized, the rot was David. After a while you didn't notice so much, but she had been away. Flies buzzed around his head in a cloud.

A year or two ago, David took up the practice of squeezing blood from the hearts of his victims into his hair. He was a furry man and any one heart yielded only a few tablespoons, but of course they added up quickly. Over time, the combination of hair and blood hardened into something like a helmet. Once, curious, she asked Peter how strong this would be. Peter, whose catalog included mathematics and engineering, looked up at the ceiling for a moment, thinking. "Pretty strong," he said meditatively. "Clotted blood is harder than you'd think, but it's brittle.

The strands of hair would tend to alleviate that. It's the same principle as rebar in concrete. Hmm." He bent to his pad and scribbled numbers for a moment, then nodded. "Yeah. Pretty strong. It would probably stop a twenty-two. Maybe even a nine-millimeter." For a while David had dripped it into his beard as well, but Father made him chisel this off when it became difficult to turn his head. All that was left was a longish Fu Manchu mustache.

"Where were you?" David demanded, shaking Michael by the shoulders. He spoke in Pelapi, which bore no resemblance at all to English, or any other modern language. "You've been off playing in the woods, haven't you? You finished up weeks ago! Don't lie to me!"

Michael was close to panic—his eyes rolled wildly, and he spoke in fits and starts, conjuring the words with great effort. "I was . . . uh-way."

"Uh-way? Uh-way? You mean *away*? Away where?"

"I was with . . . with . . . the small things. Father *said*. Father said to study the ways of the humble and the small."

"Father wanted him to learn about mice," Jennifer translated, calling over her shoulder, grunting at the weight of her rock. "How they move. Hiding and the like."

"Back to work!" David screamed at her. "You're wasting daylight!"

Jennifer plodded back to the pile and hoisted another rock, groaning under the load. David, six-foot-four and very muscular, tracked this with his eyes. Carolyn thought he smiled slightly. Then, turning back to Michael: "Gah. Mice, of all things." He shook his head. "You know, I wouldn't have thought it possible, but you might be even more useless than Carolyn."

Carolyn, safe in her hiding blind, made a rude gesture.

Jennifer dropped another rock into the underbrush with a dry crash. She straightened up, panting, and wiped her forehead with a trembling hand.

"Carolyn? What? I . . . not know . . . I . . ."

"Stop talking," David said. "So, let me get this straight—while the rest of us have been killing ourselves trying to find Father, you were off playing with a bunch of *mice*?"

"Mice . . . yes. I thought—"

A flat crack rang out across the clearing. Carolyn, who had long experience of David's slaps, winced again. *He leaned into that one.*

"I did not ask what you *thought*," David said. "Animals don't *think*. Isn't that what you want to be, Michael? An animal? Come to that, isn't it what you actually are?"

"As you say," Michael said softly.

David's back was to her, but Carolyn could picture his face clearly. He would be smiling, at least a bit. *If the slap drew blood, perhaps he'll be giving us a look at his dimples as well.*

"Just . . . shut up. You're giving me a headache. Go help Jennifer or something."

One of Michael's cougars rumbled. Michael interrupted it with a low yowl, and it went silent.

Carolyn's eyes narrowed. Behind David, she saw from the grasses on the western edge of the valley that the wind was shifting. In a moment the three of them would be downwind of *her*, rather than vice versa. In her time among the Americans Carolyn had gotten acclimated to the extent that their smells—Marlboro, Chanel, Vidal Sassoon—no longer made her eyes water, but Michael and David had not. With the wind coming from the west she would not stay hidden long.

She took the risk of staring directly at their eyes—Isha had taught her that to do so was to invite notice, but sometimes it was unavoidable. Now she was hoping for them to be distracted by something north of her. Sure enough, after a moment Michael's glance was drawn to a moth fluttering to a landing on the cairn. David and the cougars followed his gaze, as predators will do. Carolyn took advantage of the moment to slip back into the underbrush.

She circled down the hill, south and east. When she was a quarter mile distant she doubled back, this time walking without any particular caution, and announced her arrival by purposefully cracking a dry twig underfoot.

"Ah," David said. "Carolyn. You're louder and clumsier than ever. You'll be a real American soon. I heard you blundering up all the way from the bottom of the hill. Come here."

Carolyn did as she was told.

David peered into her eyes, brushed her cheek gently. His fingers were black with clotted blood. "In Father's absence, each of us must be mindful of security. The burden of caution is upon us all. You do understand?"

"Of cour—"

Still stroking her cheek, he punched her in the solar plexus with his other hand. She had been expecting this—well, this or something like it—but still the air whooshed out of her lungs. She didn't go to her knees, though. *At least there's that*, she thought, savoring the coppery taste of her hate.

David studied her for a moment with his killer's eyes. Seeing no hint of rebellion, he nodded and turned away. "Go help them with the cairn."

She forced herself to draw a deep breath. A moment later the fog around the corners of her vision cleared. She walked over to Margaret's cairn. Dry autumn grasses brushed against her bare legs. A truck roared by on Highway 78, the sound muffled by the trees. "Hello, Jen," she said. "Hello, Michael. How long has she been dead?"

Michael didn't speak, but when he came near he gave her neck an affectionate sniff. She sniffed back, as was polite.

"Hello, Carolyn," Jennifer said.

Jennifer dropped the stone she carried into the underbrush and wiped the sweat from her brow. "She's been down since the last full moon." Her eyes were very bloodshot. "So, that's what? About two weeks now."

Actually, it was closer to four weeks. *She's stoned again*, Carolyn thought, frowning a little. Then, more charitably, *But who could blame her? She's been alone with David*. All she said was, "Wow. That's quite a bit longer than usual. What's she doing?"

Jennifer gave her an odd look. "Looking for Father, of course. What did you think?"

Carolyn shrugged. "You never know." Just as Michael spent most of his time with animals, Margaret was most comfortable with the dead. "Any luck?"

"We'll see shortly," Jennifer said, and looked pointedly at the pile of rock. Carolyn, taking the hint, walked over to the pile and hefted a medium-sized stone. They worked in silence with quick, practiced efficiency. With the three of them at it, it wasn't long before the pile was gone, scattered throughout the surrounding underbrush. The ground beneath it had sunk only a little since the burial. It was still relatively soft. They squatted down on their knees and dug at it with their hands. Six inches down, the smell of Margaret's body was thick. Carolyn, who hadn't done this in some time, stifled a gag. She was careful to make sure David didn't see. When the hole was about two feet deep she touched something squishy. "Got her," she said.

Michael helped brush away the dirt. Margaret was bloated, purple, rotting. The sockets of her eyes boiled with maggots. Jennifer hoisted herself out of the grave and went to gather her things. As soon as Margaret's face and hands were uncovered, Carolyn and Michael wasted no time getting out of the pit.

Jennifer took a little silver pipe out of her bag, lit it with a match, and took a deep hit. Then, with a sigh, she hopped down and began her work. Stoned or not, she was very gifted. A year ago Father had paid her the ultimate compliment, surrendering the white sash of healing to her. She, not Father, was now the master of her catalog. She was the only one of them he had honored in this way.

This time the murder wound was a vertical trench in Margaret's heart, precisely the width and depth of David's knife. Jennifer straddled the corpse and laid her hand over the wound. She held it there for the span of three breaths. Carolyn watched this with interest, noting the stages at which Jennifer said *mind*, *body*, and *spirit* under her breath. Carolyn was careful to give no outward sign of what she was doing. Studying outside your catalog was—well, it wasn't something you wanted to be caught at.

Michael moved to the other side of the clearing, away from the smell, and wrestled with his cougars, smiling. He paid the rest of them no attention. Carolyn sat with her back against one of the bull's bronze legs, close enough to watch as Jennifer worked. When Jennifer took her hand away the wound in Margaret's chest was gone.

Jennifer stood up in the grave. Carolyn guessed this was to get a bit of fresh air rather than for any clinical purpose. The stench was bad enough over where Carolyn was, but in the pit it would be overwhelming. Jennifer took a deep breath, then knelt again. She furrowed her brow, brushed away most of the insects, then knelt and put her warm mouth over Margaret's cold one. She held the embrace for three breaths, then drew back, gagging, and set about rubbing various lotions on Margaret's skin. Interestingly, she applied the lotion in patterns, the glyphs of written Pelapi—first *ambition*, then *perception*, and finally *regret*.

When that was done, Jennifer stood up and scrambled out of the grave. She started toward Carolyn and Michael, but after two steps her eyes widened. She cupped her hand over her mouth, bolted into the underbrush, and retched. When her stomach was empty she walked over to join Carolyn. Her steps were slower and shakier than before. A thin film of sweat glistened on her brow.

"Bad?" Carolyn asked.

By way of answer Jennifer turned her head and spat. She sat down close and laid her head on Carolyn's shoulder for a moment. Then she fished out her little silver pipe—American, a gift from Carolyn—and fired it up again. Marijuana smoke, thick and sweet, filled the clearing. She offered it to Carolyn.

"No thanks."

Jennifer shrugged, then took a second, deeper drag. The coal of the pipe flared in the polished bronze of the bull's belly. "Sometimes I wonder . . ."

"Wonder what?"

"If we should bother. Looking for Father, I mean."

Carolyn drew back. "Are you serious?"

"Yeah, I—" Jennifer sighed. "No. Maybe. I don't know. It's just . . . I wonder. Would it really be that much worse? If we just . . . let it go? Let the Duke, or whoever, take over?"

"If the Duke repairs himself to the point where he can start feeding again, complex life will be history. It wouldn't take long, either. Five years, probably. Maybe ten."

"Yeah, I know." Jennifer fired up her pipe again. "So instead we have Father. The Duke . . . well, at least his way would be painless. Peaceful, even."

Carolyn made a sour face, then smiled. "Had a rough couple of weeks with David, did you?"

"No, that isn't—" Jennifer said. "Well, maybe. It actually *was* a pretty goddamn rough couple of weeks, now that you mention it. And where have you been, anyway? I could have used your help."

Carolyn patted her shoulder. "I'm sorry. Here, give me that." Jennifer passed the pipe. She took a small puff.

"Still, though," Jennifer said. "Doesn't it ever get to you? Serious question."

"What?"

Jennifer waved her arm, a gesture that took in the grave, Garrison Oaks, the bull. "All of it."

Carolyn thought about it for a minute. "No. Not really. Not any-more." She looked at Jennifer's hair and picked a maggot out. It squirmed on the end of her finger. "It used to, but I adjusted." She crushed the mag-got. "You can adjust to almost anything."

"You can, maybe." She took the pipe back. "I sometimes think the two of us are the only ones who are still sane."

It crossed Carolyn's mind to pat Jennifer's shoulder or hug her or something, but she decided against it. The conversation was already more touchy-feely than she was really comfortable with. Instead, by way of changing the subject, she nodded in the direction of the grave. "How long will it be before . . . ?"

"I'm not sure," Jennifer said. "Probably a while. She's never been down this long before." She grimaced and spat again. "Blech."

"Here," Carolyn said. "I brought you something." She rummaged in her plastic shopping bag and pulled out a half-empty bottle of Listerine.

Jennifer took the bottle. "What is it?"

"Put some in your mouth and swish it around. Don't swallow it. After a few seconds spit it out."

Jennifer looked at it, dubious, trying to decide if she were being made fun of.

"Trust me," Carolyn said.

Jennifer hesitated for a moment, then took a sip. Her eyes went wide.

"Swish it around," Carolyn said and demonstrated by puffing out first her left cheek, then her right. Jennifer mimicked her. "Now, spit it out." Jennifer did. "Better?"

"Wow!" Jennifer said. "That's—" She looked over her shoulder at David. He wasn't looking, but she lowered her voice anyway. "That's amazing. It usually takes me hours to get the taste out of my mouth!"

"I know," Carolyn said. "It's an American thing. It's called mouth-wash."

Jennifer ran her fingers over the label for a moment, an expression of childlike wonder on her face. Then, with obvious reluctance, she held the bottle out to Carolyn.

"No," Carolyn said. "Keep it. I got it for you."

Jennifer didn't say anything, but she smiled.

"Are you done?"

Jennifer nodded. "I think so. Margaret is set, at any rate. She's heard the call." She raised her voice. "David? Will there be anything else?"

David's back was to them. He was standing at the edge of the bluff, looking across Highway 78 to the entrance to Garrison Oaks. He waved his hand distractedly.

Jennifer shrugged. "I guess that means I'm done." She turned to Carolyn. "So, what do you think?"

"I'm not sure," Carolyn said. "If Father is out among the Americans, I can't find him. Have you learned anything?"

"Michael says he's not among the beasts, living or dead."

"And the others?"

Jennifer shrugged. "So far it's just us three. They'll be along presently." She stretched out on the grass and rested her head on Carolyn's lap. "Thank you for the—what did you call it?"

"Listerine."

"Lis-ter-ine," Jennifer said. "Thank you." She closed her eyes.

All that afternoon the other librarians filtered in, singly and in pairs. Some carried burdens. Alicia held the black candle, still burning as it had in the golden ruin at the end of time. Rachel and her phantom children whispered among themselves of the futures that would never be. The twins, Peter and Richard, watched intently as the librarians filled out the twelve points of the abbreviated circle, studying some deep order that everyone else was blind to. The sweat on their ebony skin glistened in the firelight.

Finally, just before sunset, Margaret stretched a pale, trembling hand up into the light.

"She's back," Jennifer said to no one in particular.

David walked over to the grave, smiling. He reached down and took Margaret's hand. With his help she rose on shaky legs, dirt raining down around her. David lifted her out of the grave. "Hello, my love!"

She stood before him, no taller than his chest, and tilted her head back, smiling. David dusted off the worst of the dirt, then lifted her by the hips and kissed her, long and deep. Her small feet dangled limp six inches over the black earth. It occurred to Carolyn that she could not think what color garment Margaret had been buried in. It might have been ash-gray, or the bleached-out-flesh tones of a child's doll left too long in the sun. Whatever color it actually was, it had blended well against Margaret herself. *She is barely here anymore. All that's really left of her is the smell.*

Margaret wobbled for a moment, then sat down in the pile of soft earth next to the grave. David tipped her a wink and ran his tongue along his teeth. Margaret giggled. Jennifer gagged again.

David squatted down next to Margaret and ruffled her dusty black hair. "Well?" he called out to Richard and Peter and the rest, "What are you waiting for? Everyone's here now. Take your places."

They were gathered into a rough circle. Carolyn watched David. He eyed the bull, uneasy, and in the end stood so that his back was to it. *Even now, he doesn't like looking at it.* Not that she blamed him.

"Very well," he said. "You have all had your month. Who has answers for me?"

No one spoke.

"Margaret? Where is Father?"

"I do not know," she said. "He is not in the forgotten lands. He does not wander the outer darkness."

"So, he's not dead, then."

"Perhaps not."

"*Perhaps?* What does that mean?"

Margaret was silent for a long moment. "If he died in the Library, it would be different."

"Different how? He wouldn't go to the forgotten lands?"

"No."

"What, then?"

Margaret looked shifty. "I shouldn't say."

David rubbed his temples. "Look, I'm not asking you to talk about your catalog, but . . . he's been gone a long time. We have to consider all possibilities. Just in general terms, what would happen if he *had* died inside the Library? Would he—"

"Don't be *ridiculous*," Carolyn said, not quite shouting. Her face was red. "Father can't be *dead*—not in the Library, and not anywhere bloody else!" The others muttered agreement. "He's . . . he's *Father*."

David's face clouded, but he let it go. "Margaret? What do you think?"

Margaret shrugged, not really interested. "Carolyn is probably right."

"Mmm." He didn't seem convinced. "Rachel? Where is Father?"

"We do not know," she said, spreading her hands out to indicate the silent ranks of ghost children arrayed behind her. "He is in no possible future that we can see."

"Alicia? What about the actual future? Is he there?"

"No." She ran her fingers through her dirty-blond hair, nervous. "I checked all the way to the heat death of normal space. Nothing."

"He's not in any futures and he's not dead. How is that possible?"

Alicia and Rachel looked at each other and shrugged. "It is indeed a riddle," Rachel said. "I cannot account for it."

"That's not much of an answer."

"Perhaps you ask the wrong questions."

"Do I?" David walked over to her, grinning dangerously, jaw muscles jumping. "Do I *really*?"

Rachel went pale. "I didn't mean—"

David let her grovel for a moment, then touched a finger to her lips. "Later." She sank to the ground, trembling visibly in the moonlight.

"Peter, you're meant to be good with all that abstract crap. Figures and so forth. What do you think?"

Peter hesitated. "There are aspects of Father's work that I was never allowed to see—"

"Father kept things from all of us. Answer my question."

"When he disappeared he was working on something called regression completeness," Peter said. "It's the notion that the universe is structured in such a way that no matter how many mysteries you solve, there is always a deeper mystery behind it. Father seemed very—"

"Oh, for fuck's sake. Do you know where Father is or don't you?"

"Not exactly, but if you follow that line of thinking, it might explain—"

"Never mind."

"But—"

"*Stop talking.* Carolyn, get with Peter later and translate whatever he says into something normal people can understand."

"Of course," she said.

"Michael, what about the Far Hill? Was there any sign there?"

The Far Hill was the heaven of the Forest God, where all the clever little beasts went when they died—something like that, at any rate. Carolyn hadn't been aware that it was real. For that matter, she hadn't been certain that the Forest God was real until just now.

"No. Not there." His speech was better now.

"And the Forest God? Is he—"

"The Forest God is sleeping. He has massed no armies against us. Among his pack there were the usual intrigues, but nothing that concerns us directly. I see no reason to think—"

"Think? You? That's almost funny." He turned away. "Emily, what about—"

"There's something else," Michael said. "We are to have a visitor."

David glared at him. "A visitor? Why didn't you tell me earlier?"

"You hit me in the mouth," Michael said. "You told me to be quiet."

David's jaw muscles jumped again. "Now I'm telling you to not be quiet," he said. "Who is coming?"

"Nobununga."

"What? *Here?*"

"He is concerned for Father's safety," Michael said. "He wishes to investigate."

"Oh *fuck,*" said Carolyn. This was startled out of her—she hadn't expected Nobununga quite so soon. But she had the presence of mind to speak softly, and in English. No one noticed.

"When will he arrive?"

Michael's brow furrowed. "He . . . he will arrive, um . . . when he gets here?"

David gritted his teeth. "Do we have any idea when that might be?"

"It will be later."

"Like, when, exactly?" His hand curled into a fist.

"He doesn't understand, David," Jennifer said softly. "He doesn't see time the way people do. Not anymore. Hitting him won't change that."

Michael, panicky now, flitted his eyes from Jennifer to David. "The mice have seen him! He approaches!"

David unclenched his fist. He rubbed his temples. "Never mind," he said. "It doesn't matter. He's even right. Nobununga will arrive when he arrives. All we can do is make him welcome. Peter, Richard—collect the totems." The twins bounced up, scrambling to obey.

"Carolyn—I need you to go back into America. We need an innocent heart. We will offer it to Nobununga when he arrives. Do you think you can handle that?"

"An innocent heart? In America?" She hesitated. "Possibly."

Misunderstanding, he said, "It's easy. Just cut through the ribs." He scissored his fingers through the air. "Like so. If you can't get it out yourself, send for me."

"Yes, David."

"That will be all for tonight. Carolyn, you can go whenever you're ready. The rest of you stay close." He glanced at the bull, uneasy. "Richard, Peter, be quick about it. I want to, um, get back to Mrs. McGillicutty's," he said, winking at Margaret. "Dinner will be ready soon."

Rachel sat down on the ground. Her children crowded around her. In a moment she was entirely hidden behind them. Carolyn wanted to speak with Michael, but he and his cougars had faded into the woods. Jennifer unrolled her sleeping skins and lay back on them with a groan. Margaret drifted into orbit around David.

David rummaged around in his knapsack for a moment. "Here you go, Margaret," he said. "I brought you a gift." He pulled out the severed head of an old man, hoisting him by his long, wispy beard. He swung the head back and forth a couple of times, then tossed it to her.

Margaret caught it with both hands, grunting a bit at the weight. She grinned, delighted. Her teeth were black. "Thank you."

David sat down beside her and brushed the hair out of her eyes. "How long will it be?" he called over his shoulder.

"An hour," Richard said, running his fingers through the bowl of totems—Michael's hair of the Forest God, the black candle, the scrap of Carolyn's dress, stiff with blood, a drop of wax from the black candle. These would be used as nodes of an n-dimensional tracking tool that they were quite sure—well . . . fairly sure, at least—would point them toward Father. Well . . . probably. Carolyn had her doubts.

"No more than that," Peter agreed.

Margaret took the head into her lap and began fussing over it—caressing its cheeks, cooing at it, smoothing its bushy eyebrows. After a moment of her attentions the dead man's eyelids fluttered, then opened.

"Blue eyes!" Margaret exclaimed. "Oh, David, thank you!"

David shrugged.

Carolyn snuck a peek. Perhaps the man's eyes had been blue once, but now mostly what they were was sunken and filmed over. But she recognized him. He had been a minor courtier in one of Father's cabinets and, once, the prime minister of Japan. Normally such a man would be protected. *David must be feeling bold.* The head blinked again and fastened his eyes upon Margaret. His tongue stirred and his lips began to move, though of course without lungs he could make no sound.

"What is he saying?" David asked. After six weeks of banishment, most of them had picked up at least a smattering of American, but Carolyn was the only one who spoke Japanese.

Carolyn leaned in close, her nose wrinkling at the smell. She tilted her head and touched the man's cheeks. "*Moo ichido itte kudasai, Yamada-san.*" The dead man tried again, pleading to her with sightless eyes.

Carolyn sat back and arranged her hands in her lap demurely, left over right, in such a way that the palm of each hand concealed the fingers of the other from view. Her expression was peaceful, even pleasant. She knew that Emily could read her thoughts easily. David, too, could sense thoughts, at least the basic flavor. He knew when someone bore him ill will. In battle he could peer into the minds of his enemies and see their strategies, see the weapons that might be raised against him. Carolyn suspected that he might be able to look deeper if there were a need. But it didn't matter. If Emily or David chose to look into Carolyn's thoughts, they would find only the desire to help.

Of course, *genuine* emotion is the very essence of self. It cannot ever be unfelt, cannot be ignored, cannot even be rechanneled for very long.

But with practice and care, it may be hidden.

"He is asking about Chieko and Kiko-chan," Carolyn said. "I think they are his daughters. He wants to know if they are safe."

"Ah," David said. "Tell him I gutted them for the practice. Their mother as well."

"Is it true?"

David shrugged.

"*Sorera wa anzen desu, Yamada-san. Ima yasumu desu nee,*" Carolyn said, telling him that they were safe, telling him that he could rest now. The dead man allowed his eyes to droop. A single tear trembled on the edge of his left eyelid. Margaret studied it with bright, greedy eyes. When it broke free and ran down Yamada's cheek she dipped her head, birdlike, and licked it up with a single deft flick of her tongue.

The dead man puffed his cheeks and blew them out, the softest, saddest sound Carolyn had ever heard. David and Margaret laughed together.

Carolyn's smile was just the right amount of forced. Perhaps she was overcome with pity for the poor man? Or maybe it was the smell. Again, anyone who bothered to peek in on her thoughts would find only concern for Father and a sincere—if slightly nervous—desire to please David. But her fingertips trembled with the memory of faint, fading vibrations carried down the shaft of a brass spear, and in her heart the hate of them blazed like a black sun.

Chapter 2

Buddhism for Assholes

I

"So," she said, "do you want to break into a house?"

Steve froze for a long moment, his mouth hanging open. Over by the bar he heard a series of clicks in the bowels of the Automated Musical Instruments juke. Somebody had dropped in a penny. He set his Coors back down on the table un-sipped. *What's her name again? Christy? Cathy?*

"Beg pardon?" he said finally. Then it came to him: *Carolyn*. "You're kidding, right?"

She took a drag off her cigarette. The coal flared, casting an orange glow over a half dozen greasy shot glasses and a small pile of chicken bones. "Nope. I'm completely serious."

The AMI juke whirred. A moment later the opening thunder of Benny Goodman's "Sing, Sing, Sing" boomed out across the bar like the war drums of some savage lost tribe. All of a sudden Steve's heart was thudding in his chest.

"OK. Fine. You're not kidding. So, what you're talking about is a pretty serious felony."

She said nothing. She only looked at him.

He scrambled for something clever to say. But what came out was "I'm a plumber."

"You weren't always."

Steve stared at her. That *was* true, but there was no way in the world she could have known it. He'd had nightmares about this sort of conversation. Trying to camouflage his horror, he grabbed the last wing off the plate and dipped it in bleu cheese, but stopped short of actually eating it. The wings there did not mess around. The smell of vinegar and pepper drifted up to him like a warning. "I can't," he said. "I've gotta get home and feed Petey."

"Who?"

"My dog. Petey. He's a cocker sp—"

She shook her head. "That can wait."

Change the subject. "How do you like this place?" he said, grinning and desperate.

"Quite a lot, actually," she said, fingering the magazine Steve had been reading. "What's it called again?"

"Warwick Hall. It used to be an actual speakeasy, back in the twenties. Cath—the lady who runs the place—inherited it from her grandfather, along with some old photos of how it used to look. She's a big jazz fan, so when she retired she restored it and opened it as a private club."

"Right." Carolyn sipped her beer, then looked around at the framed posters—Lonnie Johnson, Roy Eldridge holding his trumpet, an ad for a Theatrical Clam Bake on October 3 and 4, 1920-something. "It's different."

"It is that." Steve shook out a cigarette and offered her the pack. As she took it, he noticed that although the nails of her right hand were unpainted and gnawed away almost to the quick, the ones on her left were long and manicured, lacquered red. *Weird.* He lit their cigarettes off a single match. "I started coming here because it was the only bar around you can still smoke in, but it grew on me."

"Why don't I give you a minute to chew on the idea," Carolyn said. "I know I sprang it on you out of the blue. Where's the ladies' room?"

"No need to think it over. The answer is no. Ladies' is back that way." He jerked a thumb over his shoulder. "I've never been in there, but on the urinals in the men's room you have to pull a brass chain to flush. It took me a minute to figure that out." He paused. "Who are you, exactly?"

"I told you," Carolyn said. "I'm a librarian."

"OK." At first, the way she looked—Christmas sweater, complete with reindeer, over Spandex bicycle shorts, red rubber galoshes with

1980s leg warmers—made him think she was schizophrenic. Now he doubted that was it.

OK, he thought, *not schizophrenic. What, then?* Carolyn wasn't unduly burdened with good grooming, but neither was she unattractive. He got the impression that she was also very smart. About an hour and a half earlier she'd sauntered up with a couple of beers, introduced herself, and asked if she could sit down. Steve, a bachelor with no attachments other than his dog, had said sure. They talked for a while. She peppered him with questions and answered his own questions vaguely. All the while she studied him with dark-brown eyes.

Steve had kinda-sorta gathered the impression that she worked at the university, maybe as some sort of linguist? She spoke French to Cath, and surprised another regular, Eddie Hu, by being fluent in Chinese. *Librarian kind of fits too, though.* He imagined her, frizzy-haired, surrounded by teetering stacks of books, muttering into a stained mug of staff lounge coffee as she schemed her burglary. He grinned and shook his head. *No way.* He ordered another pitcher.

The beer beat Carolyn back to the table by a good couple of minutes. Steve poured himself another glass. As he drank, he decided to change his diagnosis from schizophrenic to "doesn't give a fuck about clothes." A lot of people *claimed* not to give a fuck about clothes, but those who actually didn't were rare. *Not entirely unheard-of, though.*

A guy Steve had gone to high school with, Bob-something, spent two years on a South Pacific island as part of some weirdly successful drug-running scheme. When he got back he was rich as hell—*two* Ferraris, for chrissakes—but he would wear any old thing. Bob, he remembered, had once—

"I'm back," she said. "Sorry." She had a pretty smile.

"Hope you're up for another round," he said, nodding at the pitcher.

"Sure."

He poured for her. "If you don't mind me saying so, this is weird."

"How do you mean?"

"The librarians I know are into, like, I dunno, tea and cozy mysteries, not breaking and entering."

"Yeah, well. This is a different kind of library."

"I'm afraid I'm going to need a bit more in the way of explanation." As soon as the question was out of his mouth he regretted it. *You're not actually considering this, are you?* He took a quick spiritual inventory. *No. I'm not.* He *was* curious though.

"I've got a problem," Carolyn said. "My sister said you might have the sort of experience required to solve it."

"Like, what sort of experience are we talking about?"

"Residential locks—nothing special—and a Lorex alarm."

"That's it?" His mind went out to the toolbox in the back of his truck. He had his plumbing tools, sure—torch, solder, pipe cutter, wrench— but there were other things as well. Wire cutters, crowbar, a multimeter, a small metal ruler that he could use to—*No.* He clamped down on the thought, but it was too late. Something inside him had come awake and was beginning to stir.

"That's it," she said. "Easy-peasy."

"Who's your sister?"

"Her name's Rachel. You wouldn't know her."

He thought about it. "You're right. I don't recall meeting anyone by that name." She certainly wasn't part of the small—*very* small—circle of people who knew about his former career. "So, how does this Rachel person know so much about me?"

"I'm honestly not clear on it myself. But she's very good at finding things out."

"And what, exactly, did she find out about me?"

Carolyn lit another cigarette and blew twin columns of smoke out of her nostrils. "She said you've got a knack for mechanical things and an outlaw streak. And that you've committed over a hundred burglaries. A hundred and twelve, I think she said."

That was true, if almost ten years out of date. Suddenly his stomach was in knots. The things he had done and, worse, the things he *hadn't* done back then were always circling, never far from his thoughts. At her words they landed, tore into him. "I'd like you to go now," he said quietly. "Please."

He wanted to read *Sports Illustrated*. He wanted to think about the Colts' offensive line, not about how he could bump through a residential Kwikset in thirty seconds even *without* proper tools. He wanted to—

"Relax. This could be very good for you." She slid something across the floor to him. He peeked under the table and saw a blue duffel bag. "Look inside."

He picked the bag up by the handle. Already half suspecting what he might find, he unzipped it and peeked inside. Cash. Lots of it. Mostly fifties and hundreds.

Steve set the bag down and pushed it back across the floor. "How much is in there?"

"Three hundred and twenty-seven thousand dollars." She stubbed out her cigarette. "-ish."

"That's an odd amount."

"I'm an odd person."

Steve sighed. "You have my attention."

"Then you'll do it?"

"No. Absolutely not." *The Buddhist undertakes to refrain from taking that which is not given.* He paused, grimaced. The previous year he had declared $58,000 on his taxes. His credit card debt was just slightly less than that. "Maybe." He lit another cigarette. "That's a lot of money."

"Is it? I suppose."

"It is to me, anyway. You rich?"

She shrugged. "My Father."

"Ah." *Rich daddy.* That explained some of it, anyway. "How'd you come up with—how much did you say it was?"

"Three hundred and twenty-seven thousand dollars. I went to the bank. Money really isn't a problem for me. Will that be enough? I can get more."

"It should cover it," he said. "I used to know people—qualified people—who would do a job like this for three *hundred* dollars." He waited, not unhopefully, for her to rescind the offer, or maybe ask for an introduction to the qualified people. Instead they stared at each other for a while.

"You're the one I want," she said. "If it's not the money, then what's holding you back?"

He thought of explaining to her how he was trying to do better. He could say, *Sometimes I feel like a new plant, like I just sprouted from the dirt, like I'm trying to stretch up to the sun.* Instead what he said was "I'm trying to figure out what you get out of this. Is it some kind of rich-kid extreme sport? You bored?"

She snorted laughter. "No. I'm the exact opposite of bored."

"What, then?"

"Something was taken from me a number of years ago. Something precious." She gave him a flinty smile. "I mean to have it back."

"I'll need a little more detail. What are we talking about? Diamonds? Jewels?" He hesitated. "Drugs?"

"Nothing like that. More like sentimental value. That's all I can tell you."

"And why me?"

"You come highly recommended."

Steve considered. Over Carolyn's shoulder, on the dance floor, Eddie Hu and Cath were practicing the Charleston. *They're getting pretty good, too.* Steve remembered what it felt like to be good at something. For a time, in some circles, he had been a little bit well-known. *Maybe somebody remembered.* "All right," he said finally. "I can accept that, I guess. Couple more questions, though."

"Shoot."

"You're sure that whatever it is, we'll just be dealing with basic, residential alarms? No safes, no exotic locks, nothing like that?"

"I'm sure."

"How do you know?"

"My sister again."

Steve opened his mouth to wonder about the quality of her information. Then it occurred to him that he couldn't have told you exactly how many jobs he'd done if you put a gun to his head. *One hundred and twelve sounds about right, though.* So, instead, he said, "Last question. What if whatever it is you're after isn't there?"

"You get the cash anyway." She smiled slightly and leaned in a little closer. "Maybe even a bonus." She cocked an eyebrow, smiled just a little flirtatiously.

Steve considered this. Before she dropped the burglary bombshell he'd been hoping that the conversation might head toward flirty land. But now . . . "Let's keep it simple," he said. "The money should do me just fine. When do you want to go?"

"You'll do it then?" Her legs were strong and tan. When she moved you could see the muscles working under her skin.

"Yeah," he said, already knowing in his heart what a terrible idea it was. "I guess."

"No time like the present."

II

One of the things Steve liked about Warwick Hall was how clean it was. Everything was polished wood, glowing brass, well-sprung leather seats shaped like a friendly invitation for your ass, black-and-white tile laid out on the floor in a way that would have tickled Euclid.

That atmosphere broke as soon as you went out the front door, though. To get back to the modern world you had to climb a couple of flights of greasy concrete steps up to the street. The stairwell was black with ancient dirt, the sort of place stray cats go to die. Drifts of McCrap accumulated in the corners—cigarette butts, fast food bags, a Dasani bottle half full of tobacco spit. Tonight it was chilly, which kept the smell down, but in the summer he held his breath while he climbed.

Carolyn didn't like it either. She had removed her rubber boots in the bar, but put them back on at the threshold, then took them off again at the top of the stairs. Her leg warmers were candy-striped in the many colors of the unfashionable rainbow. *Oh hell, I've got to ask.* "Where did you even get those things, anyway?"

"Hmm?"

He pointed at the galoshes.

"I'm staying with a lady. She had them in her closet." Without the rain boots her feet were bare. The parking lot was crushed gravel. Walking on it didn't seem to bother her.

"That's my truck over there." It was a white work truck, a couple of years old, HODGSON PLUMBING stenciled in red letters on the door. The locks on his equipment cases were Medeco, the best. "Chicks dig it, I know. Try to contain yourself." It had turned cold after the sun went down. His breath puffed white as he spoke.

She tilted her head at him, a quizzical expression on her face.

"Not funny. Never mind." He got in the driver's side. She fumbled at the door handle.

"Is it jammed?"

She gave a small, nervous smile and fumbled harder. He reached across the seat and opened the door from the inside.

"Thanks." She tossed her galoshes and the bag with the $327,000 onto the floorboard, there to languish among the Mountain Dew bottles and empty bags of beef jerky. She curled up on the bench seat, legs folded beneath her, flexible as an eight-year-old.

"I got a spare jacket in the back. You want to borrow it? It's chilly out."

She shook her head. "No, thanks. I'm fine."

Steve cranked the truck. It rumbled to life. Cold air began to pour out of the vents. *Last chance*, he thought. *Last chance to back out of this*. He glanced at the floorboard. In the phlegmy yellow glow of the streetlamp he could see a bundle of money outlined against the canvas of the bag. He grimaced the way you do when you swallow medicine. "You got an address for this place?"

"No."

"Then how am I—"

"Take a left out of the parking lot. Go two miles and—"

He held up a hand. "Not yet."

"I thought we were doing it tonight?"

"We are. But first we've got to talk."

"Ah. OK."

"You ever done this before?"

"Not exactly. No."

"You the high-strung type? Nervous?"

She flashed a small, wry smile. "You know, I'm honestly not sure. If I am, I've got it under control."

"Well, that's good. I don't know what you're expecting, but this isn't going to be like bungee jumping. As a first-timer, you might be a little tense. That's normal. But after the first couple of times, it's actually pretty boring, more like helping a buddy move to a new apartment than anything you'd see in the movies."

She was nodding. "I get that. I—"

He held up a hand. "However. There are a couple of things to keep in mind. You got a cell phone?"

She looked confused for a moment, then shook her head.

"Really?"

"Really. I don't have any kind of phone. Is that a problem?"

"Nope. I was going to have you get rid of it. They can be tracked. It's just that everyone seems to have them these days. You got gloves?"

"No."

"I got a pair you can use. You'll need to put your galoshes back on too—footprints. They're probably not going to give the full *CSI* hair-and-fiber treatment, not for a simple burglary, but they might dust for prints. Other than that, just follow my lead and try not to touch anything you don't have to. You don't have any guns, right?"

"Nope."

"OK, good. Guns are bad news." Aside from not wanting to hurt anyone, Steve was a convicted felon. If he were caught in possession of a gun he'd be looking at five years, minimum.

"Let me get some things." Steve took his own cell phone out of his pocket and removed the SIM card. He knew that cops could put together a pretty accurate map of where a person had been by the cell towers their phone connected to as they moved around. *If I remove the card, that should make it impossible, right?* He wasn't sure. Back when he used to do this, cell phones didn't exist. It crossed his mind to put the phone in one of the equipment lockers in the back of the truck. He figured that would work about like an elevator in terms of insulating the signal. *But you never know. Ah, fuck it,* he thought. *I'll just smash the thing.* Probably that was overkill, but if he was going to do this he was going to do it right.

He was parked in the back corner of the lot—under a light, but away from everybody else, and mostly out of sight. *Old habits die hard.* He smiled a little. The metal locker over the wheel well swung open on well-oiled hinges.

He started pulling out tools. A cordless Makita drill, a couple of screwdrivers, a small crowbar, a five-pound hammer, and a slim jim he had made himself out of sheet steel from Ace Hardware. Just, y'know, for practice. He wrapped his cell phone in a towel and ruined it with two whacks from the hammer. The rest of the stuff he put into his tool belt along with a couple of pairs of leather work gloves, then stuck the tool belt in a knapsack. *Long time since I put a kit together.* He felt a burst of something like nostalgia and squashed it down hard. He *hated* how he missed this so much. He wanted to do better and, mostly, he did. Even after ten years the slap that ended his burglary career, and the accompanying verdict—*You little asshole*—were never far from his thoughts.

But . . . three hundred grand. He sighed. "How far is it?"

"About twenty minutes."

"What kind of place is it? House? Apartment?"

"It's a house."

"Stand-alone? Not a duplex or anything?"

"Yeah, stand-alone. It's in a subdivision, but the neighborhood is mostly empty. The owner works night shift, so we should have all the time we need."

"All right. First thing is, I've got to get us another car."

"Why?"

"Well, among other things, this one has my name on the door."

"Oh. OK."

They drove to the airport. He parked in short-term parking, then slung the knapsack over his shoulder. They walked into the terminal and out the other side, then took a shuttle to long-term parking. He walked down the rows until he found a car with the ticket stub in plain sight. It was a dark-blue Toyota Camry, just about the blandest car on the road. The owner had dropped it off the day before. *Perfect.*

"Stand there, would you?" he said.

Carolyn took her place in front of the wheel well. He hung the crowbar from a belt loop and put the wire cutters in his back pocket. Then he took the long strip of sheet steel out of the knapsack, slid it in between the rubber and the window, and slipped open the lock. He was ready for the car alarm to go off, but it never did. He popped the trunk from inside the car and tossed his knapsack in there. "You coming?"

She walked around and got in on the passenger side. "That was quick," she said. "My sister was right about you."

"That's why they pay me the big bucks." He popped the cover off the steering column with the crowbar and used the screwdriver to pop out the ignition locking bolt. The Toyota started on the first try. Some of the exits from the lot were automated, but the electronic trail that his credit card would leave if he swiped it would be more or less conclusive proof of grand-theft Camry. So instead he replaced the metal cover on the steering column and had cash ready when he got to the window. He needn't have bothered. The lot attendant, a bored-looking black guy in his fifties, was watching TV. He never looked up.

They slipped out into the night.

III

I n his secret heart, Steve fancied that he was a Buddhist.

A couple of years ago, following a whim, he'd picked up a copy of *Buddhism for Dummies* at the bookstore. He kept it under the bed. Now it was dog-eared, the pages stained with the pizza grease and spilled Coke of repeated readings. Sometimes when he couldn't sleep he fantasized about giving up all his worldly belongings and moving to Tibet. He would join a monastery, ideally one about halfway up a mountain. He would shave his head. There would be bamboo, pandas, and tea. He would wear an orange robe. Probably in the afternoon there would be chanting.

Buddhism, he thought, *is a clean religion.* You never heard about how eight people—two of them children—just got blown the fuck up as part of the long-standing conflict between Buddhists and whoever. Buddhists never knocked on your door just when the game was getting good to hand you a tract about what a great guy Prince Siddhartha was. Maybe it was just the fact that he didn't know any Buddhists in real life, but he clung to the hope that they might really be different.

Probably that was bullshit. Probably if you actually went to a Buddhist service you'd find out that they were just as petty and fucked-up as everyone else. Maybe between chants they talked about how so-and-so was wearing last season's robe, or how the incense little Zhang Wei burned the other day was the shitty, cheap stuff because his family was so poor, ha-ha-ha. But this was Virginia and he was a plumber. Why not pretend?

He never went so far as to even fantasize about buying a plane ticket, of course. He wasn't stupid. Pretend for the sake of argument that his vision of the Buddhist ideal had a basis in reality. The fact that he himself was still just a piece of shit with a shaved head and an orange robe was bound to come out sooner or later.

Probably sooner, he thought. The Buddha was pretty clear on the subject of stealing. "If you kill, lie, or steal . . . you dig up your own roots. And if you cannot master yourself, the harm you do turns against you Grievously." The *g* in "Grievously" was capitalized.

And yet, he thought, with the mental equivalent of a sigh, *here I am.*

"—left up there," Carolyn said.

"Say again, please?"

"I said turn left up there, by the red car."

They had been driving about twenty minutes, Carolyn giving directions. "Left here. Right on the big road. Whoops, sorry, turn around." Her voice was low and throaty. It was hypnotic. Also, Steve's sense of direction was crap. Five minutes out from the airport he'd already been utterly lost. They might as well have been in Fiji. Nagoya. The moon. "Are you sure you know where you're going?"

"Oh yes."

"Are we getting close?"

"Another few minutes. Not long."

She was sitting curled up in the passenger seat with her back to the door. Her posture, together with her tight bicycle shorts, showed a lot of leg. He was having trouble not staring at that leg. Every time they drove past a billboard or road sign on her side he'd sneak a peek. She didn't seem to mind or, indeed, notice.

"Turn there," she said.

"Here?"

"No, next one down. Where that—yes." She smiled at him, her eyes feral in the moonlight. "We're close now."

The road ahead was dark. They were well outside the city, edging into farm country. They drove into a mostly empty subdivision. It was big, or designed to be big—it had enough acreage for maybe a hundred houses with postage-stamp-sized yards. There were a few finished ones here and there, a few more poured foundations with weeds sprouting from the cracks. But mostly the lots stood empty.

"Perfect," Steve muttered.

"There." She pointed. "That one."

Steve followed her finger out to a smallish ranch house painted a pale shade of green, hideous even in the dark. The driveway was empty. The only source of light was a lonely-looking streetlamp on the corner.

He rolled past the yard slowly, which reminded him in some non-specific way of a rap video, which made him feel ridiculous. A hundred yards farther down the road curved just enough that the house vanished from sight behind a stand of trees. He parked there and turned to look at Carolyn.

"Last chance," he said. "You're sure you want to do this? If you'll tell me what it is you're after I can—"

Her eyes flared in the moonlight. "No. I have to go with you."

"All righty, then." He snuck another peek at her legs, then got out. The soft thunk of the door shutting sounded satisfactorily covert. He walked around to the back of the car and retrieved the knapsack. "Are you—"

She brushed the back of his neck with her fingertips. He shivered, the little hairs standing up. He turned around to find her very close, close enough that he could smell her. She smelled a bit like she hadn't bathed in . . . well, a while—but it was a *good* kind of hadn't bathed in a while—musky, feminine. His nostrils flared.

"Come on," she said. She had put the galoshes back on over the leg warmers.

When they reached the house, Steve checked inside the mailbox. It was stuffed full, easily a week's worth of junk. *Owner hasn't been home in a while*, he thought. *Perfect.* He pulled out a magazine and angled it in the moonlight until he could read the cover. It read *Police Chief Magazine* in big blue letters, and was addressed to . . . "Detective Marvin Miner." He looked at Carolyn. "This guy's a cop?"

"Looks that way."

"What'd he do to you?"

"Ruined my silk dress."

"How'd he do that?"

"He got blood on it."

"Hmm. Did you try rinsing it with club so—"

"Yeah, it was too far gone. Are you in or not?"

"Well . . . I guess it doesn't make much difference, if we do it right. Anyway, it doesn't look like Detective Miner is home."

"Mmm."

Steve hesitated, then stepped onto the driveway. He walked up to the front door and rang the bell. No response from inside the house.

"Why'd you do that?"

"I wasn't expecting anybody, but if there's a Rottweiler or something it would be good to know about it now."

"Ah. Good thought." Her voice dripped with distaste.

"You don't like dogs?"

She shook her head. "They're dangerous."

Steve gave her a quizzical look. Most nights when he got home his cocker spaniel, Petey, wagged his tail so hard his whole butt wiggled. *Maybe when this is done me and Petey will go to Tibet.* He imagined hiking up the hill to the monastery on a bright spring day, Petey bouncing along beside him, Inner Peace waiting for them at the top of the hill.

Business first. Steve picked up the doormat, looking for a key. Nothing. He slid his finger across the top of the frame. Carolyn looked at him quizzically. "A lot of times people keep spare keys sitting out." The tips of his gloves came away dusty. There was no key. "Oh well," he said. "Have to do this the hard way."

They walked around to the back. Steve took out the crowbar and muscled it in between the door and jamb at the level of the bolt.

He slipped a Phillips and a flathead into his pocket, along with a pair of wire cutters. "If the alarm is set you usually get a full minute to disarm it," he said. "That should be plenty of time. You wait out here, though. I don't want to be tripping over you."

She nodded.

Steve pulled at the crowbar, grunted. The doorjamb bent open an inch or so, enough that the bolt slipped free of its housing. The door popped open into darkness. Warm air rolled out from inside. He waited, but nothing beeped.

"I think we caught a break. The alarm isn't set."

Inside, it was very dark. All the windows were curtained—thick heavy things that the moonlight and that lonely streetlamp couldn't penetrate. The only light in the living room came from an enormous stereo rack, fully as tall as Steve himself. The pale blue LEDs of the receiver shone down over a La-Z-Boy recliner rising up out of a sea of crumpled Busch cans.

"What are you waiting for?" Carolyn asked. The sound of her voice came from in front of him. Steve didn't quite jump, but he was startled. He hadn't heard her move.

"Just giving my eyes a chance to adjust," Steve said. He glanced around. The microwave in the kitchen blinked endless green midnight over a greasy pizza box and a small mountain of crumpled paper towels. "Hmm." He padded into the kitchen and pulled open the fridge, squeezing one eye shut so as not to re-blind himself. The white light of the fridge was startling in the dark. It was mostly empty of food—just a half-empty jar of relish and a plastic squeeze bottle of French's mustard in the door—but there was a box of beer in the back. Steve, thirsty, considered the question this posed for a moment, then shut the door and drank a plastic cup of water from the sink.

"Carolyn? You thirsty?"

She didn't answer.

He poked his head out of the kitchen. "Carolyn?"

"Yes?" She had moved again. Now her voice came from behind him. This time he did jump. He turned to look at her. She was very close.

"Do you want . . ." His voice trailed off.

She moved in closer, ran her fingers down his chest. "Want what?"

"Hmm?"

"You asked me what I *wanted*." Faint emphasis on the last word.

"Oh. Right. Sorry. Lost my train of thought." He paused. "You want me to help you look for . . . whatever it is?"

She said something he didn't understand.

"What was that?"

"Chinese. Sorry. So many languages. Sometimes when I get excited the words blend."

Her touch was electric on his chest. He backed away from it. His eyes had adjusted to the darkness. Where before there had only been vague shapes, he now saw couch and television, chair and table. He walked over to a cabinet next to the television and opened it. "Not bad," he said. The receiver was a German brand, much nicer than the house warranted. "You want a stereo?"

"No."

Steve's own stereo, never particularly high-end, had developed some sort of short. He reached out for this one—*Hey, it's a burglary, right?* His hand hovered over the power cord for a moment . . . and then he pulled back, mentally kicking himself in the ass. *If you kill, lie, or steal . . . you dig up your own roots.* When he looked up, Carolyn was gone. "Hey," he said. "Where'd you go?"

"It's in here," she said. "I found it."

Her voice came from a different, adjoining room. Steve flinched again.

Found what? He followed the sound. She was in the dining room. She sat on a long, formal table, feet dangling, silhouetted against the pale light of the streetlamp. The china cabinet loomed behind her like a black throne.

"Carolyn?"

"Come here," she said. Her legs were slightly parted. He went and stood before her.

"Where is it?"

"Here," she said. She reached out to him, slid her hand around the back of his neck, pulled him in close.

"Wait," Steve said, not resisting much. "What?"

She tilted her head a little, leaned forward, kissed him. Her lips were full, soft. She tasted of salt and copper. For a moment, he let himself go, sank down into the kiss. But it was in his nature that he did not close his eyes.

Behind her, reflected in the glass plate of the china cabinet, something moved.

Steve jerked away, spun around. In the shadows at the corner of the room stood a man. He was holding a long gun.

"Whoa," Steve said, raising his hands. "Wait a minute . . ."

"I'm sorry, Steve," Carolyn said. Somehow she had managed to slip off the table and move to the other side of the room.

"You're under arrest," the man said. He leveled the gun at Steve.

"Yeah," Steve said. He raised his hands slowly. "OK. No problem."

The man stepped forward into the pale light of the streetlamp. His hair stood on end. His eyes rolled wildly in their sockets. *What the hell is wrong with him? Thorazine? Brain damage?*

"You're under arrest," the man said again, raising the gun to his shoulder.

"Right," Steve said. "OK. Should I turn around now, or . . . ?"

"Stop or I'll shoot," the man said. A trickle of drool ran down the side of his mouth.

"*Wait! Wait, I'll—*"

"Do it," Carolyn said.

The man fired. The muzzle flash was huge and bright in the small room, but Steve seemed not to hear the shot at all. When his vision cleared he was on his back, looking up. Behind him he heard a small, tinkling sound. He rolled his eyes toward it, saw a chunk of glass fall out of the china cabinet. It made a pretty sound. *What's that on the plates?* he wondered. *It's all dark and drippy.*

Carolyn leaned into his field of vision. "I'm sorry," she said again.

"I . . . help . . . I gotta get home . . . gotta feed Petey . . . got . . . go . . ."

She reached down, touched his cheek.

Darkness.

IV

When Steve was dead, Carolyn took a moment to get hold of herself. She squeezed her eyes shut and blew out a long breath.

"You're under arrest," Detective Miner said again. He had resumed tottering around. Now he was in the corner, his back to her. He took a step forward and bumped into the wall. She walked over to him, turned him around gently, took the shotgun from him. He surrendered it without protest.

She gave it an expert pump, jacking another round into the chamber, then set it on the dining-room table. She was careful not to look at Steve's body. Then she took Detective Miner by the shoulders and steered him into the archway between the dining room and the kitchen.

"Stand here," she said.

He focused on her for a moment, then rolled his eyes again. "You're under arrest," he said. He didn't move, though.

Carolyn walked around to Steve's right side. She picked up the shotgun and wrapped the dead fingers of his left hand around the pump, holding it in place with her own. She put his right index finger on the trigger. She aimed the gun at Detective Miner.

Miner watched this without much interest. "Stop or I'll shoot."

She pulled the trigger. The blast caught Miner in the chest, obliterating his heart and lungs and sending a good bit of tissue out a fist-sized hole in his back. He dropped to the floor.

She set the gun down and walked over to the light switch. There she took off her right glove and rolled her thumb across the brass plate around the switch, careful not to smear. When she was done she put the glove back on.

Finished now, she took her hands away, leaving the gun in Steve's grip. She turned around and faced him. Even now she did not allow herself to weep. Instead, with infinite gentleness, she reached down and shut his eyes. "*Dui bu chi,*" she said, touching the skin of his cheek. "*U kamakutu nu,*" she said. "*Je suis désolée*" and "*Ek het jou lief*" and "*Lo siento,*" "*Mainū māfa kara dēvō*" and "*Het spijt me*" and "*Je mi líto,*" "*Ik hald fan di*" and "*Ben bunu çȫecektir*" and "*A tahn nagara*" and on and on.

She sat beside Steve's body, rocking back and forth a little, hugging herself. She took his head in her lap. Silver moonlight lit the room full of broken things. Alone, she dispensed with lies. All that night she held him, brushing his hair with her fingertips, speaking softly, saying, "I'm sorry," saying, "forgive me," saying, "I'll make it better" and "I promise it will be OK," over and over and over again in every language that there ever was.

INTERLUDE I

✳

FROM THE EAST, THUNDER

After Isha and Asha were killed, David brought the two deer carcasses back with him to the Library, one over each shoulder. The next morning he skinned them in what had been the driveway of Lisa's parents. Father insisted that Carolyn help. She did this without complaint, delivering the rubbery, bloody pelts of her friends to Lisa for their leather, their intestines to Richard for bow strings. Father himself took the carcasses. That afternoon he spitted them, rubbed them with sugar and cumin, and roasted them in his bronze bull.

Carolyn asked Father not to make a big deal about her homecoming, but he insisted. Everyone who was anyone in Father's court attended. The ambassador of the forgotten lands came bearing the regrets of his mistress. He wore a black robe, smoking hot against the cold of the living world. The last Monstruwaken made an appearance as well, which was a great honor. He lived barricaded in the crown of the black pyramid at the end of time, and rarely manifested in the former world. Some said that he was just an older incarnation of Father himself. Carolyn watched closely for signs of this either way, but saw nothing. There were others as well, two dozen in all—the Duke, Liesel, others she did not yet know. The noble guests laughed and bantered among themselves as they ate. In the firelight the deer grease was shiny on their cheeks.

Carolyn did not eat. Even before all of the guests had arrived, she asked to be excused to her cell. She wished, she said, to catch up with her studies. Father peered at her for a moment, then nodded. A week or so later he tested her, quizzing her about the events of the summer, first in

Mandarin and then in the argot of low dragons. Father said that he was pleased with her progress. Carolyn smiled and thanked him.

Life went on this way for some time.

The day Michael knocked on her door was perhaps a year after the banquet. She would have been about ten years old then. Carolyn's chamber beneath the jade floor of the Library was cool and dark, but out in Garrison Oaks the summer solstice was approaching. They were allowed to go outside in the evenings, but after what had happened the week before, she did not want to. She shuddered. *Not after Rachel.*

Rachel's catalog was concerned with the prediction and manipulation of possible futures. Sometimes this was accomplished via mathematical calculation. Other times she would read portents in the clouds, the waves. But for the most part, Rachel learned of the future by sending out agents. The agents were her children or, rather, their ghosts. In order to make agents of them, Father required that Rachel strangle them in their cribs, usually at about the age of nine months. It was important, Father said, that she do this herself.

Rachel first came to understand this on her twelfth birthday, three weeks previous. Two weeks later she attempted to escape. One night when Father was away she ran for it, darting through the long shadows of summer twilight, bare feet crunching down on lawns grown yellow and brittle in the drought. Thane saw her, of course. He and the other sentinels took her down just short of the subdivision sign. They ripped her to bits as the children watched.

Rachel's right hand, bloody, poked up out of the mass of furry bodies. Two fingers were gone. She grasped for—

There was a sound at Carolyn's door, very soft, like the brush of a paw against wood. For a moment she considered ignoring it. Father was away on some errand. David had begun to look at her in ways that made her uncomfortable. The cell doors locked from inside as well as out, and if she—

"Carolyn?" It was Michael.

Carolyn smiled. She undid the bolts that barred the door on her side and opened the door a crack. Michael stood in the hallway, naked and sunburned. On his shoulders she saw a fine white crust. *Salt?* He was clutching a scrap of paper. She waved him in, then shut the door behind him and locked it up again.

Her cell was about four paces on a side, lined with bookshelves on every wall. The shelves were filled with Father's texts and Carolyn's notes on them. There were no windows, of course. She might have decorated—it wasn't forbidden, and most of the others had a painting or two—but she didn't. Her desk was the only furniture to speak of. The desk also stood out for being a notch or two above strictly utilitarian—cherry wood, leather top, and some scrollwork. Her sleeping roll was merely comfortable. But the wall shelves were filled to bursting with books, and knee-high stacks teetered here and there across the floor.

"Michael!" She hugged him, unmindful of his nakedness. "It's been ages! Where have you been?"

"In the . . ." His mouth opened and shut a couple of times. No sound came out. After a few seconds of this he waved his hand vaguely behind him.

"The forest?" she suggested.

"No. Not forest." He pantomimed swimming.

"The ocean?"

"Yes. That." Michael smiled at her, grateful for the help. "I learn with—*study* with—Diver Eye." Diver Eye, a sea tortoise, was one of Father's ministers. Loyal and ancient, he had sole charge of the Pacific Ocean, and sole responsibility for guarding against the things in the Sea of Okhotsk. Michael touched Carolyn's cheek with one salty hand. "Missed you."

"I missed you, too. How was the outside world?" Carolyn spent almost all of her time inside the Library itself, with only occasional field trips to test her fluency in a new language.

Michael's face was troubled. "Different. Not like here. The ocean is very deep."

Carolyn thought about this for a moment. There didn't seem to be anything to say to that. "Yes. Yes, it is."

"How is here?"

"Beg pardon?"

"How . . . how *have* . . . it been here?"

"Oh! Well, about the same. Maybe a little worse, lately. Margaret keeps waking everyone up with her screaming. Honestly, I think she's going nuts. It must be all those horrible cobwebby books Father has her read. Lately she's convinced Father's going to murder her soon." Carolyn rolled her eyes. "She's so melodramatic."

"Oh. That is sad. And David?" Michael and David had been good friends, back when they were Americans. They still played together when they could.

"Oh, you know David. Just a big goofball, he *looooves* everybody." Carolyn rolled her eyes. "He's nice enough, but he's always so damn cheerful. It gets old."

"Yes. The wolves have a saying——" Here Michael made wolf noises.

"Um. Yes."

"It means, uh, 'heart too big for the hunt.' David is, maybe, too friendly? Too kind to be a fight?"

"I think the word is *'fighter,'*" she said gently. "But you may be right. Father said something very similar a few weeks back."

"And you?"

"Could be worse." This was true, but she didn't know that yet. She thought she was lying. Then, to change the subject, "What do you have there?" She pointed at a scrap of paper he was holding.

Michael held it up and looked at it. His brow wrinkled. The paper was covered in writing—cuneiform, she saw. Not Pelapi. "Father says . . ." He waved his hand up and down the paper, then handed it to her.

"Of course." It was fairly common for Father to send one child or another in to her for translations, and Michael could barely remember *Pelapi* words. Most of his education came from the woods and the creatures therein, not books. She took the paper from him and scanned it for a moment. "Shall I read you the whole thing?"

Michael looked pained. "Could you . . ." He made a squishing gesture with his hands and looked at her hopelessly. "I not . . . words are hard, now. For me."

"I know." Her tone was soft. "I'll summarize it for you." He looked blank. "Fewer words. Give me a minute." She skimmed the document with a practiced eye. "This is old," she said. "Well, it's a copy. But it's talking about a battle that happened in the second century, maybe sixty-five thousand years ago." He didn't understand that, either. She tried again. "Long, long ago. Many winters, many lifetimes."

"Oh," he said. "Yes."

"It's about a . . . hmmm. Give me a second." She went to the rear wall and took down an ancient, dusty scroll. She scanned it quickly, looking something up. She nodded. "It's about Father, sort of."

"Father?"

"Well, kind of. It says here that, mmm, originally the dawning didn't go as planned." "The dawning" was what everyone called the battle that marked the end of the third age. Everything after that was considered part of the fourth age, the current one, the age of Father's reign. "The first sunrise worked OK, and the um, Silent Ones—I think it's Silent Ones?—were driven into shadow. But when Father prosecuted the final attack against the Emperor—whoa! it says here that Father was 'cast down and broken.'" She looked at Michael, eyebrows raised.

He gave her a blank look. "I not . . . I *do* not—"

"It means that Father was getting his ass kicked."

"*Father?*" He looked shocked.

She shrugged. "That's what it says here. Anyway, so Father was getting his ass kicked by this Emperor guy." Carolyn had heard of the Emperor before, but beyond the fact that he existed and that he had ruled the third age, not much was known. *He must have been quite a character to go around casting Father down, though.* "Blah, blah . . . smite, smite . . . looking pretty bad for Father . . . and then . . ." Carolyn trailed off.

"What?"

She looked up. "Sorry." She read aloud: "'And then, from the east, thunder. And at the sound of this Ablakha'—that's something they used to call Father—'Ablakha did rise up. And looking to the east, Ablakha did see that the thunder was a voice of a man, and that this man was known to him. This one had been the . . .' Um, I don't know what this word means. 'This man had been the something-or-other of the Emperor, and his trusted confidant. But now this one had seen wisdom, and cast his lot in with Ablakha. And seeing this, Ablakha's . . .' mmm, fury? No, not fury. His warlike heart.

" 'Seeing this, Ablakha's warlike heart was renewed, and he did rise up. So too did the armies of Ablakha that had been rent asunder'—killed, I guess?—'rise up anew.' Blah, blah . . . smite, smite, smite . . . 'and thus did dawn the fourth age of the world, which is the age of Ablakha.' " She handed the paper back to Michael. "Did that make sense?"

He nodded.

"OK, good. So what's all this for, anyway?"

Michael shrugged. "I am to meet this one tomorrow—begin my learning with him."

"Oh." Her heart sank. Michael was the closest thing she had to a friend. She thought about asking how long he would be away, but he wouldn't know. *Well*, she thought, *at least we've got tonight.* In the Library you took your good times where you could find them.

"Name," Michael says. "What was his name?"

"Father?"

"No. The thunder of the east. Him."

Carolyn squinted down at the manuscript in her small hands, already dry and permanently stained with ink.

"Nobununga," she said. "His name was Nobununga."

Chapter 3

The Denial That Shreds

I

On the morning after she murdered Detective Miner for the second time, Carolyn came awake on the floor of Mrs. McGillicutty's living room. It was shortly after dawn. As was her habit, she lay very still at first, eyes closed, careful not to give any sign that she was conscious. Mornings were always hardest for her. As far as she knew, no one—not Father, not David, not even Emily—could see into her sleeping mind, so it was only there that she did her *real* planning. But when she was fresh out of sleep it was difficult to keep the truth of her heart from tangling in the lies of her conscious mind, and her fingertips often trembled.

She sniffed the air in the room, learning what she could that way. Michael was gone. As they agreed, he had left before sunrise. They would meet later at the bronze bull.

Most of the others were still there, still sleeping. Faintly, from the back bedroom, she caught a whiff of sour sweat and fresh blood—David. Mingled with that, the smell of brown earth and rotting meat—Margaret. Alicia was closer, just back from the far future and still smelling of methane. Mrs. McGillicutty was making food in the kitchen—coffee, potatoes frying in garlic, some kind of sauce.

Carolyn opened her eyes the barest crack. This American room still looked alien to her, like a half-remembered dream. In calendar years, Carolyn was something like thirty years old, but calendar years were only part of it. By the time it occurred to her to wonder what her true age was, she could only make the roughest guess. She understood all languages—past and present, human and beast, real and imagined. She could speak most of them as well, though some required special equipment. How many in all? Tens of thousands? Hundreds of thousands? And how long to learn them? Even these days, it still took her most of a week to master a new one. But when she looked in the mirror she saw a young woman. Father had given her things to improve her memory, to help her mind work more quickly. But it was also true that time worked differently in the Library. And Carolyn, more than any of them, had passed her life in there.

So the America that had once been her home now felt exotic. The thing called a "couch," while comfortable enough, was far too tall, much higher than the pillows she was used to. In the corner was a box called a "television" or "teevee" that could show moving pictures, but you couldn't step inside it or touch things. There were no candles, no oil lamps. And so on.

Mrs. McGillicutty was a living woman, an American, who had taken them into her home of her own free will. *Well . . . more or less.* Lisa had had a chat with her, but the effects of that were only temporary. Also, Jennifer gave her a blue powder that made her less curious about their eccentricities. But it was also true that Mrs. McGillicutty, a widow who lived alone, liked having the company.

They had been there about six weeks. By the second night of their banishment from Garrison Oaks and the Library, it became clear that the whatever-it-was keeping them out of Garrison Oaks wasn't going away. Peter and a couple of others had been grumbling about sleeping rough. Everybody was hungry. They might have gone to one of Father's courtiers, but David thought it was unwise. "Until we know who is behind this, we keep to ourselves."

On the horizon, the lights of America glittered.

So they set out en masse, walking east down the westbound lane of Highway 78. A mile or so outside of their valley, they walked up a hill, turned into the first neighborhood they found, and knocked on a door at random. It was just before midnight. Carolyn stood in front. David towered behind her, spear in hand.

Mrs. McGillicutty, a widow whose only son didn't ever call, came to the door in her housecoat.

"Hi!" Carolyn said brightly. "We're foreign exchange students! There's been some sort of mix-up with the program, and we don't have a place to stay! We were wondering if you might put us up for the night?"

Carolyn wore her student robe, a gray-green cotton thing along the lines of a kimono with a hood, tied at the waist with a sash. The others were dressed similarly. They did not look like foreign exchange students.

"Smile," Carolyn said under her breath, in Pelapi. They all did. Mrs. McGillicutty was not reassured.

Oh well, Carolyn thought. *It was worth a shot*. A lot of cultures had a tradition of sheltering strangers. *Evidently not America, though*.

"Er . . . I think there's a Holiday Inn just down the road, there," Mrs. McGillicutty said. "On the left."

"Yeah," Carolyn said. "That probably won't work out." Then, in Pelapi, "Lisa, can you . . . ?"

Lisa stepped forward and touched Mrs. McGillicutty on the cheek. The older woman flinched at first, but when Lisa spoke her face softened. The sounds Lisa made weren't in any language that Carolyn knew, and if there were any sort of grammar or even a pattern to them, she had never noticed it. Whatever it was, it was outside of her catalog. But it worked on the old woman just as it did on all Americans. After a moment she said, "Of course, dear. Won't you please come in?"

They did.

Even under the effects of Lisa's whatever-it-was, Mrs. McGillicutty was cool to them at first. Carolyn could see that she was afraid. She asked a lot of questions, and didn't seem satisfied with Carolyn's answers. Then the subject of food came up.

"You're hungry?" Mrs. McGillicutty said. "Really?"

"Yes. If it isn't too much trouble, anything you have would be—"

"I'll make a lasagna!" She grinned, perhaps for the first time in years. "No, two lasagnas! Growing boys! Won't take but a moment!"

Actually, it was more like a couple of hours, but she also put together some things she called amuse-bouche, which meant "mouth amusement," a term Carolyn rather liked. These were bite-sized snacks of cheese, olives, salami, bread fried in oil and garlic, things like that. She had wine as well. Jennifer's silver pipe made a few rounds. By three a.m., when the lasagna arrived, they were all pleasantly buzzed and laughing, temporarily carefree.

There was only one bad moment. David, done with his olives, went to the counter for more wine. He dipped his finger in the cheese mixture and slurped off a bit of goo. Mrs. McGillicutty slapped his hand.

Everyone froze.

Ah, shit, Carolyn thought. *This was going so well.*

David's face clouded. He towered over the old woman. She tilted her head back and met his eyes. By now she understood that they did not speak English, at least not well. She waggled her finger in his face. David's eyes widened.

Carolyn looked away and braced herself for blood.

Mrs. McGillicutty pointed at the sink. David looked confused. Everyone was confused actually . . . but at least the old woman was still alive.

"Um . . . David?" Richard said after a moment.

David glared at him.

"I think she wants you to turn on the taps? To wash your hands?" He pantomimed doing this.

David thought about this for a moment, then nodded. He walked over to the sink and turned on the water. *Oh no,* Carolyn thought, despairing. *He's going to drown her in it. Boil her. Something.*

But he didn't. Instead, David washed his hands, first letting the clear water rinse off the caked dirt and clotted blood, then giving them a good lather with something called Palmolive. When he was done his hands were shiny and clean halfway to his elbows. He showed them to Mrs. McGillicutty.

"You're a good boy," she said in English. "What's his name, dear?"

"David," Carolyn said. Her lips felt numb. "His name is David."

"You're a good boy, David."

David smiled at her. Then, perhaps the most amazing thing Carolyn ever witnessed happened. David mined the Paleolithic depths of his memory and returned with an English phrase: "Tanks . . . gamma."

Mrs. McGillicutty grinned.

David grinned.

Mrs. McGillicutty presented her cheek.

David, bending almost to the level of his waist, kissed it.

Jennifer looked at her little pipe, blinked, looked back up. "Are you guys seeing this?"

"*Seeing*, yes," Peter said.

Mrs. McGillicutty got a clean spoon and scooped out a bit of the cheese-and-egg mixture. She fed it to David, then used the spoon to wipe a little dribble off his chin. He rubbed his tummy and made "yum" noises.

Carolyn looked around Mrs. McGillicutty's kitchen table. All she saw were wide eyes and slack jaws.

David filled his wineglass and came back to the table. "What?" he said, looking at them. "Oh, for gosh sakes. You guys always act like I'm some kind of ogre."

II

Now, just over a month later, Carolyn rose and tiptoed between sleeping bodies to Mrs. McGillicutty's sanctum sanctorum. Some yellow sauce bubbled gently on the stove next to the ingredients—cream, eggs, butter. Mrs. McGillicutty stood before her encyclopedic spice rack, tapping her cheek with a finger, considering. "I'm out of the fresh ones," she said apologetically, waggling a little plastic lemon.

Carolyn smiled. Mrs. McGillicutty was a gentle soul. All she really wanted out of life was to be feeding someone. *And she's* really *good at it too.* Breakfast turned out to be something called Eggs Benedict. Carolyn, normally indifferent to food, had two helpings. When she could eat no more she waddled off to clean herself up.

Coming out of the bathroom she saw that Peter's eyes were open, watching her. Silently, she held one finger at a particular angle on her chest. This angle corresponded to the height that the sun would be in the sky at around ten a.m.

That was when Peter would meet her and Michael at the bull.

According to Rachel's ghost children, Nobununga would arrive sometime today. He would meet with all of them eventually, but Carolyn had arranged that she, Michael, Peter, and Alicia would have a private word first. Peter nodded silent understanding. Alicia wasn't awake yet, but Peter would pass the word along.

When she got back to the kitchen, Jennifer was at the table. In front of her sat a steaming mug of black coffee.

"Good morning," Jennifer said in Pelapi.

"Good morning. Did you sleep well?" Her smile was warm and genuine but, even though they had their privacy, she did not show Jennifer the sign she had exchanged with Peter. She liked Jennifer well enough, but at the meeting with Nobununga they would discuss matters of life and death. In Carolyn's estimation, Jennifer had drowned in her smoke and her fear a long time ago. *She is of no use.*

Mrs. McGillicutty looked over her shoulder at Carolyn. "Could you ask your friend if she's hungry?"

"She'll have some." Then, to Jennifer, "I hope you're hungry."

Jennifer groaned. "I'm still recovering from dinner. Is it *really* good?"

Carolyn gave her a grave nod. "It's ridiculous. I don't know how she does it."

With real glee, Mrs. McGillicutty stirred a pot of simmering water and cracked an egg into the vortex.

Jennifer sighed. "OK. Fine." She opened up the little leather pouch she kept her drugs in and sighed. It was almost empty. "I don't suppose you thought to—"

"Yeah," Carolyn said. "Matter of fact, I did."

Jennifer grinned. "My hero!"

Carolyn went to her bag and pulled out a foil-wrapped brick about the size of a paperback. She tossed it to Jennifer. "There you go, Smoky."

Jennifer turned the brick over in her hands, eyeing it doubtfully. "What's this?"

"It's called hashish," Carolyn said. "I think you'll like it. It's the same stuff you usually get, but more concentrated or something."

Jennifer unwrapped the brick, sniffed it, pinched off a piece. She crumbled it into her pipe and lit it. A moment later: "Whoa!"

"You like?"

She nodded. Smoke trickled out of her nostrils. She coughed a little, then blew out the smoke with a satisfied sigh. "My hero," she said again. She took another puff, then offered the pipe to Carolyn.

"No, thanks," she said. "Bit early for me."

"Suit yourself." She took one last puff, then stashed the gear in her pouch. They sat in silence for a while, watching Mrs. McGillicutty cook.

"The poor woman," Jennifer said in Pelapi. She was shaking her head.

"How do you mean?"

"She has a heart coal. It's very distinct."

"She has a what?"

Jennifer gave her a quizzical look. "I thought you spoke all languages?"

"I do and I don't," Carolyn said. "I mean, I understand the words you used, but they don't mean a lot to me. I'm guessing it's a technical term? Something . . . from your catalog?" Then, hurriedly, "I'm not asking you to explain!"

Talking about your catalog was the one thing truly and enthusiastically forbidden to them. Father never said why, exactly, but he was *very* serious about it. The general thinking was that he didn't want any one of them growing too powerful, but after what happened to David, no one ever dared ask.

"It's OK," Jennifer said. "The rules are a little different for me. I can talk about medical conditions, about their symptoms, diagnosis, likely outcome, anything a patient might have a legitimate interest in. I just can't go into any kind of technical detail about treatments."

"Oh? I didn't know that." She and Jennifer didn't talk much, hadn't in years. "So it's . . . what? A bad valve, or something?"

"No, no. Nothing physical. 'Heart coal' is just a term for the syndrome."

"Awfully flowery."

Jennifer shrugged. "Father has a poetic streak."

Carolyn stared at her. "If you say so. So, what's wrong with her?"

Jennifer pursed her lips, searching for the right words. "She makes 'brah-neez.'"

"*'Brah-neez?'* You mean brownies?"

"Right!" Jennifer nodded. "That! You *do* understand."

"Er . . . no, Jennifer. I'm sorry. I'm not following you at all."

Jennifer's face fell. "She makes brownies," she said. "She doesn't eat them herself, but she makes them anyway. She does it every few days."

"I still don't . . ."

"Sometimes she sings when she does it," Jennifer said. "That's how I know. It doesn't have to be words. Hearing someone sing or even just hum can tell me everything."

"About what?" Carolyn asked, utterly lost.

"Her pathology," Jennifer said. "The brownies aren't for her. They're for someone she lost a long time ago."

"Her husband?" Mrs. McGillicutty's husband was a couple of years dead.

"No," Jennifer said. "Not him. He spent most of their marriage at work. That was what defined him. And he had other women. Once she tried to talk to him about it and he beat her for it."

"Lovely."

Mrs. McGillicutty bustled in the kitchen, her eyes far away.

"But there was a child once. She doesn't even know it herself, but the brownies are for him."

"What happened?"

"The boy liked getting fucked in the ass," Jennifer said. "This made his father very angry. One day the two of them came home and found him doing it on the couch. It was an older man, one of his father's friends. She wouldn't have minded, not much, but it made the boy's father crazy. He beat the child rather badly, broke his left tibia and the mandible in two places. He was in the hospital for a long time, but the bones eventually healed. The damage to his spirit was catastrophic, though. The boy and his father had been close, when he was younger. The beating broke him. He started taking drugs—amphetamines, mostly, but anything he could get his hands on. He withdrew. He stayed away for days at a time. Then one day he didn't come home. They spoke to him once or twice after that—" Jennifer pointed at the thing on the wall.

"It's called a telephone," Carolyn said. She had gotten Miner to explain about telephones before she killed him the first time.

"Right. That. They spoke twice on the tel-oh-phone, and once there was a note. He was in a place called Denver, then another one called Miami. Then they didn't get any more phone calls. That was ten years ago."

"Where is he?"

Jennifer shook her head. "Dead, probably. No one really knows. At first this was agony for her. Every phone call, every knock on the door ripped open the wound. She lay awake every night for years. Her husband recovered . . . moved on, forgot. He was a man who never felt anything very deeply, just as Mrs. McGillicutty's own father was. But Eunice cannot move on. She lies alone in the dark and waits for her little boy to come home. The waiting is all that she has now."

Carolyn looked at the sad woman bustling about in her kitchen and felt something stir inside herself. It was compassion, though she did not recognize it as such. It was not something she felt often. "Oh," she said softly, "I see."

"She thinks that if her son were to come home now it would be like waking from a dream. She would feel again. But the boy will not come home, and though she will not allow herself to know this, she knows it anyway. And so she makes brownies for the memory of her baby. She can't help herself—faint comfort is better than no comfort at all, you see? Her world is very cold, and this is the thing she warms herself over with."

Jennifer looked at the old woman cooking eggs in the kitchen and smiled sadly. "It is a heart coal."

"We should do something," Carolyn said. Her right index finger trembled, just the tiniest bit. "Rachel could find her son. Even if he's dead, you could—"

Jennifer looked at her, surprised. "That's kind of you, Carolyn." She shook her head. "It wouldn't help, though. It never works out the way you would think. The problem with a heart coal is that the memory *always* diverges from the actual thing. She remembers an idealized version of her son. She's forgotten that he was selfish, that he enjoyed giving little offenses. It wasn't really an accident that they saw him and the other man fucking on the couch. If he came back now it wouldn't help. He would be gone again soon enough, only this time she would no longer have the comfort of the illusion. Probably that would destroy her. She isn't very strong."

"What then? Is there anything that can be done?"

Jennifer shook her head. "No. Not for this. She will either find a way to let the boy go, or she will die of the memory."

"I see." After that they sat in silence. Jennifer drank her coffee and asked for seconds. Carolyn sipped her lemon soda.

The others were waking up, drifting in. Carolyn translated breakfast orders between them and Mrs. McGillicutty, relayed thanks, helped wash things when it seemed appropriate. Then she announced that she was going to go for a walk and slipped into the woods heading west, toward the bull.

As Carolyn walked, she felt the coal of her own heart acutely. She wondered if she had ever hummed or sung around Jennifer. Certainly she wouldn't have done so in the last ten years, not since the plan began to come together, but before that she just couldn't remember. *If Jennifer knew, she gave no sign, but* . . . She turned it over in her mind for a little while, then put the question aside. Jennifer might know, or she might suspect. Or she might not. It didn't matter.

It was far too late to turn back now.

III

An hour later she stood on the ridge of the clearing, overlooking Highway 78. On the far side of the road down below, the weathered wooden Garrison Oaks sign creaked in the wind. It was ostentatious, in the way of real-estate signs, but now the raised wooden letters were silvery and cracked with age. *Perfect, really.* Among his other skills, Father was very good at camouflage.

She was a bit early, so she stopped there to collect her thoughts. The bronze bull loomed behind her, shiny clean and horrible, not quite out of sight behind the trees. That was where they were to meet, but she didn't want to be near it for any longer than she had to.

She was thinking about Nobununga. It was crucial that this informal meeting go well, and she was trying to think of things she might do to ingratiate herself with their noble guest. Ideally, she would have liked to have brought along Steve's heart—currently marinating in a Ziploc bag in Mrs. McGillicutty's vegetable crisper—but of course that would tip David off that things were taking place behind his back.

Beyond that, she couldn't think of much. She and Nobununga had never met, and she didn't know much about him other than what she'd heard from Michael. He apparently had an appetite for raw meat, as did many of Father's ministers. There was the bit about "thunder of the east," of course, but that was a long time ago. A very long time, actually. Unlike most of Father's early allies, Nobununga had never fallen from favor, never been stripped of his rank. *He will be loyal, then. Unshakably so.* Of course, there was more to it than that. Supposedly he and Father were friends as well, which was strange to think of. But Michael loved him without reservation, so probably he was a decent sort. And he was reputed to be clever. *Possibly we can—*

Far behind her, from deep in the forest, came the sound of cracking wood.

Carolyn tilted her head, suddenly alert. *That sounded big.* She remembered enough from her time with Isha and Asha to be certain that this was not a falling tree. *No. That was a branch cracking.* Cracking under the foot of something very large indeed, by the sound. *Barry O'Shea, maybe? Surely it's too soon for—*

She twisted on the rock to get a better angle, then let her eyes unfocus. She put all of herself into the act of listening. On the road below a car passed by, pleasantly distant. Not far off a whippoorwill called out something that she couldn't quite understand at the moment. It sounded urgent. *Michael would know.*

Crack.

This time it was closer.

She hopped down off the boulder, suddenly wary. Isha and Asha had lived in fear of bears. She had never seen one, but Michael agreed that there were a few around, and a few unnatural creatures as well—pneumovores and the like. *They weren't any danger when Father was nearby, but now . . . time to go, I think.*

Even so, she wasn't especially worried. Anything unnatural would smell the Library on her, and be afraid. About the worst possibility was a hungry bear, and after the week she'd had she couldn't quite manage to be afraid of something like that.

Another crack.

The whippoorwill screamed again. A rabbit darted out of the underbrush, panicky, heading for the bluff.

Whatever it is, it's definitely coming my way.

She sighed and set out toward the bull at a trot. She moved with all the craft Isha had taught her, and more she had learned on her own. She was very quick, and she made absolutely no sound. She still wasn't especially worried. The bull had a presence on several planes other than the physical. Animals sensed this more than humans, and it made them uncomfortable. No natural beast would approach it. If she got within a stone's throw she would be safe.

Off to her side she heard a rustling, slight but unmistakable. *Is that . . . is it* stalking *me?*

Surely not.

Then, a hundred yards away, half-hidden behind a stand of crocus, she saw what was hunting her.

A tiger? *Really? In Virginia?*

Their eyes met. The tiger nudged aside the spiky leaves of a datura stem that had broken up the lines of his face. He allowed her a brief look at the whole of him—orange fur, black stripes, white underbelly—then set out toward her. He trotted, hypnotically graceful, green eyes flicking here and there. His nostrils flared. Three feet of tail swished gently in his wake.

Her instinct was to skid to a stop and run the other way as fast as possible. Instead, she turned *toward* it and sped up a little, involuntarily, as the adrenaline hit. She drew the obsidian knife from its sheath in the small of her back. Now she did scream, but it was a war cry, not panic, a low and brutal human sound.

The tiger's eyes widened ever so slightly.

Then, suddenly, she was gone from its sight. With a single bound she broke left, hidden behind a thick pine. When she could no longer see it—and, more important, *it* could not see *her*—she launched herself at a second, smaller pine. She hit it a good five feet off the ground, wrapped her legs around it, then her arms. She began to shimmy up. The bark was rough against her chest, her belly, her thighs. It crumbled into her eyes as she climbed.

A few seconds later she chanced a look down and was surprised to see that she was almost thirty feet up in the air. The ground below her was empty. For a moment she entertained the thought that she had imagined the whole thing, that it was—

Nope, she thought, *that's a tiger, sure enough.*

It sidled out from behind the thick pine, languid. Even listening closely, she could hear no sound. *It must have been toying with me earlier*, she thought. *Making little sounds, cracking branches, to see what I would do. It must have been—*

The tiger looked up at her and roared. Carolyn fought the urge to wet herself. She moved two more feet up the tree, as high as she dared. The trunk was getting thinner here, and she was concerned that her weight might—

The tiger sat back on its haunches. It lifted one massive paw, inspected it, gave it a lick.

A moment later, Michael stepped into view. "Carolyn?" he said. His speech was stilted, halting, the way it was when he had been conversing with animals. "Why are you in the tree?"

She squeezed her eyes shut, gritted her teeth. "Hello, Michael," she said. "I'm just out for some fresh air and exercise. I thought it might be fun to climb a tree. How are you today?"

"I am well," Michael said, clearly confused by the anger in her voice. "You should come down, Carolyn. You look silly."

"Yes. Yes, I don't doubt that I do." She began to inch her way down the tree.

When her feet touched the earth Michael and the tiger watched her for a moment. Michael nodded at the ground. She looked blankly at him, not understanding. He pointed at the ground again, then patted his belly.

Oh, Carolyn thought. *Right.* She lay on her back and showed her belly to the tiger. He nuzzled her, taking a sniff here and there. When that was done Carolyn stood.

"Our Lord Nobununga honors us with his visit," she said.

Michael translated, surprisingly deep rumbles booming from his small chest.

Then, as an aside to Michael, "You might have told me he was a fucking tiger, Michael."

Michael blinked at her. His expression was blank, guileless. In that moment she could have strangled him and smiled as she did it.

"You didn't know? I thought everyone knew."

IV

With Nobununga's blessing, Carolyn backtracked a little bit to meet Peter and Alicia. She wanted to give them a bit of warning about Nobununga, spare them the sort of fright she'd had. Everyone was on edge already. She intercepted them at the bluff, half a mile or so back, walking together. That was a surprise.

"What did you tell David?" she asked. Peter's catalog was mathematics. Alicia explored the permutations of the future. She could think of no business that might plausibly have required both of them to go out together.

They exchanged a glance.

"We, ah . . ." Peter began, then trailed off. He was blushing.

Alicia took his hand, laced her fingers through his. "We've been taking little walks together every so often for a while now, Carolyn," she said dryly. "No one thought much of it today. I just sort of assumed that you knew?"

"Why do you take—oh! I, ah . . . oh. I see." Carolyn rubbed her forehead. "Sorry. The evidence is mounting that I need to be a bit more observant. But never mind that. Nobununga is here."

"He is? Where?"

Carolyn pointed down at Highway 78. Nobununga was padding down the eastbound lane. A car zipped by in the other direction. The driver,

Carolyn saw, was yawning. Father had done something to make sure the neighborhood never seemed very interesting to Americans, but no one was quite sure what.

"That's *him*?" Alicia said.

"He's a *tiger*?"

"Oh, sorry guys," Carolyn said brightly. "I just sort of assumed that you knew! Yeah, that's him. Quite the specimen, isn't he?"

"I don't think I've ever seen a tiger up close before," Peter said.

"You have," Carolyn said. "Me too, actually. There was one at the feast when I got back from . . . from my summer away." Her summer with Isha and Asha. "That almost had to have been him. But I left early. If we were introduced, I don't remember it."

"Oh, right," Peter said. "I remember now."

"*That's* what—who—Michael has been apprenticing with?" Alicia said. "I thought Nobununga was, you know . . . a guy." She watched him walk for a moment. "Wow. Just . . . wow."

"Not *only* Nobununga, I think," Carolyn said. "Every time I talk to Michael he's back from somewhere different—Africa, China, Australia— but Nobununga always makes the introductions. He's well regarded."

"Fierce-looking fellow, isn't he?"

Carolyn nodded. "Yeah. Really, you have no idea." She paused. Then, almost idly, "I wonder if it might have been him."

"What do you mean?"

Carolyn rubbed her temples. "I hate to admit it, but David has a point. Father has never been away this long." She gave them a long, level look. "It's conceivable that something has happened to him. Something bad. Fatal, even."

"You don't seriously think—"

"I just said 'maybe.'" Her fingertips were trembling again. She pressed them into her palm. "But . . . I think you'll agree that the pool of creatures who might do violence to Father is relatively small. Off the top of my head I can think of only three—David, the Duke, and Nobununga."

"There might be others," Alicia said. "Some of the ones we don't see much. Q-33 North, maybe?" But she was looking at Nobununga, thoughtful.

"Is he the one with the tentacles?"

"No, that's Barry O'Shea. Q-33 North is the sort of iceberg with legs, remember? Up in Norway."

"Oh, right."

"I still think it had to be David," Peter said. "You remember what—"

"I remember," Carolyn said. "On balance, I think I agree with you. It almost *had* to be David. That's why I suggested that we meet—if David has moved against Father, he must have some sort of plan for dealing with Nobununga as well. Nobununga needs to be made aware of that. He could be walking into a trap."

"Nobununga is old," Alicia said. "Some say sixty thousand years. Some say a lot more. I myself am not quite thirty, Carolyn. In his eyes we're barely children. Are you sure he needs advice from us?"

"Father was old too," Carolyn said. "Where is he now?" She waited, but no one had an answer for that. "Come on," she said finally. "We don't want to be late."

They set out toward the bull, following along the edge of the bluff. All three of them watched Nobununga as they walked, fascinated. He had walked down the steps and across the road. He was standing in front of the Garrison Oaks sign. A pickup truck zipped by on Highway 78. The dog in the back gave a couple of bewildered barks, but the driver didn't seem to notice.

Nobununga paced back and forth in front of the sign—once, twice, three times. Peter was enchanted by the sight of him. Alicia had to pull him back from walking off the edge of the bluff.

When they were about two hundred yards away, Nobununga roared, calling out to Michael. Michael scrambled down the steps and across the street to attend his master. They spoke to each other for a time, deep growls that Carolyn couldn't quite hear, and gestures. Then Nobununga rubbed his shoulder against Michael's chest.

Michael flailed about, wild, obviously upset. The tiger let him carry on for a moment, then roared. Michael went silent. He walked back across the road and squatted down on the lowest of the steps to the bull, head in hands, dejected.

I wonder what that was about.

Nobununga turned his back to the highway. He faced Garrison Oaks and set one massive paw on the road that led to the Library.

Slowly and deliberately, he began to walk forward.

"Wait . . . what's he doing?"

"What does it look like?" Alicia said. "He's going to look for Father."

"But," Peter said, "if the . . . whatever-it-is . . ."

"Yes," Carolyn said. "There *is* that." She called out to Michael. "Michael, did you tell him about—"

"Be *quiet*, Carolyn!" Michael screamed. Carolyn was a little alarmed to see that he was crying. "Be *quiet*! He has to *concentrate*!"

Carolyn nodded, more grimly this time. "He is. He's doing it. He's going to look for Father."

The sign at the entrance to the subdivision marked the boundary of the barrier keeping them from the Library. A step or two past the sign and you'd begin to feel the effects—headache, numbness, shortness of breath, sweating, whatever. It was different for everybody—everybody affected by it, at least. Not everyone was. The others held their collective breath, waiting to see whether Nobununga would be immune. Carolyn, fingertips trembling under the weight of her lies, pretended to hold hers as well.

Nobununga walked past the sign slowly, with no obvious symptoms of distress.

"He's really doing it," Alicia said, awed. When she'd tried, she had made it two steps past the sign. There her eyeballs began to bleed. She turned back after that, and though Jennifer had stopped the bleeding, she hadn't really seen well for days.

David made it the farthest—eight steps. Then he turned back, blood streaming out of his ears, eyes, nose. He hadn't screamed—it took a lot to make David scream—but at the farthest point, just before he turned back, he had made a little moan, a suffering animal noise.

With four long strides Nobununga was past the point that had stopped David.

"It doesn't seem to be affecting him," Peter said.

"Possibly not," Carolyn said.

It was about three blocks from the gateway to the entrance to the Library. Nobununga made his way down the first block without showing any signs of distress. He stopped at the first intersection and looked back over his shoulder at Michael.

"This is *reissak ayrial*," the tiger called out. He spoke not in the language of tigers, but in their common language of Pelapi. His voice was a little growly, but perfectly understandable. "I understand this now. It is the will of Ablakha that I hunt the token—and destroy it, if I am able."

"He can talk?" Peter said.

"What's *reissak ayrial*?" said Alicia.

"It means 'the denial that shreds,'" Carolyn said. "Shh! I want to watch."

Nobununga took another step.

"He *is* immune," Alicia said, hope rising in her voice. "I knew it. It looks like we're going to go home after—"

"Look," Carolyn said.

Three steps past the stop sign marking the first intersection, Nobununga paused. He lifted one massive paw. Carolyn, whose vision was very good, saw that he was trembling.

Nobununga turned again to Michael. Now tears of blood dripped from his green eyes, ran down his muzzle.

"No!" Michael screamed, then said something in the language of tigers. He set off running.

"Michael!" Carolyn screamed in her turn, "No!" She watched, transfixed with dread, as Michael sprinted toward Garrison Oaks. She had thought she was ready for what came next, the things she had to do, but . . .

Not Michael. Not yet.

She set off after him. She was quick—Carolyn was quicker than any of them except David—but Michael was far ahead. She scrambled down the steep bluff, almost falling. But by the time she reached the asphalt, Michael was across the road.

"No!"

Michael covered the twenty feet or so between the road and the Garrison Oaks sign too fast for Carolyn to intercept. Momentum carried him another eight feet or so beyond that.

"*No!*"

Then he fell as if he had been shot in the brain. He lay very still.

"Michael!" Carolyn screamed again, real anguish in her voice. She flashed on the day he had come back from the ocean to visit her, his skinny arms golden tan, the salt smell of his skin. A gold BMW bore down on her, coming fast, horn wailing. She shrieked back at it, teeth bared, apelike. The driver swerved onto the shoulder, not quite losing control, then sped off in a spray of gravel. She covered the hundred feet between her and Michael in a matter of seconds, sprinted past the boundary and, precisely as Michael had done—she hoped, anyway—fell flat on her face on the concrete.

But where Michael only lay still, Carolyn rose up.

She lifted herself onto her elbows, her knees. Her nose was broken. Blood streamed down her face from gashes in her nose and cheek. She crawled one step forward, then another. Her motion was spastic, halting, as if her nerves were no longer firing properly. She thought it was a good performance. Her twitches were indistinguishable from the real thing, and had the side benefit of camouflaging the completely genuine tremble in her fingertips.

A third step. Two more and Michael's ankle was in reach.

She grabbed him by the ankle, then vomited up a flood of lemon soda and egg. When she had a good grip she turned and began moving back toward the main road, dragging Michael after her.

Inch by inch, she muscled the two of them to safety. Just outside the iron gate, right where the effects stopped, she flopped onto her belly, exhausted. A moment later Peter and Alicia approached, slow and cautious.

"Are you OK?" Alicia asked.

Carolyn rolled over on her belly and dry heaved a couple of times. Her face was covered in blood. "I will be, I think," she said. "Michael . . . ?"

Michael coughed, gagged.

"Turn him . . . turn him on his side. So he doesn't choke." They did. Michael coughed some more, spat out blood.

"We need to get him to Jennifer," Carolyn said. She wiped blood from her eyes with one trembling finger. "What about Nobununga? Where is—"

Peter, looking off in the distance, was shaking his head. "He made it about a block and a half before he fell over. He's lying on his side. For a while his chest was heaving but"—he glanced down at Carolyn—". . . not anymore."

Carolyn squeezed her eyes shut. "*Ebn el sharmoota!*" she said in Arabic. Then, "Fuck! *Neik! Merde!* Poopy-goddamn-cacka!" She rolled over on her side and pushed herself up to a sitting position. She squinted down the block and saw that Peter was right. *Not so much as a twitch.* She suppressed a chilly little smile. "Even if I could get in that deep, which I don't think I can, he's too heavy for me," she said. "I couldn't move him. Not alone."

Peter was looking at her with something between admiration and horror. "Is there a word that means 'brave' and 'stupid' at the same time?"

"There is," she said, "lots of them." A little irked by Peter's implied jab, she considered explaining how the American word "wussy" might be applied to *him*. She didn't, though. It would have been counterproductive. Instead she crawled over to Michael and checked his pulse with her fingertips. At her touch his eyelids fluttered. "Carolyn? Carolyn, where's—"

He read the answer from her eyes, then moaned. His mouth worked, but nothing came out. His grief was too deep for words.

"Shhh," she said, stroking his hair. "Shhh, Michael. Shhhh." It was all she could think to say.

V

A n hour or so later, it became clear Michael was going to be OK—physically, at any rate. His heart was broken. He wept the guileless, unaffected tears of a small child. Carolyn wanted to get somewhere a little less exposed—being by the road made her nervous—so together they helped Michael climb the steps that led to the clearing of the bull. But instead of making for the bull itself, they went into the woods. That was Michael's true home.

Not far away a stream flowed over a small cliff, burbling pleasantly. Carolyn remembered the spot from her summer with Isha and Asha.

Better still, you couldn't see the neighborhood from there, couldn't see Nobununga's body. The three of them helped Michael to it—he couldn't quite walk under his own power. There they lay him down by the stream to rest.

Perhaps misunderstanding, Peter and Alicia left the two of them alone.

Carolyn and Michael were not lovers. They had tried to be, once, when they were—what?—in their early twenties? That was about a decade ago, though it seemed longer. She thought that night must have been her idea, though she couldn't imagine what she might have been thinking. She had never had any real interest in sex that she could remember, certainly not after the thing with David. Had that one night been some symptom of her desperation, or maybe simple loneliness? She didn't know.

One night when the others were away she seduced him, sort of. Or at least tried to. It ended badly. For reasons she never completely understood, Michael was unable to perform. He wanted to, she could tell that from the way he kissed her, the hungry way he pawed at her once he understood what she was about. But no matter what she did, his penis stayed limp in her hands, and even her mouth. After a long, awkward time of trying Michael pushed her away, very gently. That night they slept by the same fire, but did not touch. She woke in the night and heard him crying out in his sleep. He left before dawn the next day. After that she saw him less and less.

They were still friendly, though, if not precisely close. They bore each other no grudges, and protected each other when they could. Among the Pelapi that counted for a lot. Carolyn held him in her lap all through that autumn afternoon, saying things like "I'm so very sorry" and "I know the two of you were friends." The words felt like ashes in her mouth. She knew every word that had ever been spoken, but she could think of nothing to say that might ease his grief. All she could do was wipe away his tears with the tips of her fingers.

Shortly before sunset, Michael rose. He washed his face in the creek, stood, called out to Peter and Alicia. They came a few minutes later. Both of them were flushed, and Alicia's robe was on inside out.

"Nobununga said something, before he left." Michael was sometimes childlike, but he was not weak. His voice had grown calm, controlled, despite his grief. "You all need to hear this."

"We're so sorry, Michael," Alicia began, and reached out to him.

He waved her away. "All of you know that Nobununga is—was—more than he appears, yes? He is ancient. He is wise. He told me that he understood what was going on here. He said that Father would let no harm come to him. It seems now that he was wrong about that part"—he gestured back at the neighborhood—"but, even so, we would be foolish to discount his other thoughts."

"What did he say?"

"He knew what it was," Michael said. "The thing keeping us out. He has seen such before. They were used in the third age. They are called *reissak ayrial.*"

"Yeah, we heard him say that. What is it?"

"It means 'the denial that shreds,'" Carolyn said.

"Yeah, Carolyn," Peter said. "But what *is* it?"

Carolyn shrugged, thinking of "heart coals." "Poetic license?"

"I know," Alicia said.

"You do?"

"Yeah. I wasn't going to say anything. It's part of my catalog." Alicia's catalog was the far future.

"Well, then don't—" Peter began.

She put her hand on his arm. "It's OK. Really. This *reissak* is happening *today.*"

"What do you know about it?" Carolyn said. "That you can tell us, I mean."

"Well . . ." Alicia considered. "Not much in terms of technical detail. I couldn't make one. But I know it's sort of a perimeter-defense mechanism. Basically, it's a sphere anchored in the plane of regret. There's some sort of token associated with it—"

"Token?" Peter said. "Like what?"

"It could be anything. The token needs to be an actual physical object, but all it really is, is an anchor. The closer you get to the token, the more powerful the effects are."

"That fits," Carolyn said. Her voice was meditative.

"Wait. It gets better. There's also a trigger."

"I don't understand."

"It's something about a person that brings the *reissak ayrial* into focus."

"Like what?"

"The trigger would be something internal—an emotion, an experience, a memory . . ." Alicia shrugged. "Something like that. The people who share it feel the effects of the *reissak ayrial*. For everyone else, it's like it doesn't exist."

Peter considered. "That fits too," he said.

"Who among us would know how to make such a thing?" Carolyn asked. "David?"

"Nooo . . . no. Not David. The *reissak* has defense applications, obviously, but it's not like a spear or something. It's pretty complex."

Carolyn gave her a suspicious look. "You say in the future these things are pretty common. Are they maybe for sale, or . . . something? If you wanted one, how hard would it have been to—"

"It wasn't *me*!" Alicia said. "And no. You have to alter the shape of spacetime locally—space *and* time. It's very customized. You can't just pick one up at the market, even in the future."

Carolyn continued to look at her.

"Come on, Carolyn," Peter said. "We know it's not—"

"Yeah, OK," Carolyn said. "I guess I'm inclined to believe you." When the barrier—the *reissak ayrial*—first came up, they had all tested themselves against it. Alicia came away with massive internal hemorrhaging. It wasn't immediately obvious, but within a day or so she was one big bruise. She stayed that way for weeks. Whatever the trigger was, it worked on her.

"If not David, who, then?" Peter asked.

Alicia gave him a sympathetic look. "I hate to say it, dear, but the likeliest candidate is, well . . . you?"

"*Me?* Alicia, come on, you know that—"

Alicia held up her hand. "*I* know this. Carolyn and Michael may not." She turned to them. "The *reissak* is mostly a mathematical construct." As such it would be part of Peter's catalog. "Sorry, dear."

"Guys, I've never even heard of such a thing," Peter said. "You can either believe me or not, but—"

"It's all right," Carolyn said, holding up a hand. "I remember. I believe you." On the day the *reissak* was first set, the day that Father disappeared, Peter made it two steps beyond the sign and began to smoke. By the time he came back out, his skin was already blistering.

"Who, then?" Peter asked.

"I'm not sure," Carolyn said, "but I have an idea. This trigger you were talking about—is there any way to know what it is?"

"None that I know of. Why?"

"Well," Carolyn said, "it occurs to me that the dead ones still get packages delivered most days. Also, there's always somebody driving in to deliver those big round cheese-bread things that David's fond of."

"Pizza?" Peter said. "I like that too. It's a good point. If the *reissak* worked on Americans, there'd be piles of them dead in the street by now."

"Yeah," Carolyn said. "That crossed my mind as well. You said that the token can be anything, but the field of effect is a sphere. If that's the case, we can just map the outline of the effects and we'll know pretty much where the token is. Right?"

Peter was grinning. "And if we know where it is—"

"We can find someone to *move it*," Alicia finished. She was grinning. "Carolyn, you're a genius! Library, here we come."

"Yeah, well, it's a little early to start celebrating. Among other things, we still need an American. Do you guys know anybody?"

They shook their heads in unison. "That's going to have to be on you, Carolyn. None of us even speaks the language."

"Yeah," she said. "OK. Fair enough. I'll come up with something. Also there are the sentinels to think about."

They plotted together until well after dark. Carolyn pretended to resist at first, but eventually she let them convince her that David would have to be involved as well.

INTERLUDE II

※

UZAN-IYA

I

By the third year of her apprenticeship, Carolyn had mostly forgotten the outside world. Most of the others supplemented their studies with outings, or at least vacations. Michael went to the woods or the ocean. David killed scores of men on every continent. Margaret followed them down to the forgotten lands. Jennifer called some of them back.

Carolyn's studies did not require travel. Native speakers were brought to her when she needed practice, and after the summer with Isha and Asha she no longer cared to take vacations. So her world was only the Library, her studies the only escape. She spent her childhood in a circle of golden lamplight, bounded on all sides by teetering stacks of books; folios; dusty, crumbling parchment. One day when she was about eleven years old—in calendar terms, at least—it occurred to her that she no longer remembered what her actual parents looked like. Time was different in the Library.

She lost track of the exact count of languages she was fluent in at around fifty—trophies were never her thing—but she thought that whatever the count was, it was probably pretty high. One of the more challenging was the language of the Atul, a tribe of the Himalayan steppe that had died out about six thousand years ago. The Atul had been linguistically isolated. Their grammar was nearly impenetrable, and they had some exotic cultural norms. One such was the notion of *uʒan-iya*, which was what they called the moment when an innocent heart first contemplated the act of murder. To the Atul, the crime itself was secondary to this initial corruption. Carolyn found that idea—and its implications—fascinating. She was turning this over in her mind one dry summer afternoon when she realized, with a bit of irritation, that her stomach was rumbling. When had she last eaten? The day before? The day before that?

She went down to the larder, but it was bare. She called out for Peter, whose catalog included the preparation of food. No answer. She walked to the front door and went out into Garrison Oaks.

Jennifer was sitting on the porch, studying. "Hey, Carolyn! Good to see you outside for a change."

"Is there any food?"

Jennifer laughed. "Driven out by hunger? I might have known. Yeah, I think some of the dead ones got a grocery dump last week."

"Which ones?"

"Third house down."

"Thanks. Want me to get you anything?"

"Nah, I'm good. But"—Jennifer looked up and down the street furtively—"you might want to swing by my room tonight."

"Why, what's up?"

"Michael brought this back from his last trip." She held up a little baggie with green leaves in it.

"What is it?"

"It's called marijuana. Supposedly if you smoke it, it makes you feel good. We're going to try it tonight."

Carolyn considered. "Can't. I've got a test tomorrow." The last time she missed a question, Father gave her ten lashes.

"Oh, OK. Next time?"

"Love to." Carolyn paused. "You might ask Margaret, though. I think she could use a little fun." Margaret was no longer screaming herself awake every night, which was a relief, but she'd developed a nervous giggle that was at least as bad.

Jennifer made a sour face. "I'll ask." She didn't sound happy about it.

"What's the problem? You two used to be buddies."

"Margaret *stinks*, Carolyn. And she and I haven't hung out in ages. You really need to get out of your room more."

"Oh." Come to think of it, Margaret actually *had* smelled pretty bad the last couple of times Carolyn had seen her. "Well . . . it's not really her fault."

"No. It's not. But she still stinks."

Carolyn's stomach rumbled, audible to both of them. "I've got to go get something to eat," she said apologetically. "I'll catch up with you later."

She hurried off down the street. The houses of Garrison Oaks belonged to Father now, as did the things that lived in them. Most of the homes had dead ones inside as camouflage. These were what remained of the children's actual parents, and some other neighbors who hadn't been vaporized on Adoption Day. Carolyn wasn't entirely sure how they had been transformed into dead ones, but she had a guess.

For a year or so Father had been murdering Margaret two or three times a week. He did this in various ways. The first time he snuck up behind her with an ax at dinner, startling everyone, not least Margaret herself. After that it was gunshots, poison, hanging, whatever. Sometimes it was a surprise, sometimes not. Another time Father pierced her heart with a stiletto, but only after telling her what he would do, setting the knife before her on a silver tray, and letting her contemplate it for three full days and nights. Carolyn would have supposed that the ax would be the worse of the two, but Margaret seemed to take that one in stride. After a day or so of looking at the knife, though, she started to do that giggle of hers. *And after that, she never really stopped.* Carolyn sighed. *Poor Margaret.*

But Margaret wasn't really the point. When she was dead she'd usually spend a day or two in the forgotten lands practicing whatever lesson was next in her catalog. Then Father would resurrect her. By this point Carolyn had seen enough of the resurrections to gather that they were a two-stage process.

First, Father—or, lately, Jennifer—would heal whatever wound had done it for her in the first place. Then he would call her back into her body. Once, though, he'd taken a break in the middle of all this to go use the bathroom. That time Margaret's healed body had gotten up and wandered around the room, picking up random objects and saying "Oh no" over and over again. She seemed to be not all there.

Carolyn suspected that was where the dead ones came from. They had been *reanimated* but not *resurrected*. They looked fairly normal, at least from a distance. They wandered the green lawns and grocery stores convincingly enough, but in every way that really mattered they were still in the forgotten lands. They could interact with one another and even with Americans—they exchanged casseroles, filled the cars up with gas, ordered pizza, painted the house. They did these things automatically. It was useful and, she supposed, easier than hiring a lawn service. They could also follow orders if it was something they knew how to do already, which could be handy as well. But they could not take instruction, could not learn new things.

Perhaps most important, they served as a security system. Every so often a stranger would stumble into Garrison Oaks and go about knocking on doors—salesmen, lost FedEx drivers, missionaries. For the most part these outsiders noticed nothing terribly out of the ordinary. Once, though, a burglar actually made it into one of the houses. After he saw what was inside he couldn't be allowed to return to the outside world. When he tried to sneak out the window, the dead ones were waiting for him. They fell upon him and tore him to bits. Father did to him whatever he'd done to the others and the erstwhile burglar took his place in one of the houses as someone's cousin Ed. Or whomever.

Carolyn and the other librarians could come and go as they pleased, though. Hungry, she opened the door of the house Jennifer had pointed at and went in. There were three of them inside: a little girl of about eight, a teenage boy, and an adult woman.

"Make me some food," she said to the woman.

Lately she had been focusing on mythical languages. The English felt strange on her tongue. Evidently it sounded as bad as it felt. She had to repeat herself twice before what was left of the woman understood her. Then it nodded and began pulling things from here and there—a can of fish, white stuff from a jar, some sort of green goo that smelled like vinegar.

Carolyn sat down at the table next to the little girl. It was drawing a family: mother, father, two daughters, a dog. The family stood in a park. Something that might have been the sun but wasn't blazed down on them, huge in both the sky and what passed for the little girl's memory. It was far too hot, far too close. As Carolyn watched, the little girl took a yellow crayon and added some flames to the father's back. The red O of his mouth, she suddenly realized, was a scream.

Carolyn stood up fast, the wooden chair scraping across the linoleum. She didn't want to be there anymore. She fled to the family room. There a teenage boy sat slack-jawed in front of a lighted box. *Do they still grow up, or will he be like this always?* She couldn't figure out what he was doing at first, then it came to her. *Television.* She smiled a little. *I remember television.* She sat down on the couch next to the dead boy. He didn't seem to notice. She waved her hand up and down in his field of vision.

He turned his head, looked at her without much interest, and pointed at the television. "It's time for *Transformers.*" A trickle of drool ran out the side of his mouth.

On the screen, giant robots were shooting each other with rays.

A few minutes later the woman drifted in and handed her a plate of food and a red can that said Coke. Carolyn fell on it, ravenous. The soda was sweet, delicious. She drank it too quickly and it burned in her throat. She had forgotten about Coke. The woman watched her eat, a flicker of disquiet crossing her face. "Hello," she said. "You must be . . ." She—it—trailed off. "Are you one of Dennis's friends? Dennis, is this . . ." she said to the boy. She broke off. "You're not Dennis," she—it—said to the boy. "Where is Dennis?"

Carolyn knew what this meant. When Father reanimated the neighbors he had assigned them to houses more or less at random. The boy on the couch was not actually the woman's son. Probably the girl wasn't her daughter. The man she laid down with at night wouldn't be her—

"Dennis?"

Carolyn stood up, grabbed the sandwich, and handed the plate back to the woman. "Thank you."

"You're welcome, dear," she said absently. "Dennis?"

On the television, a robot screamed. Carolyn strode back to the front door and out into the summer sunlight, slamming the door behind her. They would settle down once she was gone.

But when she saw what was waiting for her, she wished she had stayed among the dead. Halfway back to the Library black clouds boiled over the face of the sun. The pressure dropped enough to make her ears pop. The tips of the trees bent nearly double in the sudden wind. Here and there she heard flat wooden cracks as the weaker branches gave way.

Father was home.

II

They all knew from the thunder that he had returned. It was expected that they would meet him at the Library. They trickled in and gathered on the lawn—Michael from the forest, Jennifer from the meadow, and so on—all except Margaret. She was with him already.

"Look," Father said. They all did. Margaret's left arm was badly broken. It hung limp, a spur of bone poking out of her skin. Jennifer moved to help her, but Father waved her away. "Why does she not cry out?" he spoke lightly, as if talking only to the breeze.

No one answered.

"Why does she not cry out?" he asked again. This time his tone was more menacing. "Will no one answer me? Surely one of you must know."

David mumbled something.

"What? I can't hear you."

"I said, '*gahn ayrial*.'"

Carolyn's mind whirled. The words "*gahn ayrial*" meant, in a literal sense, the denial of suffering. The phrase itself was kind of meaningless—suffering existed, just look around you—but the way he pronounced the words suggested that it was the name for a skill set. *Some sort of self-anesthesia?* Carolyn knew that Father knew all sorts of things about that, and about staunching your own wounds, and healing. *But he only teaches that sort of thing to David.* With a kind of slow-boiling horror she realized what all this was about. *If Margaret knows about* gahn ayrial, *then . . .*

"Someone has been reading outside of her catalog."

The young librarians made a sound like dead leaves rustling.

"I don't really blame Margaret," Father said meditatively. "Her studies are often painful. Who could fault her for wanting to alleviate that? No. Not Margaret." He tapped his teeth with a fingernail. "Who, then?"

"Me," David whispered. "It was me."

"You?" Father spoke with mock surprise. "You? Really. Interesting. Tell me, David, why do you think that I did not teach Margaret of *gahn ayrial* myself?"

"I . . . I don't know."

"*Because I did not wish for her to learn it!*" Father thundered. All of them flinched at this—all but David. He was Father's favorite, and knew it. "Still . . . if you have chosen to teach the craft of *gahn ayrial*, then surely you have mastered it. I had no idea you were so far along in your studies. I will admit that I am impressed." He waved his arm, beckoning. "Come with me."

They all followed, afraid not to. Together they trailed Father and David down the main street of the neighborhood, past the houses of the dead, and oh how Carolyn wished then that she had died with them. She had never seen Father so angry. Whatever came next was sure to be very bad. They followed him across the road, and up the rough steps cut into the earth.

There, in the clearing at the top of the hill, they found Father's barbecue grill. Carolyn remembered the thing existed, but had never thought much of it. It was a hollow bronze cast in the shape of a cow or, rather, a bull. It was a bit larger than life-sized, made of yellowish metal about half an inch thick. When Father had been pretending to be an American he kept it in his backyard. Sometimes, at neighborhood picnics or whatever, he would cook in it, "hamburgers," or sometimes pork. *He seemed pretty normal back then.* She vaguely remembered people—maybe even her parents?—commenting on the unusual grill, but it hadn't been a big deal.

Not long after Father took them in he had the grill moved up to the clearing. She never found out why, but there must have been some sort of reason. The grill was phenomenally heavy. The dead ones gathered around it and heaved as one, sweating and straining in the summer sun. It surrendered a few slow, painful inches at a time, its hooves cutting trenches in the grass as it moved. Moving it took days, and at least a couple of reanimations.

Looking at it for the first time in years, suddenly Carolyn's only real thought was *Oh, right. That thing.* She associated it mostly with the parties of her childhood, hamburgers and barbecue. *The pork sandwiches,* she remembered, *were especially good.*

Then a darker memory surfaced. *Actually,* she thought, *the last time I saw it was at the feast of my homecoming.* She remembered seeing the hatch in the side of the grill opened, how the thick hickory smoke poured out. She remembered clamping down on her scream when the smoke cleared and she saw the meat in there, recognized the delicate curve of Asha's hindquarters, saw Isha's severed head staring back at her, skinned and sightless. It occurred to her that that moment had probably been her own *uẓan-iya.* *Yup,* she thought, *that was probably it. Up until then I was still in shock.*

It also occurred to her that the bull could be used to cook things other than pork. She looked at David. The same thought must have occurred to him. He was staring at the bull with wide, horrified eyes.

David was brave, though. He brought himself under control, grinned at Father. "C'mon," he said. "I'm sorry. I won't do it again. I didn't mean anything by it." He shadowboxed, the way they did sometimes.

Father walked to the bull and opened the hatch in its side. The outside was polished bronze—the dead ones kept it shiny—but inside it was black, black. David, a boy of at most thirteen years, held up his hands in surrender. Father pointed inside. David did not kneel, but he trembled. "Oh. Oh no."

Father raised his eyebrows, waiting for more, but David fell silent.

Carolyn's hatred of David was second only to her hatred of Father, but in that moment she could almost have felt sorry for him. The look in his eyes as he climbed inside the bull brought to mind another Atul phrase, "*waẓin nyata,*" which was the moment when the last hope dies.

The bolts Father threw to lock the hatch shut were not bronze, but thick iron, ancient and pitted. Before that moment it had never occurred to her to wonder what purpose they served. Now she understood. *Meat,* she realized, *doesn't try to climb out.*

For the next hour or so the rest of them brought cut wood up from the stockpiles around the neighborhood houses, an armful at a time. Father

called out a few of the dead ones—Mother and "Dennis" among them—
and they helped as well. He even pitched in himself.

The bull shone golden and polished under the light of the afternoon
sun. One by one they deposited their armfuls of wood around the base
of it—pine, mostly, fat and sticky with sap. Once Jennifer dropped to
her knees, sobbing. She was always the kindest of them. Michael, by
this point more accustomed to the thinking of beasts than that of men,
watched the wood pile up without understanding its implications. Margaret just looked interested.

Not long before sundown, Father struck a match. They had kindled
well. The pile of wood caught quickly, going from a few tongues of flame
to a full-on bonfire in a matter of minutes. Smoke came from the bull's
nostrils—first a trickle, then a stream.

They continued feeding the fire through sunset, expecting all the
while to hear him cry out, but David was so *very* strong. The heat was
such that by dark Carolyn could approach the bull no closer than ten feet
or so. From there she pitched her logs into the flame as best she could.
Even then, the heat scorched the hairs on her arm. The dead ones continued their slow slog to the fire, oblivious, their skin reddening and
blistering.

But David was so *very* strong. It was not until full dark, when the
bronze belly of the bull began to glow a dull orange, that he began to
shriek.

Whenever she thought of Father's face, it was by the light of that fire.

How rare it was to see him smile.

III

Just before dawn the next day there were still small sounds coming
from the bull, mostly from the head and neck. Carolyn wondered at
this until she noticed that the bull's nostrils were actual openings; flues
for those times the coals lay inside. The air from those openings must
have seemed relatively cool, the only hint of mercy in all David's world.

How is he not dead by now?

But of course, it was his catalog. Father had trained him to survive grievous wounds and fight on. Also there were potions, tonics, injections. Like all of them, David was what Father had made. So however badly he might need to die, he could not.

Even so, by noon he had gone mercifully silent. Father kept them feeding the fire until just before dark. David, he said, was still alive. Carolyn didn't doubt that he really *could* tell somehow.

Father told them to stop feeding the fire shortly after twilight of the second day. It was out by midnight. By morning of the third day the bull had cooled enough to open, though the metal was still hot enough to leave a blister on Carolyn's forearm when she brushed against it.

What was left inside wasn't as bad to look at as she had feared. More than most of them, David was a devoted pupil. His craft was already very strong, second only to Father's.

He had cooked away almost to the bone before he died.

She and Michael helped Jennifer take him out. What was left was surprisingly light, dry and brittle. They put him on a makeshift stretcher made from an ironing board and hauled him down to one of the empty houses. There they laid him out in a large room on the main floor with dusty, moldering furniture piled in one corner. *This is what Americans call the "living room,"* Carolyn thought, and giggled. Margaret smiled too. The others looked at her strangely.

Margaret examined the charred remains of David's skull, his arms pulled up into a boxer's stance by the heat of the fire, his mouth still open in his last scream. "He will be very deep." She turned to Father. "May I join him? Help him find his way back?"

Father shook his head. "Let him wander."

Carolyn wondered at this. She thought that Margaret meant David would be deep in the "forgotten lands," which, she'd gathered, was where you were both before you were born and after you died. But would he be deep because he had never died before, or because he had died so horribly? Or perhaps—

Father was glaring at her. When he saw that he had her attention he glanced significantly. She followed his gaze back up the hill, to the bull.

The question, of course, was outside her catalog. *He knows*, she thought, despairing. *How can he know what I am thinking?* She put the thought aside, but Father still glared. The pupils of his eyes reminded her of the greasy blackness of the bull's interior. Pinned by his stare, for a moment she imagined herself inside the thing, her ears ringing from the clang as the door swung shut. The only light would be a faint or orange glow visible through the nostrils as the heat began to rise. It would be warm at first, then a little uncomfortable, and then—

"Never!" she hissed, desperate. *I'll never think of it again! Never, never!*

Only then did Father look away. She felt his gaze fall from her as if it were a physical thing. *This is how the field mouse feels, when the shadow of the hawk passes him by.*

"Jennifer. Attend me," Father said.

Jennifer, whose catalog was healing, bustled to her feet, stood before him.

"You will bring him back. Make him whole again."

Up until then Jennifer had worked the craft of resurrection mostly with animals, and those only slightly dead—roadkill and the like. "I'll try," she said, casting a doubtful glance at the corpse. "But I—"

"Try hard." He said it with an edge in his voice. "The rest of you help. Bring her what she asks for."

Jennifer set to work. She dug three big bags of colored powder from her kit and set them around David's body. The rest of them fetched for her—mostly water, but other things as well; salt, honey, a goat penis, several feet of eight-track tape. Jennifer chewed the tape in her mouth until it came away clear, then spat brownish stuff into David's eye sockets. Carolyn had no idea what this might be in aid of. Remembering Father's glare, she forbade herself to wonder.

Jennifer worked all through the night. Margaret sat up with her, though Carolyn and the others rested.

When she woke the next morning, David had begun to fill back in. The withered flesh of his torso had inflated a bit. A hint of pink was now discernible here and there in all the black. By the afternoon of the fourth day this was true of the skin of his arms, then his legs. That evening his lungs became distinguishable, then his heart, though it did not yet beat. By the fifth day he had flesh over most of his body, though it was still black and charred.

On the sixth day he moaned. Jennifer sent Margaret to ask Father if she might do something to ease his pain. Margaret went to ask with a speed that Carolyn found rather touching. She returned with a nod. Jennifer touched David's forehead with a tool she kept in her pouch and, a moment later, his moaning ceased. He didn't thank her, probably couldn't, not yet, but when he rolled his lidless eyes toward Jennifer, Carolyn saw gratitude in them.

By the morning of the seventh day he was, to Carolyn's eye, completely healed. Perhaps that wasn't true, not yet, but it was close. He slept. His chest rose and fell in slow, even breaths. Jennifer was asleep as well, her first real rest in five days. Seeing Carolyn wake, Michael laid a finger against his lips. Carolyn nodded, then sat down near him.

Father threw the door open around midmorning, momentarily blinding Carolyn with the sunlight. He walked over to David and kicked him awake. David snapped to his feet, lightning-fast once again, if slightly dazed and blinky. Father said something to him in the language of murder, which Carolyn did not yet speak. David hesitated for a bare instant, then went to his knees. Father asked him something. David answered. She didn't know what was said, but his tone was perfectly humble, perfectly respectful.

Then, in Pelapi, "And there will be no more sharing of catalogs." Father surveyed the room. "Is that clear? Am I understood?"

All of them nodded. Carolyn thought that, without exception, they all meant it. She certainly did.

Father nodded then, satisfied. He left without shutting the door. When he was gone, Margaret went to David. She stood before him shyly, arms first dangling, then hugging herself. Then, surprising them all, she stretched her neck out and bit him on the ear, not quite hard enough to draw blood. "You sang so *beautifully*!" she said. She ran away, blushing.

"I think she likes you," Jennifer said, deadpan. They all laughed.

David got quieter after that, more reserved, less prone to grin and tell jokes. A month or so later he broke Michael's arm for, he said, cheating on a wager, an archery contest between the two of them. Michael swore he had done no such thing. Jennifer fixed his arm without comment. Michael and David didn't hang around as much after that.

The following month, the final Monstruwaken paid them a visit. He was one of Father's favorite courtiers. They celebrated the visit with a feast. The pig, Carolyn was relieved to see, was dead before they roasted it. These feasts were always a big deal, even to her. If nothing else, the food was very good. But this time she thought the other children's celebrations were somewhat muted. The tongues of flame licking at the bull's belly reminded them of bad things.

Once, just for an instant, out of the corner of her eye, she caught David looking at the fire in a particular way. David did not notice her noticing him, nor did Margaret, standing next to him now. Carolyn did not say "*uzan-iya*" out loud, or even think it very clearly—she was learning— but for the rest of the night the phrase was never far from the surface of her thoughts. She recognized the look in David's eyes immediately. She had seen it many times, reflected in the black pools of her own heart.

The child who went into the bull had been aggressive, and sometimes casually cruel to the rest of them. But David had truly loved Father. But Carolyn knew for an absolute certainty that that was no longer true. *Uzan-iya*, they called it on the Himalayan steppe six thousand years ago. *Uzan-iya*—the moment when the heart turned first to murder.

One day David would move to kill Father. She could not guess when that day would be. She knew only that it would come.

For the first time, it occurred to her to wonder whether David might be of some use.

She pondered on this for many months.

Chapter 4

Thunder

I

E rwin Charles Leffington was an unusual guy. He knew that about himself. For one thing, he insisted that people call him Erwin. He wouldn't accept Charles or E.C., and never, ever Chuck. Erwin. As a little kid he had gone by Chuck for the first seven years or so. Then he started taking classes two years ahead of his age group on account of because he was so *smart* and the teacher let his legal name slip. So, it was "Errrrrrrrrrrrrrrwiiiiiiiiiiiiiiiiiin" that the McClusky twins screeched when they ambushed him after class, "Erwiiiiiiiiiiiinnnnnnnnnnn!" when they pushed his wadded-up A+ in algebra through his pinched lips and into his mouth, "Errrrrrrrrrrrwinnnnnnnnnnnnnnn!!!!!!!" as they worked his jaw, "ERRRRRRRRRRRRRRWIIIIIIIIIIIIIINNNNNNNNNNNNNNNN!" as they made him swallow, "Erwin" in a casual, almost friendly, tone while they beat him until he smiled and said thank you. After he grew up into a badass it crossed his mind to go back and pay the McClusky twins a visit, but in the end he decided against it. They had taught him a valuable life lesson at a young age, and on balance he was grateful.

Erwin had fight in him and, as luck would have it, he grew up to be a big motherfucker. *Erwin* was what the crowd chanted when he ground his way through the defensive line and scored the winning touchdown at the homecoming game in his junior year. Erwin was what they called him at Fort Bragg from the day he enlisted—well, almost—right up to the day he retired. Part of it was that "Sergeant Major" or "Command Sergeant Major" was a fucking mouthful and he didn't want to inflict that on his men. But mostly it was because he liked telling officers to call him Erwin, liked the way some of them got a little flicker in their eyes when he said it, but they did it anyway.

Erwin wasn't in the Army anymore. Thirteen years in—just after his third tour in Afghanistan—he'd decided he'd killed enough people. He wasn't post-traumatic or anything. He still loved his men. He still thought the enemy were a bunch of assholes. He was just done with it. It was a Tuesday and he'd seen an Apache gunship basically disintegrate a sixteen-year-old knucklehead. It was the right thing to do, he was grateful to the guy flying the Apache for doing it—the kid was toting a Dragunov sniper rifle, a little banged up but perfectly serviceable, and he probably wasn't going into the hills to hunt goats. Given the same circumstances he'd cheerfully have massacred the little bastard himself. He just didn't want to be in those circumstances anymore.

So a little while later he took a discharge and went out into the world. There he ended up teaching middle school art. That was some soothing shit right there. Not exactly what he was expecting to do, but it turned out he had nothing against tempera paint. He actually kind of liked making clay pots. What's more, he was surprised to discover that he was good at it. And the kids loved him. They respected him too. Not once did he ever have to raise a hand to even a single one of the little bastards. Truth to tell, most of them seemed a little scared of him. Teachers too, for that matter. And the school board, once or twice. Did they see smoldering bodies piled ten deep when they looked in his eyes? Was he flanked by ghosts when he walked down the hall? He didn't know. But once they realized he wasn't going to stab them in the face or blow them up, they relaxed. *Well, they relaxed a little bit. Most of them.*

After a while he relaxed too. He loved the kids—he *allowed* himself to love them—in a way he hadn't thought he was capable of anymore. When he got back from the war, his ability to love was in serious doubt—all you had to do was take one look at the smoking ruin of his marriage or maybe ask his half-forgotten family. In the civilian world, the volume was a lot lower, but he was still shouting. He knew that, he just couldn't seem to do anything about it. It crossed his mind to eat a shotgun. But after he thought about it he decided to take a chance. Really, what did he have to lose? So one time when he caught this little dude named Dashaen Morning Flower Menendez—he would never forget that name, why the fuck would you do that to a kid?—when he caught little Dashaen eyeing the little plastic dish of mac-and-cheese on his desk the same way the skinnies in Somalia had looked at his MREs, he took the kid aside thinking maybe he was poor or his mom was a junkie or some sad shit like that. Who the fuck couldn't come up with the money for a goddamn sandwich? This was America, for chrissakes.

But it turned out little Dashaen's mom had plenty of money. She was a phlebotomist or some shit. Money wasn't the problem. The problem was that the kid's dad was in some kind of hippie religion and he'd taught little Dashaen about nonviolence and talking through your problems and all that other crap. Erwin had pointed out what a dumb idea this was at the parent-teacher conference and the crazy fuck brought up Gandhi. Clearly the man was insane, and little Dashaen was suffering for it. Erwin, himself no stranger to the problems of insane parents, took pity on him. It turned out he wasn't a nerd or anything like that, he'd just been handicapped by poor upbringing. All he needed was a clue. Once Erwin figured that out, he muttered a prayer of thanks to a God he didn't really believe in and set about *providing* said clue. He taught Dashaen how to kick the other little bastards in the balls, bloody their noses, sneak up behind them and clap both hands over their ears—all the basics. Actually, he might have gone a bit far with that last one; Dashaen overdid it and one of the other mini dudes ended up with a little bit of permanent hearing loss. But after that everybody liked Dashaen and no one stole his lunch money, so basically it was a happy ending. Little Dashaen moved on to high school the following year. Erwin figured he'd seen the last of him. But then one rainy day in December he headed out to the mailbox in front of the duplex where he was staying. He remembered it perfectly. It was the eighteenth, a Saturday. School was out on winter break. The people next door, the Michaelsens, had two little kids, and they were all decorating their tree. It was two in the afternoon. He was on his eighth scotch. He could hear Christmas carols through the wall, that one about Good King Wenceslas, Jingle Bells, Gramma Got Run Over by a Fucking Reindeer. That shit didn't bother him. He wasn't jealous of the Michaelsens. He was happy for them. He didn't feel like he'd fucked up in life. Getting apocalyptically drunk by yourself was just the sort of thing bachelors did around Christmas. Also, he wasn't thinking of the shotgun in the corner of his closet. At all. Then he opened the mailbox and, *mirabile visu*, little Dashaen had sent him a Christmas card. He took that card out of the mailbox with trembling hands, opened the envelope, and read it standing right there at the mailbox. It said

> Dear Erwin,
> Merry Christmas! I know it's not "cool" but I wanted to
> send you this card so you'd know all is good wit me. High
> scool sucks but it's also pretty cool, if you know what
> I mean. Probly it wouldn't of been if I hadn't met you.
> Wanted you to know I knew that. Wanted to say thanks.
> I'd invite you over for X-Mas dinner but I think my Dad
> is still mad.
>
>   Dashaen
> p.s. - I got me a girlfriend. That's her in the picture. Hawt
> ain't she?

When he was done reading it, Erwin went back into his half of the duplex and wept, the only time in his adult life he would ever do so. He wept for a good solid hour, then poured the rest of the scotch down the drain and turned on the TV and watched Charlie Brown. Before he went to bed he folded the card up and put it in his wallet. It would be there until the day he died.

Not long after that he felt better, more like himself, more able to do the sort of work he was good at. He resigned his teaching job at the end of the school year. Most everyone was relieved, though they were too polite to say anything. Or nervous.

Whatever.

II

Now, on a sunny October morning with the last breath of Virginia summer hanging in the air, Erwin aimed his rental—a shitty little Ford Taurus—at an empty spot in the parking lot and slid to a stop with a spray of gravel. This drew glares from a couple of cops smoking and swapping lies around the corner of the jail. Erwin grinned at them and waved. He didn't give a fuck.

He got out of the car and looked around, then spat in the general direction of the sign reading COUNTY JAIL. He called out to the two guys sucking on their Marlboros, "That shit'll kill ya, y'know," then tipped his hat and grinned at them. "Just sayin'."

The younger cop peered over the top of his sunglasses at Erwin like he couldn't believe what he was seeing. The older one laughed. "I'll keep it in mind," he said. Actually, Erwin was wrong. The cops had less than two hours to live, but smoking would not be a factor.

The lobby of the jail was about like every other government building built in the past twenty years: cinder-block walls painted light-tan or dark-pale or something like that, linoleum floors—cheap but damn shiny—and a gray water fountain that dispensed lukewarm water that tasted like piss. Erwin drank it anyway. He was thirsty, and he'd had worse.

Looking around the lobby he counted at least half a dozen meth heads in various stages of strung-out, two drunks, and a redheaded kid who, in Erwin's opinion, was fucking schizophrenic.

He walked up to the window under the sign that said VISITORS REGISTER HERE and took out his badge. "Yeah, I'm Erwin," he began. "I'm with Homeland S'curity. I'm here to see—"

The attendant, a pudgy man in a green uniform that said VIRGINIA DEPARTMENT OF CORRECTIONS on one pocket and ROGERS on the other, didn't look up. "Fill this out," he said, pushing a clipboard through a slot in the glass.

"Can I get—"

"Fill it out," said the deputy. "Then we'll talk."

Erwin sighed. The form ran three pages long, back and front. By the time he got done, a goodish line had formed ahead of him. He took his place behind a fat lady with dirty feet and a skinny girl of about sixteen with a bad Lynyrd Skynyrd tattoo on her back. Erwin was a little surprised to see that tattoo. Ronnie Van Zant had to have been in his grave ten years or more when the kid was born. *But,* he reflected, *for a certain demographic Skynyrd is gonna be timeless. Like Elvis or the Virgin Mary.* To whatever degree such a demographic existed, these two were definitely part of it. The fat lady had a kid named Billy who got caught with a truckload of stolen cheese.

Cheese?

It emerged that this was Billy's third time receiving stolen goods, so he was looking at a good long stretch. Momma wept steadily and noisily, saying things like "I raised them boys raht!" every so often. The skinny girl doled out Kleenex. Every so often she'd say something like "I just don't know what he was thinking," and pat her belly protectively. Erwin guessed that there would be another doomed idiot to take Billy's place in the trailer park in six months or so.

Fifteen sniffly minutes later he was back at the window. He didn't bother trying to talk, just passed the form in and waited for the verdict. As a thirteen-year veteran of Army bureaucracy he was pretty sure he'd filled it out properly, but with a certain species of asshole you could never really be sure.

The pudgy cop scanned the form carefully, all three pages, back and front. After a moment he nodded. "Looks good," he said, clearly disappointed. "I'll need to see two forms of identification, Officer"—he broke off and squinted at the form—"Leffington? *Erwin* Leffington?" He looked up for the first time.

"That's me," Erwin said. He held his badge up.

"Are you . . . you're not *the* Erwin Leffington, are you?"

Ah, fuck, he thought. *Here we go.* If he had one regret in life—which he did—it was letting that fucker write the book about him. It seemed harmless at the time, but the book was what led to the movie. When the movie came out, that was basically all she wrote. "Prolly not."

"*Command Sergeant* Major Erwin Leffington? B Company, Second Battalion?"

Erwin just looked at him. For the first time in a good long while the taste of dust and cordite came back to him. He tried to cling to the image of little Dashaen, to the Christmas card, but all of a sudden he was drowning.

"Second Battalion of the *Fifteenth*?"

"Not for a while," Erwin said. He spoke very softly. "If we could just—"

"My brother is Jim Rogers," the fat guy said.

Erwin looked up at that, no longer drowning. "How is Sergeant Rogers?"

"He's better, sir. It was rough going for a while, but he's doing well now. He just had a son, born last May."

"Don't call me sir." Then, after a moment, "How's his leg?"

"He gets around OK. Now, anyway. Took the VA a while to get it adjusted right."

The news that Rogers was doing well helped, a little. "Your brother is a good man," he said. "You tell him I asked after him. Now, if we could—"

"Sir, he told us about you," the fat deputy said. "He told us what you done."

Erwin shuffled his feet. Shit like this always made him uncomfortable. The silence stretched out. "Your brother is a good man," he repeated.

"My brother says the same about you. No, that ain't true. He says you're a *great* man. He says you're about the best soldier who ever wore a uniform, and a certified badass to boot." The fat deputy was looking at him with worship in his eyes. His voice trembled as he spoke. "He says you saved his life, his and everybody—"

"*Thanks*," Erwin growled. Then, calmer, "All that, yeah, that was overhyped."

"My brother says different, sir." Then something horrible occurred to him. "I'm sorry about making you fill out them forms! If I'da known you was *you* I never woulda done that." His lips trembled. "I'm real sorry."

"S'aright."

"Who you here to see?"

"A guy named Steve Hodgson."

The deputy's face darkened. "The cop killer? What you want with him?"

Erwin, clever, saw his way out. "Can't talk about it," he lied. "National security."

"For real?"

"Oh yeah." He could see that Rogers's brother believed this completely. That made him feel a little bad. Not as bad as he would have felt continuing the conversation, but bad. "Yeah. It's all real fucking classified and shit. Tell Sergeant Rogers I asked after him."

"I will, sir." He hesitated. "Could I . . . could I maybe get your autograph?"

Erwin weighed his options. One of them was to beat the guy a little bit unconscious. That worked sometimes. *Usually after they get a autograph they let me go, though.* Plus the lobby was full of security cameras. "Yeah. Sure."

The deputy passed out a clipboard with a blank sheet of typing paper. Erwin signed it, passed it back. Rogers's brother took the autograph and put it in a drawer with trembling hands. "I'm gonna have to put you in the chapel."

"The chapel?"

"Yeah. Visitation room is full, unless you want to wait."

"The chapel's fine." The toilet would have been fine. He just wanted out, away from Rogers's brother and the endless parade of awful shit that lurked, trembling and eager, just beneath the surface of his babble.

III

Rogers's brother searched Erwin's bag and took his weapon, but let him keep the laptop and manila folders. As they searched, another deputy skittered around whispering. So Erwin wasn't surprised when a different guy—a sheriff's lieutenant, no less—handed him his guest ID and walked him down the long hall to the chapel. *He's probably the highest-ranking guy in the building,* Erwin thought, bracing himself.

Sure enough, when they got to the steel door: "I, uh. I read. I read that book they wrote about you. Well, mostly. About what you did in—how do you pronounce that place?"

"Natanz," Erwin said.

"Is it really true that—"

"Nope," Erwin said. He could go weeks at a time without anyone recognizing him, but there were also days where it seemed like everybody he ran into with even the *tiniest* connection to the military turned out to have read the book, or seen the movie, or that thing on the History Channel. Today was shaping up to be one of those. "It's total bullshit." *Maybe I should grow a beard?*

"Oh. I don't read much, but—"

Erwin strode into the chapel, shut the door behind him. Inside, he looked around. His job carried him into the occasional jail, but this was his very first jail chapel. It was maybe twenty feet on a side and windowless. It smelled of paint. He had expected rows of metal folding chairs—it was that kind of building—but instead he saw six concrete benches set into the floor, each wide enough for three or four guys. Interestingly, there were no crosses in sight. *Political correctness, maybe?* The only real features were a plain pine podium at the front of the room and a framed painting on the wall.

With nothing better to do and not eager to settle his middle-aged ass onto the concrete bench, Erwin walked over to check the painting out. It wasn't bad, but it wasn't good, either. It had the simple, blocky representationalism of medieval iconography and prison tattoos. A small man with nut-brown skin—Jesus? Mohammed? Other?—stood in the center of the picture. The sun burned down behind him, leaving his face in shadow. He held out his hands, blessing a motley array of people and animals gathered in the light. The holy dude and his supplicants were surrounded by darkness.

The chapel door opened. A middle-aged guy in khakis and a grease-spotted Izod walked in. "You Leffington?"

"Call me Erwin. Yeah."

"I'm Larry Dorn."

"Yeah, hi. Where's the kid?" Dorn was Steve Hodgson's public defender.

"He'll be along. I asked them to give us a minute first. I wanted to talk to you."

"Sure," Erwin said. "Be happy to." This was a lie. They had spoken on the phone a couple of times. Dorn came across as sort of a sack of shit, in Erwin's opinion. But he controlled access to the Hodgson kid.

While Dorn looked the papers over, Erwin occupied himself with staring at the painting. At first glance the surrounding darkness was completely black, but from the right angle you could see that it wasn't, not really. The paint was layered. If you looked at it right you could see figures in the darkness, devils maybe, and—

"Everything looks in order," Dorn said.

"Yeah. For what it's worth, I don't give much of a shit about your boy. Only reason I'm talking to him is that he might know something about another case."

"What a relief," Dorn said. His voice fairly dripped with sarcasm.

"Not real fond of him?"

"Nope. I knew Detective Miner. Our daughters played together sometimes."

"That gonna be a problem for you, defending him?"

Dorn shrugged. "What's to defend? They found him passed out drunk on Miner's dining-room table. The gun that killed Miner was in his hands. It had his prints on it." Dorn looked like he wanted to strangle his own client. *It ain't looking real good for the defense.*

"Just his prints?"

"No. Miner's too. And a thumb print on the light switch from a third party we haven't made yet."

Yeah, we have, Erwin thought. *You just don't know it yet.*

"Anything else?"

"Like what?"

"Like anything."

Dorn pursed his lips for a moment, considering. Then he shrugged. "Yeah. There was this." He rooted around in a folder and handed over a stack of 8 x 10 glossies of the crime scene.

"Lotta guts on that china cabinet," Erwin said. "We know who they belonged to?" *Carolyn, maybe? Or maybe Lisa?*

"We're still waiting on the lab work."

"It was a shotgun what did it, though. The same one?"

Dorn popped an eyebrow. "Good eye. You in forensics?"

"Not really." He had killed a lot of people with shotguns. "That there's a piece of lung, looks like. It ain't the victim's"—his lungs were mostly in the kitchen—"and this Steve kid is up and walking around, so it probably ain't his either. You guys wonder about that?"

"Not really, no. What are you getting at?"

Erwin sighed. *How'd this guy make it through law school?* "Anybody gone looking for this mystery chick of his?"

"Who?" Dorn said. "The one at the bar? He made her up."

"I thought you had witnesses who saw the two of them together."

"We do. But that's all we have. If she was ever at Miner's house, she didn't leave any fingerprints, any footprints, not so much as a stray hair. Do you know how hard it is to walk through someone's house and not leave any trace?"

"I dunno. Pretty hard, I guess. Thing is, though, she *did* leave a print."

Dorn's face clouded. "You're kidding me."

"Nope."

"Which, the one on the light switch? It wasn't in IAFIS," Dorn said, meaning the FBI's Integrated Automated Fingerprint Identification System.

"That's right," Erwin said. "It wasn't." He was going to let the phrase hang there, pregnant with all sorts of sinister implications about the information he had access to, but just then the door to the chapel clanged open. This disappointed Erwin. It spoiled the fucking moment.

A different deputy walked in clutching a skinny white guy with short brown hair. Erwin recognized Steve Hodgson from his mug shot. The deputy shoved him at Erwin the way you'd push a sack of trash into a landfill.

Erwin looked him over. *Is that him? Is that all there is?* He wasn't quite a kid, not anymore. *Early thirties, maybe?* He was in an orange jail jumpsuit, faded and fraying at the edges. No visible tattoos. He didn't look like a junkie, but his eyes jumped around, alert and maybe a little shell-shocked.

Dorn nodded at the guard. "Thanks."

"I gotta lock you in Mr. Leffington, sir," the guard said. "I'm real sorry. I gotta say, though, it's a honor to—"

"It's no problem," Dorn said. "Thanks."

Looking thwarted, the guard shut the door.

The Hodgson kid immediately started asking Dorn about someone named Petey, whether Dorn had heard anything about him. *Who the fuck is Petey?* He made a mental note but didn't interrupt.

Dorn looked at the guy like he was a fucking idiot. "Don't you have bigger things to worry about?"

Erwin could see desperation in Steve's eyes, but he kept it out of his voice. "Yeah. I know. I just wondered if—"

"Yeah. OK. Fine. Your friend called. He said he picked up your dog. That's all I got."

Hodgson nodded, smiled a little. Tension visibly slid off him. He shuffled over to one of the concrete benches, his thin blue prison slippers scuffing against the shiny linoleum. The manacles didn't leave him much room to move.

Up for murder one and all he cares about is his dog? When he got close enough Erwin stood up and held out his hand. Steve looked startled, but after a moment he reached out to the length of the chain and gave Erwin a little shake.

"I'm Erwin," Erwin said.

"Steve Hodgson." He thought about it for a second. " 'Pleased to meet you,' isn't quite right, but I'll admit I'm curious. What can I do for you, Mr.—"

"It's Erwin," Erwin said. "Always call me Erwin." Steve's eyes narrowed at this. *Probably wondering if I'm playing "good cop."* "I was hoping I could ask you a couple of questions. You mind if I call you Steve?"

"Sure. Whatever." Steve sat on one of the benches. "I don't suppose you've got a cigarette, do you? I'd drop-kick the baby Jesus for a Marlboro."

"Sorry. Don't smoke. Want a dip?" Erwin noticed that Steve took a couple of extra steps so that he could sit with his back to the wall. Erwin had done the same thing.

Steve considered. "I'll pass. Thanks, though."

"I've read your case file," Erwin said. "If what you say is true, sounds like you got well and truly fucked over."

Steve gave him a wry smile. "Yeah. Oddly enough, I had that same thought."

"Any idea why she'd want to do such a thing?"

Again, Steve looked startled. "You believe me?"

"Dunno yet. You ain't said much."

Steve gave Dorn a resentful look. Dorn hadn't made a secret of the fact that he thought the woman, if she existed at all, was awfully convenient. "Up until now no one seemed interested. But to answer your question, no. I have no idea why she'd want to do something like this to me. Or anyone else, for that matter." But something flickered in his eyes as he said it.

"You got a clean conscience, do ya?"

Steve gave him a long, appraising look. "You don't miss much, do you? No. I don't have a clean conscience. I did something a long time ago. A friend of mine got hurt. Probably his parents hated me enough to do something like this, if they would have thought of it, but Celia died of a heart attack seven years ago and Martin shot himself the year after."

"That's a sad fucking story," Erwin said.

"You making fun of me?"

"I am not," Erwin said. "For what it's worth, I get it. I've got plenty of shit I wish I could take back. Keeps me up some nights."

Steve studied him for a moment, then relaxed a little. "OK. Sorry."

"You think this Carolyn chick has anything to do with that?"

Steve's brow wrinkled. "I don't see how she could," he said. "But there's a whole lot about her that I don't understand at all."

"Why don't you start at the beginning," Erwin said. "Tell me everything you remember. Take your time. I got all day."

IV

"Then I heard a guy behind me," Steve was saying. He had been speaking for almost an hour. He had a good memory for visual detail, less so for the exact wording of conversations. His description of the woman's funky attire—bicycle shorts and leg warmers?—was both interesting and surprisingly detailed. Also in Erwin's professional opinion, it had the ring of truth. *If this guy is lying, he doesn't know it.* He simply had no idea what had been done to him, or why. It made Erwin feel fucking sad.

"Then the guy—Miner—he said something along the lines of 'You're under arrest.' He said it at least twice. He acted kind of weird, like he wasn't sure what was going on. In a daze, you know?"

"What happened next?" Erwin asked.

Steve looked down. Erwin noticed that he avoided looking at the chain around his ankles. "I honestly don't remember. I remember thinking, *Oh, shit, he's got a gun,* and I can kind of picture his face, so I must have turned around. But my next *clear* memory is waking up on the floor. I had no idea where I was, and some guy was hollering at me."

"That would be Detective Jacobsen," Dorn said. "He and Miner were friends. They were supposed to go out fishing that morning. He discovered Miner's body, and performed the initial arrest."

"Thanks," Erwin lied. He didn't give a fuck about Jacobsen. He tapped his pen against the concrete bench, thinking. "So you deny killing him? Miner?"

"Does it matter?"

"Prolly not," Erwin said. "But I'm curious."

"I guess I do. Deny it, I mean."

"You *guess*?" Dorn said, incredulous.

Steve shrugged. "Like I said, I don't remember. The last clear memory I have, he was alive. When I came to the next morning he was dead. I had no grudge against the guy." He sighed. "I really wish I'd just gone home and gone to bed. Dunno if it would've helped *him* much, but I'd probably be at home with my dog."

"You think she'd have killed him anyway?"

"Dude," Steve said with truly epic sincerity, "I've got no fucking idea."

Erwin waited for more, but that was it. *He's empty.* He considered. "OK," he said after a moment. "I think you've been pretty straight with me. I appreciate that. A lot of the guys I talk to, they lie just 'cause they like the sound of it. So I'm going to spare you my dance moves. I got some information about this woman—not much, but some—that might be of use in your case. Maybe."

Steve blinked. "Go on."

Dorn looked up from his papers.

"I'm fairly sure that the woman you met is named Carolyn Sopaski. And what you said dovetails with the little bit we know about her."

Steve looked attentive, maybe even hopeful. He didn't speak.

"I'm listening," Dorn said.

"Like I said, I work for Homeland Security. I'm a special agent. It's kind of like an FBI special agent, except we ain't gotta wear a suit if we don't want to." Today he was in a gray T-shirt and a navy-blue zip-up hoodie. The jeans he had on were the same size as the ones he wore to his high school graduation thirty years ago.

"So what do you do, exactly?"

"It depends. A lot of times I just follow up on interesting coincidences."

"How do you mean?"

"Well, these days Homeland Security is tied into pretty much everything. You know that, right? Phone records, Internet searches, library books, bank stuff . . . everything. All that goes into this big air-conditioned room that they got up in Utah. What comes out the other end is a pile of weird coincidences that might be of interest to guys like me. So, like, if the same dude buys one bag of fertilizer at fifteen or twenty different Home Depots, this system might notice that. You follow?"

"I guess."

"Or, like in this case, say a cop writes a report. They're forever writing reports, poor fucks. In addition to all the normal shit that happens with it—prosecutors and lawyers and dust-gathering—there's also a copy that goes in to these machines in Virginia. And on the last run one of the cases that popped out was—"

"Mine?" said Steve, suddenly eager. "You found something that clears me?"

"Nope. Yours didn't get picked up. Nothing unexplained there. The connection that ended up on my desk had to do with a bank robbery. A really fucking weird bank robbery."

"Weird how?"

"Part of it was the size of the haul," Erwin said. "Most robberies, the guy gets ten, maybe fifteen thousand. A lot of times it's not even that much. But this one was more like three hundred thousand."

"Three hundred twenty-seven thousand," Steve said, "-ish?" Quoting the amount his mystery woman had said was in the blue duffel bag.

Erwin nodded. "Actually, yeah. Same thought crossed my mind. Anyway, that's a pretty successful robbery. A lot more successful than most of them. It's unusual. So the computer took an interest, kicked it up to me. One thing that might have explained it was if the people who did it were trained."

Steve wrinkled his forehead. "Trained? You mean, like, government trained?"

"Believe it or not, yeah. KGB ran a course on that very thing back in the '70s. Insurgent training or some shit. We did too, as part of the Green Beret Q Course. Not anymore, but a lot of the know-how is still floating around. Anyway, that's why I got called in. We get one like this every couple of months. Usually it turns out to be nothing.

"That's true here as well, at least in that we don't have any reason to think Ms. Sopaski is into any kind of terrorist shit. What's less clear is what exactly she *is* involved in. I mean, the bank tellers *helped* her do the fuckin' robbery. What's up with that?"

"What do you mean?" Dorn asked.

Erwin shrugged. "Just what I said. At around three p.m., Ms. Sopaski—your Carolyn—and another chick, identity unconfirmed, walked into the Oak Street branch of Midwest Regional in downtown Chicago. We got 'em on the lobby camera. They waited in line like good little customers for just over three minutes. When their turn came the two of them approached the teller, a Miz"—Erwin squinted at his notes—"Amrita Krishnamurti. The unidentified woman spoke with her calmly for thirty-seven seconds. Then—well, never mind. Watch it yourself."

Erwin fired up his laptop. He punched up Microsoft something-or-other, spent a couple of seconds closing out porn, then pressed Play. "Security-camera footage," he said. "From the bank."

Steve set the laptop on one of the concrete benches. Dorn watched over his shoulder.

"Why is she dressed like that?" Dorn asked. Carolyn looked more or less reasonable, if a bit dated—jeans and a man's button-down, barefoot—but the other woman was in a bathrobe and cowboy hat.

"I ain't got a fuckin' clue," Erwin said. "My first thought was meth, but I don't think that's it. She looks too sleepy."

"Plus she still has all her teeth," Dorn agreed. "Could be LSD, though."

Erwin and Steve looked at him.

Dorn shrugged. "About half the people who get booked tripping on acid are wearing bathrobes. It's, like, a thing."

They considered this for a few moments, then Erwin nodded back at the laptop. "It's about to get good." The woman in the bathrobe was speaking to Amrita Krishnamurti. Carolyn handed her a blue duffel bag, like one you'd use to take stuff to the gym. Ms. Krishnamurti motioned to the other two tellers and they gathered round to listen. The bathrobe woman spoke for a few more seconds, then touched each of them on the cheek.

Then the tellers split up and started filling bags of money. They worked quickly, slowing only to toss out dye packs and the occasional bill.

"Are those the marked bills?" Dorn asked.

Erwin nodded.

The video ran for just under three minutes. When it was over Steve handed the computer back.

"They all helped," Dorn said.

"Yeah." Erwin bit back the urge to salute Captain Obvious. He needed Dorn. "They did. That Krishnamurti lady was the, whatchacallit, branch manager. She worked there about twelve years. The other two had been there about a year each. None of them was fixing to go bankrupt or any shit like that. And they couldn't have got the job in the first place if they had criminal records. But they was just *awful* eager to fill up that bag, don't you think?"

Dorn nodded. "It's weird."

Erwin thought, but did not say, *Maybe a little bit like a guy who'd kept his nose clean for ten years all of a sudden deciding to commit burglary and kill a cop?* Or maybe not. But he'd bring that up later. "Yeah, I thought so too. So I went and talked to them a little bit. They seemed nice enough. They all remembered where the alarm buttons were, didn't panic or anything like that, but not a one of them pushed one."

"Did they say why?"

"Not at first. They lawyered up. But once I convinced them they weren't going to jail, one of the younger ones talked to me. She said she didn't set off any of the alarms 'because I was just too busy hunting for dye packs and radio transmitters.' Real matter-of-fact, see? I asked her why she'd do such a thing, and she said she had no idea. I'm pretty sure I believe her." Erwin gave a wry smile. "I'll be honest, I'm fucking stumped. That's why I came here."

"How do you mean?" Steve asked.

"I was hoping you might have some bright ideas."

"Me?"

Erwin nodded. "You spent more time with her than anybody. Anything about that video jump out at you? Jog your memory, like?" Erwin gave him a minute to think about it. His eye drifted once again to that fucked-up painting. *The shapes in the darkness were black on black, but you could almost—*

"You don't think the tellers are in on it?"

"Nah," Erwin said. "I don't. I did what I could for them. They lost their jobs, but I don't think there's going to be a trial."

"And you're sure the woman in the video was Carolyn?"

"The prints match."

"How did you get her name? Matching prints would give you a connection between the two cases, but for the name you'd need something else."

Smart kid. "Birth records," Erwin said. "Hospital."

Dorn's eyes narrowed. "I didn't know that was technically possible."

Erwin shrugged. "Learn something every day, dontcha? I'm Big Brother, more or less. I've got access to all sorts of shit you wouldn't think. We couldn't find much on her, though, and our computer guys are pretty good. Whadda they call it, data mining?" Erwin said, playing dumb. He'd published papers on data mining.

"I've heard of it," Dorn said. Erwin was pretty sure he was lying.

"Whatever. Point is, them nerds just about always come back with *something*. Not this time, though. I'm about convinced they came up dry because past a certain age there's just nothing out there to find on Miz Sopaski."

"What do you mean, 'past a certain age'?" Steve asked.

"Well, up until she turned eight or so, she shows up in the record about like any other kid. Birth records, shots, school . . ." He rummaged around in his folder and dug out an 8x10, slid it across the table. "That's Mrs. Gillespie's second-grade class. Carolyn's on the back row."

Steve examined the picture.

Erwin waited for a lightbulb to go on, but it didn't. "You notice anything else in that picture?"

"Should I?"

"Maybe not. I've had a lot longer to look at it than you. And I might be seeing things. But take a look at the girl in the second row, third from the right. She remind you of anybody?"

It took Steve another couple of seconds. "Is it . . . the kid looks like the other lady from the bank robbery. The one who did all the talking. Same nose, same shape of her face . . ."

"Yeah," Erwin said. "I thought so too. The kid's name is Lisa Garza. We're trying to find out what she's been up to for the last quarter century or so." He gave them a level gaze. "Haven't found anything on her, either. Ab-so-lutely nothing."

Dorn let out a low whistle.

Seeing that they were ready, Erwin dug out the pièce de résistance. It was a photograph from a newspaper. The caption underneath it said

"Beating the Summer Heat! Carolyn Sopaski, 7, takes her turn on the water slide." A grinning girl with a missing front tooth was sliding down a long piece of plastic, haloed by a sparkling spray of water. In the background a small crowd of kids milled around, waiting their turn.

"What about that one?" he asked. "You notice anything—" He broke off. He sniffed the air. He couldn't identify the smell at first, and then he could. *Blood*. All of a sudden he was back in Afghanistan. He reached out for an M16 that wasn't there.

In the distance he heard a woman scream, then a gunshot. Then two more gunshots and a deep, booming laugh.

Then, screaming.

V

Thirty seconds later Erwin heard keys clattering in the lock. "Aw fuck."

The door swung open on Sergeant Rogers's brother kneeling on the floor, head hung low, cheeks streaked with tears. He pointed at Steve with his left hand. His right, Erwin saw, was broken in at least two places. "That's him," he said. "Please. I got a baby . . ."

Erwin just had time to register the words when Rogers's head exploded. He crumpled the rest of the way to the floor, his short, dumb life mercifully over. Then the craziest looking asshole Erwin had ever seen stepped over the body into the chapel.

He was a white guy, tall and muscular, a "healthy specimen" as they had said back in the day. Erwin's first thought was that the guy had done himself up in red body paint like one of those tribes in Colombia. *No. Not body paint. Blood.* He was covered in blood from head to toe. Here and there bits of meat were stuck to him as well. A couple of feet of someone's small intestine dangled from his shoulder.

The big guy was spinning a pyramid-shaped weight on the end of a long chain. At the other end of the chain was a machete-sized knife mounted on a yellow metal shaft. *Is that bronze?* Also—*What the fuck?* At first Erwin refused to believe what his eyes were telling him, but the guy was, in fact, wearing a tutu. *Hmm*, Erwin thought. *There's something you don't see every day.*

"Eshteeeeve?" the big guy said. His eyes tracked back and forth between Erwin, Steve, and Dorn, reminding Erwin of the forward-mounted gun on an Apache. He had a strange accent, one Erwin couldn't place. The *s* sounded more like "esh" and he dragged his *e* out too long.

"Uh . . . Steve?" said Dorn. "You're looking for Steve?"

"Don't, Counselor," Erwin said.

The big guy's eyes locked onto Dorn. "Eshteeve?"

"That's him!" Dorn said, pointing at Steve.

The guy gave Dorn a big smile. His teeth were brown. "Eshteeeve?"

Dorn nodded his head with comical enthusiasm, looking for a moment more like a headbanger than an attorney. "Yeah," he said, jabbing his finger into the air in Steve's direction, "that's him!"

"Counselor, I don't think—"

Quick as a panther, the big guy was at Steve's side. He put an arm around him, stroked his cheek with the blade of the knife. Erwin's professional eye noted that the blade was hand-forged. *Don't see that much either.* It looked very sharp.

"Eshteeeve?"

"Um . . . yeah," Steve said. "That's me."

The big guy continued running the knife up and down Steve's cheek, not quite hard enough to draw blood. Then, with a movement so fast that Erwin's eye could not track it, the weighted end of the chain smashed out and obliterated Dorn's lower jaw. It literally disappeared. Probably part of it was mashed back into his throat, but other bits scattered hither and yon.

"Gubboy," the big guy said to Steve. "You come."

From the look in his eyes, Dorn realized that something had happened but not exactly what. He reached up and probed tenderly at the bottom half of his face. About the time he realized something was missing the first drops of blood began to rain down on his shirt. His eyes widened. "OOOGH!" he said. "OOOOOOOGH!" He began bouncing up and down on the bench like a little kid who needs to use the bathroom. "OOOGH! OOOOOOGH!"

Both Steve and the big guy were looking at Dorn, Steve in horror, the big guy with a slight, amused smile that brought out his dimples. After a moment of this he began to imitate Dorn's bouncing. He glanced at Steve and Erwin the way a man will when he is laughing among friends. He pointed at Dorn and said, "Oogh! Oogh!"

Steve didn't seem to notice. His eyes were fixed on the ruin of Dorn's face. The big guy's smile faded a bit. He turned to Erwin. He didn't like what he saw there, either. His smile disappeared. He shrugged. A split second later the spear on the other end of the chain flashed out and buried itself to the hilt in Dorn's eye socket. The pointy end of the blade poked out the back of Dorn's skull, yellow and bloody. After an interval just long enough for Erwin to register the fine silver chain running from the hilt to the big guy's hand it flashed back again. Dorn fell forward, his head hitting the concrete bench with a solid clunk. Blood and aqueous humor leaked from his eye and began puddling.

The silence seemed very loud.

The big guy savored the looks on their faces for a moment. He gave Erwin a wink, then began to spin the weighted end of the chain again.

Erwin realized he was about to die. Then his mind—his clever little mind, which had been so good to him over the years—came through again. He looked at the big guy's ridiculous dress—brown loafers with the toes cut out, purple tutu—*a tutu? Da fuck?*—flak jacket, probably Israeli, and red tie. He thought of the woman who had done the bank robbery in a bathrobe and a cowboy hat. "Say," he said, "you wouldn't happen to know a chick named Carolyn, would you?"

The big guy raised his eyebrow in surprise. "Carolyn?" The rotation of the chain slowed, just a little.

Erwin, whose instincts had been honed to exquisite sharpness through a decade-long association with murderous men, thought, *The trick now is not to show panic. If he sees fear, it will excite him.* "Yeah," he said casually. "Carolyn. Lisa, too."

"Wussay Carolyn?"

"Eh?" He put his hand to his ear. "Say again, chum?"

"Wut . . . say . . . Carolyn." He wiggled the knife for emphasis.

With a knot in his stomach that reminded him of the one and only time he had gone deep-sea fishing and hooked a "big'un," Erwin said, "Oh yeah, Carolyn and me go waaaaaay back. If she's told me one time she's told me a thousand, 'Erwin, if you ever need anything, anything at all, you just have to say my name—Carolyn—and I'll come a-running.' We're real good friends, me and Carolyn.'"

The big guy scrunched up his face, confused. "Carolyn?"

"Oh yeah." Erwin nodded. "Carolyn."

The big guy narrowed his eyes suspiciously. "Nobununga?"

"Yup. Nobunaga. Him too, yup."

He realized immediately that he had said the wrong thing. *Not Nobu-nag-a, Nobu-nun-ga. Ah, fuck.* The big guy's eyes narrowed. He resumed spinning his pyramid. Erwin was thinking, *When he throws it I'll twist right, twist right and grab the chain if I can but he's* so *fucking* fast—

The big guy blinked. He leaned forward, brow furrowed. Then his eyes flew open wide, reminding Erwin of how Rogers's brother looked when he recognized Erwin's name on the form. He pointed. "You . . . Erwin?"

"Umm . . ."

"Natanz?" The big guy held his hand to his shoulder as if it were wounded, then pantomimed working a squad automatic weapon, sweeping it back and forth, singlehandedly suppressing an attack by a vastly superior force.

Erwin considered his answer in light of the Israeli flak jacket, the guy's obvious insanity. *Ah, fuck it,* he thought. "Yeah. Natanz."

The big guy drew in breath. He stopped spinning the pyramid, then snapped to something almost but not quite like the US military's version of attention—his feet were a bit too wide, his chest poked out a bit too far for the Army. Then, holding the spear perfectly vertical with his left hand—parade rest?—he raised his right fist and banged it on his chest. He said something in a language Erwin had never heard before.

Erwin wasn't going to salute him back—not *this* guy—but he nodded again. *One of them days.*

Down the hallway he heard a clatter of bullets falling on the tile floor, a soft curse, the distinct sound of a rifle being cocked. *AR-15, prolly. The cops are still trying to fight back.* Both Erwin and the big guy glanced back at the door. The big guy frowned, not liking what he saw out there. Then, just like that, he punched Steve in the jaw. Steve slumped, dazed but not completely out of it. The big guy slung him over his shoulder. The two of them disappeared out into the hall.

Erwin heard gunfire, then screams, then a deep, booming laugh. He felt alive in a way he hadn't since Afghanistan. His veins were thrumming with energy. He got up and went looking for a gun.

The rifle he'd heard in the hall—it *was* an AR-15—was all bent-up. He found a pistol in the locker room, but by then the big guy was gone. Steve was gone with him. Erwin followed a trail of bare, bloody footprints down the hall. The security door was blocked open by the fat lady with the dirty feet. A hole the size of his hand gaped in her chest. Through it he could see a big blood vessel, probably her aorta, all shredded-up.

The skinny girl with the Skynyrd tattoo, apparently unharmed, knelt beside her, staring down with a blank expression on her face. "Bev?" she said. "Beverly?"

Erwin thought about telling the skinny girl that Beverly was with Ronnie Van Zant and Elvis, but he wasn't sure how that would go over. He settled for patting her on the shoulder.

The lobby was drenched with blood. Intestines dangled from the metal chairs, the light fixtures, the counter. Thick splinters of bulletproof glass lay strewn across the floor. He had seen that stuff break before, just once, when an Iraqi limousine got hit by a depleted uranium slug from an A-10 Thunderbolt. He made his way through the lobby, checking for pulses and finding none. The older cop he'd seen smoking outside had been decapitated. If his head were still around, Erwin didn't see it.

He stood over the dead cop for a long minute, lips pursed, considering. Lightning flashed off in the west. Someone in the lobby was screaming. He bent over and fished around in the dead cop's front pocket and retrieved a pack of Marlboro Lights and a Bic, then made his way back to the chapel.

Once inside he kicked the door shut. He moved to a spot where he could look at the painting and slid down along the wall until his ass hit the floor. The buzz of the fluorescent lights reminded him of a cloud of flies around a corpse. In a few minutes there would be sirens, ambulances,

SWAT teams, reports. He shook out a smoke, lit it, and took a deep drag, relishing the head rush from the nicotine.

On the bench in front of him sat the newspaper picture of Carolyn on the water slide. In the background of the twenty-five-year-old photo someone who looked an awful lot like Steve Hodgson, aged about ten, waited for his turn. *Shit*, Erwin thought. *I really wanted to ask him about that.* Up on the wall Jesus—or whomever—held his hands out, keeping the dark things of creation at bay. He heard the rumble again, from the east, closer now.

Thunder.

Chapter 5

The Luckiest Chicken in the World

I

"Wow," Aliane said. "You weren't kidding. You *do* have lions in your backyard."

"Yeah," Marcus said. "Just like in *Scarface*!" He grinned, exposing what Aliane judged to be about twenty thousand Brazilian reis' worth of gold grills on his teeth.

How much would that be in dollars? More than Aliane's mother had made in a year of scrubbing floors, anyway. Aliane was only vaguely familiar with *Scarface*, but she could tell from his tone she was supposed to be impressed. "Ooooh, baby," she said, smiling, and ran a fingernail down his forearm.

She could still hear the party a couple hundred meters behind them—thumping bass, laughter, people splashing in the pool—but they were far enough away that she could no longer see Marcus's mansion through the trees. They stood on a concrete walkway between two deep, lighted pits filled with fake rocks and a few bushes. Marcus faced her, standing a little bit inside of the invisible we're-just-friends line.

"The big male is Dresden. That one"—he pointed at the one on her left—"is called Nagasaki. Naga for short."

"I thought lions were supposed to have a mane?"

Marcus shook his head. "Only the males. Don't you watch the Discovery Channel?"

Aliane forced a smile. Growing up she was too poor to have a TV. "She's small, too."

"She's only about half-grown. We think she's his daughter."

She turned and looked into the other pit, the one with the male. The sound of their voices had disturbed his sleep. He was awake now, studying her with unblinking yellow eyes. She shivered and stepped in a little closer to Marcus. "He's really big."

"I'm living large." Marcus puffed his cigar and spread his arms wide, a gesture that took in the lion pit, the forty landscaped acres, the ten-foot concrete wall surrounding the grounds. Marcus—Little Z to the hip-hop cognoscenti—lived on a Connecticut estate that had once been the weekend getaway of a hedge-fund manager. He put his arm around Aliane's shoulders and pulled her forward to look down at the male.

"Hey, you want me to wake her up too?"

"No!" Aliane said, a little too quickly. "No . . . I mean, that's OK. Let it sleep." The big lion put his head back down, closed his eyes. She snuggled in close, stifling a cigar-smoke sneeze.

"What's the matter?"

"Nothing." But when she looked at the sleeping lion, some deep part of her stirred. Before she'd become a model she lived in a small village in Brazil, near the Pantanal. Jaguar attacks were not unheard-of. A boy in her fourth-grade class had been killed. Once she saw a farmer with his scalp hanging loose, his face drenched with blood. "Can they, you know, get out?"

Marcus shook his head. "No way. That pit is fifteen feet deep. You can't tell from up here, but the walls slope back towards the inside. So, like, there's no way to get a grip or anything. Ain't no *way* they're climbing out of there."

"Oh. Well . . . good," she said, trying to sound convinced. "Wow, baby. That's really cool. Can we go back to the party?"

"In a minute. Gotta feed them first." He grinned. "You wanna go fishing?"

"Fishing?"

"Come with me." He circled around the side of the pit to a trail that led deeper into the woods.

"I don't know, Marcus . . . it's pretty dark." She glanced back at the house. The party was in full swing. Marcus's latest single—"Pimp Hand"—was blaring out over the stereo. "I'm out of wine."

"We'll get you some more wine in a minute. Come on, you really want to see this. It's the funniest thing ever."

The forest behind him was very dark, but his watch was a Patek Philippe. *And he's going to put me in a video. Maybe.*

"OK," she said. "Fine."

II

The big lion's dream was the same every night. Golden grass brushed at his whiskers. The breeze carried the scent of wildebeest and zebra. The sun hung low on the horizon, and the shadows of the baobab trees lay long.

Home.

In Dresden's dream his daughter was still very small. She paced him as he walked, moving in his shadow just as Dresden had done with his own father. He was teaching her the rudiments of their craft: the location of the drinking holes, the proper way to drift in from downwind of one's prey, the words to show respect to the Forest God after a kill. It was a good memory, a good dream.

But then it turned.

Dresden froze in his tracks, one forepaw hanging just above the ground. He perked his ears up and leaned forward, straining to catch a scrap of sound carried by the breeze. Naga heard it too, deep and buzzy, a bit like a roar and a bit like the sound of angry bees except not at all like either one. It sounded like metal.

It sounded like men.

Wait, he said to Naga. *Watch.* She swished her tail, acknowledging the order. But Dresden was older than was common for a new father, and he had mostly forgotten what it was to be young and playful. He did not see the mischief in her eyes. He left her then, moving through the grasses, low and slow and silent. In the dream he was not afraid, not yet. But the part of him that was not dreaming ached to do something else, *anything* else, to take his cub and flee, to rip and tear, to shred those things that brought the sounds of men into his world. But of course he could do nothing. That was the way of this dream.

Dresden rose up in the grass to stand at his full height. His eyes glinted in the twilight, twin bright points framed by the inky shadows of his mane. The gazelle they had been stalking caught sight of him and fled. He did not care. His attention was all on the buzzing sound and, a moment later, on the brown cloud of dust that accompanied it.

Dresden watched them, uneasy. He knew of men, and he understood their guns well enough.

Then unease turned to terror. Naga had not waited. Naga had not watched. Instead she approached the men with all the bravado of youth. As he watched, a man raised a gun to his shoulder and, with a puff and a crack, Naga fell. Dresden, roaring, charged across the veldt for the last time, not caring about the danger, wanting only to seize the prey that dared hurt his daughter, to rend and tear, to shred its life.

Instead, mid-charge, he watched as the men raised the sticks to their shoulders, felt the sting of the needles in his back, his neck. Suddenly he could no longer stand.

Dresden, dreaming, understood he would wake in a distant land, wake in a high-walled trap, slick beyond climbing, tall beyond jumping. There would be no escape. The rest of his life stretched out before him, worse than any nightmare. Worse, they would take *Naga* as well. He had failed his cub. That knowledge bore down on his heart like a stone.

He and his cub would wake under strange stars, and all the days and nights of her life would be poisoned by the sounds and smells of men.

Now, SEASONS LATER and an ocean away, Dresden jerked awake. He saw humans in the pit with him, three of them, very close.

Dresden wondered if he might still be dreaming. He raised his head, sniffed the night air. It stank of smoke. The horizon glowed with unnatural light. Not far away, machines roared and clanked. *This is real, then.* He gathered his feet under him and stood, rumbling a little deep in his chest. His craft stirred in him for the first time in a very long while. If they came just a bit closer, he would spring. If not, then he would sidle up to them, pretending to be—

"Good evening," one of the three said. "Please pardon our intrusion. We mean no disrespect." He spoke in the language of the hunt, spoke it *perfectly*, though perhaps with the tiniest hint of tiger accent. "Are you the one they call the Thorn of Dawn?"

Dresden blinked. Thorn of Dawn was the name his father had given him. He thought he would never hear it again. Astonished, he swished his tail. *Yes.*

"Good. I thought that it might be you. I am called Michael. I hunted for a time with the pride of the Red Wind." He glanced around the pit. "It was there that I heard of your troubles."

For a moment, Dresden was speechless. The Red Wind lived a long run or so to the west of his home. They were fierce, and well respected. *Hunted* with them? A *man*? After a moment's consideration he made the sound he might have made if he saw another lion in the distance: *Who are you? What do you want?*

"That is a bit involved. Let me begin by saying that I am the adopted son of Ablakha, and apprentice to the tiger Nobununga. I bear Nobununga's scent, and hunt at his side. This is my brother David, who is the slave of murder, and my sister Carolyn, also of the house of Ablakha. We come bearing news of Nobununga. May we approach?"

Ablakha? Dresden knew the name. He was a heretic, an enemy of the Forest God. But Nobununga was a different matter. He was an ancient tiger, said to be the ruler of all the forests of the world. Dresden padded over to the man and sniffed him, just as he might have done when receiving a fellow lion. And, sure enough, the man did smell of tiger. *Hmm.*

Dresden decided to err on the side of courtesy—if even half of what he heard about Nobununga was true, that would be the wisest course. He froze and allowed himself to be scented in turn. The man gave his mane a quick sniff and backed away. This was exactly the proper thing for a junior hunter to do in these circumstances.

Dresden furrowed his brow. He had no love for men in general, and Ablakha was an enemy of God. But each night he spent under these strange stars, Dresden had prayed himself to sleep. He did not bemoan the fate that had fallen to him, did not protest that his lifelong piety was rewarded in this way. He asked nothing for himself. He prayed only that his cub be given a chance at life beyond this cage. Each night Dresden begged God to grant him this one prayer, to accept his own life as forfeit. He could not think how this might possibly be related . . . but God had surprised him before.

Dresden settled back on his haunches and lifted his forepaw, gave it a quick lick. This was a respectful gesture, if not quite a welcome.

Despite himself, he was curious to hear what the *man* had to say.

III

"—and that motherfuckin' lion dropped not *five feet* away from me, I kid you not," Marcus was saying. "He was *pissed*. If my third shot hadn't caught him just right . . ."

"For real?" Aliane said.

"For real."

The little patch of forest they were in was supposed to look wild. It pretty much did from a distance. Up close, not so much. Even if you discounted the little Christmas-tree lights marking the path, something about it said "landscaping." The palms were too evenly spaced, or something. But wild or not, Marcus's walled forest was plenty big. She could barely make out the sounds of the party.

"Anyway, once the big lion was asleep, I just walked over and picked up the cub. She was little-bitty then. And then when I did that, I heard this roar and here comes *momma* running after me now."

"What'd you do?"

"Well, I put down the cub. But it was too late. Momma was a crafty bitch—she snuck in a lot closer than the daddy had been, and all our tranquilizer guns were empty. So one of the native guys, he pulls out a rifle and shoots her."

"Aww! You *shot* her? She was just trying to protect her baby."

"Yeah, we shot her! She was fixin' to eat my ass. And lucky we did, too. She landed on one of them dudes we had toting our tents and tore his arm all up before she died. I heard later it had to get amputated."

Some of what Aliane felt must have shown on her face.

"It's OK. I gave him some money." Marcus looked at her. "What?"

"Nothing," she said. Then, in hopes of changing the subject, "How long ago was this?"

"Mmm . . . this was maybe a month after I got off tour, so I guess it must be coming up on a year now. Naga—she was the cub—has grown a lot. Back at the house I got a picture of me standing with my foot on her dad while I'm holding her. Now she's pushing two hundred pounds, and she's only half-grown."

"Damn. How big's the daddy?"

"Like, maybe four hundred pounds? It took four people to lift him. Twelve hours later we was all on a plane back to Connecticut."

"They let you bring lions in?"

"I got a permit. This here's a zoo."

Aliane looked around her and shivered. The weed was doing its thing, but not in a good way. The landscaped forest seemed very dark, very deep. She could hardly hear the party at all anymore. For some reason she thought of Mae, her mother, thought of their last fight. Aliane had come home from the city to visit, but she had not brought enough drugs. After two days she grew sick. She lost control of her bowels, became weak. She huddled on the mat where she had slept as a child, sweating, shaking. Mae brought her a bowl of *feijoada*, a glass of water, and a cool cloth, her face soft and compassionate in the light of the candle. She remembered the hurt on Mae's face when she slapped the bowl out of her hands. She didn't want food. *Food* was not what she needed. She left the next morning without saying good-bye, fled to São Paolo, to the lights and the nightclubs and the men who would give her things if she would do things for them. She didn't mind. Anything was better than growing old in a simple shack on the edge of the Pantanal, wasting her life the way Mae had done. But here in the shadows Mae's face came to her again.

"Let's go back," Aliane said. "I'm, um, cold."

"In a minute. We're almost there."

A few steps later the path ended in a small clearing. Marcus opened up a panel in what had looked like a tree. All of a sudden the clearing was flooded with light.

"Whoa." She blinked. "What's that building?" It looked like a garden shed, except on stilts.

"Chicken coop," he said. "The zoo guy said to keep it way over here so they can't smell the lions. It gets 'em all riled-up."

Just like the towels and the marble foyer, the door to the chicken coop had been stamped with Marcus's initials, written in flowery Old English script. *On a chicken coop?* "*Palhaço,*" she said, louder than she intended.

"What?"

"Nothing." She gave him her best cover-girl smile.

Marcus smiled back. "Here, take this." He handed her a long bamboo pole with a length of thin rope tied to one end.

"What's this for?"

"Told you," he said. "We're going fishing." He grinned. "You'll probably want to wait out here. It's pretty smelly inside." A moment later she heard a wild cacophony from inside the shed, five parts angry chicken noises and one part irritated rap star.

"C'mere, you little shit!"

Squawk, flutter, cackle.

"Goddammit!"

After a couple of minutes of this the door opened and Marcus emerged holding a wire cage containing two chickens. The birds' wings flapped quite a bit, but they were reasonably calm, all things considered.

"Gimme that," he said.

She handed over the bamboo rod. Marcus put it over his shoulder like a fishing pole. The cage in his other hand reminded her of a tackle box. He made a lasso out of the string on the end of the pole and slipped it around one chicken's foot.

All of a sudden it dawned on her what he was going to do. "Oh, Marcus, no . . ."

He flashed her his album-cover grin, his gold grill shiny against his white skin. "Gangsta, baby. Come on." He headed back the way they had come. She followed, then stopped. "Marcus?"

"What?"

"I thought I saw something move over there."

He squinted out into the night. "Probably a monkey," he said. "We got a couple of monkeys in the trees. They won't bother you. Come on."

Aliane walked behind him, feeling sick. It seemed to her that the chickens grew agitated as they approached the lion pit. Only a little, though. *If it was me getting fed to that cat I'd be squawking my head off*, she thought. *They're lucky they're so dumb.*

A minute or so later they emerged in the small clearing. Marcus walked out onto the bridge between the two lion pits and dangled the chicken over the edge. He let out some slack in the line. The chicken flapped its wings, helpless. It squawked in terror.

"Oh, Marcus, don't do this. . . ."

"Just watch!" He snickered. "It's hilarious." He bounced the chicken at the end of the string. "C'mere, Dresden," Marcus called. "C'mere, big guy! Suppertime."

"Baby, please, why don't we go back to the—" She broke off. Marcus wasn't smiling anymore. "Baby, what's wrong?"

"Dresden?" Marcus said. "C'mere, big guy." He looked back and forth across the pit. Aliane followed his gaze. The pit was an oval shape, deep but not terribly big. It was about forty feet across at its widest point. There was grass on the bottom, some concrete boulders, a couple of sawed-off tree trunks that were supposed to look natural but didn't. You could see every inch of the pit from where they were standing.

"Where's the lion?" she asked.

Marcus just looked at her. His eyes were very wide. The chicken dangling at the end of its string squawked again, outraged. Marcus dropped the pole. The bird fell five feet or so. The loop came off its foot. With a bit of fluttering it freed itself, then stomped around, making outraged clucks.

Nothing came to see what the fuss was about.

"Marcus, where's the lion?"

"Shhhh," Marcus said. He held one manicured finger up to his lips. His brow was knotted. He lifted up the back of his shirt and pulled out a pearl-handled 9mm automatic.

"Are you saying it got *out?*" she whispered. "How could it get *out?* You said there was no way—"

"Shh!" Marcus's face was strained. It was too dark to see much, but he could still listen. After a moment, Aliane listened with him.

Crickets. The soft echoes of cars on the freeway. Up by the house, there was a big splash as someone fell into the pool. Laughter.

Then, closer in—not far away at all, really—a branch cracked.

"Marcus?" she said softly.

He turned and looked at her. There was no need for him to speak. The look on his face said it all.

The pit was empty.

The pit was empty and something was moving out in the night.

IV

"Marcus, *o que é que é?*"

"I don't know," said Marcus. He didn't speak Portuguese but, really, there was only one thing she could be asking about. But he *did* know. A stick had cracked, close by, a big one. He jacked the slide back on his pistol, cocking it. In the distance, up at the house, a bunch of asshole freeloaders were laughing. By now the album was on to the third track, something called "Money Shot" that his A&R man liked quite a bit and, oh, something was moving out there in the night.

"What do we do?"

Marcus rocked his head in time with "Money Shot," thinking. Then it came to him: "The Husbandry Room," he said. The zoo guy had shown it to him. It was an underground room between the two lion pits, very solid, with poured concrete walls and metal doors. There was a slit in the wall with a metal slide in it for watching the lions, like the slit in the door of a jail cell. "We can get in there and . . ." What? Make a call? Hide out? It didn't matter. He would be safe. "Come on."

"Yeah, fuck that," Aliane said behind him. "I'm going back to the—" She stopped and gasped. "Marcus?"

Something in her tone made him turn. Just in front of her, less than five feet away, stood the lion she had come to see. His muzzle wrinkled back over thick yellow fangs.

Aliane turned toward him. Her expression was dreamlike. "Tell Mae that I—"

Dresden sprang. The two of them went to the ground together, wrapped in a cloud of dust and small rocks. Aliane's head bounced off the ground. She squirmed a bit, but the lion gripped her with forepaws the size of shovel blades. Then it had its jaws around her neck. The angle at which it held her was such that she was looking directly at Marcus. She seemed resigned, even peaceful.

A few moments later Marcus was a member of a fairly exclusive club. He had no idea how many people had been firsthand witnesses to not one but *two* lion attacks, but he thought that the number would be very, very small. *Gangsta, baby,* he thought, and wet himself.

About two hundred yards away he could hear the party going on. Some chick with a thick Bronx accent was saying "Oh. My. Gawd" over and over. The sound of her voice was like ice picks in his ears. *I fucking HATE my friends,* he thought. *Fuck it. I quit. No more rap-star bullshit for me. Starting tomorrow I'm going to flight school.* The rapper thing had never been his first love. He sort of fell into it after a talent show in high school. *If David Lee Roth can be a paramedic, I can be a pilot.*

The lion, his muzzle bloodied, looked up from Aliane's body. He roared.

Marcus screamed. He felt sudden weight in his boxers. He squeezed off three quick shots from his nine, kicking up dirt high and wide of the lion. The stink of his shit hung in the warm night air.

Marcus moaned, thinking about the Husbandry Room. The entrance was on the far side of the lion pits, a closet-sized cinder-block building built to keep the rain off the stairs. The door to this stair house was thick steel. No lion could claw through it.

I'll be safe in there.

Marcus turned his back on Aliane without a second thought. He sprinted off the path and into the dark. The small, tasteful lights lining the path blinked off. The stair house entrance was well off the path, hidden behind a tall hedge, surrounded by undergrowth. Marcus didn't quite see it in time. He crashed into the metal door, splitting his lip open. He didn't even notice. The pain in his mouth was eclipsed by a terrible vision—his key ring, hanging from a peg in the kitchen.

"Ah no," he said. "No, no, no, no."

He fumbled at the door handle, sure that it would be locked. But the handle turned easily in his hand. "Thank you, Jesus," he whispered, yanking it open. "Thank you, thank—"

Then he screamed, as much from surprise as terror.

There was a man just inside the door, standing on the top stair. *He's blocking my waaaay*, Marcus thought. Even his thoughts were moans now. Time seemed very slow. The guy was enormous, both in height and muscle, but—*what the fuck?*—he was wearing a lavender tutu.

How the hell did he get in there? Marcus wondered. Then, on the heels of that, *A tutu?* Marcus briefly entertained the idea that he was dreaming. *It doesn't matter.* All that mattered was that he was in the way. Marcus lifted his left hand to push the man aside, simultaneously raising his right to threaten him with the gun. *Threaten my ass*, Marcus thought. *I'll shoot him if I—*

There was a sudden, bright explosion of motion. He felt a sort of pressure on the fingers of his gun hand, then found himself sitting on his ass in the dirt. He looked down and saw that his two smallest fingers were dangling at an odd angle. A splinter of bone poked out of his pinkie. Seeing this, he felt the first twinge of pain.

He looked up. The man in the tutu was examining Marcus's pistol. He ejected the magazine and twirled it between his fingers like the flourish at the end of a magician's trick.

He flashed Marcus a grin. His teeth were very dark, almost black. He stepped out of the stairwell and circled around behind Marcus, dropping the unloaded pistol in his lap as he passed.

Another man, this one completely naked, climbed up out of the dark stairwell.

"Are y'all with the party?" It occurred to Marcus that someone might have spiked his wine cooler. *That's it! I bet Wilson slipped some of that PCP in my Bayberry fizz.* Good old Wilson. They would laugh about this later.

"You best not be butt-fucking down there! I don't want no faggot shit around up in *my*—"

"Shhh," said a woman's voice from the darkness. "Out there. Lions."

Marcus opened his mouth, then shut it. It wasn't an unreasonable point. When he spoke again his tone was softer. "Who the fuck are you?"

The woman stepped forward. "I am Carolyn. This is Michael. That is my brother David."

"Yeah, hi, pleezdameetcha, now gimme a goddamn hand so we can get down in—"

She shook her head. "No."

"What do you mean, 'no'?" Something occurred to him. "Heyyyy . . . are y'all the ones who let my lions out?"

"We are."

"Why the hell would you— Are you crazy? Are you with PETA?"

She shook her head. "I don't know what that is. No."

"Never fucking mind. Just get out of my way."

"No."

"Suit yourself." He put his left hand on the ground, prepared to stand. *If that bitch gets in my way, I will knock her on her—*

A shadow fell over him. Marcus looked up.

"If you try to go downstairs, David will hurt you," she said. "Maybe just a little, maybe a great deal. You should not try."

Marcus looked the big man up and down, gauging his chances. His shoulders slumped. "What do you *want?*" All the fight was gone from his voice.

David smiled.

"I am to give you a message," the woman said.

"From who?"

"The message is from Dresden."

For a moment, he thought she meant the city. "You talking about the *lion? That* Dresden?"

"Yes. Why do you call them that?"

"Dresden and Nagasaki? From, like, in the war . . ."

Off to his side he heard laughter. He turned. The big man, David, made a ka-boom sound. He held his hands up in the air and drew them out as if there were a fireball between them.

"Yeah," Marcus said. "Ka-boom."

Still chuckling, the big guy patted him on the shoulder. Marcus answered him with a small but sincere smile. *Finally. Someone gets it.* That moment ended up being the high point of his day.

The woman squatted down to be at eye level with him. "Do you watch television?"

The question took a moment to sink in. "Why the fuck you care?"

She repeated herself, patiently enough. "Do you watch television?"

"I . . ." Marcus's eyes darted around, looking for safety. All around him the jungle pressed in. *Humor the crazy people.* "Yeah, man, I watch TV."

"You have seen it when the television shows the hunt? In Africa? When a lion brings down a zebra, or a wildebeest?"

Marcus didn't like where this was going. "I . . . yeah . . . I guess so." It wasn't a zebra that he had seen, but a gazelle. *Close enough.*

"Good. What you saw was called"—she twittered something at the naked guy, and he rumbled deep in his chest. He sounded *exactly* like a lion. The hair on the back of Marcus's neck rose.

"In the language of the hunt, that word describes a specific way of killing," the woman said. "It is a thing of respect. Most times, the hunter has no wish to hurt his prey. It is only that he is hungry, that this is the way of things. When you were watching television, did you notice that past a certain moment, the zebra doesn't resist?"

Marcus had not seen that, exactly, but he remembered seeing the gazelle with three lions burrowing around in its guts. He'd thought it was dead. Then it lifted its head, looked down at what was being done to it, and looked away. He'd been smoked-up when he saw this, and it freaked him out enough that he had to change the channel.

"Good. You do know. The prey doesn't move because it feels no pain. The lion touches it in a certain way, and unbinds it from the plane of anguish. This is part of the craft of hunters. When the kill is this way, the lions say . . ." She nodded at the naked man.

He rumbled again, eerily lionlike.

"Your woman died in this way, if it matters to you. She didn't suffer at all."

Marcus thought of the gazelle, staring into the camera, thought of the light receding from Aliane's green eyes.

"But there is another way of killing. This is done when the lion hunts out of hate, rather than hunger. For such times the big cats have a touch that *enhances* suffering rather than relieves it. Under this touch the prey's spirit is bound to the plane of anguish. The pain is like drowning. Often the damage to their spirit is such that there is not enough left of them to return to the forgotten lands. Those killed in this way are ruined forever. It is as if they were never born." Her eyes crinkled. "I saw this done once. It was a terrible thing." She touched his arm with real sympathy. "The lion wishes me to inform you that this is how you will die."

Marcus's eyes flicked back and forth among the three of them, looking for some sign that this was a joke. The woman's face was grave. The guy in the tutu watched him avidly, his eyes cruel and alive. Marcus wasn't sure what was worse.

"So . . . you're just going to *feed* me to that thing?"

"We are, yes."

"Why?" Marcus whispered. "Why would you do something like that?"

"Because that is what the hunter wants," she said. "We came to an arrangement, you see. This is his price."

The big man in the tutu smiled at him. Moonlight glinted off the blade of his spear.

"If we free his daughter and give him the time to kill you as he wishes, he will help us. He will protect our agent as if he were his own cub." She shrugged, stood. "What he asks isn't so much. It is fair, even."

"*Fair?* . . . I . . ."

"You what?" She looked down, her face mostly in shadow. The compassion he had seen before was gone. "You invaded the lion's home. You murdered his mate, the mother of his cub. You kidnapped him and his daughter here and cast them down in a pit. Is that about right?"

"Yeah, but . . . I mean . . ."

"And why did you do this? To what purpose? You were going to steal their lives so they could growl and roar for the amusement of your whores?"

"Sort of . . . I guess. But I mean, you saw *Scarface*, right? It was—"

"Stop talking." She spoke to the naked man in a language he did not understand. He said something back to her, then made a sound amazingly like a lion's roar. "Please excuse me," she said. "I'd rather not watch."

"Hang on!" Marcus said. "I got a *lot* of money! We could—"

She and the naked man faded back into the stairwell and started down to the Husbandry Room. They shut the door behind them. The big man in the tutu smiled down at him. "Hey, man," Marcus said. "Help me out, here. You want to get into show business? I could—"

The big man smiled wider. He pointed over Marcus's shoulder, back into the woods.

Not wanting to, Marcus turned to look. Dresden and his daughter stood just behind him, closer than he would have thought possible. Somewhere out in the impossible distances of the night he heard the Bronx chick saying "Oh. My. Gawd."

Down in the pit, safe and comfortable, the chicken squawked.

Chapter 6

About Half a Fuckton of Lying-Ass Lies

I

Steve woke up in 1987, more or less.

It was a teenager's bedroom. He was pretty sure about that part. The walls were covered with posters of singers—Wham!, the B-52's, Boy George, others—that he vaguely remembered from high school. A rack of cassette tapes hung across from the bed and, next to it, a collage of Polaroids. Teenage boys in acid-wash jeans and parachute pants mugged for the camera—fake-singing, flexing their muscles, that sort of thing. In one of the Polaroids two boys were kissing.

Steve blinked. *Where the hell am I?* He remembered being in the jail chapel, remembered the stinky dude in the tutu killing Dorn and the guard. Thinking of the tutu and the two guys kissing in the Polaroid, a horrible thought bubbled up: *Maybe Tutu Guy kidnapped me as some sort of sex slave? Like that guy in* Pulp Fiction*?*

But that was too terrible to contemplate. *Think, think.* He remembered getting slugged in the chapel. A few seconds later he was moving down the tile corridor, slung over the guy's shoulder, watching guts and severed limbs roll by like he was on the Horrible Shit ride at a high-end amusement park.

Someone's arm had been lying on the floor—just the arm, nothing else. It looked surprisingly un-gross—not much blood, and muscles like a medical drawing. A few paces farther down most of another guard came into view. He was an older dude, fiftyish, cut neatly in half just above the belly button. *What did that?* Steve remembered wondering. *Giant scissors?* The half of his face that Steve could see was bloodless and unmarked, eyes open. Steve remembered recognizing him, remembered squirming, and . . .

And then I woke up here.

The alarm clock on the nightstand pretty much had to be from 1987 as well. *No one makes stuff out of wood-grain plastic anymore, right?* The clock didn't work, though. Someone had stomped a crater in it, then drawn a circle around it in what looked like corn flour.

Steve blinked at this for a few seconds, trying to imagine a remotely plausible reason why someone might do such a thing.

Steve sat up and peeped out through the venetian blinds at the foot of the bed, wincing at the metal rattle they made. His head hurt. The sun was either just coming up or about to go down. At first he wasn't sure which, but then a couple of houses down some guy came home from work and got the mail. Kids were playing ball in the dude's backyard. *Not dawn, then. I slept through the day.*

Questions answered, Steve let the blinds fall closed. If he had known that this sunset would be the last he would ever see, he probably would have taken a couple of seconds to savor it.

He still had on the jail coveralls. That was sort of a relief, in light of his fears about becoming a butt slave, but still not ideal. The closet turned out to be full of things like parachute pants and acid-wash jeans. After a brief rummage he put on some black sweatpants—tightish, but serviceable—and a gray concert T-shirt. The logo of the band Heart was stenciled across the chest in bright-orange letters, glowing like a coal.

He followed the sound of voices out into the hall. Out there it was warmer than in the bedroom. It smelled good, like freshly baked something-or-other—bread, maybe, or sweet rolls? His stomach rumbled.

But under that was a bad smell, something he didn't quite recognize. There was a metallic sound as well. *Clink. Scratch. Click.* It was vaguely familiar. *Clink. Scratch. Click.*

Steve peeped around the corner into the living room. The big guy in the tutu was asleep on the floor in front of the TV. The sound was off, but Nazi artillery rumbled across North Africa on the History Channel.

Steve wondered at this for a minute. *TV? He doesn't speak English, does he?* On-screen Rommel held binoculars to his face. *I bet he does like tanks, though.* Next to the tutu guy a halfway demolished pile of brownies rested on a white plate. Brown crumbs stuck to the dried blood in his mustache and on his chest. His bronze sword thingy with the chain lay at his fingertips.

Half a dozen other people, some almost as weird, sat here and there in the living room as well. They glanced at Steve without much interest as he walked in.

Next to the couch stood a man in brown business slacks, cut off ragged at the knees, one pant leg a couple of inches higher than the other. His bare chest was tattooed with dozens of triangles, the smaller ones inscribed in the larger, down to a black dot at the midpoint of his breastbone.

Seeing Steve, he put his hand on the shoulder of a woman sitting on the couch. She had dirty-blond hair, hacked short and carelessly. She wore what looked like the top half of a black one-piece bathing suit, cut into a sort of sports bra. She put her hand over the man's, laced her fingers in his.

Clink. Scratch. Click. In the darkest corner of the room a woman sat on the floor, knees huddled up to her chin. Skeletal arms poked out from the remains of an apocalyptically filthy gray dress. Half a dozen flies buzzed around her head. As Steve watched, she flipped open a Zippo. *Clink.* Lit it. *Scratch.* Closed it up again. *Click.*

Her eyes never wavered from the place of the flame. Unsettled now, Steve jerked when a new person entered the room. He recognized the Christmas sweater and bicycle shorts immediately.

"*You.*" Small knuckle pops as his hands clenched into fists.

Carolyn held her finger to her lips. "Shh." She pointed at the bloody man in the tutu sleeping on the floor between the knife and the brownies. She jerked her thumb back over her shoulder toward the kitchen.

Steve opened his mouth to yell at her, then, with a glance at the napping murderer, nodded instead. He tiptoed around the couch as quietly as he was able. The couple stood up and followed in his wake. The woman with the lighter went *clink, scratch, click.*

There was another person in the kitchen, an older woman, kneading dough. To Steve's mild surprise she was dressed normally; floor-length fleece housecoat, a bit faded but clean, and slippers.

"Hello, there!" She spoke in a half-whisper. "I'm Eunice McGillicutty. Would you like a cinnamon roll? They're just out of the oven."

"Steve Hodgson. Uh, pleased to meet you." Somewhat to his surprise, he realized this was true. Unlike the others, she didn't seem like the sort of person who might keep a guy chained up in her basement. He briefly considered thanking her for this, but gave up when he couldn't think of a delicate way to phrase it. "Sure. A cinnamon roll would be great."

The old lady smiled, pleased. She pointed at a baking dish. "Coffee over there," she said. Steve grabbed a mug off a wooden peg and helped himself to a cup.

"Hello, Steve," Carolyn said, her voice not quite a whisper.

"Hi!" he said, a little too brightly.

"That's Mrs. McGillicutty. She speaks English."

"Yes. Yes, she certainly does."

Carolyn jerked her thumb at the couple behind her. "These are Peter and Alicia. They don't speak English. Not much, anyway."

"What about the big guy out in the living room?"

"That's David. His English is pretty bad as well."

"And the other one? The one who keeps playing with the lighter?"

"That's Margaret."

"No English?"

"Hardly any anything. She almost never talks."

"Can I ask you something?"

"Sure."

"Can you think of any reason I shouldn't grab one of those kitchen knives and stab you in the fucking neck?"

Carolyn pursed her lips, considering. "You might get blood on the cinnamon rolls."

"I'm only partly kidding."

"OK," she said. "Fair enough. I can see why you might be a little upset."

His rage flared. Steve glanced at the knives, almost not kidding anymore. "*A little upset?*" he hissed. "You framed me for murder! Of a fucking cop! They're talking about the *death penalty*, Carolyn! Lethal. Fucking. Injection. *Life* in *prison*! If I'm *lucky*!

"Try to keep it down," Carolyn said. "You don't want to wake up David."

No, Steve thought, thinking of the swinging intestine that dangled from the ceiling outside the jail chapel, *I probably don't.* "OK," he said in a fierce whisper. "Fair enough. Why don't you quietly explain why you'd do such a thing to me? What did I ever do to piss you off?"

Carolyn winced a little. "Nothing," she said. "I'm not angry at you. That's absolutely the last thing that I am." She hesitated. "For what it's worth, there are some sound reasons for all this. I can't go into details, but I really am sorry. I can see where it might be a bit . . . upsetting."

"Upsetting," Steve marveled, unable to believe that he had heard right. "Well, that is one way of putting it. Another way of putting it would be that you permanently and completely ruined my life. That's the version that I sort of prefer."

Carolyn rolled her eyes. "Don't be so melodramatic. You're not in jail anymore, are you?" She pointed at the tray. "Have another cinnamon roll. They're good."

Mrs. McGillicutty looked over her shoulder. "Help yourself, dear."

Steve felt like his heart was boiling. "Melodramatic?" His hand drifted, unbidden, toward the block of kitchen knives. *"Melodramatic?"*

"Calm down," Carolyn said. "It's not as bad as all that."

"What do you mean it's not—"

"Quiet, Steve. Shut up for a second and I'll explain. I have a plan. If you'll do a small service for me, I can make every single one of these problems you've mentioned go away."

"Oh?"

"Yup." Carolyn rummaged around in the refrigerator and came out with a plastic bottle of orange juice. She twirled off the top and lifted it to her mouth.

"Glasses are over there, dear," Mrs. McGillicutty said pointedly.

"Sorry." Carolyn got a glass.

Steve considered. "You can make a murder charge go away? A *death penalty* case?"

Carolyn poured some orange juice and took a swig. "Yup."

"And how, pray tell, might you be planning to do that?"

"Grab me one of those cinnamon rolls and pull up a chair. I'll show you."

II

Carolyn stood up and disappeared into the nether reaches of the house. While she was away, Steve went to the refrigerator looking for a Coke. All they had in the main compartment was diet, but he spotted something approximately the same shade of red as a Coke can in the vegetable crisper.

Carolyn padded up behind him a moment later. "Steve, this is—"

"Hold up a second," he said, staring into the crisper. "Is this a heart?"
It's definitely not a Coke.

Carolyn didn't answer immediately. "Beg pardon?"

"In this bag here. In the fridge. Is this a heart? Like, a person's heart? It looks like a person's heart in your refrigerator, Carolyn."

"Um . . . no. I mean, yes, it's a heart. But not a person's. It's from a cow. A bull. David was going to make an hors d'oeuvre for a guest, but he had to cancel."

"Yeah, um, no." Steve turned. "That's nowhere near big enough to be a bull's—whoa."

Next to Carolyn stood a blond woman who Steve hadn't seen before. Three children, silent and pale, clung to the woman's waist. One of the kids, a little boy, had huge purple bruises all around his neck. The girl next to him had a deep dent in her forehead.

Steve knelt down in front of the children. "You guys OK? Are you, like . . . hurt?" He reached out to touch the crater in the girl's skull. She cringed back.

"They only speak to their mother," Carolyn said. "Steve, this is Rachel."

"Well, that's fucking weird. What the hell happened to the girl's head?"

"It was, um, an accident. She fell. Off her bike." Then, hissing, "Don't *say* anything, Steve. You'll embarrass her."

"And the boy?"

"Football," Carolyn said, deadpan. The boy peeped out from behind his mother's waist and gave a small nod.

"Hmm." Then, pointing at Rachel, "What about her? No English?"

"No English," Carolyn confirmed. She and Rachel spoke for a moment in a vaguely singsongy language that sounded like the illegitimate child of Vietnamese and a catfight.

"What's she doing here, then?"

"Rachel is good with secrets," Carolyn said. She lifted Mrs. McGillicutty's telephone receiver and set it down on the kitchen table. "You still want me to fix your legal troubles, right?"

Steve looked at the heart in the vegetable crisper, opened his mouth, then shut it with a click of his teeth. He shut the refrigerator door. "Yes, please."

"Then make it be loud," Carolyn said, pointing at the phone.

"What?"

"So everyone can hear."

"Oh. Yeah, sure." He studied the receiver for a minute, then punched the Speaker Phone button.

"Now make it be the directory."

"What?"

"Where you tell them the name, and they give you the number."

Steve dialed three digits.

"What city?" said a mechanical voice.

"Washington, DC," Carolyn said.

"What listing?"

"White House switchboard."

Steve raised an eyebrow.

The machine reeled off the numbers. When it asked if she wanted to be connected for an additional charge of fifty cents, Carolyn said yes. The operator picked up on the third ring.

"My name is Carolyn," she said. "I'd like to be connected with the president."

Steve gaped at her.

"Last name, please?"

Carolyn's brow furrowed. "I'm not sure. Does it matter?"

The operator sounded bored. "I'm sorry, Ma'am. The president is unavailable at the moment. If you'd care to leave a message I'll see that—"

"He'll speak to me," Carolyn said. "Prepare to authenticate. Today's code word is 'bolt.'"

"Oh!" the operator said. "Hang on. I'll transfer you."

"Could it be Sopaski?" Steve said, remembering what Erwin had told him.

"What?"

"Your last name. Could it be Sopaski?"

Carolyn thought about it for a second. "Actually, yeah. That sounds—"

A man's voice boomed out of the headset. "This is Sergeant Davis," he said. "Please authenticate."

Carolyn pointed at Rachel and raised her eyebrows quizzically. Rachel beckoned to a little girl in a grimy gray sundress. The child whispered something in her ear. Rachel relayed it to Carolyn in that singsong language.

"The code is 'bear 723 walking 33744 dawn,'" Carolyn said, translating.

"Please hold." There was a sound of typing. A moment later the man said, "I'll connect you to Mr. Hamann's office."

Steve thought about this for a moment, then his eyes opened wide. "The *chief of staff*?"

"Shh!" Carolyn said. For about a minute they were in limbo—no hold music, no recorded messages, just silence. Then, "This is Bryan Hamann," a voice said.

Are you fucking kidding me? Steve took a breath, focused on trying to appear calm. He wasn't sure, but he suspected he was doing a really shitty job of this.

"Mr. Hamann, I need you to get the president for me," Carolyn said. "Thanks so much."

"I'm afraid that won't be possible, Miss, ah"—there was a sound of computery clicking—"Carolyn. The president is in a meeting. Is there something that I—"

"Get him out of the meeting."

For a moment there was silence on the other end of the line. Steve suspected that the man was simply having trouble crediting what his ears were telling him. He sympathized. Carolyn let him have a moment.

"Lady, there are exactly three people on the planet who are authorized to use the code you just provided, and I happen to know that you aren't any of them. Now, unless you tell me exactly who you are and how you came by those codes, you're going to be in for some extremely serious trouble. Either way, you've gotten as far up the chain as you're going to." There was a slight clicking on the line.

"I think they're tracing the call," Steve said. He felt like this was a valuable contribution.

"Hush," Carolyn said. She turned to Rachel. The two of them spoke for a few moments. The sound of it put Steve in mind of tropical birds fighting. "Mr. Hamann, please pardon me for being blunt. You seem like a decent man, but I'm pressed for time. I know where the president was on the night of March 28, 1993. I know why Alyson Majors is so quiet these days. I even have access to photographs. If I'm not speaking to the man himself in one minute I'm going to hang up. My next call will be to the *Washington Post*."

There was a brief pause, perhaps two seconds. Hamann didn't bother to put the call on hold, he just dropped the receiver. Steve heard the sound of a door hitting a wall. There was a few seconds of silence, a distant commotion. Next he heard Hamann say, "Clear out. Now. We need the room." There was the sound of a door shutting, then, "This is the president."

Oh-ho! Steve thought. *There's something you don't hear every day.* He took a bite of his cinnamon roll. It was his third. *They really are quite good.*

Carolyn smiled. "How do you do, Mr. President? I'm sorry to be so pushy, but I'm afraid these are unusual circumstances. My name is Carolyn Sopaski."

There was a long silence. "I'm afraid that I don't—"

"My Father is called Adam Black."

There was a very long silence. "Can you repeat that, please?"

She did.

Another pause, shorter this time. "There are a lot of men named—"

"Yes, but my Father is the Adam Black who was mentioned in the folder waiting for you on your desk on the day when you first took office. The yellowish paper, handwritten by Mr. Carter, I believe? Do you remember it?"

"I do," the president said. His voice was faint.

"Excellent. I thought you might. Would you like to know what became of the piece of Air Force hardware with the number 11807-A1 stenciled on the side? I can tell you exactly. I was there."

The president made a whooshing sound. "I see." His voice was weak. "I—that is, my understanding was that a condition of the treaty was that there was to be no contact between—"

Carolyn laughed. "Is that what you call it? A 'treaty'? That's rather grandiose of you, isn't it? The way I recall it, my Father told Mr. Carter to see to it that he was not bothered anymore. Mr. Carter said that he would be happy to take care of it, and be sure to call again if there was ever anything else he could do. My Father said we would. Now I am. Adam Black would be very grateful if you would do him a small favor. A service."

"A service?"

"Yes. My understanding is that you have the power to issue criminal pardons. Is that correct?"

"I do . . ."

"Excellent. I'll send you the details. Thank you, Mr. Pr—"

"May, ah, madam, if I may—may I ask the nature of the offense?"

Carolyn's eyes narrowed. She didn't answer immediately. When she did her tone was noticeably cooler. "Why would that matter?"

"It, ah, it might have bearing on—"

Carolyn sighed. "The man in question hasn't been charged yet, but I'm told that it's just a matter of time. The incident revolves around the murder of a police officer. There are also likely to be some incidental charges—breaking and entering, burglary, things of that nature. Oh, and escape. He left jail yesterday without permission. Some people died. I assume that's some sort of crime as well?"

The president, a former editor of the *Harvard Law Review*, agreed that it probably was.

"But it's the death-penalty case that we're primarily concerned with."

"Death penalty," the president said flatly.

"Yes." Carolyn paused. "If it eases the sting any, I happen to know that the man being charged is quite innocent. I know this for an absolute fact."

"May I ask how?"

"Because I was the one who killed Detective Miner," Carolyn said. "Mr. Hodgson was present but . . . unaware that anything of the kind was going on. Legal technicalities aside, he is completely innocent."

"I see," the president said at length. "Even so, Ms. Sopaski, this could be politically very—"

"My understanding is that when you took office you were briefed on, among other things, a file with the code name Cold Home. The file had blue and red stripes along the border. It was about an inch thick and just chock-full of unanswered questions. Is that correct?"

The president was silent for a beat. "How could you *possibly* know about that?" he hissed.

Carolyn laughed. "I'm afraid that will have to be another unanswered question," she said, and winked at Rachel. "Add it to the file, why don't you? But the fact is that I *do* know, Mr. President. And if you've read the file on Cold Home then you have some idea of what my Father is capable of. I can assure you from my own personal experience that he is not a man you want to make angry. All I'm asking is that you sign a piece of paper. For what it's worth, I consider it very unlikely that the fact you did so would ever be made public."

After a moment the president, who was not a fool, said, "Very well."

"Thank you! I'll be sure to inform Father that you've been very helpful."

"That's very kind of you. Ms. Sopaski, this administration would very much like to open a dialogue with your father. We could—"

"I'm sorry, Mr. President. I'm afraid that will not be possible."

"But—" said the president.

"There is one other thing you can do for me though. When is your next press appearance?"

There was a pause. Someone in the background said, "Tomorrow morning." The president said, "Tomorrow morning, I believe."

Carolyn thought about it for a moment. "Sorry. That's not quick enough. Arrange one for tonight."

"I'm afraid that won't be—"

"That wasn't a request." Her tone was frosty.

There was a long silence at the other end of the line. Steve stared at her, slack-jawed.

"Very well," the president said softly.

"Good. When you're giving that speech I want you to say something for me. Say, mmm, oh, I don't know. Say 'Auld lang syne.' Do you think you could work that into your remarks without raising too many eyebrows?"

"I suppose I *could*," the president said slowly. "May I ask why?"

"Because at some point in the next few minutes it's going to occur to the person you're about to pardon that *mmmmaybe* I'm talking to a man who just *sounds* like you. When he sees you say 'Auld lang syne' on live TV, that will go a long way toward alleviating those doubts."

"I see. Yes, I suppose that can be arranged."

"Excellent!" Carolyn said. "Thank you, Mr. President. That will be all."

She hung up.

III

An hour or so later Steve and Carolyn were alone in the living room. Not long after Carolyn had hung up on the president, the big bloody guy woke up and ate a couple of cinnamon rolls. Then he went to the stinky woman in the corner and took the lighter from her. She seemed to come out of herself then. She smiled up at him. The two of them moved to the back bedroom about the time the president came on.

Steve wanted to focus on the press conference, but he was having trouble. The big guy and the smelly woman were having some truly epic sex back there. It started with squeaking bedsprings, but those were eventually drowned out by bear noises and something not unlike yodeling. The smell of sex and rotting meat wafted throughout the house. Mrs. McGillicutty's bed evidently wasn't rated for stunt fucking, though. Right before the big finish it collapsed with a splintery, wrenching sound. Steve, not unimpressed, noted that the happy couple didn't so much as skip a beat.

He looked around to see if Carolyn or any of the others were as amused by this as he was, but the only one who seemed aware anything was going on was Punkin Tinkletoes, the old lady's pet cat. He had been sleeping by the wall opposite the bedroom. When they bounced off it hard enough to make family photos rain down, the cat sauntered over to join Steve on the couch.

Carolyn waved a hand in front of Steve's eyes and looked pointedly at the TV. "Pay attention, OK? I don't want to have to call him back."

"Sorry."

For the last twenty minutes or so, the president had been yapping about some sort of bill that was supposed to stimulate the economy. He wanted to raise taxes, or maybe lower them. Now he was taking questions.

Steve watched diligently for a couple of minutes. Then the big guy, wrapped in a bedsheet, walked back through the living room into the kitchen. He grabbed two brownies, a bottle of Wesson oil, and—*oh, gosh*—kitchen tongs. Then, grinning like a fiend, he sank back into the bedroom. Punkin Tinkletoes tracked this. Steve thought he might be wondering about the tongs as well. When the big guy disappeared around the corner, the cat turned to Steve with a quizzical blink.

Steve shrugged. "You got me, dude," he whispered. "Honestly, I'm not sure I want to—"

Carolyn poked him again, and Steve shut up. On TV, one of the reporters asked about an upcoming arms summit with the Russians. The president said that the location wasn't fixed yet, but that both he and the Russian liked the idea of doing it in Reykjavik, "if nothing else, for auld lang syne." All the reporter people laughed.

Steve didn't get the joke. *That's the president, though, for really real.* He felt dazed. Mrs. McGillicutty got all the cable channels, and the press conference was covered live on two of them. When it had started, he'd flipped back and forth between C-SPAN and Fox News, thinking maybe it was some sort of elaborate hoax, that they'd just gotten an actor who . . .

Carolyn was looking at him.

"OK," Steve said. "Let's say I believe that you *can* get the president to sign a pardon for me." He was surprised to realize he actually did believe that. "We still have a problem."

"Which is?"

"I have no reason at all to think that you *will*. You may remember, the last time I agreed to run an errand for you I ended up in jail. The day before yesterday my asshole lawyer said, and I quote, I was 'on a fast track to death row.' "

Carolyn's brow furrowed. She brushed her hair back with her fingers. "I'm sorry about that. Really. It was unavoidable. If you do this for me, I *can* and *will* make it better." She reached behind the couch and tossed him the duffel bag full of money she had brought to the bar. "Here's your cash, by the way."

Steve looked down at the bag, then back up at her. The way she tossed it to him suggested a couple of possibilities. One was that she didn't give a fuck about $327,000. Another was that she knew Steve wasn't going to be around long enough to spend it. *Still,* he told himself, *it's not like you have a lot of choices.*

They'd been watching the news for an hour or so. Prior to the surprise press conference, one of the big stories had been his "escape"—Steve thought "kidnapping" would be more accurate, but no one asked him— from jail. Apparently the body count was up in the thirties. CNN was speculating that Steve might be the head of some hitherto unsuspected drug cartel. Fox thought he was probably part of a terrorist organization. Everybody seemed to agree that he was really, really dangerous. They flashed his mug shot about every ten minutes.

The big guy came back out of the room again. He wasn't grinning anymore. As he walked past, he glowered in a way that made Steve distinctly uneasy. He grabbed a couple of candles off the dining-room table and disappeared again, muttering under his breath.

When he was gone, Steve turned to Carolyn. "What did he say?"

"Hmm? Who?"

"Tutu Guy. He keeps grabbing stuff. I'm just curious—what did he say?"

"Oh." Distracted, she searched her memory for a moment. "He said, 'I just can't reach her. Not anymore. I just can't.'"

"Huh." Steve, baffled, meditated on this for a moment. "Any idea what he means by—"

"Would you like a brownie?" Mrs. McGillicutty asked.

Steve opened his mouth to say *No, thanks*, but what came out was "Don't mind if I do!" Three weeks of jail food had left him with an appetite. Plus, the brownies were ridiculously good. Mrs. McGillicutty brought him some milk as well. When he was done he turned to Carolyn. "I don't suppose you've got a cigarette?"

"Sure." She rooted around in her sweater and fished out a pack of Marlboros with some matches tucked into the cellophane. "Can you pay attention now? Pretty please?"

"Yeah, all right." They glared at each other as they lit up. "So, what exactly is it that you want?"

"How good of you to ask. Finally. The reason we broke you out of jail is that we want you to go for a jog."

Steve blinked, thumped his cigarette. "Say again?"

"You're a jogger, right?" He did vaguely remember mentioning something of the sort when they talked at the bar. "We'd like for you to go for a jog."

"That's *it*?"

"And pick something up."

Here it comes, he thought. "What sort of something?"

"We don't know, exactly. We know with a very high degree of precision where it is, but it could look like anything."

"OK . . ." Steve said. "But it will in *fact* be . . . what? Drugs? High explosives?" A horrible thought occurred to him. "Not some sort of nuclear shit?"

Carolyn rolled her eyes, a don't-be-an-idiot look, and fluttered her hand. "No, no. Of course not. Nothing like that. It's—how can I put this?—think of it as a very advanced system of perimeter defense."

"You want me to go get you a land mine? No. Actually, hell no. I'll take my chances in jail."

"It's not a 'land mine,'" Carolyn said. "It's absolutely nothing at all like a land mine. What it is, is a kind of, um . . . do you know what a gravity well is? It's kind of like that, except in reverse, and it only works on certain people."

"I have no idea what that's supposed to mean."

"Hmm. OK, think of it this way. Do you know how microwaves work?"

"No."

"It's based on microwaves."

"Oh, wait. I just remembered. I do know how microwaves work, and what you're saying is bullshit."

"Fine. It isn't microwaves. But how it works really doesn't matter."

"If it doesn't matter, then why don't you tell me?"

"Because it's *very advanced*. You don't have the background. Trust me, please?"

"Fuck no. So, you're . . . what? Some sort of weapons researcher?" That, he could almost believe. "Weird professor type" covered a lot of ground. "Look, I'm not going to even consider this until you tell me what it is I'm picking up."

"You wouldn't—"

"Try me."

She sighed. "It's called a *reissak ayrial*. Its essence is a mathematical construct, a self-referencing tautology, consecrated in the plane of regret. The *reissak* works because the target has the trigger because the *reissak* works. The physical token that you'll be picking up is the *reissak*'s projection into normal space. Do you see?"

Steve stared at her. "You invented this thing?"

"Not me. I'm more of a linguist. Can we get back to the point now?"

Steve grimaced. "Sure." *Thwarted by technobabble.*

"The token that serves as the *reissak*'s nexus is just sitting somewhere, probably out in the open. It could be a Coke can, a McDonald's bag, a mailbox, anything. And for most people—almost certainly including you, Steve—that's all that it actually is."

"But?"

"But not everyone. For some people, it's like poison. The closer you get to it, the worse it hurts, the more damage it does. If you get close enough, it kills you."

"So, it's radioactive? I'm not picking up any radioactive crap."

"No. It's not radioactive."

"What if I don't believe you?"

"Then I guess you're going back to jail, aren't you?" she said brightly.

Steve gritted his teeth.

"It isn't radioactive. I promise." She sniffed, a little offended. "Nothing so crude as that."

"How do you know this thing, whatever it is, won't work on me?"

"Well . . . we don't. Not for sure. But the only ones it does seem to work on are the people connected to Father. Regular people, people like you—FedEx drivers, pizza delivery guys, regular Americans—come and go all the time. It doesn't seem to have any effect on them."

"That's why you did all this to me? You just picked me at random? Because I'm a regular guy?"

Carolyn nodded. "That's about it, yeah."

"Bullshit."

She raised an eyebrow. "I'm not sure that I unders—"

"I mean," Steve said, smiling, "that you are fucking lying to me, you lying-ass liar."

"Steve, I can assure you that—"

"Save it."

"Beg pardon?"

"Don't bother. I'm sure they're very nice lies but, really, don't bother. I'll do it."

She raised an eyebrow again.

"Discounting that duffel bag full of cash, which I seriously doubt you'd let me walk out of here with, I've got no money, no car, no ID, and no one I'm even *close* to close enough to go to for help. I figure I'd last twenty-four hours on my own, tops. Then I'd either be back in jail or, more likely, shot resisting arrest." *And if I say no, you'll probably have that big guy cut my throat, or whatever. I don't think he'd mind at all.*

"Well," she said, "I guess that's good news."

"I'm sure you can see the joy in my eyes. I have some questions, though."

"Of course."

"What's the deal with the jogging? Why don't I just drive in? It'd be quicker, and if this whatever-it-is turns out to be too heavy to carry, then I can—"

"Welllll . . . it's kind of a safety precaution."

"Oh?" He leaned forward, smiling ferociously. "Do tell."

"If"—she held up a finger—"*if* you did turn out to be susceptible to the effects, of the, ah, perimeter defense, then you wouldn't want to be in a car. At the speeds they move, you could hit a fatal depth before you really knew what was happening. On foot, you can just turn around if you start feeling sick."

"Sick how?"

"It's different for everybody. David got a brutal headache. My face started bleeding. Peter caught on fire. Basically, if you're moving along feeling fine and you all of a sudden start feeling pain, turn back before it gets any worse."

"What if I *do* turn out to be susceptible? Do I still get the pardon and the cash?" He wouldn't believe her answer, but he was curious to hear what it was.

"As to the pardon, sure. All we ask is that you try. And, like I said, the money is already yours."

"That was very convincing."

She rubbed her forehead. "Steve, I don't know what to say to—"

"Save it. You said you know *where* this thing is, but not *what* it is? Can you explain that to me?"

"Sure. Because of the way the perimeter-defense system works, the area that is affected is in the shape of a sphere. Basically we got a map and walked the perimeter of the circle. It has to be in the center of that."

He thought this over. "What if it's in a tree or buried or something? It doesn't have to be at ground level."

"Fair point, but we tested for that, as well."

"How?"

"Very carefully. Look, we can go into the methods if you want, but I promise you, the object is at 222 Garrison Drive, fifty-seven feet back from the curb of the street, sitting about two feet off the ground."

"Two feet off the ground? Is it floating?"

"It's on the porch."

"And you have no idea what the object is?"

She shook her head. "It could be anything. Probably it will be something small, innocuous. That porch is usually empty."

"How do you know?"

She scrunched up her face, considering how to answer. "Because it's my house."

"*Your* house?"

"Why does that surprise you?"

"From the way you dress I figured you were homeless."

She frowned. "Well, I'm not. The house belongs to our Father, but we all live there."

"All who?"

She gestured at the room behind her. "My family."

"Yeah . . . you keep calling these guys your family. You don't look much alike."

"We're adopted."

"All of you?"

"Yes. Father took us in when our parents died."

"Sounds like a real prince."

"That's why we're so anxious to be sure he's OK," she said dryly.

"So . . . you think, what? Somebody is trying to keep you out of your own house?"

"It appears that way, yes."

"Any idea why?"

"Father is a more important person than he lets on. He's . . . something of a kingmaker. He has powerful friends."

That, Steve decided, might be true as well. Certainly the president had jumped when the man's daughter said "frog." "And powerful enemies?"

She nodded. "Yes. Some of them might like to inspect things he kept in the house. Books."

So . . . what? Mob accountant? A Meyer Lansky type? "What sort of people are we talking about here? If it's drug cartels, I think I'd just as soon take my—"

Carolyn snorted laughter.

"What's funny?"

"I'm trying to imagine Father involved in a drug deal. No. That isn't it."

"Who, then?"

"I'm really not at liberty to say." She offered a frosty smile.

"Right." Steve sighed. "So you think one of these enemies of your dad snuck in and set your perimeter-defense system?"

"Possibly. Somebody had to put it there. The porch was empty when I left that morning. I'm sure of it. All we really know is that Father hasn't been seen since the perimeter-defense system was set." She fished a crooked Marlboro out of the pack and popped a wooden match alight against her lacquered thumbnail. The flame flickered a little as she held it under the end of the cigarette, amplifying a nearly imperceptible tremble.

"Maybe he was the one who set it. Did you ever think of that?"

She frowned. "That is conceivable. I really can't imagine why he'd do something like that, but . . . maybe. If so, we'd like to go to him and very politely ask him why. Basically we need to get into the Library and look around. There are also reference materials there that may be of use. If you can help us with that, I absolutely guarantee you'll walk away unharmed, wealthy, and free of criminal entanglements."

"We'll pretend for the moment that I believe you. Anything else?"

She bent over and unzipped the duffel bag. There was a holstered pistol inside. "You might need this."

"Oh."

"Is that a problem?"

"No. It's actually sort of weirdly reassuring. Up until now this was sounding way too good to be true. Who might I be shooting, do you think?"

"Well . . . again, very probably no one. But as I said, Father is a powerful man. He has . . . bodyguards. It is possible—not likely, but possible—that they might see you jogging and take it as a threat. In that case," she shrugged, "better to have it and not need it than need it and not have it."

He glanced at the case. It was an HK 9mm semiautomatic. "Three magazines? That's a lot of bullets."

"You might be a lousy shot."

"It so happens that I am. Which means I'm less than enthusiastic about shooting it out with professional bodyguards."

She opened her mouth, hesitated, then shut it.

"What?"

She shook her head.

"*What*, Carolyn?"

"If it came down to a . . . an open conflict with the sentinels . . . you would not be alone."

"Oh? And who, pray tell, would be helping me?"

"Friends of my brother. They're very skilled, I promise. If it comes to that they can and will protect you. You would be safe."

"I don't doubt they're very good." *And probably weird as hell.* "Do you mind if I look at the gun?"

She slid the duffel bag across the table. He took the pistol out of the holster and examined it. He slipped a magazine in, cocked it, pointed it at her. "What if I just shoot you and take the money?"

She gave him a bright smile. "Then I'd be out of this nightmare, I suppose. And my brother David would kill you. He'd probably take his time about it. And we'd find someone else to do the job instead."

She didn't seem even a little nervous. The sounds of sex emanating from the back room stopped. A moment later the big guy, David, peeped around the corner. He smiled at Steve. He said something to Carolyn in that birdsong language of theirs. She answered in kind.

Steve smiled back, wide and reassuring. "Just asking." He lowered the pistol. David watched him for a moment, then grabbed another brownie and went away again. "Anything else?"

"No . . . no."

"What?"

"I just . . . I wish there was a way to keep in touch with you while you're out there. Doing the run. I just can't think of anything we could . . ." She trailed off. "What?"

Steve was staring at her. He was thinking, *This woman is . . . not insane, exactly . . . something else?* What he said was, "Have you not heard of cell phones?"

"Oh," she said. She nodded, wide-eyed and, to Steve's increasingly practiced eye, completely full of shit. "Yeah. Sure. Lots of times."

PART II

THE ANATOMY
OF LIONS

Chapter 7

Garrison Oaks

I

About ten the next morning Steve jogged into the weeds on the shoulder of Highway 78 and slowed to a stop. Acutely aware of his mug shot on CNN, he pretended to be really interested in something in the woods until the car coming up behind him passed. It was a cool, gray morning, just right for a run.

Garrison Oaks came into view as he rounded this last bend, half a mile away and a little downhill. It didn't look like anything special. A couple dozen houses flanked the main drive in neat rows. Three secondary roads branched off it, terminating in culs-de-sac. Some guy was out mowing his lawn. Yawn.

Steve's burglar instincts reared up momentarily. The houses were *OK*, if a trifle on the modest side, but most of the cars out front were fading relics—a 1977 Cutlass Supreme, a blue Datsun, even a station wagon. *Do they even* make *those anymore?* A good rule of thumb, he'd found, was that if a dude has enough cash to drop on a new car, he's also got enough to drop on electronic gizmos, jewelry for the wife, and other pawnable stuff. The converse, he'd found, was also true. *Nah*, he thought. *This place isn't worth robbing.*

Of course, this was no normal burglary. Among other things, he'd never carried a gun before. Carolyn hadn't thought to provide a holster, but twenty minutes or so in Mrs. McGillicutty's garage took care of that. *How*, he wondered, *did humanity ever get along without duct tape?* The makeshift holster was comfortable enough, but the thought of the pistol smoldered in the back of his mind. Dry leaves swirled around his feet as he moved, blown down from the bluff that flanked his course on the left.

When he was a hundred yards or so from the subdivision sign he slowed to a walk, then unclipped Mrs. McGillicutty's cell phone from the top of his sweatpants and punched number 1 on the speed dial: "Home." Number 2 was someone named Cathy. The third slot was a funeral home. The other five slots were empty. He felt a little bad for Mrs. McGillicutty.

Carolyn picked up on the first ring. "Steve?"

"Yeah."

"Where are you?"

"About fifty yards out," he said, clipping the phone back in his waistband. Mrs. McGillicutty also had a Bluetooth headset, which he had found unopened in the box. Now it was clipped to his ear. Between that and the pistol he felt like a mall ninja pretending to be a Secret Service agent.

"OK. Remember, when you get near the gate, you want to enter gradually. If you feel anything out of the ordinary, turn around and head back the way you came."

"Understood," he said. He brushed the Garrison Oaks sign with his fingertips as he passed. "I'm in."

"Feel anything?" *Clink.*

"Nope. Nothing." Two steps, three. He thought about asking her if she was sure the whole thing wasn't in her head. Then he looked down. The asphalt under his feet was dark with congealed blood. There was a lot of it. The question died in his mouth.

"How far in are you?" *Clink.*

"Twenty feet or so."

"OK," she said clinically. "That means you don't have the trigger. If you did you'd be feeling it by now." *Clink.*

"If you say so. Hey, what's that clinking sound I keep hearing?"

"Margaret is playing with her lighter." Carolyn said something in angry tones. The clinking stopped. "Do you see anything unusual?" Her voice was tense.

"The guy on the corner has a lot of dandelions in his yard," Steve said. "A real infestation."

"I mean is there anyone watching you? Anything like that?" She spoke pleasantly enough, but it sounded like she was gritting her teeth.

Steve, pleased to be getting under her skin, smiled in a way the Buddha would have disapproved of. "Nope. There's a guy out mowing his lawn. He's the only one I see."

"What about dogs?"

"Nope. Oh, wait . . . there is one." Deep in the shadows of someone's front porch there was a silhouette. And eyes, watching him.

"What does it look like?"

"He's a pretty good size—maybe eighty or ninety pounds?—black, white, and tan fur. What do you call that breed? Bernese mountain dog, I think."

"Does he have one blue eye and one brown?"

"I can't tell . . . wait." The dog stood up, moved into sunlight. "Yeah. How'd you know?"

"Thane," Carolyn said under her breath.

"What?"

"The dog's name is Thane," she said. "He's the lord."

"The what?"

"The pack lord. It's what they call—never mind. He's the alpha dog. What's he doing?"

"He's walking out into the yard," Steve said. Thinking of Petey, Steve waved. "Hey, buddy!"

"Are you *insane*? Don't engage him, Steve!"

"What? Why not?"

Carolyn sighed. "Just trust me, please? Ignore the dog. Ignore any dogs you see." She was gritting her teeth again.

"OK," Steve said, amiably enough. He continued walking. After a few steps he was in front of someone else's yard, this a red brick house of odd design, carved double doors in front, dark windows. It looked very familiar to him, though he didn't recall ever having been there before.

The mountain dog followed him. He barked, just once. In response another dog, a fat beagle, came trotting out from behind this house. It ran up to Steve on comically stubby legs and set about giving high alert.

Pretty good set of pipes on him for a little dude, Steve thought.

Carolyn heard the barking. "Is that a beagle?"

"Yeah."

Steve quickened his pace a little, hoping the dogs would leave him alone once he was out of the beagle's yard. But they followed, the beagle barking his surprisingly baritone bark, Thane watching him with one ice-blue eye.

"Do you see any others?"

Steve didn't really want to take his eyes off the two immediate problems, but he heard the urgency in her voice. He glanced on the other side of the street. A little ways ahead a pair of Labrador retrievers, one black and one yellow, trotted alongside each other. *They're pacing me.* The hair on the back of his neck stood up. Motion caught his eye. As he watched, a smallish German shepherd crested the hill in front of him. Seeing him, it barked once. "Yeah," Steve said. "Three more. Lotta dogs in this neighborhood."

"Only three?"

"Yeah. Well, five in all."

"How far in are you?"

"Almost a block. Coming up on the first intersection." He paused. "Are these dogs known to, you know . . . bite?"

"Almost never."

"*Almost* never?"

"Let me know when you get to the intersection. We'll see how they act then."

Steve continued walking. Thane and the beagle continued to follow alongside though, thankfully, the beagle shut up when they were well outside of his territory. The Labs paced him on the other side of the street.

Now he was up to the old guy mowing his yard. He was a sixtyish man, probably retired, wearing a ball cap and work boots.

"Are these your dogs?" Steve called, forgetting momentarily that he was a fugitive who didn't want to draw attention to himself.

The old guy waved.

"Hey, buddy, can you call off your dogs for me?"

The old guy wrinkled his face in confusion, put his hand to his ear. *I can't hear you!* He didn't shut off the mower.

"Can. You. Call off. Your DOGS," Steve said, louder.

The old man shook his head again, smiled, pointed at the noisy engine.

"Asshole," Steve muttered. He was walking very slowly now. The mower noise receded as the old guy moved down to the far end of his yard. The dogs matched Steve inch for inch.

"What did you say?"

"Nothing, never mind. I'm almost there. OK, I'm at the intersection."

"Hold up there for a second. What are the dogs doing?"

"Uh . . . the two Labs have trotted up to the German shepherd. And there's a new one in the mix, some sort of black-and-white breed, maybe an English spaniel, mid-size. Are these, like, guard dogs?"

"Not the way you mean. Try taking a couple of steps forward."

Steve did. The reaction was immediate and furious. The four dogs in front of him went from passively watching to full-on attack, barking, sprinting at him. At the same time the big mountain dog leaped up and clamped down on Steve's arm. The beagle latched on to the tongue of Mrs. McGillicutty's son's Reebok.

"Aaaah!" Steve screamed as much out of surprise as actual pain. The pain arrived in a second, though. Thane, the mountain dog, had sunk his teeth into the meat of Steve's upper right arm. Now he dangled there, all ninety pounds of him pulling on the triceps. Steve elbowed him furiously, then reached around with his left hand to loosen the jaws. The dog's brown eye rolled at him, darkly furious. Steve's blood stained the white fur of his muzzle.

"What's happening?" Carolyn said. "Steve?'

He was making some progress on dislodging the mountain dog when the other four hit. The yellow Lab bit down on his left forearm. The black Lab latched on to his left ankle. The shepherd went for his left butt cheek but mostly just got the cloth of his sweatpants. It whipped its head back and forth. Steve heard cloth tear, felt cool autumn air on his ass.

"Steve? Steve, answer me! What's happening? Is it the dogs, Steve?"

These dogs mean to kill me. The thought carried a burst of adrenaline. He twisted, gyrated, trying to shake them loose, but they hung on him like Christmas ornaments. He lurched a step back in the direction that he had come, thinking hysterically that that might do the trick, convince

them to let him go. All this happened in silence. The dogs weren't barking anymore, because they had their mouths full. The pain was not yet so
bad that he needed to scream again. The only sound was the lawn mower.
He took another step. The beagle let go of his shoe and clamped down on
Steve's Achilles tendon. The pain drove him to his knees, or maybe he
tripped. The mountain dog let go of his right arm and bit at his ear, his
scalp, his face.

Steve struck out blindly, punching with his right hand. Now he was
screaming.

"That's it," Carolyn said. "I'm sending in the backup."

II

Facedown on the asphalt, buried under the marauding dogs, Steve felt
surprisingly peaceful. He heard the blood roaring in his ears but felt
no real pain. *Probably I'm dying.* He noticed a piece of gypsum baked into
the asphalt of the road, inches away from his eye. It was very interesting.

Then, as if from a great distance, he heard a sound that was not a dog,
not a lawn mower. It was a bass rumble, a roar. He felt it in the depths of
his chest.

A moment later the shadow of the mountain dog—*Thane*, Steve
thought, *his name is Thane*—fell away from his face. Unexpectedly, he
was in daylight again. The dog on his right arm fell away. Then his left
leg was free.

"—an you hear me, Steve? Answer me! Are you—"

Steve, dazed, put his right hand down on the asphalt and examined it.
He had a good, wide gash in his arm. When he flexed his fingers he could
see the muscle work. *Not much blood, though.* The muscle of his forearm
looked a lot like raw chicken. He found this very interesting as well, and
clenched his hand a couple of times to watch it work.

"The gun, Steve! Use the gun!"

Hey . . . that's a pretty good idea. He put a hand down and pushed himself off the asphalt. The old guy mowing his lawn was headed his direction. Steve waved him over for help with one bloody, shredded hand. The

old guy smiled and waved back. He cupped a hand to his ear and shook his head, pointing at the mower.

What . . . the . . . fuck? That was weird enough to bring him back to himself, at least a little. He got to one knee, took a quick inventory. His right leg worked. The beagle hadn't been able to do much damage to his ankle. *Not for lack of effort, though.* His left, not so much. He'd been badly bitten in the calf. It hurt to put weight on it. *Wonder what happened there?*

"The gun, Steve! The gun! Shoot the dogs!"

That did it. Steve, fully conscious again, remembered who—what— had done this to him. He was suddenly and acutely aware of the slavering dogs at his back. Black murder bubbled up into his heart, the Buddha's message of compassion for all life temporarily forgotten.

"C'mere, Thane," he said, drawing the pistol. "I got a treat for you, buddy."

Wow, he thought, *that's a* really *big dog. Must be—what?—four hundred pounds or so. Maybe five hundred.*

But of course it was not a dog. It was a lion. Two of them actually, an adult male with a thick brown mane and a smaller female, standing between him and the dogs. *Lions, huh? That's kind of unusual.*

He pulled the slide back on the HK, cocking it. He leveled it, aiming at the center of the big lion's mane and carefully squeezed off a shot. He missed completely. The bullet went between the two lions and ricocheted off the asphalt, kicking up a small spark.

The big lion turned around and roared at him.

"Steve," Carolyn's voice came in his ear, "what are you doing? Don't be an idiot! They're there to protect you! They're your backup!"

"Say again, please?"

"The lions *saved* you. They're the *backup.* Do not shoot them."

"How did you know I tried—"

The big lion roared again.

"He says there's more dogs on the way. Can you shoot? Use the gun. But be careful. How many dogs are there?"

Steve took stock. The beagle lay dead in the road, his back broken. Thane, bleeding from a wound in his ass, the fur on the back of his neck high, paced back and forth in front of the lions, studying them with his eerie mismatched eyes. Behind him the other four dogs stood, growling, slightly wounded, uncertain. Three new ones, two Rottweilers and a poodle, had arrived while Steve was out of it. As he watched a golden retriever crested the hill. "I count nine."

"Shoot!" Carolyn said. "You're going to have to fight your way up the street."

Steve squeezed off a shot at the English spaniel. He missed this time too, but it was a more credible effort. The big lion glanced over his shoulder and moved farther out of Steve's field of fire.

The spaniel was growling, growling, its muzzle wrinkled back, stained red with Steve's blood. It barked, took a half step forward—

—and Steve shot it right between the eyes.

The lions roared their approval. Steve glanced off to his right. The guy with the mower had completed another row and turned around. This time he waved twice as he passed by, once at Steve and once at the lions.

Steve shot the yellow Lab in the side. It took a couple steps forward and fell on its side, ribs heaving. *I'm getting the hang of this.* He fired at the black dog and missed completely, then shot it in the hip. It screamed, then began limping toward him. He shot it in the breastbone and it fell down dead.

The remaining six dogs charged. Three of them attacked the female lion, swarming her. She roared with pain, but Steve didn't care because the other three charged him, bypassing the male lion. Steve didn't really blame them. It was becoming evident that he wasn't much of a shot.

He shot the poodle in the chest. *Not bad . . .* He shot at Thane, missing him completely. The shepherd, snarling and yellow-eyed, launched herself at him. He held his wounded arm up to block and she latched onto it, sharp white teeth sinking into exposed muscle. Steve screamed. He jammed the pistol into her belly and pulled the trigger. Guts showered out the other side, but the shepherd didn't let go. Now a pit bull was gnawing at the ankle that the beagle had been on.

He shot again, higher on the shepherd's body. The hammer clicked down on an empty chamber. The dog had to be nearly dead but it just wouldn't let go. The bite felt like being on fire. Steve screamed again, clubbing her in the head with the butt of his gun.

"Yaah!" he screamed. "Fucking get off me, asshole!"

With a look of surprise, the shepherd fell away. Steve plopped down on his ass and began kicking at the pit bull with his free foot. It growled at him and sunk its teeth in deeper. Steve screamed.

Then the two lions landed on the pit bull, a split second apart. Steve screamed again—lion attacks will do that to a person—but they didn't touch him at all. Instead they took the dog's spine in their jaws, one near the neck and one near the tail, and crunched down. Now it was the dog's turn to scream.

"Yaaah, you FUCKER!"

When they dropped the dog, it didn't move.

The lions turned and stood over him, *inches* away now. Their yellow eyes bored into him. They were panting. He felt their breath over his wounds, the slick sweat of his brow. It smelled of blood and rotting meat. Steve held up the empty pistol, then lowered it again. The big one rumbled a little, swished his tail. He took a step back, then raised his head and looked down the street. His brow furrowed.

Not wanting to, Steve twisted to follow his gaze.

Behind him there were a dozen more dogs, ten at least. Behind *them*, dozens or even hundreds more were on the way. They flowed out of the woods half a mile away like a river of murder, across the hay field, down the main road. The clicking of their toenails on asphalt sounded like a stampede.

"Oh shit," Steve whispered.

The lion roared.

Steve stood up. He fumbled at his back. Carolyn had duct taped the two extra magazines there, like Bruce Willis did in the original *Die Hard*. It seemed like a good idea at the time, but when he grabbed at one of the magazines it wouldn't come unstuck. He pulled again, harder this time. This time it came loose, but the magazines Carolyn had given him were slick with gun oil. It slipped out of his grip and clattered across the road, coming to rest not far from the streetlamp.

"Oh *shit!*" Steve said again.

"What happened? What's going on?"

"They're coming! There's hundreds of them! And . . . and I dropped the fucking magazine." As he spoke he reached around, carefully this time, and put his hands on the final magazine taped to his back. He wrapped his fingers around it, gently but firmly, and pulled it free.

Carolyn exhaled softly. "You have to get indoors," she said. "Get inside, Steve! Get inside!"

"Where?"

"Anywhere! Whatever's closest! They're not locked! Go!"

Steve took off, limping as best he was able across the half-mowed yard. As he moved, he took the duct tape still clinging to the full magazine in his teeth and pulled. It came off.

Behind him he heard the thunder of running dogs, a hundred more reinforcements coming to join the dozens already standing shoulder to shoulder twenty yards away. Only the lions stood between them and him. The old guy mowing the yard waved again.

"You're an asshole!" Steve screamed.

The old guy cupped a hand to his ear, then pointed at the mower and shook his head.

"Steve, get indoors!" Carolyn's voice was thick with tension. "You have to get indoors *now*."

Still moving, Steve ejected the spent magazine, let it drop into the grass. *I hope it messes up his mower blade.* He slammed the full magazine home and jacked the slide back, cocking the gun. Now he was on the porch. He put his hand on the knob, fully prepared to shoot it if it was locked. *Surely that would work? It always does in the movies.* But the door opened easily into an unremarkable foyer—linoleum floor, floral wallpaper, dusty umbrella stand.

"What about the lions?"

"Leave them. They're disposable. Just get indoors."

Steve lurched inside, shutting the door behind him. "I'm in."

"OK, you're safe. Which house are you in?"

"Uhh . . . the outside is white brick?"

"Perfect. There's food, water, and medical supplies in the living room. Stay there. You'll be safe inside. I'll get you out of there as soon as I can, but it may be a day or two." She hung up.

III

"Shit," Carolyn said in Pelapi as she hung up the phone. She, Jennifer, David, Margaret, Rachel, and Peter were sitting around Mrs. McGillicutty's kitchen table.

The others could tell from her tone that things had gone bad, but none of them understood more than a smattering of English.

"What happened?" David rumbled.

"He ducked in to one of the houses." She stood and walked over to the wall, where the phone's cradle hung. When she seated the phone she also unplugged the jack. No one noticed. The librarians weren't much good with technology, nor was Mrs. McGillicutty. Nor was she, for that matter, but she'd had time to read up on telephones. The other phone jacks in the house were already unplugged.

"Well," David said reflectively, "I suppose it was going to be one of the two. Margaret, which do you think would be worse? Ripped apart by dogs, or gummed to death by the dead ones?" He tickled her. She giggled and squirmed, unsettling a small cloud of flies. "You'd know, wouldn't you?" She giggled again.

Jennifer slapped her forehead. "Oh, no! Didn't you warn him? Are you going to want him back, Carolyn? Because that's going to be a real mess." The dead ones would be friendly to strangers they encountered outside their houses, if somewhat odd. But on the rare occasion that some unfortunate soul from the outside world made it indoors, they fell on him with teeth, hands, clubs, kitchen tools, whatever was handy. Unless someone intervened quickly, there usually wasn't much left.

Carolyn shrugged. "He's disposable. If we get in there in the next little bit, maybe. Otherwise, as far as I'm concerned he can stay dead."

"So . . . new plan?"

"Oh, I don't know. I think the basic plan is solid. The problem was that he didn't ignore the sentries."

"What did he do?"

"He spoke to Thane, almost first thing."

Jennifer winced.

Carolyn felt her index finger about to tremble. "It never occurred to me to warn him." This was plausible. Most of the librarians had a horror of the neighborhood dogs that dated back to childhood. Even Michael tended to keep his distance. But Americans, for some reason, seemed to love the furry little bastards. It was one of their unfathomable quirks.

"So, what then?"

"Unless anybody can think of something better, I guess I'll go out and see if I can round up another American," she lied. "David? Does that suit you?"

David, perhaps thinking of the bloodbath at the jail, blessed this with a shallow nod.

"When will you go?" Jennifer asked.

Carolyn thought about it. "Now, I suppose."

"Want to wait a bit? There will be food soon." Mrs. McGillicutty was bustling in the kitchen.

Carolyn groaned. "No! I've already eaten twice today. And I may have to do bar snacks. Has anyone seen those boots I had on? And the blue duffel bag with all the green paper? I'll need it as bait."

Carolyn collected her things and emerged into the afternoon sunshine. *That went rather well,* she thought. *Mission accomplished, and Steve is in a safe place.* It was true that the dead ones were fierce defenders of their quarters. It had to be that way. Their private lives could not bear much inspection. But there were exceptions. The librarians could come and go as they pleased, as could others who had been resurrected.

Steve would be fine.

The others did not know this, of course.

IV

Steve gave the interior of the house a quick glance—weirdly empty—and turned to the door. It had one of those little peephole things that gave a fish-eye view of the outside. The two lions were about five yards from the porch, backing up slowly.

It wasn't hard to see why. Now there were at least a hundred dogs in the street of all sizes and description—Dobermans; Jack Russell terriers; poodles both large and small; German shepherds; Labs of the chocolate, yellow, and black variety; dozens of other breeds. They were advancing on the lions.

The big male looked back and forth over the assembled dogs and gave a full-throated roar. The sound echoed down the street, bouncing off the houses of Garrison Oaks. The female looked over her shoulder at the door. Her gaze seemed to bore into Steve.

The look in her eyes reminded Steve of something, but he couldn't quite think what.

Fuck, fuck, fuck. What do I do here? The lions had saved him. *But, y'know, they're fucking* lions. Still, he had been down for the count, barely conscious as the dogs tore into him.

That reminds me—he looked down. He was dripping blood on the floor, but not actually spraying it, as far as he could tell. That was probably good. And Carolyn had said there were medical supplies. "*Medical* supplies?" *That's suspiciously convenient.* Then, *God, I hate her. A lot.*

Outside the door a low rumble was building, the sound of a hundred dogs growling at once. Over that, the lawn mower. The female lion stood in the old man's path, teeth bared, fur up. He just steered around her. He didn't seem to notice the dogs at all.

The male lion took another half-step back. Thane advanced two steps, the rest of the dogs close behind him. One of the Rottweilers barked mechanically, over and over, spraying flecks of white foam. The yard was a sea of wrinkled muzzles, fangs, savage eyes.

Yeah, they're fucked. Even if the lions had somewhere to run, which they didn't—they had cornered themselves covering Steve's retreat—he had no doubt that at least some of the dogs could outrun them. *And there were so many.* Steve pounded the wall. "Fuck, fuck, *fuck*!"

He thought about dialing Carolyn back, but there wasn't time. The big lion took another step back, roared again. The Rottweiler charged him and he swatted it, sent it flying into the crowd. The female looked over her shoulder again. Steve would have sworn he saw reproach in those eyes.

Wasn't there a thing on YouTube a couple of years back about lions and some English dudes buddying up? Steve thought hysterically. *Ah, fuck it.*

He opened the door.

The female lion looked at him. Possibly he was kidding himself, but he thought she looked grateful. "Get in here! What are you waiting for?"

She tried to bound, but her hind leg wasn't quite up to it. She did a belly flop onto the brick porch steps, then scrambled up. The male wasn't wounded, but he waited for her to get inside. Some of the dogs were just inches from him. He held them at bay with swipes of his paw and, Steve thought, the force of his personality.

"Come on!"

The male spun and was through the door in two quick leaps. Steve, standing behind the door, tried to slam it shut, but was thwarted by the dogs. Two of them, both greyhounds, were pinned neck-deep between the door and the jamb. They snarled, snapped. Steve kicked at their heads with his good leg, holding himself up with the door. He kicked the top greyhound unconscious, or possibly to death. When he let the pressure off the door the other one backed out. He was able to shut the door then; there were a lot of dogs outside, but for whatever reason only a couple of them had come onto the porch. They scrabbled ineffectually against the door with their toenails.

He made extra-special sure that the latch caught, then released the handle. He locked it, then threw the deadbolt for good measure. The dogs outside clambered at the door, barking. Steve leaned against the wall and turned to see if the lions would eat him now.

They didn't. They ignored him completely, actually. The female had collapsed in the living room. She had a biggish chunk missing from her left rear leg. Blood wasn't spurting from the wound, but it oozed out in a steady stream. A red trail led from the foyer to where she lay.

Right, Steve thought. *Medical supplies.* Carefully, keeping one eye on the lions, he limped into the living room. It was still bright outside, but in the house it felt like twilight. Thick curtains hung over all the windows, and there were no lights on. He fumbled around on the wall until he found a row of switches and flipped them at random until one worked.

A single anemic bulb came on overhead, its dull ochre glow further diluted by the husks of dead insects in the fixture.

"Whoa," Steve said.

The living room was flat, empty space about the size of a two-car garage. All the furniture was heaped in the corner—couch standing on one end, squished lamp shade poking out from a splintered bookcase, end-table legs jutting up like skeletal fingers. The ghost of the couch lingered as a cleaner spot on filthy carpet.

The framed photographs and art were in the pile as well, but the room was not undecorated. Most of the wall space was covered with crude paintings that looked like the work of a talented kindergartener. *No*, Steve thought. *That's not quite right. They look like cave paintings.*

These images had the same crude style, but they were not of animals. *Well, mostly not.* He saw a few four-legged beasties here and there, possibly dogs. But mostly these cave paintings were of modern things—he recognized the square brown of a UPS truck, a small car with a sign on the roof, a stick-figure man bearing pizza beside it. A mail truck. A basketball hoop. A bicycle. But among the recognizable and commonplace stuff of American life, there were inexplicable things as well—a black pyramid, a yellow bull standing in a fire, angry calamari bobbing in green waves.

He found the supplies Carolyn had mentioned stacked neatly in the corner opposite the furniture—two cases of Dasani water, a case of Johnson & Johnson sterile gauze, two industrial-sized boxes of Band-Aids, a plastic bag full of beef jerky, what looked like a tackle box with a red cross stenciled on it. A plain white box held a collection of less-familiar things, neatly wrapped in an old wedding dress; three clay pots, a Styrofoam tray of glass ampoules, tiny bowls of powder. *This stuff's fresh, looks like. It's been here a day or two at most.* Steve walked over and spun the cap off a Dasani, guzzled it. He opened a Band-Aid box, peeled one, and stuck it over a small bite mark on his finger. Another box said AMOXICILLIN. He opened it and found a dozen syringes.

"Oh, hello!"

Steve started, spun around. It was an older woman, mid-sixties, in a flower-print skirt-and-pants combo, mostly purple. She herself was very pale, her lips a cyanotic blue. "How lovely to see you! Won't you come in? May I take your coat?"

"Oh . . . hi. I didn't realize anyone was here. I'm sorry to break in. Really. There are dogs—"

"Won't you come in?"

"I don't—" He stopped, squinted at her. He thought of how the mower guy kept pantomiming deafness, pointing at the mower over and over like it was the first time. *His wife, maybe? They're perfect for each other.*

"Won't you come in?" she said again. "How lovely to see you." The lion walked over, sniffed her. She looked down at the four-hundred-pound cat bleeding in her foyer and patted his thick, dusty mane. "May I take your coat?"

The lion looked over his shoulder at Steve and gave a dubious rumble. Steve shook his head. "Beats the shit out of me, man."

The big cat swished his tail at Steve's words, agreeably enough, as if he understood—maybe not the words, but the gist of his thoughts, the sentiment. For some reason this struck Steve as funny. When the sound of his chuckle prompted the woman to ask again if she might take his coat, he laughed long and loud.

Maybe he was getting the hang of this weird-ass day.

Chapter 8

Cold Home

I

The secretary was a middle-aged black lady with a friendly face and eyes like ice. She'd tracked Erwin's approach the way a panther might watch a goat sidle up to a water hole. Behind her, a tall window overlooked a perfectly manicured garden. Erwin looked out that window with real longing. It was clear and sunny, cool but not chilly, maybe the best day of the fall. Erwin wanted to be out hiking in the woods, kicking his way through crunchy leaves.

Instead he walked up and laid his visitor's badge on her desk. "I'm Erwin," he said. He jerked a thumb at the curved door to his right. "Got a call that he wants to see me."

"Erwin *what*?" the secretary said, running her finger down a printed list of names. Erwin didn't answer. His last name was on the badge. She was just being a bitch.

"Ma'am, *that* is Erwin Leffington," said a voice behind him. "*The* Erwin Leffington."

Erwin turned. A fit-looking middle-aged man in an Army general's uniform sat on the couch behind him. In his briefcase Erwin saw a number of file folders with black borders. *Hmmm.* He was aware that such classifications existed, but he'd never been in the room with one before.

"Ah," the secretary said, thwarted. "I see. You're connected with . . . the emergency?"

"I guess," Erwin said.

The secretary pursed her lips. She consulted a different, shorter list, gave a curt nod. "He is expecting you," she admitted. "Have a seat, please."

Erwin nodded in return.

Behind him, the general had gathered up the papers he was looking at and put them away in a briefcase cuffed to his wrist. Then he stood, smiling broadly, and walked over to greet Erwin. "I'm Dan Thorpe," he said, holding out his hand to shake. "It's a real honor to meet you, Sergeant."

Out of habit, Erwin skimmed Thorpe's decorations—an Airborne patch, the crossed arrows of Special Operations, a whole bunch of campaign ribbons. He knew the Joint Special Operations commander by reputation, though they had never met. Supposedly he was a pretty good guy. Erwin shook his hand. "Meetcha," he said. "Sir."

"Captain Tanaka said to say hello," Thorpe said. "He wanted to come himself but he's . . . otherwise occupied. Mission planning. He insisted that I bring you down for a beer when all this is over."

Erwin warmed a little. "Yeah? You know Yo?" He and Yoshitaka had served together in Iraq. "Didn't realize he was with you guys."

"For about a year now. How come you never came out for selection?" Thorpe asked. "I know Clint invited—"

"The president will see you now," the secretary said. She stood up and walked over to the oddly shaped door and opened it for them.

The door wasn't very wide. Erwin, who'd retired as a command sergeant major, deferred to General Thorpe's rank, letting him go through first, then followed him into the Oval Office.

II

It was Erwin's first time in the sanctum sanctorum. He'd been to the White House before, once as part of a tour group and once when he and a couple of other guys swung by to pick up some Distinguished Service Crosses. Erwin, who gave no fucks about medals, had come close to skipping that last. At the time, though, he'd been remodeling his house.

He was curious to see how the carpenters handled the baseboards and crown molding on the curved walls of the Oval Office. But it kinda sucked. The ceremony had been in the Rose Garden, not the Oval Office, and the president—not this guy, the one before last—turned out to be a douche. He showed up drunk and spent most of his time drooling over the niece of a Marine pilot. As soon as she made it clear she didn't love her country in *that* way, Scotchy McPolitics disappeared. Also he got the pilot's name wrong during the ceremony.

Anyway, nine years and two presidents later, here he was in the Room itself. It wasn't small, but it wasn't quite as big as he would have expected. *But . . . really nice job on the baseboards.* Perfectly molded plinth blocks, good clean shoe molding, and nearly invisible joins on the scalloping up above. He looked around. The rest of the room was fancy too. Regal blue carpeting, alternating gold-and-cream stripe pattern on the walls. His eye lingered on the president's desk, an elaborately carved teak thing that depicted some sort of naval battle. *Nice detailing*, he thought. *And can you even* get *teak anymore?* He considered. *Probably it's a antique or some shit.*

"—nd this is Erwin Leffington," Thorpe was saying. "Formerly with the Eighty-Second, now a special investigator with Homeland Security."

Erwin looked up. In front of the desk two gold couches faced each other, a coffee table between them. The president and a bunch of guys he vaguely recognized from the news were sprawled out on them. They looked tense. Mentally, Erwin rolled his eyes. *Here we go.*

"Why is he here?" asked an older woman, looking down at him over the top of her glasses. A classified-documents folder lay open in her lap. *Another black border*, Erwin saw. *La-di-da.* The label inside the jacket read COLD HOME.

"A number of reasons, Madam Secretary," Thorpe said. "Sergeant— sorry, *Special Agent* Leffington has proven to be well ahead of the curve on this one. Prior to yesterday's, ah, events, he was conducting an investigation of a related crime, a bank robbery. Leffington was also interrogating the escapee at the time of his prison break. He's the only person known to have seen the operatives and lived."

"It was just the one guy."

"Beg pardon?" said the lady in glasses.

Erwin jerked a thumb at Thorpe. "He said 'operatives.' But it was just the one guy. That I saw, anyway."

"Just one? What about the one who escaped custody?" He rustled papers in his black bordered folder. "Steve, ah . . . Hodgson? The one you were interviewing?"

"I wouldn't necessarily say 'escaped custody,'" Erwin said. "Looked more like 'kidnapped out of custody' to me."

"How so?"

Erwin shrugged. "Well, he was surprised as shit when the guy in the tutu showed up. We all were. Our jaws was all hanging open like we was morons." Erwin especially relished that last phrase. *'Like we was morons.'* He only trotted it out on special occasions. "Plus the guy in the tutu had to knock the fuck out of Hodgson to get him to stop squirmin'."

"Excuse me," said a tall guy with coppery red hair. "Did you say tutu?"

Erwin dredged his memory and came up with a name. *Bryan Hamann,* he thought. *White House chief of staff.* "Yup. Purple tutu and a flak jacket. Israeli, I think. That and a knife. He was barefoot too." Erwin shook his head a little. "Fucking weird."

"So . . . he was unarmed?" Thorpe said slowly.

"It was a pretty big knife. But no guns, if that's what you mean."

"And there were how many casualties?" the president asked, ruffling through papers.

"Thirty-seven," Erwin said, without looking at any notes.

"They were armed?"

"Lots of 'em were, yeah. Didn't seem to help much. One guy in the hall, he had a forty-caliber Glock stuffed up his ass, way past the trigger guard. Only thing poking out was the butt of the magazine."

The secretary of state paused with a china cup halfway to her mouth, then set it back down, coffee unsipped. "But he let you live," she said. "Why is that, do you think?"

Erwin shrugged. "Fanboy."

"Beg pardon?"

"It's kind of a long story." Erwin hated people who told long stories without an invitation. He scanned the room. The president made a come-on gesture. "So, like, the guy in the tutu kicks in the door of the chapel and kills the cop that brung him there pretty much straight off." Erwin took his Copenhagen out of his shirt pocket, thumped it a couple of times to settle the tobacco, and put in a dip. "Then, he asked which one of us was Steve." He imitated the big guy's voice: "'Eshteeeeeeve?' Like that. Hodgson's lawyer blabbed—he was a pussy—and the big guy killed him, too, with like a weight on the end of a chain." Erwin put the Copenhagen back in his pocket. "*Man* that guy was quick," he said, looking at Thorpe significantly. "I ain't never seen nobody that fuckin' fast in my life."

Thorpe nodded. *Message received*.

"Anyway, I figured I was next. So I started thinking fast. And I asked him if he knew a chick named Carolyn. He recognized the name. I think that almost got me off the hook."

"What made you think to do that?" the secretary of state asked.

Erwin shrugged. "Her and him both dressed weird."

They were all looking at him now.

"Weird how?" asked Hamann.

"Well, he was in the tutu." He scanned their faces. "And Hodgson had said that this chick Carolyn was going around in a wool sweater and bike pants, them Spandexy things, the night he met her. And leg warmers. That was weird too. So that had already reminded me how one of them ladies who robbed the bank did it in a bathrobe and cowboy hat. It wasn't so much a connection as they just kinda reminded me of each other. Kinda thin, but I figured if he was getting ready to kill me anyway it couldn't hurt to try. So I asked if he knew her."

"And that worked?"

Erwin shrugged. "Almost. Slowed him down for a second, anyway. He didn't speak English, but I could tell he knew the name."

"What *did* he speak?"

"Dunno. Funny accent. Couldn't place it. But when I said 'Carolyn,' he sat up and took notice. Then he said 'Nobununga'—or something like that. I pretended like I knew him, too."

"Nobunaga?" the president asked. "Where do I know that name?"

Erwin was surprised. *Oh right*, he thought. *He was a history major.* "Oda Nobunaga. Yeah, he was my first thought too."

The president snapped his fingers. "Right. That's it."

"Pardon me," said the secretary of state, "but who are we talking about?"

"Oda Nobunaga," Erwin explained. "In sixteenth-century Japan he unified the shogunate. Mostly, anyways."

They were all staring at him now, the way dumb shits sometimes did when you surprised them. All except the president himself. He was smiling a little. "Go on," he said.

"But I got it wrong," Erwin said. "It wasn't No-bu-*na*-ga. He said No-bu-*nun*-ga."

"Who the hell's that?" Hamann asked.

Erwin shrugged. "Not a fuckin' clue. Maybe it was a code word, or some stupid shit like that." He nodded at the director of Central Intelligence. "No offense."

The DCI shook his head. *None taken.*

"Anyway, I fucked up. When I said the wrong name, the guy in the tutu figured out I was trying to bullshit him. He was fixin' to kill me with that spear of his—or try, anyway. But it turned out he was a fanboy. I dunno who was more surprised, him or me."

"A 'fanboy'?" the secretary of state asked. "So . . . you two know each other? I don't understand."

"Nah. It's just sometimes—"

Thorpe's tone was cold. "Madam Secretary, Command Sergeant Major Leffington is well-known within military circles. 'Living legend' is probably a fair description of his status. At Natanz, while wounded, he singlehandedly—"

"Yeah, anyway," Erwin said, "he'd heard of me. You get to where you recognize the look."

"I see. And you think that's why he spared your life?"

"Well, I wasn't gonna just sit there and let him kill me. But yeah. After he recognized me he just grabbed the Hodgson kid and took off."

"Did you pursue him?"

"I gave it a shot." Erwin shook his head. "*Man* that guy was quick." He looked at the president. "Hey, you got a trash can or something? I gotta spit." He pointed at the wad of Copenhagen in his lip.

Thorpe looked at him, wide-eyed, then stifled a grin.

"Under the desk," the president said.

"Thanks." Erwin walked around behind the president's desk, retrieved his trash can, and spat a brown stream in it. He set the can on the desk. *Might need it again in a minute.* "Say, can I ask you a question?"

The president waggled his fingers in a come-on gesture.

"Why do you give a fuck?"

"OK, that's about *enough* of—" Hamann began.

The president held up his hand. "How do you mean, Agent Leffington?"

Hamann's face was really red now. *Yup*, Erwin thought. *Asshole.* "Call me Erwin," he said to the president. "Yeah, what I mean is, why do you give a fuck? I mean, it was all horrific and shit, but ain't it a little below your pay grade?" He meant this sincerely. *A thirty-person massacre ain't so much, as presidents go.*

The president and Hamann exchanged a glance. The president gave a small nod. "Mr. Leffington—" Hamann began.

"It's Erwin," Erwin said.

Hamann's face got redder still. Erwin gave no fucks.

"Erwin, then," Hamann said, smiling through gritted teeth, "do you have a security clearance?"

"Sure," Erwin said. He had one from the Homeland Security gig. He told them the level. It wasn't especially high.

Hamann looked smug for a moment, but when he glanced at the president his face fell.

"Tell him anyway," the president said.

"Sir, I don't think—"

The president gave him a look.

"Right," Hamann said. "Ah, yesterday, this office received a call from a member of the terrorist organization. A woman."

"Carolyn? *She* called *here?*"

They all looked at him again. "That's correct," Hamann said.

"Nooooooo shit," Erwin said softly. "Huh. What'd she want to talk about?"

"Steve Hodgson was the reason she called," the president said.

"I ain't followin'."

"She wanted me to arrange a pardon for him," the president said.

"*Oh?*" Erwin said, very interested now. "*You* talked to her? Yourself? Personal-like?"

"She had the access codes," Hamann said. He and the president exchanged another glance.

Erwin waited, but neither of them said anything more. *He's holding something back*, Erwin thought. *Access codes will only get you so far. What did she say? What did she say to make that asshole put the president on the phone?* He suddenly thought of the tellers at the bank robbery, of Amrita Krishnamurti, that spotless employee of twelve years, tossing away dye packs, marked bills, her career. But someone was speaking to him. The question was a good one, though. He tucked it away for later examination. "Sorry," Erwin said. "Say again?"

The president didn't seem too put out about Erwin zoning out. Erwin provisionally decided that he liked the guy. "I *said*," the president said again, "what made you take an interest in her in the first place?"

"She did a bank robbery three, four weeks back, her and some other lady. Left prints all over the place, at the bank. Everywhere, like. Then, just one single print at the house where they found this Hodgson guy."

"Just the one print?" the president asked. He sounded like he understood why this was weird, which surprised Erwin again.

Oh. Right. He was a prosecutor. "Yeah. Just the one. Weird, huh? Usually you either get lots of 'em, or none at all, if they wear gloves. But this time, just one. It was perfect, too. They found it on the plate over the light switch in the dining room, like she rolled it out on a pad."

"So she wanted us to find it," the president said. "Why?"

"Don't know," Erwin allowed. "Good question, though. Wanted us to connect her with this Hodgson guy, maybe?"

"We keep coming back to him. Who is he?"

"Nobody in particular, so far as I can tell. He's a plumber."

The secretary of state, regal, studied him over the top of her glasses. "A plumber?"

"Yeah," Erwin said. He spat in the president's trash can. "You know—them guys who make the toilets work? He seemed pretty normal, though," he said meditatively. "Not like them bank-robber ladies or the tutu guy."

"Did anything strike you about him?" the president asked.

Erwin considered the question. "I didn't have a whole lot of time with him. But I don't think he had any more idea what was going on than I do. He seemed all guilty about *something*, though. I couldn't figure out what. He got busted selling a little weed when he was a kid, did two years when he wouldn't roll over on his supplier. No arrests after that, but he got mentioned in a lot of other guys' files."

"And now?"

"These days he's clean, best I can tell. Other than the dead cop, I mean. And he denies that."

"Do you believe him?" the president asked.

"Yeah," Erwin said. "I do. I think she set him up."

"Why?"

"Leverage, I 'spect. What'd you say when she asked about the pardon?" The president didn't answer. His eyes were like ice. *He said yes, then.* "Never mind. None-a my fucking business. Sorry."

"You might be right," the president said. "Leverage. Hmmm. What would she want from him?"

"Dunno. Seems like a lotta trouble to get him to fix a faucet. Does it matter?"

"How do you mean?"

"Well, you got Thorpe over there. He ain't much of a negotiator. You gonna kill 'em?"

Everyone was very quiet. Then, after a moment, Hamann spoke. "Thank you, Erwin. That will be all."

Erwin waited a second, but this time the president didn't override him. "Yeah. Sure." He spat again. "I wouldn't."

Now both Hamann and the secretary of state were glaring at him.

"Why not?" the president said.

"I think it's what they want," Erwin said. "What *she* wants. Whoever she is, she's not dumb. She had to know you'd trace the call, right? And she had to know it would piss you off, getting your cage rattled."

"She didn't rattle—" Hamann began.

"Yeah. Whatever. So, way I see it, you can either go skip-skip-skippin' down this merry trail she's blazed for you, or you can lay back in the tall grass for a while, see if maybe you can figure out what the fuck is going on."

The president eyeballed him for a long moment. "Duly noted," he said. "I'll think it over."

"You do that. You done with me?"

"Yes."

Everyone looked relieved.

"Erwin, can you wait for me in the lobby?" Thorpe said. "I'd like a chance to debrief you on a couple other details."

"Yeah," Erwin said. He sighed inside, thinking of the fall leaves. "Sure." He walked out the funky curved door, pausing just a moment to run his fingers across the perfect wainscoting.

III

They conspired for another hour or so. Erwin, irritated, amused himself by annoying the secretary. Eventually the door opened. The herd of assholes spilled out, most of them glaring at Erwin as they left.

Thorpe was one of the last ones to leave. He walked up to Erwin, eyes wide. "You know," he said, "they talk about you, in the Unit. Yoshitaka and the others. I'd heard some of the stories. But before today, I never really believed—"

"Hey," the president called through the open door. "Erwin? Got a second?"

Erwin and Thorpe exchanged a look. "He can't kill me," Erwin said with a shrug. "I got the Distinguished Service Cross."

"Two of them. And the Medal of Honor."

"Yeah, well, that one got all blown out of proportion." Erwin went back into the Oval Office. "Yes, sir?"

"I wanted to thank you for your help today," the president said, "and your service to your country, of course." He paused. "It's been very memorable, meeting you."

"Yeah. Nice meetin' you, too." He waved a hand dismissively. "Happy to help and shit." Erwin paused. "Say, you mind if I ask you something?"

The president gave the question serious consideration before he answered. "Go ahead. I may take the fifth, though."

Erwin didn't smile. "I didn't vote for you." He waited for a reaction. There wasn't one. "Reason was, all the time you talked on TV, you always sounded like a dumbass. It was really convincing."

"Erwin, we should probably—" Thorpe said, from out in the lobby.

"Years of practice," the president said. "What's your question?"

"I was just wondering why you did that. Pretend to be a dipshit, I mean."

The president grinned. "Prolly the same fuckin' reason you do."

They looked at each other for a second, then both of them laughed, long and loud.

"Yeah," Erwin said. "OK. I'm convinced. Good luck in November!"

"Thanks," the president said. "I won't need it."

They both laughed again. Erwin stepped back out into the bitchy secretary's lobby.

"Hey! Erwin?"

He turned around. "Yeah?"

"We do a card game, every other Tuesday. If you're in town, I'd love to have you sit in."

Erwin considered this. "No ya wouldn't. I'll clean yer fuckin' clock."

"I can print money," the president said, grinning again.

"Hmm. Yeah. Good point. OK, I'm in. What time?"

"Around six, usually."

"See you."

"Phyllis?" The president's secretary looked up. "Add Erwin to the Tuesday list. If I'm tied up, have Harold take him over to the residence."

She glowered, then jotted a note down on a legal pad. "Yes, sir."

Thorpe was looking at Erwin with something like awe. "Be looking forward to it," Erwin said.

He kinda was, too.

INTERLUDE III

✳

JACK

Steve had been about twelve when he was orphaned. Even now, he remembered life with his birth parents fairly well. But the car accident that killed them and put him in a coma was a blank, his memory completely gone after breakfast cornflakes three days prior. They told him this was common with violent brain injury. He remembered waking up in a hospital room. It was night, and he had been alone, though his aunt Mary showed up an hour or so later, all tears and hugs. His parents were dead. Steve himself had been in a coma.

He'd gotten a bad concussion. That led to swelling of the brain, hence the coma. If there was permanent damage, no one could find it. Other than his long nap—a little over six weeks—and some minor burns, he was unhurt, remarkably so considering the ferocity of the crash. Years later, in his senior year of high school, Steve tracked down a newspaper photo of the wreckage. A tractor trailer had run a stop sign on a back road, speeding. It smacked into the front end of his mom's Cadillac, essentially flattening the front half. This made jelly of his parents and catapulted Steve into a new life, quite different from the one he was used to.

After an additional two-week hospital stay that ate up his father's life-insurance policy, Aunt Mary brought Steve home to her single-wide trailer. Steve, devastated, tripped over his grief with every thought: my-teeth-feel-fuzzy-better-brush-'em-because-*Mom-says*, I'm-hungry-wonder-if-*Dad*-will-get-pizza. The loss throbbed in the core of him like a toothache.

Aunt Mary didn't let this ruin her plans. The night she brought Steve home she went out to a roadside bar called Lee's Stack and got very drunk.

Around two a.m. she rolled back in with a guy named Clem. Steve, done with crying, watched the moon through the window as he listened to Mary and Clem bang the headboard on the other side of the flimsy plastic wall.

The next day Clem drove Steve back to his old house in Mary's aging, rattletrap Dodge. The estate was in bankruptcy—apparently Steve's dad, a real-estate guy, had made some boo-boos. A trustee let them in with a key. Steve got to keep his Commodore 64 computer, his clothes, and a box full of comic books. There were other toys, but he had to pick and choose because space at Mary's place was limited. He wanted to get the television, but Clem snagged it for himself. The trustee hustled them out before the auction started.

Predictably enough, Steve became an angry kid. Commuting to his old school was out of the question, so along with his parents he lost the friends he had known since childhood. Steve was still growing, but clothes were listed well below vodka and cigarettes on Mary's shopping list. A kindly English teacher noticed this and took him out to the Salvation Army, and bought him clothes that fit with her own money. Steve hated her for it, more so when the other kids figured out what was going on.

There were some jokes about that, but they didn't last. When Steve nearly drowned a well-dressed eighth-grader with a smart mouth in an unflushed toilet bowl, he was suspended for two weeks. The kid's parents, red-faced and screaming, wanted him arrested. No one said anything about his clothes after that. Not to his face, anyway.

He started shoplifting almost immediately—books, cassettes, candy, whatever—but it wasn't until a year or so after his parents' death that he committed his first burglary. In his freshman year in high school, on the Friday night of the football team's homecoming, Steve put on his Salvation Army sneakers and jogged through the back woods to an expensive neighborhood eight miles away. That night there was a faint glow in the east, near the neighborhood where he lived when he was young.

He selected a dark house at random, came out of the woods, and hopped the privacy fence around the pool. He carried a hammer and screwdriver, but ended up not needing them. The back door was unlocked. When Steve stepped over the threshold the dry husk of his old life fell away and was abandoned. He moved through the empty house with the savage glee of a marauding Hun. He'd brought a black pillowcase along with him to carry the loot. It fluttered from his hand as he moved, the flag of his new nation.

Steve, childlike, stole what his eye was drawn to. A box of Milky Ways. Some Atari cartridges. Cassette tapes. Then, in the master bedroom, he happened on the object that set the course of his life. It was a lacquered wood jewelry box. Steve remembered gasping when he opened it. What lay inside glittered like a dragon's hoard: silver chain, diamond earrings, golden rings. As he stole these things his hands trembled the way a newly frocked priest's might, pouring the chalice of his first communion.

Later, alone in his room in the single wide, Steve spread the gold out on his rickety bed and wept, smiling as he did so. In that moment he did not miss his parents at all.

Some months later, he was the veteran of a dozen burglaries, and no longer quite so poor. Mostly through luck he had found an actual fence. Quiet Lou, fat and diabetic, lurked in the very darkest corner of a downtown pawn shop, his face lit from below by closed-circuit television monitors. Lou smoked vile cigars, and his shop had a permanent blanket of smoke floating at eye level. Many pawn-shop owners were legitimate, or mostly so. Lou was not one of these. He and Steve never became friends, but they understood each other.

Not everything Steve stole went to Lou, though. Sometimes he kept things he particularly liked—not smart, but it never completely blew up in his face, either. One such was a leather jacket. It was quilted and heavy, very thick, and smelled of pipe tobacco. Steve kept it for himself.

A week later he met Jack. He was peeing in the boys' bathroom at school, later than usual for class that morning. One other kid was in there sneaking a smoke. Steve knew Jack slightly from a common gym class, but Jack was a junior, and rich. The gulf between them might as well have been the Grand Canyon . . . except for the fact that Jack, the clean-cut scion of two devout Mormons, also had a feral streak.

"Nice jacket," Jack said, over the sound of urine on porcelain.

Steve didn't look around. "Thanks."

"Where'd you get it, if you don't mind my asking?"

Steve shook off and zipped up. "The store."

"Oh yeah? Which one?"

"I forget." Steve could feel his pulse pounding in his neck, in his temples.

"It wouldn't be the 'Maurley house' store would it? 'Cause I know a guy over at Kennedy whose dad had a jacket just like that. Same stain on the elbow and everything. Somebody robbed his house a couple weeks back. They got the jacket."

Steve turned to Jack, looked at him.

Jack's grin faded. "Relax, man. I ain't gonna say nothing. The kid's an asshole anyway."

"Thanks."

"Tell you what—why don't you meet me after class? We can go hit the mall or something. You can tell me all about how you got that jacket. Maybe we'll burn one."

A cautious smile flickered on Steve's face. "Yeah?"

"Yeah."

As it turned out, they burned not one but two joints on the way to the mall, and wandered through the stores high as kings. They didn't come home with Jack's trunk bulging with loot that time, but they did the next day and a lot of days after that.

Jack was an easygoing, wry guy. His own amorality flowed from a different place than Steve's. Steve, by nature an introvert, had long since figured out the basics of his own psychology. Jack he never quite understood. Jack's parents were solid, churchgoing types. To all appearances they were happy, and Steve got a pretty close look. Jack's brother was a church youth-group type.

Jack could be raw, angry. His temper snapped at unpredictable times. Steve once saw him beat the shit out of a guy behind a movie theater for spilling popcorn—not on Jack himself, or even a person, just on the floor. He and Steve got into it more than a couple of times as well, blacking eyes, bloodying noses. Usually Jack started it, and he always came over to Steve's place afterward, shame-faced, and apologized. It got to where Steve would roll the joint in anticipation of his arrival and wave off the actual apology.

Within six months or so, Jack's family semi-adopted him. He spent three nights a week at their house, sleeping on the floor in Jack's room or in the bedroom down the hall. Jack's parents never said anything, but Steve got the feeling that they knew his situation, perhaps pitied him. Steve resented that at first, but Martin and Celia were so old-fashioned nice that he just couldn't dislike them. They bought him presents on his birthday, for fuck's sake.

Steve had done dozens of burglaries by then, enough that it got written up in the paper. Jack was with him on seven of them. By the last two, Steve thought that Celia and Martin were beginning to suspect that something was up, but they never really probed. Steve figured they were afraid of what they might find out.

Perhaps they were wiser than they knew. On the most recent burglary Jack had suggested that they use gasoline from the garage to burn the place down. "We should torch the place, man! Cover our tracks!"

Steve, the acknowledged leader on the burglaries, vetoed this. That night he slept at Mary's trailer for the first time in several days. He lay awake in the moonlight until almost dawn, flopping around in the bed, wondering if his friend might be crazy. Two weeks later Jack shat on an old lady's bed and wiped his ass with her aging, yellowed wedding photo.

Jack funneled some of the pawn profits into a sideline business, buying small quantities of pot from a guy Steve knew, cutting it with oregano, selling it to other high school kids. It was a solid if unremarkable stream of spending money. Then one of their clients, a freshman girl, got caught with a baggie in her purse. In tears, she promptly confessed who she bought it from. The police showed up at Jack's house and searched his room. Jack left with them, in handcuffs.

The legal trouble ended up being not that big of a deal—juvenile court, record expunged, blah-blah—but from the standpoint of Jack's family it might as well have been Armageddon.

Naturally enough, Celia and Martin blamed Steve. Probably, he thought now, there was some justification for this. At the time, though, it seemed like the grossest injustice. They forbade Jack from hanging out with Steve. He was barred from the house, exiled back to Mary's trailer.

The two of them still hung out, of course, but now they had to be circumspect. No more trips to the mall, at least not in Jack's car. Steve started thinking about ways to get his own car, started scanning the classifieds with a pen in his hand. But the numbers were oppressive. He could probably figure out a way to steal one—it wasn't his specialty, but he was becoming very good with locks. Registering it would be another matter, however. Something decent would probably cost around $2,000, five times as much money as he had on hand. Steve went to Quiet Lou. They talked numbers. Lou mentioned pharmacies.

A month later he and Jack climbed up the back of an independent pharmacy with a diamond-tipped circular saw normally used for cutting through concrete. Quiet Lou had sold them the saw at a good price, and promised to buy it back when they no longer needed it. It was noisy, but it got the job done. Three quick strokes cut a black triangle out of the roof. If that had tripped the alarm, there was no sign.

Steve had tied footholds into eighty feet of strong nylon rope. One at a time they climbed down between the shelves, silent as wraiths. In residential burglaries Steve made a habit of turning on the lights—flashlights bobbing through darkened houses would look odd to the neighbors—but here he didn't have that option. He never found out for sure, but he thought it was their flashlights that had betrayed them. A neighbor? A passing car? Who knew.

The layout was unfamiliar, and it took time to locate the bottles that Lou was interested in. They split up and scanned the shelves in parallel. Steve's heart thumped in his chest. Jack whistled. One at a time the prizes fell to their search—valium, Xanax, Vicodin, morphine sulfate, cough syrup, brand-name and generic, many doses, many bottles. Steve was still using the black pillowcase. Soon it bulged.

After about fifteen minutes, Steve judged they had enough. Lou was a skinflint, but he never tried to cheat them. Steve's cut would be well over two thousand. With that, he could have his car. He had not told Jack this, but that meant something else to him as well. With his own wheels, he would not be so reliant on Jack for transportation. They could begin to go their separate ways.

Steve went up first, pulling himself up the rope with his shoulders. Jack, still in darkness, tied the pillowcase to the end of the rope. Steve hauled up the loot.

He was getting it untangled when he saw the flashing blue lights in the distance. They weren't using sirens. For a long minute he hoped that it was just coincidence, but as they bore down he knew in his heart that it wasn't.

"Cops," he hissed to Jack.

"What? How far?"

"Not far. Hurry."

"Ah, shit."

A minute later Jack was halfway up the rope. "Dude," Steve said, "they're about two blocks away."

Jack looked up at him, his face pale in the moonlight. He seemed resigned, and not especially worried. Steve was scared enough for both of them.

"Go," Jack said. "I'll catch up."

"Seriously?"

"Seriously."

Steve thought about it for a second, then took off. He left the bag on the roof. In later years he would lie awake in the dark and wonder why he had done that. The possibility of leaving Jack holding the bag—literally, ha-ha—either had occurred to him in that moment, or it had not. He simply could not remember.

Then the blue lights were bearing down on him, too close for anything but flight. He climbed over the side of the roof, dangled, dropped, bypassing the storm drain he and Jack had climbed up. He darted into the shadows behind the strip mall a second and a half before the lights turned into the parking lot. He hid behind a Dumpster as the first car did a tentative probe. Steve could hear the radio through the squad car's open window. "Suspect in custody." It did a U-turn and circled back to the pharmacy.

This time there would be no juvenile court, no pre-trial intervention. That ship had sailed. Jack was charged as an adult with burglary. He might have lessened his sentence if he ratted Steve out, but he didn't. Martin and Celia got him a good lawyer, though. They pleaded it down to three years, out in eighteen months on good behavior. It wasn't such a long time as these things go, but even from the first visit, Steve could tell it wasn't going well. The prison was medium-security, but Jack was young, relatively good-looking, and white. Quiet Lou had explained that he would be a prize, explained what that would mean. After only three days, Jack looked back at him with haunted eyes.

He lasted three months, then hanged himself with his underwear. Steve didn't go to the funeral, but he attended the graveside service. He watched from a hundred yards away, behind a tree. Celia saw him anyway. After she buried her oldest son she bore down on Steve, eyes bright, like a hawk descending on a field mouse. She didn't say anything. The woman who had bought him his one and only fifteenth-birthday present slapped him hard across one cheek and then the other and delivered her verdict.

"You . . . you little . . . you *asshole*."

She was crying. Steve didn't stop her, didn't try to say anything. There was nothing to say.

As the days and weeks and seasons wore on he found himself repeating this nothing, not wanting to. Gradually he came to understand that this particular nothing was all that he could really say now. He chanted it to himself in cell blocks and dingy apartments, recited it like a litany, ripped himself to rags against the sharp and ugly poetry of it. It echoed down the grimy hallways and squandered moments of his life, the answer to every question, the lyric of all songs.

Chapter 9

A Bone That Cannot Be Cracked

I

An hour or so after Steve and the lions took shelter in the room with the cave paintings, Mrs. McGillicutty's cell phone rang. Steve was sitting next to the female lion, checking her bandages. He stood with a grunt, limped across the room, and answered it on the fifth ring. "Hello?"

"Hi, Steve. It's Carolyn."

"Of course it is." He rummaged around in the supply pile for another piece of beef jerky. It was homemade, and very good. "Who else would it be, really?" He noticed that he was slurring a little. *Probably the pain pills. Or maybe the blood loss.*

"How are you?"

"Oh, I'm *great*," he said, putting a little edge in his voice. "Thanks to you, I mean. I found the bandages and whatnot. Very helpful. I think the bleeding has stopped."

"Well, that's good."

"Yes. Yes, it is. And suspiciously convenient."

Long pause.

"There's a little clay pot with a cork in it," Carolyn said. "Did you see that?"

"Matter of fact, I did. Right next to the syringes? I wondered about what it was."

"That's the one. I got it from my sister. What's in there will help you with blood loss." She paused. "If, um, you know . . . if that's a problem."

"As it happens, yes. I believe that it is. However could you have guessed? I'm pretty light-headed, and I don't think it's just the pain pills. So, what . . . do I chew up the little round things in the pot, or . . . ?"

"Umm . . . no."

"What, then?"

"Well, you, ah, that is . . . it's a suppository."

"I see. So I should stick it up my ass, then?"

"Yes."

"Interesting."

"What?"

"*I was just thinking the same thing about you,*" Steve roared. "*Cram it up your ass, you crazy, horrible bitch!*" He reached for the Off button, then something occurred to him. "Quick question, though, before I hang up on you." He waited for a long time. "You still there?"

"Yes."

"Does the stuff work on lions?"

"Lions?"

"Yes. Lions. My *backup*. Thanks for them as well, by the way. Those guys were awesome. They got here just in the proverbial nick of fucking time. But the female is banged up pretty bad. She's lost a lot of blood. I put a couple of those pressure bandages on her, but I think she's still bleeding."

"They're not dead?"

"Nope," Steve said, proud of himself for the first time in decades, "I let them in."

"But . . . I told you . . ."

"Yes. You mentioned that they were 'disposable.' I'm pretty sure that was your word. But seeing as how they'd just saved my life, I didn't feel like *leaving them out there to fucking die* was the dao way."

"The what?"

"The dao way. It's Chinese. I meant it wasn't the right thing to do."

"Oh. Your pronunciation . . ."

"What?"

"Never mind. But to answer your question, yes. It should work on lions as well."

Steve was quiet for a long time.

"Are you still there?"

"What? Yes. Sorry. I was trying imagine sticking something up a lion's ass. I don't think I'm quite there yet."

"Oh. Well . . . it's up to you. Like I said, at this point they're disposable. But they won't hurt you. They've given their word."

"I see. Gave their word, did they? To you?"

"Not me. My brother."

"The big scary guy?"

"No. My other brother. Michael. He talked with the lions. He told them to look after you."

"Talked with the lions, did he?"

"Yes. We made a deal. They will protect you as if you were their own cub."

"Maybe they were just being polite."

"No," she said seriously. "Dresden may be in exile, but he is still king. In his language the word for 'promise' is the same as the word for 'a bone that cannot be cracked.' He will do as he says."

Steve considered this. When he spoke, some of the joking was gone from his voice. "If you say so. That seems to be what they're doing. And honestly, I'd almost figured out that they weren't going to hurt me." He paused. "It just takes a while to wrap your head around the idea. When I got up this morning I was under the impression that lions were scary." He patted Dresden's mane, offered him the rest of the beef jerky.

The big lion sniffed, then took it gingerly from his hands, exposing canines thicker than Steve's thumb.

"These two seem OK, though. We've struck a mighty blow against prejudice this day." A thought occurred to him. "Say, do you know the female's name?"

She didn't answer at first. Then, he heard a deep, bass rumble that sounded exactly like a lion. Steve held the receiver away from his head, eyebrows raised. The male lion looked up at the sound, interested. "Is there another lion with you?"

"No. That was me. That's her name."

"Oh." Steve paused. "I don't think I can pronounce that right."

"Probably not. Theoretically I can't either."

"What do you mean, 'theoretically'? I just—"

"Never mind. It takes practice. And minor surgery, to really get it right. But . . . you might call her Nagasaki. Naga for short. That was what the guy who kidnapped them did. They don't like those names, but they'd recognize them. They'd know who you meant."

"Dresden and Nagasaki, huh? Cute. Are they married, or whatever you call it?"

"No. Naga's his cub."

"Pretty big for a cub."

"Well, his child. But she'll get bigger. She won't be full-grown for another couple of years."

"If she makes it that long."

"What do you mean?"

"Like I said, she's lost a lot of blood. And I can't go anywhere because of the dogs. There's at least a couple hundred of them out there. How are you planning to get me out of here?"

"We'll walk. But it won't be until tomorrow, at the earliest."

"She—Naga—she's not going to make it that long. And what the hell do you mean 'we'll' walk? I thought you couldn't—"

"We'll talk about it when I get there. Maybe I can—"

"Can't you alter your schedule or something? This lion . . . I mean, she saved my life." For a moment he saw Jack's face through the hole in the roof of the pharmacy, trapped in a darkness he would never leave. *Go. I'll catch up.*

"I'm sorry, Steve. I just can't. But the lion isn't important."

"Yeah, well, maybe she's important to me." He hung up. "And fuck you." She called back, then called back again. After the third time he turned the phone off.

II

When he hung up, the female lion—*Naga*, Steve thought, *her name is Naga*—was still conscious, but only just. Despite his best efforts and admirable patience on her part, blood was still leaking out from under the bandage. More important, she seemed to be getting worse. Putting on the pressure bandage had obviously hurt her, but she hadn't mauled him, hadn't even growled.

Talked with the lions, did they? He could almost believe it. Not quite, but almost.

But maybe on some level he *did* believe it, because when he lifted the thick flesh of Naga's muzzle to check her capillary response, he really wasn't afraid at all. Steve wasn't a veterinarian, but he'd had a lot of dogs over the years, including one who got run over. He knew that one way to check for blood loss in animals was to push your thumb into the gums and watch how fast the color returns. If it comes back fast, that's a good sign. If it takes a while, like it had on Angie after she got hit by the car, not so much.

He didn't think Naga was quite as far gone as Angie had been, not yet, but she was getting there fast.

So, as an experiment, he shook one of the suppositories out of the little clay jug that Carolyn left for him and took it into the bathroom. There he bent over and used one trembling finger to cram it up his own ass. When he turned on the tap to wash his hands afterward, nothing came out. He used a couple of bottles of Dasani instead, lathering up a dry, ancient bar of Ivory soap gathering dust in a dish over the sink. By the time he got the stink off his index finger he felt better. A lot better, actually. Even the slurring in his voice was gone. But he was really thirsty. He guzzled two more bottles of water and half of a third before he stopped feeling parched.

Then, with a sigh, he pulled the cork out of the little clay jug and shook out another suppository. "Heeere, kitty-kitty," he whispered under his breath.

Dresden looked at him quizzically.

"Sorry, big guy," Steve said. "Bad joke." He limped across the room. Naga lay in a fairly sizable pool of her own blood. He didn't want to sit in it and soak his pants, and with the way his ankle and calf were torn up he couldn't squat. Naga herself was no longer conscious, but Steve felt the eyes of her father on him, yellow and alien in the dim light of the overhead.

When he was ready, he bent at the waist and lifted her tail, exposing her rectum. She gave no response at first, but when Steve placed the small white globe against the puckered flesh and pushed it in, she trembled in her sleep. Dresden's brow furrowed. He took a step forward and showed Steve a flash of teeth.

Steve stood up rapidly, held his palms out to Dresden. "All done," he said. "Sorry." He took a step back. Dresden, to his relief, didn't follow. "I'm gonna go see if I can find a bowl," he said. "If this works, she's liable to be awfully thirsty."

The old woman was in the kitchen. Her husband, done with his mowing, was milling around on the porch with a couple of dogs. He seemed lost, bumping here and there among the dogs like a pinball, jiggling the locked door handle every so often. Inside, his wife stood at the kitchen sink dry-washing ancient, dusty dishes with a rotting sponge.

"Um . . . excuse me?"

"Supper isn't quite ready, dear. Why don't you go watch the game?"

"Do you have a bowl I could borrow? A biggish one? A mixing bowl, maybe?"

She blinked. "Why . . . yes. Yes I do." She sounded almost as surprised as Steve was. She pointed at a cabinet under the stove. "There."

"Thanks." Steve opened the cabinet door and rummaged around inside. There was a stack of bowls—ceramic, stainless steel, plastic. With a clatter he slipped a good-sized one out of the pile.

"Supper isn't quite ready, dear."

"I'll go watch the game."

She smiled, nodded. He limped back into the living room. To his amazement, Naga was standing. As Steve watched, she took a single step. She wobbled but did not fall. Dresden moved to her hindquarters and sniffed at her butt with a quizzical look on his face.

"Feeling better?" Steve heard real relief in his own voice. "Awesome."

Probably the lions heard it too. They swished their tails, accidentally and amusingly in sync. Steve went to the supply pile and emptied half a dozen bottles of water into the bowl. Naga's nostrils flared as he did this, and she took another step. This time when she lost her balance she did fall.

"Don't try to do too much," Steve said. "I'll bring it to you." He set the bowl down in front of her. She lapped at it greedily until more than half was gone, then lay on her side.

Hesitantly, Steve touched her muzzle. She pulled away, causing Steve to jerk his hand back. *You could call it overreaction, but if ever there was a good time to be jumpy, it's when fiddling around with a lion's mouth.* Then she leaned forward and licked his knuckles. Dresden, watching this, swished his tail again.

"Do you mind if I . . . ?" Tentatively, he touched her muzzle again. When she didn't draw back, he lifted her lip and pressed his thumb into the gum just behind her left incisor. He tested twice, comparing it against the same test done on his own fingernail. He judged her to be better, but not quite well.

He slid around to her hindquarters and inspected the pressure bandages on her hip. The bandage was bloated and dripping blood, saturated. Steve debated changing it, then settled for tying a third one, his last, over the first two. He pressed down on this, hoping that the direct pressure would help. It seemed like the sort of thing they did on doctor shows.

III

An hour later he was still pressing down. Naga's bleeding was better, but it hadn't completely stopped. There was one more suppository left in the little clay jug. He went back and forth about when to use it. Now? Or at the last minute? He had no idea how the thing worked, so he couldn't begin to guess. Was it like a video game where if you drink your health potion too soon you waste some of the benefit? Or was it like sharpening a knife, where it was best to put forth a little effort to whet the edge every time you used it rather than waiting until it got really dull before you trotted out the sharpening stone? He didn't know.

What he did know was that if he couldn't get the bleeding to stop, Naga was unlikely to be around for Carolyn's return. "And you won't want to miss that," Steve whispered. "It's *bound* to be weird."

As he waited, his mind drifted back to Jack, who had also been kind to him, and to whom he had brought ruin. Thinking this, looking down at Naga's wounded body, it came to him that there might be a new way to say the nothing that had weighed on his heart for so very long. He touched Naga's neck, gently. She lifted her head a little, looked at him.

"I'm going to get you out of here."

His words hung in the dusty silence of the living room. Dresden turned at the sound, golden eyes solemn over his blood-caked muzzle. Carolyn's words echoed in his mind. *He is still king. His word for 'promise' also means 'a bone that cannot be cracked.'* Steve met the lion's gaze. "Yeah. I'm going to get her out of here if it fucking kills me."

Steve stood and went back into the kitchen. The woman wasn't doing dishes anymore. Instead she stood at the wall, scraping away the dirt and the paint in lines shaped like a cave man's image of a dog. "Supper isn't quite ready, dear."

"That's OK. I need to borrow your car." He looked around. He was hoping for her purse, or a bowl. Then his eye happened upon a peg with spare keys dangling from it. One of them was a leather tab with the Ford logo on it. "Gotcha."

He hadn't paid a lot of attention to the house when he was outdoors, but he vaguely remembered the garage being on the far end. There was a hall leading in that direction, but it was dark. He found a switch and flipped it, but no light followed. He wandered down the hall in darkness, feeling ahead with his fingers.

The first room he came to was a bedroom that had been converted into an artist's studio. Someone—the woman?—had once used it for painting still life in oils—flowers, fruit, a random jumble of costume jewelry. Most of them were rather good. Steve thought of the kindergarten scribbles lining the living-room wall. He shivered as he shut the door behind him.

The next room was indeed the garage, and the Ford was there, but it sat on four completely flat tires. The dust on the hood was so thick it was difficult to tell what color the car was. Steve tried the key anyway, but it didn't so much as click.

"Shit." He pounded the steering wheel. *What, then?* He shut the door to the garage and made his way back to the relative brightness of the living room. Dresden stood over Naga. The puddle of her blood was wider. Her sides heaved. Steve rattled the last suppository out of the little clay jug and crammed it up her butt next to the other one. He wiped his finger on the carpet and rinsed it off with half a bottle of Dasani, then drank the rest.

He limped back into the dim, windowless foyer. Then, from outside, he heard an engine. *Carolyn?* He ducked into the kitchen and looked out the window over the sink. Not Carolyn, but one of those little white jeeps that the Post Office uses. It was two houses away. Lawn-mower guy was nowhere in sight.

Uncounted dozens of dogs lay in the yard and nearby on the street. They watched the truck approach. Steve wondered what they would do.

The mailman was one house away now. He put the mail in the mailbox, but did not continue down the road, only sat there, engine idling. *He's seen them.* After a long moment, the mail guy rolled up his window. He turned into the driveway next door, then backed out of it pointing in the opposite direction. He drove off down the street.

"Shit." He couldn't think what help the mailman might conceivably have offered, but he sure did hate to see him go.

The dogs watched the jeep depart but did not follow. After it turned onto the main road they seemed to lose interest. Also, instead of just sitting on the lawn and staring at the house, now some of them were doing dog stuff—humping each other, playing bite-tag or whatever that was, scratching at fleas. Over the next fifteen minutes or so, more than half of them wandered off. *That's progress.*

Not all, though. Thane and a couple dozen others kept vigil on the yard. As Steve watched, a big dog—Rottweiler, maybe?—trotted up to the porch and sat down. "Fuck." He went to the door and looked out through the peephole. His ankle was starting to throb. *Well,* he thought, *I guess you could always call 911. They'd probably get you out of here.*

He snapped his fingers and turned Mrs. McGillicutty's phone back on. When he had a good signal he dialed 411. A computer asked him, "What city?" Steve answered it, careful to enunciate clearly.

"What listing?"

"Any taxi service."

Behind him, from the porch, came a low deep growl. Steve moved away from the door.

The mechanical voice recited a nine-digit number, then asked if Steve would like to be connected for an additional charge of fifty cents. Steve said yes.

The phone rang once, twice, three times. *Come on, come on*, Steve thought. Four, five. He was just about to hang up and try a different service when someone answered the phone.

"Yucatan Taxi," a man said. He spoke with an Indian accent, thick and musical. "*Se habla español.*"

"How about English?" Steve asked.

"Of course," the man said. He sounded slightly hurt that Steve would ask.

"Great," Steve said. "I need a cab. A big one. You got a minivan, something like that?"

"I have two, but only one driver at the moment. She's just heading out on a call. Can you wait about an hour?"

Behind him the Rottweiler barked, scrabbled at the door. Naga's blood pooled at his feet.

"I'm afraid that's not convenient," Steve said, struggling to sound natural. "Tell you what. I'll make it worth your while. How about a hundred bucks? We're not going far." He had no money, but there was the gun. He would apologize later. "You'll be a couple minutes late for your other call, that's all."

"Sorry sir, but I cannot—"

"I'm really in a rush. Me and the kids are meeting my in-laws. My car won't start. There'll be hell to pay if I'm late. Tell you what—five hundred."

"Five hundred dollars?" the man asked. "Ah. Now I understand. In my village we called people like yourself the 'shepherds of the shit mountain.' Such men were often caned. Good-b—"

"No, wait!" Steve said. "Five hundred dollars, cash! Really. Solemn promise. Plus whatever the fare costs. It won't be even a five-minute ride, I swear."

The man thought about it. "Possibly. What is the address, please?"

That was a tough one. Steve thought frantically. He limped to the kitchen window, peeked out at the mailbox. "Two-eleven Garrison Drive," he said. "In the Garrison Oaks subdivision. Do you know it?"

"Garrison Oaks . . ." the man said. His voice sounded distant.

"Yeah," Steve said. "Smallish neighborhood, just off Highway 78. Do you know it?"

"Oh, right," he said vaguely. "You know, I do not think I've ever been in there before."

"I'm not surprised," Steve said.

On the other side of the door the dog gave off a low, throaty bark. Another joined in, then another. Soon they were all barking.

"What is that noise?" the cabbie asked.

"Nothing, just my dog."

"He sounds like a very big dog indeed."

"Yeah," Steve said. "He's pretty big. He has separation anxiety. He hates it when I leave him alone."

"You cannot bring this dog in my cab, you understand."

"Wouldn't dream of it," Steve said.

"All right," the guy said. "For five hundred, I will come myself. I will be there in ten minutes."

"Look, there's one other thing. My, ah, friend is coming with me. He's sort of agoraphobic and—"

"What? He's sick? I do not want a sick man in my taxi, sir."

"No, no. He's not sick. Agoraphobic means he doesn't like being outside. When you get here, pull up as close as you can get, open the door, and honk. Can you do that?"

Long silence. "I do not think I like this, sir."

"What's not to like?" Steve said, eyes squeezed shut, brow furrowed. "Five hundred dollars is a pretty good tip." He forced himself to stop talking, gripped the phone with white knuckles.

The dispatcher thought about it for a while. "I'll be there in ten minutes," he said. "Make sure you have the money."

"It's a white-brick house."

"I'm sure it is a very nice one. Make sure you have the money."

The cab pulled up eleven minutes later, a white minivan with a photograph of the Mayan pyramid at Chichén Itzá on the side. The driver honked. He didn't pull around to the front door, though. *Of course not*, Steve thought. *That would have been too easy.* The dogs lounging in the yard watched all this, but they didn't bark, didn't growl.

Steve, desperate, scrabbled for an idea. Even with just six dogs on the lawn, the thirty feet or so might as well have been a thousand miles. He wouldn't have tried to run for it even if he had been *able* to run. Limping, carrying a half-grown lion, he would stand absolutely no chance whatsoever.

The cabdriver honked again. Dresden padded over to the front door, sniffed, rumbled. He looked at Steve.

"I'm thinking, dammit!" Seconds dragged out. He looked out the kitchen window. *Maybe we could go out through the garage. There was an electric door opener, and—*

The cabdriver knocked at the door.

Steve and Dresden looked at each other. Steve grinned. "Coming!"

"Sir, please can you hurry? I need to return to my office quickly."

Steve hobbled to the front door and looked out the peephole. The Rottweiler was the only dog on the porch. Thane and five others stood on the lawn, watchful, under sunny blue autumn sky. Steve took the gun out of the holster, put his hand on the doorknob, did a mental count. *Three, two, . . .*

Steve, bloody and bandaged, yanked the door open with his right hand and shot the Rottweiler. The dog's head exploded in a crash of blood and thunder. Steve grabbed the cabdriver by the shirt. "Get in!"

Out on the lawn Thane barked, furious.

The cabdriver instinctively raised his hands and went into a little half crouch. "Do not shoot!" He tried to back away. Steve leaned backward with all his weight, yanking the two of them into the foyer. His ankle gave out and he fell over backward. The cabdriver almost fell with him, but recovered.

The dogs were charging the door. Thane's ice-blue eye bore down on him. When his feet touched the sidewalk, Thane leaped and—

Steve kicked the door shut with his good foot, as hard as he was able. It slammed shut. A tiny fraction of a second later there was a meaty thud as Thane impacted the door.

Still on his back, Steve spun around on the linoleum to deal with the driver. "Don't move!"

But the man *wasn't* moving. Dresden, all four hundred pounds of him, stood inches away. The cabdriver was a short, slight Indian man with caramel-colored skin. His eyes stretched wide in terror. His hands hovered near his face in a gesture of surrender, or perhaps self-defense. He was trembling.

"Don't worry," Steve said, striving for a comforting tone. "He doesn't bite."

The cabdriver looked at Steve. "That is a lion."

"Yes. Yes, it is."

"You have a gun."

"That's true too."

"Well," the cabdriver said, speaking as if to a very dull child, "why don't you shoot the lion?"

Steve laughed. "Are you kidding? Dresden's my buddy." Then it came to him. *YouTube. Christian the lion.* "Don't you watch the Internet?"

"What?"

"Never mind. I need your keys."

"What?"

"The keys. To your cab. Give them to me." Steve waggled the gun.

The driver's face fell. "What about my five hundred dollars?"

"Yeah, it turns out I was lying about that. Sorry." He thought for a moment. "Look, I actually *am* kind of sorry." He gestured at Naga with the gun. "If I don't get her out of here soon, then—never mind. Long story. But supposedly there's a duffel bag full of cash waiting for me back at the other place. How about I mail it to you? I'll make it a thousand."

"I think that you are lying again."

"No, I will. Soon as I can, promise." He would, too. "But right now, I'm going to need your keys. Sorry."

"You will not shoot me?"

"Absolutely not."

The driver glanced down at Dresden. "What about him?"

"He's coming with me. Both of them are."

"Oh. Then, by all fucking means . . ." The cabdriver fished around in his pocket for his keys and handed them over. They jingled like the bells of heaven in Steve's hand.

"Thanks, man," Steve said. "Really sorry about all this." Something else occurred to him. "You got a cell phone?" He didn't want the guy to call 911.

"In the cab."

The key was the old-fashioned kind, just a metal key, no Lock or Unlock buttons. "Is the cab locked?"

"No."

Steve gestured with the gun. "You better not be lying to me."

"Why would I lock it? I was just going to the front door."

"Yeah, OK." Steve squeezed his eyes shut, thought for a moment. "OK, there's a bathroom right around that corner there. Go inside and shut the door." He saw that the guy's knees were literally trembling. "Look, man . . . for what it's worth, I'm really sorry about all this. I'm in sort of a situation, and—"

"Yes, I am quite sure. Please go fuck yourself." The guy backed up a single cautious step. Dresden rumbled a warning.

"No, it's OK, big guy," Steve said. The lion looked at him, confused. Steve put his arm around the smaller man's shoulders, gave him a little man-hug. "It's OK. He's a friend, see?" Then, to the cabdriver. "Go on. Shoo."

The cabbie took one cautious step away, then another, his eyes never leaving Dresden. When he was close enough, he jumped inside the bathroom and slammed the door shut. Steve heard it lock.

Naga was conscious, but she didn't look like she could stand. Steve checked her capillary response again—it was just OK. She had lost some ground. He checked the magazine on the gun—eight rounds, plus one in the chamber. There were seven dogs left. He went back into the living room and sat on the floor next to Naga. He slipped his hands under her, testing her weight. She was very heavy, two hundred pounds or so, but Steve thought he could probably lift her.

"OK," he said to Dresden, "you ready?"

Dresden looked at him quizzically.

Steve jingled the keys, the way he had done when he was going to take Petey for a ride in the car. For a moment his heart ached. He wondered if he would ever see his dog again.

Dresden looked at the keys, still confused.

Steve holstered the gun. He turned to look Dresden in the face. He took a handful of the big lion's mane in his right hand and patted Naga's side with his left. "I. Am. Going. To. Get. Her"—here he patted Naga again—"Out. Of. Here." He pointed at the front door.

Dresden's brow unfurrowed. He roared a little bit, scaring the shit out of Steve. Then he stretched out and licked Steve's cheek.

Good enough, Steve thought. He got his arms under Naga. She seemed confused, only semiconscious. *I hope she doesn't forget that we're buddies*, he thought, and lifted her. She squirmed a bit, then half stood, lifting her forequarters off the living-room floor. Steve ducked under her, lifting at the same time, and managed to get her over his left shoulder in a half-assed, crouched version of a fireman's carry. *Lift with your legs, not your back*, he thought, and tittered hysterically. He strained against her weight, pushing with his good leg and his bad. The pain was exquisite, blinding. He flashed on Carolyn's face and thought, *I fucking* hate *that bitch!* The adrenaline burst from this was just enough to get the lion up.

Once he was standing, it was easier. He took a single cautious step. He held his balance, but only just. He took a second, smaller step, almost hopping with his good leg, dragging the bad one behind him. That was better, if not exactly graceful. Naga, dangling over his back, made some cranky-sounding lion noises. Steve told her to shut the fuck up.

He inched his way to the door, Dresden following at his flank. The lion's eyes were fixed on the door, and what lay beyond. *Yeah, he knows*, Steve thought. *He understands what we're going to do.*

Still weighted down by Naga, he turned and squinted out the peephole. They were now down to six dogs on the lawn, including Thane. *Even so. Six is a lot of dogs. This is* so *going to suck*, Steve thought. He looked down at Dresden. "You ready?"

The big lion swished his tail. He did not look at Steve. His face was like something cast in stone. Balancing Naga on his shoulder with his left hand, Steve slipped the pistol out of the holster and held it with his teeth. He tasted gun oil, metallic and alien. He put his hand on the doorknob, squeezed his eyes shut, then opened them. "Showtime," he grunted, throwing the door open.

Thane stood first, barked. Steve took the gun out of his mouth, aimed carefully, and shot him right between the blue and brown eye.

Dresden charged out, roaring. Seeing him, one of the dogs turned and ran the other way. Steve limped across the porch. Dresden launched himself at a big Doberman and landed on it. A second later Steve heard the dog scream. The other three dogs, all big, tore into Dresden wherever they could find a spot—his shoulder, his front leg, his back.

Steve, clutching the iron railing, limped down first one step, then two. Now he was on the sidewalk. On his shoulder, Naga stirred. "Easy girl," he said. The cab was perhaps thirty feet away.

When the Doberman was dead, Dresden turned his attention to the dog biting his right foreleg, a big German shepherd. He lifted his paw, exposing the dog's flank, and tried biting her. He missed the first time, but with his second bite he clamped down on the dog's hind leg. Steve heard a crack. The shepherd screamed.

Three down! Steve thought. *We're doing this!* He inched his way down the front walk, past one rose bush, then a second. He was twenty feet away from the cab.

Dresden was having trouble reaching the dog on his back. Steve considered shooting it, then decided that, based on his record, he was just as likely to hit the lion as the dog. After a moment, Dresden retargeted. He bent to his right and snapped at the dog on his hindquarters. The dog let go and backed off, circling. It noticed Steve and gave its "Alert!" bark.

The sound of it—*rowrowrowrowrowrowrow*—echoed down the street. A second later Steve heard toenails clicking on asphalt, first one set, then two, then a stampede. *Oh, shit.* He was fifteen feet away from the cab.

Dresden pounced on the dog who had given the alert. Steve was past them now, so he couldn't see what was happening, but two steps later he heard another scream. Dresden's answering roar burbled through something wet.

Ten feet left.

Steve risked a glance over his shoulder. There was one dog still on Dresden, hanging from his back ... but behind him, on the hill, dozens—*hundreds*—more of them streamed in to take his place. *Where could they all be coming from?* Steve wondered. There were far too many. Even Dresden could not stand long against such a horde.

"Come on, big guy! Time to get out of here!" Only two feet remained between him and the cab. The cab's door was blessedly, wonderfully unlocked. Steve turned.

Dresden only looked at him. He was surrounded by corpses. The final dog, a Doberman, hung from his mane, scrabbling and growling. The lion made no move.

"Come on!" Steve screamed again. He took another step and bumped into the cab, almost losing his balance. Muscles trembling against Naga's weight, he slid the minivan's door back. "Come *on!*"

Steve looked over his shoulder to see what was keeping the lion. "What the hell are you *doing?* Come *on!*"

Dresden shrugged off the Doberman. Victorious now, he watched as Steve lay his daughter down in the backseat with a whoosh of deflating vinyl upholstery, watched as Steve slid the door shut. *She is safe now.* His yellow eyes met Steve's. Dresden, who was a king as of the old age, swished his tail—just once. Then, deliberately, he turned to face the coming dogs. Every muscle stood out in stark relief. He roared. The sound echoed down the street, bouncing off the neat suburban houses and well-manicured hedges with the force of dynamite. The dogs flowed at him like a tide, bottomless and unstoppable.

Dresden charged them.

Steve froze for a moment, feeling small, unable to look away from the forces at work before him. Carolyn's words came to him. *They will protect you as if you were their own cub.* Dresden smashed into the wave of dogs, a cannon shot of fury and blood. *He's stalling them. He's delaying them for Naga ... and for me.* Then, channeling Celia's voice: *Don't waste it, asshole.*

Steve shook his head, forced himself to look away, opened the door, took his place in the driver's seat.

The dogs were on Dresden now. First one, then three, then a dozen, then two dozen with a hundred more on the way. Together they formed a living wall of muscle and fur. *The cab couldn't push through that*, Steve thought. *A* tank *couldn't push through that.* He slammed the cab door. Now Dresden was buried under them, invisible under a roiling mountain of fur and teeth—Labs, poodles, Dobermans, Rottweilers, black, yellow, brown. The cabdriver's pale face watched all this from the bathroom window. Steve rolled down the van's window, frantic, then drew the pistol and steadied himself. He took careful aim, fired. A dog fell, screaming, and was replaced by three more. He fired again, fired until the pin clicked down on an empty chamber. "Fuck you!" he screamed. "Fuck you, fuck you, FUCK YOU!"

One or two of the dogs looked up at this. A chocolate Lab barked, then ran for the van. Steve rolled the window back up, but he wasn't quick enough. The dog hung on to the window by furry brown paws, barking and snapping, hind legs scrabbling at the door. There were only about three inches of room between the top of the glass and the door frame, not enough to get at Steve, but the dog's weight was such that he couldn't roll the window up. He flipped the dog the bird, put the key in the ignition.

The cab started immediately. He backed out of the driveway. The brown dog still clung to the window, blocking his view. Steve leaned back in the seat to check if, by some miracle, Dresden had emerged from the pile.

He had not.

Steve pointed the cab at the exit and floored it. A few seconds later he squealed to a stop at the gate, tires smoking. He put on his blinker, turned right onto Highway 78, floored it again.

The Garrison Oaks sign dwindled in his rearview mirror.

IV

The cabdriver's name was Harshen Patel. Two hours later, cowering behind a shower curtain in a dusty green bathtub, he heard a woman's voice.

"Steve?"

"Be careful!" Patel said. "I think that they are crazy!" He cradled his left hand, bandaged in a roll of bloody toilet paper and what was left of his shirt.

"Steve?" Her tone was doubtful now.

"I do not know who that is. If you're looking for the lying asshole with the two lions, he left."

"He *left*?" She sounded incredulous.

"Yes. A couple hours ago."

"How?"

"He stole my taxi."

She chuckled. "He's resourceful. I'll give him that."

"You should be very careful," Harshen said. "There are two of them, an old man and a woman. She came to me and said, 'Supper is ready!' and then they both started . . . started . . . *biting* me." He heard the edge of a scream in his voice and clamped down on it. "They have eaten my left pinkie finger. And part of my thumb. They might still be out there. You should—"

"It's OK," the woman said. She rattled the doorknob. "Can you open this, please?"

Harshen considered this for several seconds, then reached out with a shaking hand and opened the door.

The woman in the hall was on the small side, frizzy-haired, barefoot. She carried a blue duffel bag slung over her shoulder. She looked him up and down, surveying the wounds in his shoulder, his neck, his crotch. Her brown eyes were dark and intense, difficult to meet. "You'll live."

"Do you think so?"

"Yeah. You were lucky. Not a lot of people get to visit in this neighborhood."

Harshen nodded, miserable. "I believe you. I wonder . . . may we please leave now?"

She thought about it. "Sure." She shrugged. "I'll walk you out. What's your name?"

He told her. They stepped out into the light together.

"Nice to meet you. I'm Carolyn."

"Do you . . . do you live here?"

"Not in this one." She jerked her thumb down the street. "I'm a couple blocks deeper."

"Oh." He looked at her, horrified.

"Relax. I won't hurt you. You helped Steve." She shook her head, smiling. "He really is ever so good at slipping out of these *petonsha*, don't you think?"

"These what?"

"Sorry. That isn't English. They all start to blur after a while. I said '*petonsha*.' It means 'little traps.'"

"Oh."

They walked in silence for a block or so.

She spoke next. "Still . . . you did help Steve. I should repay the favor." She considered. "Do you have a family? Do you live in the city?"

"My wife. Esperanza. We have two boys. But no, we're out in—"

She waved her hand, cutting him off. "I don't care at all. When we get to the end of the street, I'm going to disappear. When that happens, put your family in your car and—"

"I can't."

"What?"

"I can't put my family in my car. He stole it. I don't know where it is."

"Who stole it? Steve?"

"Is he the lion man?"

"Yes."

"Yes. Him. He is the motherfucker who stole my cab."

"Oh. Hmm." Carolyn thought about it for a second, then handed him the blue duffel bag. "Here. Take this. Buy another one."

He unzipped the bag, looked inside. *Money.* "Oh!"

"Yeah. Spend it fast. It won't be worth much in a week or two—Barry O'Shea is out of hiding. Once he's established, there will be a sort of, umm, plague."

"What? What plague? Who is—"

"It doesn't matter. Pack up your wife and kids. Buy food, water, weapons. A generator, maybe. Go into the city—someplace with a lot of electric lights, and a good power supply. Get indoors, on the top floor of a tall building, if you can. Stay away from windows. And if you see people with tentacles, stay away. Don't let them touch you."

Harshen gaped at her. She spoke of insanities, but her voice was calm and certain. Her expression reminded him of a painting that frightened him as a child—Kali the annihilator, smiling as small things died.

"It's about to get very dark, you see."

Chapter 10

Asuras

I

Two miles west, Highway 78 merged into a four-lane that led into town, such as it was—basically a couple of strip malls between Steve and more empty road. The speed-limit sign said 45. He glanced down and saw he was doing 80, the rattletrap taxi shaking like the magic fingers at a cheap motel. He rolled to a stop at the first red light, a little jerkily.

There's blood on the windshield, he thought. *How did that get there?* He squirted wiper fluid on it, hoping it would clean off some of the dog blood. It didn't, just smeared it around a little. He felt dazed.

In the back, Naga lifted her head and looked around, blinking.

"Feeling better?" He thought the second suppository might be doing its thing. "Don't try to move. We're out. No more dogs!"

She twitched her tail a little, then bent around to her hindquarters and sniffed the bandages.

"Well, yeah," Steve sighed. "There is that." *Where the hell do you take a wounded lion? The zoo?*

A black Toyota truck inched to a stop beside him. Steve glanced over at it and found himself at eye level with the mud flaps. It was jacked up so high you'd almost need a ladder to get in and out. *Do you call that a monster truck? What's the dividing line?* Steve wondered. *How big does it have to get before it becomes a monster? Is it just x number of inches higher than factory, or do the tires have to—*

The truck honked. Steve looked up. Three or four feet up, some guy in the passenger seat was gesturing for Steve to roll down his window. Steve did. "Yes?"

The passenger was a kid, about eighteen or twenty. His baseball cap was on backward. "Yo, man," he said. "You got, like, half a dog hanging off your back bumper."

"Do I?"

"Yeah. Did you drive over it? On purpose, like?"

"No. The Buddha teaches respect for all life." Then, under his breath. "I guess I did shoot a couple though."

"There's blood all over your fuckin' door too, man. You get in a assident or something?"

"Nope. Dog fight." Something occurred to him. "Hey, is there a vet around here?"

The kid looked at him like he was crazy. "Man, ain't no vet gonna help *that* dog. He's cut in *half*, yo!"

"It's not for him," Steve said. "It's for her."

"What?"

Steve jerked his thumb at the backseat. The kid leaned out and down, peeping. "Whoa!" Then, to the driver, "Hey, Frank, that guy got a fucking lion in his cab!"

The driver leaned forward. "Say whaaaaat? Lean back, I can't—"

Maybe you should work harder on keeping a low profile, fugitive boy.

"Holy shit!" the driver said. "I know you! You that guy from Fox News!"

"Nope!" Steve said. "Not me! I get that a lot, though! Ha-ha!" *This goddamn light is taking forever.* He considered running it, just to get away from the kids in the truck. *Nah. Bad idea.* Instead he rolled up the window—this actually helped; it was crusty with dog slobber—and pretended to study the strip-mall sign a quarter mile up. He squinted. There was a Bi-Lo, a Walmart, some restaurant called Monsieur Taco—*What the fuck?*—and the Black Path Animal Hospital.

Steve considered. He figured it was about 50/50 that the guys in the truck would call 911. He needed to get off the road, fast. *On the other hand, there's Naga.* She was nibbling at her bandages. They were saturated, dripping. The suppository had helped, but it wouldn't last.

The light turned green.

"Fuck it," he said. " 'The true Buddhist will not be a moral and intellectual coward.' " He waited for the guys in the truck to roll away, then pulled in behind them. Half a block later he turned left into the strip mall, badly. The cab was a Chrysler Voyager minivan, a four-cylinder. It had a lot less power than his plumbing truck. Steve misjudged the gap to an oncoming BMW, obliging its driver to screech to a halt. She and Steve exchanged one-finger salutes. Naga lifted her head up again and roared. That startled him enough that he hopped the curb, clipped a hedge, and nearly T-boned a truck full of landscapers pulling out of the McDonald's drive-thru. "Aaagh!"

Naga roared again.

"Shut up! I'm driving!"

In the rearview, Naga gave him a reproachful look. Steve slowed to a walking speed and crossed the rest of the parking lot carefully, looking both ways at junctions, finally coasting to a stop in front of a vet. A sign out front read GET KITTY A FLEA DIP!

"Wait here," Steve said to Naga. "I'll be right back." He put the pistol in the back waistband of his sweatpants and pulled his concert shirt down over it. Walking around the back of the taxi, he saw that there was indeed half of a dog dangling from the tailpipe. It was too bloody to be sure, but he thought it might have been the chocolate Lab that had latched onto his window. *Maybe it got wedged under the muffler somehow?* He vaguely remembered bumps in the road as he pulled out of Garrison Oaks.

Thinking that the veterinarian might not approve, he spent a second trying to get the corpse a little more out of sight, but it was both deeply, deeply disgusting and wedged solidly in place. When gall rose in his throat he gave up, wiped his hand on the back of his sweats, and limped to the office.

The waiting room had a tile floor and smelled like cat food. A fussy-looking man in a bow tie held a Yorkshire terrier on a short leash. Opposite him a middle-aged hippie sat with a cat carrier on her lap.

Steve leaned against the receptionist's desk, his hands crusty with dried blood. "I need to see one of the doctors." Panting. "It's urgent."

The Yorkie, small and immaculate, barked at him.

"You'll need to fill this out," the receptionist said, eyeing him cautiously. "And I'm afraid these two people are both ahead of you. Do you have an appointment?"

He laughed, not quite hysterical. "It's kind of an emergency. Have you got a stretcher? A big stretcher?"

"Emergency?"

"Ohhh, yeah." He rocked his head up and down. "*Big*-time."

"It's OK," said the woman with the cat carrier. "I'm not in a hurry." The guy with the Yorkie gave her a dour look.

"Gimme a sec," the receptionist said. She picked up the phone. "Hey, Jer? We got a guy up here with an emergency. Can you grab Allie and bring the stretcher? Thanks."

"No," Steve said sincerely, "thank *you*. Really." He almost added "And I'm sorry," then thought better of it. He *was* sorry, though. He thought that the rest of the afternoon was liable to suck for everyone in the room.

A moment later two youngish women in green scrubs trotted up. One of them carried a good-sized stretcher. "Where is he? It's your dog, right?"

"Umm . . . she's in the car," Steve said. "This way."

They followed him out. In the parking lot he saw that the guys in the jacked-up black truck had circled back. They idled in the parking lot in front of Walmart, watching, the rumble of their monster truck faint but still audible. Steve groaned.

"What's wrong?" the taller vet tech asked.

"Nothing. My foot is sore." His foot actually did hurt. "She's over here." He opened the sliding door of the minivan and stepped back behind the women. Naga raised her head, groggy but interested.

"Holy cow!" the shorter one said.

"Is that a lion?"

"Ha-ha! We get that a lot. She's actually a Labradoodle. We just shaved her like a lion. Pretty funny, huh?"

The two of them peered at Naga. Steve held his breath. The tall tech said, "We"—she pointed at the shorter tech—"are veterinary students. You understand that, right?"

"Yeah," said the shorter one, nodding. "Bullshit." They both turned around to look at him. "What do you think we are, idi—Oh."

Now Steve was holding the empty pistol, not pointing it at anyone. "Here's what we're going to do. You hold the stretcher," he said. "I'll lift her out. She's not going to hurt anyone. Neither am I. She's lost a lot of blood. We're going to take her in there to the doctor, then you two can go."

The techs absorbed this.

"I mean it," Steve said. "Everything will be fine. I just need some help, is all. Will you guys help me? Please?" *C'mon, c'mon . . .*

They considered.

"No fucking way," said the short one. She looked at her partner for confirmation.

The tall tech was studying Naga. "You drove here with a lion in the back of your cab?"

"Pretty much, yeah."

"How do you know she's not going to bite?"

"I just do. Look, she's in a bad way. I hate doing this to you, but . . ."

The tall tech was studying him now. Steve held his breath.

After a moment, she said, "How about if we carry the lion and you hold her—her?—head."

"That works!" Steve said. "I'm going to get in the taxi now."

"OK, mister," said the short tech, much too sincerely.

"You try to run and I'll kneecap you," Steve said, waggling the empty pistol. "I mean it. I'm a marksman. I got a silver medal in the '92 Olympics. The shot won't kill you, but it'll hurt for the rest of your life."

Thwarted, she flashed a fake smile. "Wouldn't dream of it."

He stepped into the cab. "I'm going to put the gun away now." He tucked it away. "There. You won't even see it again unless you try to run."

"Good to know," said the tall tech.

"OK, get the stretcher ready."

The two techs looked at the lion, then at each other. "OK," the tall one said. "Yeah." She probed Steve with her eyes. "You hold her head, right?"

"I hold her head."

She nodded at the other tech. They lifted the stretcher to a horizontal position.

Steve smiled at them. "Thanks," he said. "Really." He stepped around them into the cab. "Hey, Naga," he said. "Hey, big girl. Almost there, sweetie." He patted her fur, made a show of checking her bandage.

The techs watched this, wide-eyed. "Dude, I don't think you should—"

"Shh!" As gently as he was able, he slid his arms under Naga. Naga rumbled a little but did not resist. He muscled her off the seat. She was very heavy. What he managed was not so much a carry as one controlled fall onto the floor of the cab and another onto the stretcher. *I must have been jacked-up out of my mind to get her out of the house.*

On the stretcher, Naga raised her head and squinted at the two techs. They blinked back at her, smiling and clearly terrified.

"Get her head," the tall tech said. She spoke with exaggerated gentleness. "Mmm-kay?"

"Step back a little," Steve said. "I can't—"

They backed away from the cab a foot or so.

He hopped out, grunting at a lightning strike of pain from his bad ankle. He slid one arm under Naga's raised head and lay the other hand over her cheek, patted her muzzle. *I couldn't possibly hold her if she decided she wanted to do something, but it might give them a second to get away.* Together they waddled across the parking lot and into the waiting room.

"We need a room . . . *right* . . . *now*," the tall tech said.

The receptionist gasped, jerked up out of her chair, dropped her pen. "Room, ah . . . Room Two."

"Coming through."

"Dude, that's a lion," the hippie with the cat carrier said conversationally. Steve ignored her. The guy with the bow tie stood up and bolted out the front door. A moment later his Yorkie followed.

"What's going on—" came a woman's voice from the back of the office. "Oh," she said. "Oh, my."

"Are you the doctor?"

She opened her mouth, shut it again.

Steve didn't really blame her. "It's OK," he said. "Naga's not going to hurt anybody."

She considered this. "Yeah, OK. I'm Dr. Alsace. Is she—what's wrong with her?"

"Dogs," Steve said. "We got in a fight with some dogs. They tore up her leg pretty bad. I think they nicked an artery. She's had two, um, transfusions, but I can't get the bleeding stopped."

"Is she restrained?"

"No," Steve said, "but she won't hurt you."

"You can't know that. I'm not doing anything until that animal is restrained."

"OK. Fine. Get whatever. I'll put it on her." He was thinking of a muzzle, or maybe some sort of straps.

"He's got a gun," the short tech said.

"I'll be leaving now," the woman with the cat carrier said.

"Sorry," Steve said. "I can't let you do that. And I *do* have a gun. I'm not here to hurt anyone, I swear, but I need help." In his mind's eye he saw Jack, trapped forever in darkness. His cheek stung with Celia's slap. He looked at the doctor, pleading.

Dr. Alsace pursed her lips, thinking it over. "OK," she said finally. "Two conditions. First, you let everyone here go. Second, *you* jab the injured lion with the syringe."

Such was Steve's gratitude that he was rendered mute. He said nothing. He nodded. The doctor made a shooing motion. The woman with the cat carrier ducked out. After a moment the receptionist followed. She turned to the techs. "You guys too."

"I'll stay," the tall one said.

"Jerri, you don't have to—"

"I'll stay. Wouldn't miss this for the world."

Everyone looked at the other tech. "You guys have fun," she said. Steve took her end of the stretcher. She bolted.

"OK." The doctor turned her attention to her patient. "Let's get her into Room Two. She's not full-grown. Any idea how old?"

Steve shook his head.

"Weight?"

"I lifted her, but it was all I could do. Two hundred, maybe?"

"I'd say two twenty-five, easy." She paused. "You *lifted* her? Alone?"

"She helped, a little." Still holding the stretcher he dipped his shoulder, pantomiming. "Fireman's carry."

"Oh-kay. So . . . what are you, a trainer, or—" She shook her head. "Never mind. Later." Inside the exam room they lay the stretcher on the table. "Jerri, go to the *Merck* and see what kind of dosage we need for a two-hundred-fifty-pound lion."

"Ketamine and xylazine?"

The doctor wrinkled her face. "Unless you know better? This is my first lion."

"That's what we used last summer. I'm on it."

"We'll also need an ET tube. Biggest we've got."

Naga's hind paws dangled off the end of the table. She lifted her head, looked around the room, rumbled. The doctor jumped back a bit.

"It's OK," Steve said. He patted Naga's neck. "Nothing to be scared of."

The tech—Jerri—returned a couple of minutes later bearing a big syringe and a bag full of plastic tubes. She handed it to the doctor.

Dr. Alsace checked the levels. "That's it?"

"We were a little short of ketamine."

The doctor raised her eyebrows.

"Just a little."

"OK. It will have to do." She looked at the lion, frowned, then handed Steve the syringe. "You ever given an injection before?"

"No."

"Nothing to it. This goes in the muscle. Jab it in quick, then inject slowly. See if you can find a spot on the back leg, away from the wound." She handed Steve the syringe, then backed up near the door. "Jerri . . . behind me."

Steve looked at Naga's hindquarter, found a spot with a good bit of muscle. He practiced jabbing. "Like this?"

The doctor nodded.

"It's like jabbing an orange," Jerri offered, from the hall.

"OK." Steve blew out a breath, focused. "Here we go." He stuck Naga in her hip. She lifted her head, bared her teeth. She *roared*.

Steve jumped back. The needle dangled from Naga's hip. He held up a finger as if disciplining an unruly child. "Bad kitty! You be good!"

Slowly, her snarl faded. Steve took a step forward, then another. "This is going to make you feel better." He laid his hand on the syringe.

Naga jerked up at his touch. With a wild yowl that made Steve's bowels feel loose, she swatted his chest with her right forepaw. Her claws dug deep trenches into the meat of him. Steve jumped back, yelling. Naga sprang from the table, landed with her paws on his shoulders, bit him in the left arm. Somebody in the hall screamed.

Steve, weirdly unafraid, worked his hands up to chest level and pushed as hard as he could, ripping Naga from his chest along with a good bit of skin from his back and shoulder. Naga bounced off the wall.

Following an instinct he didn't quite understand, Steve slapped the lion in the face. She didn't bite or claw him, possibly too surprised to do so, but she roared again.

Steve roared back. "*Go on!* You want to end up dead? You're still bleeding, *asshole!* Bite me all you want and you can bleed out in the parking lot! See if anyone lugs your huge ass to the zoo! Go on, see!" Drops of his blood fell to the floor and mingled with hers. They glared at each other. "Go on!"

After a while, Naga sank back against the wall. A second or two later she stopped snarling.

"Yeah," Steve said. "I thought so." He snatched the syringe up off the floor.

From behind him, the vet's voice. "I don't think you should—"

"Yeah, yeah, yeah." He walked up to Naga. She snarled again, long white teeth against pink healthy gums. *I bet her capillary response is pretty good now.* Ignoring the snarl, he pulled her unwounded right hip away from the wall and jabbed the needle in it. She roared again, a deep bass sound that rattled the windows.

"Shut. The fuck. Up!"

"Slowly," Dr. Alsace said. Her voice was muffled. Steve glanced back. The door was mostly shut. She peeped in, only the top of her head showing.

He pushed the plunger in, one excruciating millimeter at a time. In a few seconds it was empty. Steve pulled the syringe out, tossed it aside.

Naga looked at him, confused.

"There," Steve said, sarcastic. "Feel better now?"

Naga looked at him for a moment, then slumped. A moment later she laid her head down on the floor. Steve slumped too, back against the wall. His shoulder blades felt wet. He stood up straight again, turned and looked. Where he had leaned, there was a big bloodstain on the wall. He turned to the vet. "You guys got a Band-Aid?"

"Jerri, get me some gauze and some tape."

Naga lay on the floor, semiconscious.

"I think you can get started now," Steve said.

"Not yet. Give it about ten minutes."

"Oh. OK. Am I bleeding bad?" He walked over to her and presented his back.

She examined it. "It's not good. But I think it's superficial. Probably leave some scars, though. You're going to need stitches."

"Shouldn't be a problem. I imagine someone will be along shortly to arrest me."

"I don't doubt it. That was about the dumbest thing I've ever seen." She paused. "Not un-brave, but very, very dumb. Is that your lion?"

"Not really. Kind of. We just met a couple of hours ago."

She raised her eyebrows.

Steve shrugged. "It's been an intense couple of hours."

The vet looked at Naga. "She's bleeding pretty bad. She probably wouldn't have made it much longer."

Steve looked at her.

"I've seen worse, though. That bandage will hold it until she's anesthetized. I'm pretty sure I can stitch her up in time." She looked at him levelly. "If you were trying to save her life, you probably did."

Steve turned this notion over in his mind, examining it. He smiled. "Yeah?"

"Yeah. It really *was* dumb, though."

Steve sighed, wishing for a cigarette. "The Buddha teaches respect for all life."

"Oh." She considered this. "Are you a Buddhist?"

"No. I'm an asshole. But I keep trying."

II

Ten minutes later Naga was back on the table. They put the stretcher on the floor. Steve had muscled her onto it while she was still semiconscious. As he did this, Naga stretched her tongue out and licked blood off the back of his hand.

"It's OK," Steve said, stroking her cheek. "No big."

When Naga's eyes were shut he, Jerri, and Dr. Alsace lifted her up onto the examination table. While they were waiting for the anesthetic to fully kick in, Steve borrowed some bandages and started taping himself up.

Halfway through what was shaping up to be a really bad job, Dr. Alsace said, "Point that gun at me."

"Beg pardon?"

"Point that gun at me."

"Er . . . OK." Steve pulled the HK out of his waistband and lifted it in her general direction.

"What's that you say?" Dr. Alsace said. "If I don't bandage you up, you're going to shoot me? Well, I guess I have no choice, then."

Steve blinked, smiled at her. "Thanks."

"Jerri, turn your back. I'm about to set a bad example." Jerri obliged. Dr. Alsace cleaned out the scratches on Steve's back with a bottle of saline, then injected him with something. A minute or so later his back was numb. "Get me a rapID, would you?"

Jerri, gloved, went outside for a second and returned with a clear plastic tool about the size of a paperback book with two pinchable handles.

"What's that?"

"Staple gun."

"What?"

Ka-blap!

"Ow! Fuck!"

"Sorry. Hold still." *Ka-blap!*

"Ow! I'm not a two-by-four!"

"Don't be such a baby. I don't have time to suture."

Steve managed to keep quiet for the next couple, but his face contorted with pain. He grunted on the sixth, seventh, and eighth *ka-blaps*.

"There we go," Dr. Alsace said. "All done. Hold the gun on Jerri and tell her to bandage you up."

Steve pointed the gun at her.

"Eeek! Don't shoot. Hang on, I need to get more tape."

She returned a second later, eyes wide. "Um . . . mister?"

"My name is Steve."

"Steve? There's a guy out there. He says he wants to talk to you."

Steve's stomach knotted. "Cop?"

"I'm not sure. He has a gun."

Steve thought about this for a second. He pursed his lips, nodded. "Tell him it's OK. Tell him to come in. I won't shoot anything."

A second later Erwin walked in. "Glad to hear it," he said. He glanced at Naga. "Hmm. Nice lion."

"Thanks."

"When I heard the call come in, I had a feeling this might be you. You're really extra-fucking-special under arrest. You know that, right?" Erwin pulled a set of those plastic cuffs that looked like cable ties out of his back pocket.

Steve didn't move. He was thinking about the front door, the tree line behind the strip mall, the taxi.

"No," Erwin said, seeing him tense. "You shouldn't do that."

"No?"

"No." He pointed back in the general direction of the waiting room. "There's a guy on the roof back behind that dry cleanin' place. I used to work with him. He's a good shot. You try anything, he's going to put a bullet through your center of mass. It'll leave a hole in your back about a foot across. Half your guts'll blow out with it. You'll be dead before you even know what hit you."

Steve walked out into the lobby and peeped out the window. "Oh . . ." he said. "Oh, wow." There was indeed a guy on the roof of the cleaners with a rifle. There were also around ten squad cars in the parking lot, blue lights flashing. A hundred yards away people streamed out of Walmart, heads down, running. He scanned the roof line and saw another sniper on top of the Monsieur Taco. "Fuck," he said. "After all that."

"Yeah," Erwin said, "it's a bitch." He jiggled the plastic cuffs in the air. "You gonna let me do this, or do we gotta shoot ya?"

Steve looked at the front door, tested his weight on his bandaged ankle. *Maybe I could duck out the back and . . .*

"If you decide to run, can you give me a second first? I want to get them nice ladies out of the line of fire before the deppities start shooting. They're all excited, like. I don't think they'll be real careful when they see you come running out with a gun. Be a shame if the rest of us got killed along with you."

Steve put his palms up to his temples. He walked around the waiting room saying, "Shit, shit, shit!" He kicked a big bag of dog food. Then, with a sigh, "OK. You're right. No way out. I've still got a problem, though."

"Yeah? What's that?"

"I knew how this was probably going to end up, but I came here anyway. Now it occurs to me that if I just drop the gun—"

"Don't drop it," Erwin said. "Might go off. Set it down gentle—"

"—yeah, sure. If I just drop it—"

"People on TV are always dropping guns. I saw a guy get shot that way once."

"*OK*. Understood. I'll just set it down. If."

"If what?"

"If you"—he looked significantly at Erwin—"promise me you won't let them just come in here and kill her. Promise me you'll figure out, I dunno, something. A zoo. A circus." He searched Erwin's face. "Please. If you do that, I'll help you as much as I can."

"Help me? How?"

"I don't know a whole lot, but I do know where they are—Carolyn and the rest."

Erwin considered this. "Full cooperation? No holding back?"

Steve nodded.

"Can you sketch the interior of the place?"

"Sure."

Erwin considered for a second. "I can't take that lion back to my apartment, you understand."

"I understand that. I'm just asking you to tell me that you'll do your best."

"Yeah," Erwin said. "OK. You got my word."

Steve nodded. He held out his wrists to Erwin.

"Put down the gun first."

Steve set it on the reception desk, gently.

"Hands behind your back."

He did that too. Blue lights flashed through the windows. He tilted his head back, shut his eyes. The sound the cuffs made as they closed was just like zipping up a plastic cable tie.

"Smart," Erwin said. "They really would have killed you."

"I know."

Erwin leaned back and looked into Room Two. "That there's a big-ass lion."

Steve smiled a little. "You think *she's* big, you should have seen her dad. Full-grown male. Maybe four hundred pounds?"

"Oh?" Erwin looked mildly alarmed. "He around?"

Steve shook his head. "Nope. Didn't make it out." He raised his voice. "Hey, how's she doing, Doctor?"

They had started an IV and were giving Naga some sort of clear fluid. The bandage was off and Dr. Alsace was hunched over Naga's leg. She didn't answer. Jerri said, "Shh!" She walked over to the door and closed it, but slowly, giving the thumbs-up sign with her free hand.

Steve gave her a little nod. She nodded back, then shut the door.

"She yours?" Erwin said. "File didn't say nothing about you having a pet lion."

"Not really. We just met. We've kind of been looking after each other."

"Just ran into her on the street?"

"Actually, yeah."

Erwin looked at him, waiting for a proper answer. After a minute or so he gave up. "Any chance I can get you to give a little more detail on that?"

"Sure, sorry. Other things on my mind. I was out for a jog and a whole bunch of mean dogs—like, dozens of them—tried to eat me. I shot some, but they had me down on the ground. I was a goner. Naga and her dad kind of came in out of nowhere and pulled the dogs off me. Saved my life."

"Yeah? No shit?"

"No shit."

Erwin considered. "That's unusual."

"I thought so too." Steve shrugged. "Don't argue with Santa Claus, I guess."

"You think them lions have mebbey got something to do with this Carolyn chick of yours?"

Steve rolled his eyes. "Hmm. I don't know. Let me think about that for a second."

"Sorry. Dumb question. Do they . . . Hang on." Erwin put his hand to his ear. "I'd love to keep chattin' with ya, but them cops are getting antsy outside." He lifted his wrist and spoke into his sleeve. "Yeah, ah, suspect in custody and shit."

Two seconds later, the front door burst open. Half a dozen sheriff's deputies flowed in, guns drawn.

"Easy, fellas," Erwin said. "Everything's fine. Federal custody, remember?"

"I remember," said a guy with a lot of stripes on his sleeve. He spoke through gritted teeth. "What about the lion?"

"It's asleep," Erwin said. "Havin' an operation. That's why he came here."

"Don't hurt her, OK?" Steve said.

"What?" The cop looked at him like he was a bug on the road.

Steve felt his inner peace slip a notch. "Pretty please?"

"Animal Control is on the way. Can't keep a lion as a pet in this town, son," the cop said. "City ordinance." A couple of the other cops snickered.

Steve felt his rage boiling. "Erwin?"

"Yeah?"

"Remember what we said."

"I remember."

"Good. If you want, I can take you to where they—" The phone clipped to his waistband started ringing.

"Who's that?"

Steve thought frantically. "It's her, probably. Carolyn. She gave me the phone. She's called a couple of times already. Want me to talk to her?"

Erwin considered this. "Nah. We'll be seeing her in a minute anyway."

"You *already* know where she is?"

"Oh yeah. Nice little neighborhood about two miles from here. We've had the place surrounded since around lunchtime. We're waiting until we get all the neighbors evacuated, then we're going in."

"You don't sound too enthusiastic."

Erwin gave him a long look. "Fact is, I'm not."

"What's the matter?"

"I'm just not sure what—" Erwin cut himself off. "That's not true. I am sure. Something bad is going on, I just don't know what. I feel the way a rat must feel sniffing the peanut butter on a trap." He looked at Steve. "Is your buddy in that house?"

Steve looked at him blankly.

"The guy with the knife thing. The one who broke you out of jail. Is he there?"

"Oh. His name is David. Yeah, he's there. Last time I saw him, anyway."

Erwin frowned. "I was afraid of that."

"He's not my buddy, though," Steve said. "You're wrong about that. I've got no idea who those people are or what they want from me. And that guy's crazy. He scares the crap out of me. He scares the rest of them too, I think."

"The rest of who?"

Steve opened his mouth to speak, shut it. "What about Naga?"

"The lion? I'll try the zoo." Erwin sounded a million miles away.

Steve gave him a skeptical look.

Erwin glanced up. "You got my word. I'll figure something out."

Steve continued to look skeptical.

With a sigh, Erwin turned to the guy with all the stripes on his sleeve. "Frank? Listen up. That lion is evidence in a federal investigation. Take good care of it."

"Her," Steve said.

"The hell you say," Frank said.

"No," Erwin said. He turned to face the man. He spoke quietly. He was polite. But in that moment Steve understood for the first time how extraordinarily dangerous Erwin truly was. "I *do* say. You call the fucking zoo, you call Animal Control, you call whoever you need to call, but if anything happens to that animal . . . you and me, we're going to have a problem."

The cop was an inch or two taller than Erwin. When the two of them locked eyes, he was looking down. He held Erwin's gaze . . . but only for a moment. Then he withered visibly. His chest un-puffed. He averted his eyes. His men watched this. "All right," he said. "Yeah. OK."

Erwin turned back to Steve. "That good enough?"

"Good enough," Steve said. His mouth had gone dry. He swallowed hard. "Thank you. OK, I don't know a whole lot. The first time I ever saw him was the same time you did, at the jail. I saw what he did in the hall"—*ropey guts dangling from the fluorescents*—"and started squirming. He got pissed off and knocked me out, I think. I woke up in the house a couple miles from here, like you said. There were a bunch of them there. Carolyn said they were her brothers and sisters, but they didn't look like family to me. There were two black guys that looked like twins, and a creepy lady who smelled like dead ass—I think she was, like, Polynesian or something, except she was so pale her skin was almost blue. But I dunno, maybe they're adopted. They all spoke the same language, anyway."

"What language? Could you tell?"

Steve shook his head. "I never heard anything like it before. Maybe a little bit like Vietnamese? Except not."

"Are they like him? Carolyn and the rest? Dangerous? I'll tell you for free if my guys go in there and get hurt because you lied to us, I'll go hard on you."

Steve considered the question, and not just because Erwin had threatened him. "I don't know," he said finally. "I don't think so. They all seem really afraid of him."

"Good," Erwin said. "I'll—"

"But I think they might be dangerous in other ways," Steve said. "Everything I told you about Carolyn was true. Everything. She's not like that David guy, but I think she's got . . . something."

"Got something?"

"I don't know. She just doesn't seem, I dunno, helpless. Some of the others, sure. A couple of them I'm pretty sure *I* could take. But not that David guy, and not her. There's something about her . . ." Steve shook his head. "I don't know. I'd be careful, is all."

Erwin was studying him. "How many of them were there? The family?"

"I'm not sure. I didn't count. About a dozen, I think, give or take. Plus the old lady who owns the house. She's normal, not one of them."

Erwin clicked his tongue, deep in thought.

"Don't you believe me?"

"Yeah," Erwin said. "I think I do. A couple hours ago we had an RC-135 do a flyover. Infrared showed thirteen people inside. You didn't know that. If you were going to lie about something, that would have been a good place to start."

Infrared? But that raised another question. "Hey," Steve said, "how'd you find me, anyway?"

"You brought a lion into the vet, son. Even without the gun, a thing like that is bound to cause talk."

"So . . . you were just here on vacation or something?"

"Oh, I gotcha. No. I'm in town as sort of an expert advisor with the strike team. I'm the only one we know of who's seen him and lived. Besides you, a'course."

"'Strike team'?"

"Oh, yeah. Lotsa heavy hitters in town today. Delta, couple snipers from SEAL Six, even some Marine recon. Your Miss Sopaski, she's about to have company."

"How'd you find her?"

Erwin frowned. "Crazy bitch called up the White House. Can you believe that?"

III

E rwin walked Steve out of the vet's office and left him, handcuffed, in the backseat of a squad car for half an hour or so. At Steve's request Erwin cut off the plastic cuffs behind his back and re-cuffed him in front. That was a lot more comfortable.

Steve found that half hour or so weirdly relaxing. It was a nice autumn day. The car window was cracked enough to let in the breeze. He wasn't in immediate mortal danger. There weren't any big decisions to make. *Also, I don't have to worry about getting caught anymore. There's that, too.* He didn't quite sleep, but he might have dozed a little. Erwin did paperwork and argued with the cops. After a little while a truck stenciled with the words EASTERN EXOTIC CAT SHELTER pulled up. Steve smiled at that.

He was hoping to see Naga again, but before they brought her out Erwin opened the door of the squad car. "Wakey-wakey." He jerked a thumb over his shoulder. "Out."

Steve blinked. Maybe he *had* slept, a little. "Where to?"

"My car."

"This isn't your car?"

"Do I look like a cop?"

"Actually . . ."

Erwin gave him a look.

"No," Steve said. "Of course not."

Erwin nodded. He took Steve by the shoulder and walked him over to a nondescript Ford sedan parked thirty yards away.

"This is a State Department car. I signed for it." Erwin peered at him. "You gonna give me any shit?"

"I'm not planning on it."

"OK. You can ride in front if you want. I gotta leave the cuffs on, though."

"Sure, I understand. Hey, am I still bleeding?"

"A little. Not much. Actually . . ." Erwin rooted around in the backseat, grabbed a newspaper. He unfolded the paper and laid the sports section across the passenger side of the front seat. "OK. Sit on that."

Steve looked stung.

"Son, your shirt's a mess. And you need a fuckin' shower. Any stains get on that upholstery, I gotta clean 'em. No offense."

"Nah," Steve said. "It's OK." By now it was getting to be late afternoon, 4:13 p.m. according to the dash clock in Erwin's car. They turned out of the parking lot and headed back down Highway 78. Steve gave Monsieur Taco a longing look as they drove away. He was getting hungry. "Where we going?"

"DC."

"Seriously?"

"Yup. Lotta people want to talk with you."

"About what?"

Erwin looked at him like he was an idiot. *Which*, Steve thought, *I suppose I am.* "Sorry. I guess what I meant was, 'What do they expect me to be able to tell them?' I'm as confused as anybody. More so, probably."

"Hmmm."

"Hmmm what?"

"Just hmm. I sort of believe you, I guess."

"Yeah?" Steve felt absurdly grateful to hear this. "I appreciate that. I really do."

Unexpectedly, Erwin turned off the main road and rolled to a stop in the parking lot of a lumber yard on top of a hill. There were a couple of cars in the parking lot, but mostly the place was empty. "What are you doing?"

"Well, like I said, I'm taking you to DC. This is just a little detour."

"Detour?"

"Yeah. The Delta guys didn't want me riding along with them, even as an observer. I'm here to ID that David fella."

"They had cameras at the jail. When he broke me out, I mean. I saw them."

"Yeah. Funny thing about that. They didn't work. They were fine when I was talking with you. But when the big asshole showed up, them cameras just kinda magically broke." He gave Steve a look.

"That's kind of weird, isn't it?"

"I'd say so, yeah."

"OK, so that's why you're in town. But why are we in the parking lot?"

"Well," Erwin said. "Nobody said I couldn't watch." He pointed. They were on the edge of a steep bluff, maybe a hundred feet high and almost vertical. Below them and about a half a mile away two military vehicles were pulling up outside of a small subdivision.

"Are those *tanks*?"

"Nah. A tank's got a bigger gun. That there's a Bradley Fighting Vehicle. It's for carrying soldiers, mostly."

"What are they doing?"

"It's called 'going in hard,'" Erwin said. He pulled a big green knapsack out of the backseat and rummaged around in it, coming up with a pair of field binoculars. "I got a night scope too. You can borrow it if you want to watch. Don't need the starlight, but it'll magnify about six-X."

"Sure."

Erwin handed him a biggish rifle scope with ATN stamped on the side. Steve held it up. It magnified pretty well—too well, actually. It took him a couple of minutes of scanning to identify the house.

"What are those guys—"

"Shhh!"

Steve shushed. He heard a thumping noise, and looked up from the scope. Two black helicopters were flying in from the west, low and fast. He could see them clearly, but their rotors were muffled somehow. They weren't quite silent, but they didn't have the thunder you'd expect, either. A moment later the Bradleys started up with a puff of blue smoke.

The helicopters hovered just over Mrs. McGillicutty's house. Black ropes dropped out of each one. Men slid down the ropes, a dozen in all. Their synchronization wasn't quite perfect, but it was close—they touched ground within a second of one another. As Steve watched they lined up on either side of the French doors that opened onto Mrs. McGillicutty's back patio, black boots pounding silently over red brick in 6x magnification. The helicopters dropped back.

The men made hand gestures at one another. Two of them beat the doors in with a metal ram. A third man tossed something in. There was a flash and a bang. The men streamed into the house. Watching them, Steve thought of the dogs flowing out of the woods.

Muzzle flashes began, first one, then a long pause, then two more, then a fusillade. The explosive brightness was startling in the long, dreamy shadows of this suburban afternoon. The sound of the shots arrived a moment later, carried on still autumn air. One of Mrs. McGillicutty's windows shattered.

Faintly, from a great distance, Steve heard the sound of a woman screaming. An automatic weapon delivered a short burst of fire . . . then a much longer one. There was another scream, a man's voice. Steve heard something that sounded a little bit like Dresden's roar. It made the hair on the back of his neck stand up.

"What the hell was that?" Erwin asked.

Steve shook his head. *David, maybe?*

There was more gunfire, more flashes. Another woman screamed. More broken windows. Glass rained down on Mrs. McGillicutty's neatly trimmed lawn, flashing in the sun. Holes appeared in the wall, sending splinters of aluminum siding flying. *They're all shooting now.* Steve heard screams, men's and women's voices mingled, rising. *It must be hell in there.*

"Hmm," Erwin said.

One of the black-clad commandos dove out a small window in the back of the house. His face was covered with blood. His helmet was gone. He didn't have his gun anymore. Probably he hoped to tuck and roll before he hit the ground, but he only made it about halfway out the window before something caught him. His torso crashed against the side of the house. Screaming, arms flailing, he was yanked back inside. Steve saw a flash of gold metal, a spray of arterial scarlet. All this happened in less than a second.

Now the screams overlapped, building, rising to a crescendo.

Steve nodded at Erwin's walkie-talkie sitting in the console. "Can you hear what they're saying?"

"Nope," Erwin said. "They use encryption. I couldn't get it even if I knew what frequency they were on." He paused. "It don't look real good, though."

One of Carolyn's people, a woman in gray-green robes, fell through the French doors onto the back patio. She lay where she landed, not moving. Her chest was covered in blood.

"Hey," Steve said. "I recognize that one. I think her name is Jennifer?"

The helicopters, still trailing their long ropes, moved a bit closer. A moment later they backed off again. The two Bradleys in front of the neighborhood started rolling. Once in front of the house, they each disgorged a small horde of men in green carrying automatic weapons.

The Army guys moved toward the front door. Only a couple made it. Automatic weapons fire from the house cut the rest down in the front yard—head shots mostly, mercifully blurry at that distance. The soldiers fell in the grass, boneless. All but one lay still, but that one, a black guy, writhed and screamed. His legs didn't seem to be working.

"Holy fucking shit," Steve said. He looked over. Erwin's face was twisted with fury. His gray hair stood out wildly against his flushed red face.

"I told them," Erwin said. "I told them this was different. I fucking *told them*."

Three of the men from the Bradleys made it as far as the house. As the men from the helicopter had done, they stood on either side of the door and made hand gestures at one another. Steve thought, *They're going to do it. They're really going to go in there. On* purpose. "Daaaaaaaaaaaamn."

But they didn't. Something punched through the wall. Again Steve caught a flash of bright-yellow—brass and blood in the afternoon sunlight as a soldier's throat exploded. A moment later the other two dropped as well, one after the other in rapid succession. *He's stabbing them through the wall.* It reminded him of a sewing machine needle.

Steve heard a whirring sound. The barrel of a Bradley's main gun began to turn on the house. *They're going to blow up the house*, he thought. *They're going to blow it up, even with their own people inside.*

But they didn't. The rear doors of both Bradleys were still open, so when David streaked out the front door there was nothing to stop him.

My God, Steve thought. *He's so fast.* David disappeared inside the vehicle. A second later the hatch on the gun turret flipped up and a single hand, bloody, rose up. Fingers clawed at the air, helpless, then the hand slipped back inside.

The driver of the second Bradley began closing his back door. It was the right idea, but he wasn't quite quick enough. David dove over the back gate, smooth and graceful.

A minute or so later the back hatch opened again. Now the Bradley was red inside. David stood alone in the back, carrying his spear and—*is that somebody's head?*—something tucked under his arm. For just a moment he seemed to lock eyes with Steve, half a mile away. The hair on the back of Steve's neck went all prickly. David grinned, then turned and darted back inside the house.

The helicopters moved in close again. Their guns started up and began to whir, chewing away the roof of the house, the siding, the windows, the chimney.

Then Steve saw a man silhouetted against the blasted window of the house. He was holding a rifle. Steve hoped for a moment that it was one of the Army guys, but the fluff at his waist could only have been a tutu. David fired, just once, and sparks flew from the helicopter's tail rotor. It jerked, then spun around, level but moving backward. Its tail section crashed into the spinning rotors of the other chopper in a shower of sparks.

Both helicopters dropped the hundred feet or so to the ground. One of them landed on a neighboring house, the other landed half in and half out of the swimming pool behind it. The house exploded with an enormous gout of yellow flame and black smoke.

Then the day was silent again.

"Holy fucking shit," Steve said. He turned to Erwin, hoping he might confirm this diagnosis, perhaps weigh in with insights of his own. But Erwin was otherwise occupied. His eyes were fixed on Carolyn. She was standing a couple of feet outside the driver's-side window, pointing a pistol at Erwin's head.

"Hi," she said.

IV

"Hi yourself," Steve managed. From this angle he saw yellow hair next to her at about waist height. His first thought was that she was standing next to a blond three-year-old. But when he stretched his neck up to see better, he met yellow eyes. "Hey! Is that Naga?"

He knew as soon as it was out of his mouth that it was a dumb thing to ask—how many lions *are* there in a typical suburb? It was her. She stood on her own power, strong and alert.

"Yeah, I tracked the two of you to the vet," Carolyn said. "I figured you might want me to patch her up for you."

Steve, still cuffed, scrambled out of the car and went around to the driver's side. He was heading for Naga, but Carolyn put a hand on his shoulder and nodded at his cuffs. It took Steve a moment to recognize the thing in her hand as a stone knife. "I don't think that'll be sharp enough to—"

She cut through the tough plastic in a single swipe.

"Thanks."

Steve knelt down beside Naga, hugged her neck. Her wound was mostly healed—her fur hadn't grown back, but where only an hour ago there had been a bloody, gaping hole he now saw pink skin. She licked his cheek.

"I'm guessing you're Carolyn," Erwin said.

"Good guess," she said. "How you doing, Erwin?"

"You know me."

She didn't answer. Steve noticed that her index finger was trembling, just a little.

"You gonna shoot me with that thing?" Erwin asked.

"Don't hurt him, Carolyn," Steve said, still kneeling. "This guy's OK." Then, to Naga, who was still licking him, "C'mon, OK, that's enough."

"I wouldn't dream of it," she said. She opened the back door of the Ford and flopped down onto the backseat.

Erwin, sitting in the front seat, gave Steve a little nod.

Steve waved it away. He stood by the open back door, looking down at Carolyn. She sat leaning against the rear headrest, eyes closed. The gun lay on the seat beside her. Steve looked at the smoking ruin of Mrs. McGillicutty's house. "Were you caught up in that mess?"

Carolyn shook her head. "No. I got out about an hour before the shooting started. I was looking for you at the house." She opened her eyes and gave him a stern look. "You were supposed to wait for me there. It's not safe out here."

"Out *here*?" Steve said, incredulous. "Out here's friggin' Disneyland compared to that place. Anyway, I thought the whole point was that you couldn't go into—"

Erwin was studying her in the rearview mirror. "You knew this was going to happen, didn't you?"

She nodded again. "This or something like it. The president is a prideful man. When I rattled his cage yesterday he needed to do something to show what a scary fellow he is."

They both looked at her. "Yeah," Erwin said, all trace of the amiable hick gone from his voice, "I'd say you pretty much nailed that one. I'm curious, though—how did you get the codes to get through the switchboard?"

She fluttered a hand in the air. "I'm tricky."

"She is," Steve agreed.

"Yeah," Erwin said. "I'm starting to get that."

"What happened to the rest of them?" Steve asked. "Your, um, 'brothers and sisters'?"

Carolyn opened her eyes. "I was going to ask you," she said. "Did anyone get out? Maybe someone with an animal?"

"No one that I saw," Erwin said. "I don't think so."

Carolyn's expression was impossible to read. "Then they're almost certainly dead. That was the most likely outcome."

"There's someone on the back porch," Steve said quietly. "A woman. Blond hair, kinda short and spiky? You can borrow my scope if you—"

Carolyn shook her head and closed her eyes again. "I'd rather not, if it's all the same to you. It's Jennifer." Then, speaking to herself, "At least she went out stoned. She would have wanted it that way."

"I'm sorry to hear that, ma'am," Erwin said.

"Thanks, Erwin. That's good of you to say. Now it's just David and Margaret and me."

"Margaret?" Erwin asked.

"The one who smells bad," Steve said.

"Ah," Erwin said. "How do you know she's not dead too?"

Carolyn smiled, still holding her eyes closed. "David would never let anyone else hurt Margaret."

Steve looked through the scope. The house was quiet now. Thin trickles of smoke leaked from the windows. As he watched, Mrs. McGillicutty staggered outside. She was bloody and dazed, but very much alive. "Hey, there's the old lady! What's that she's holding!"

Carolyn took the scope and looked for herself, then handed it back. "Muffins. She's got muffins." She shook her head, smiled a little. "David must have saved her as well. Just when you think you know a person . . ."

"What do we do now?" Steve asked.

"Now we wait, for a little while."

"For what?" Steve asked.

"For David to come back."

"Back?" Erwin asked. "Where'd he go?"

"He's off to Washington."

"What for?"

"He's going to kill the president, and everyone involved in what just happened. He'll use the broadest possible definitions of 'everyone' and 'involved.' "

Steve boggled at her. "That's imposs—can he do that?"

"David? Yes. They might as well start digging the graves right now. The president's a dead man."

Steve stared at her, aghast.

"Oh, for gosh sakes. It was *his* idea to start killing people, remember? Before his Army guys showed up, everyone was just sitting around and eating brownies. Anyway, I doubt most people will even notice. They'll have bigger things to worry about."

Erwin's eyes narrowed. "What's that mean?"

"What time is it?"

"Uh," he glanced at the clock on the dashboard. "Around four fifteen?"

"Any second now." She gave a thin, feral smile.

Steve felt the hairs on the back of his neck prickle. "Carolyn, what did you do?"

She didn't answer with words, just pointed at the sky.

It was just after four in the afternoon. The sun was still well above the tree line. The sky was clear. There was no eclipse. All of these things were true, but after a few seconds Steve was forced to accept what his eyes were telling him.

The sun was going out.

V

For the next minute and a half or so the sun faded from the blazing yellow that was normal for this time of day to a mellower sunset orange, then red. Steve, watching this, thought, *It's like someone's turning the switch on one of those dimmer bulbs reeeeeally slow.*

At first Erwin hung his head out the driver's-side window to watch, but then—evidently forgetting that he was kinda-sorta in custody—he fumbled the Taurus's door open and stood in the parking lot next to Steve.

"Eclipse?" Steve said softly, knowing it wasn't.

Erwin shook his head. "Nah. Can't be. Maybe it's . . . is it shrinking, too?"

"I can't tell . . . well . . . yeah. Maybe." Steve held his thumbnail up for comparison. He could do this without even squinting. The sun had faded to a dirty and unenthusiastic brown. As it went finally to black he saw that it *did* visibly shrink, at least a little.

Then it was gone.

Steve felt the afternoon warmth fall away from his skin. The October breeze, its slight chill suddenly ominous, rustled dry leaves. *How cold can it get?* he wondered. *How cold does it get on Pluto? Oxygen is a liquid there, isn't it?* He shivered more than the breeze really warranted.

"Are you seeing this?" Erwin asked softly.

"I think so," Steve said. "Are you sure about the time?" Ignoring the evidence before his eyes, he was clinging to the notion that maybe this was just a normal sunset.

Erwin checked his watch. "Four eighteen, give or take."

"You're *sure?*" Steve said. His heart pounded in his chest. The stars were out. They burned down on him like the eyes of distant monsters, huge and merciless. A streetlamp flickered on, coating the parking lot in phlegmy yellow light. Naga looked up at the sky and rumbled, uneasy.

"Right on schedule," Carolyn said from behind him. She sounded pleased with herself.

Steve spun around. "*You* did this? That's impossible. It's got to be . . ." He fluttered his hands, helpless. "Why would you do this?"

"That's sort of a long story."

"This is real?" Erwin asked. His voice was flat, unemotional. His eyes flickered back and forth between her face and the gun in her hands. "It's not a trick?"

"I don't do tricks." She took a step back, out of range.

"Put it back!" Steve said. "Turn it on! We'll all—turn it back on!"

She shook her head. "I can't."

"Jesus *Christ*, Carolyn! You've got to! We'll . . . everybody . . . we'll freeze!"

"Not immediately," she said. "I talked it over with Peter once. The atmosphere acts like a blanket. The residual heat will fade, eventually, but we've got some time."

"What are we going to do?"

She considered. "Are you hungry? I'm starving. We've got some time to kill. I know a good Mexican place down the road. The guacamole is—"

"I'm not interested in any goddamn tacos, Carolyn!"

"Oh, c'mon. It's really good."

"Look, I'm sick of this crap. Right *now* I want you to—"

"Get me some guacamole and I'll tell you anything you want to know."

Steve, red-faced, drew in his breath to yell something else . . . then shut his mouth with an audible click of his teeth. "You will? Anything?"

She nodded. "Yup."

"OK," Steve said. "Yeah."

Carolyn turned back to Erwin. "We're going to take your car."

Erwin raised an eyebrow. He stood about six-two, Steve judged, and was in fantastic physical shape. He remembered the way the big cop had withered under his glare.

Carolyn, pistol in hand, raised her eyebrows. She smiled pleasantly.

"Keys are in it," Erwin said.

"Money," Steve said. "Did you bring the duffel bag?"

"What? Oh. No, sorry. I gave it to the cabdriver."

"To the *cabdriver*? All three hundred twenty-seven thousand?"

She shrugged. "I felt kind of sad for him. They ate some of his fingers."

"Wait, what? Who ate—" He broke off. "On second thought, never mind. I don't want to know." Steve rubbed his forehead, then looked at Erwin. "Have you got any money?"

Erwin raised both eyebrows this time. But then he shrugged and rummaged through his wallet. He handed over three twenties, a five, and a couple of ones. "That's all my cash. You want my AmEx, too?"

"No, thanks."

"Thank you, Erwin," Carolyn said. "You've been very helpful." Steve opened the Taurus's back door and patted the seat with his hand. Naga hesitated, then jumped in. Carolyn took the passenger seat. When Steve put the Ford in gear she said, "Wait."

Her HK was identical to the one she had given Steve. She thumbed the lever to drop the magazine out of it, then jacked the slide back, ejecting the round in the chamber. She clicked the loose round back into the magazine, then turned to Steve. "How do I make the window go down?"

Steve pointed at a button on the door. When the window was down she waved Erwin over. "Here," she said. She handed him the empty pistol, butt first. "For protection. There's a lot of crazy people out tonight. Be careful."

"Ain't much good without bullets," Erwin observed.

"I'll set the magazine on the sidewalk at the bottom of the hill."

Erwin nodded. "Thanks."

When they were a little ways out of the parking lot, Steve pulled into a turn lane and stopped. Carolyn laid the magazine next to a streetlight and waved at Erwin. Erwin waved back.

"What was that all about?"

"He seems nice." She gave him a vague smile.

Steve knew that she was lying again.

VI

To Steve's irritation, Carolyn was right. The guacamole really was excellent.

The restaurant she liked turned out to be Monsieur Taco, which was in the same strip mall as the vet. Carolyn had insisted that they go there, that particular restaurant and no other, even though the parking lot was still boiling with cops. She said it wouldn't be a problem. Steve had a bad moment when the big cop that Erwin had humiliated looked their way, but nothing came of it. Steve parked in back, and Carolyn rumbled something to Naga. She rumbled back and curled up in the backseat to go to sleep.

The place was weirdly upscale for strip-mall Mexican—among other things, there were valets and a doorman. Steve parked himself, though— Naga was sleeping in the backseat, and he didn't think that would go over very well. He was also worried that the fact his butt was visible through a hole in his crusty sweatpants might be a problem. But the closest anyone came to giving them trouble was the maître d'. His right arm was in a cast, and he apparently remembered Carolyn from an earlier visit. When she asked for a table for two, he screamed and bolted for the door.

Steve gave Carolyn a what-the-fuck look.

"Hmm? Oh. We came here a couple weeks ago. David doesn't understand about money. When he started to walk out without paying that guy grabbed him, and . . ." She trailed off.

"Wackiness ensued. Got it."

They ended up seating themselves at the bar.

Steve didn't think he could eat, but Carolyn insisted he try the lobster tacos. While they were waiting he drank a half pitcher of margaritas, which cooled him out some. By the time the food was actually in front of him he had rediscovered his appetite. Carolyn, however, only managed a couple of bites.

"I hate to admit it, but this actually is fantastic." Steve munched a chip and pushed the guacamole bowl an inch or two closer to her. She ate a chip or two, but only pushed her dinner around on the plate. "Something wrong? I thought you said you were starving."

"I am, but my stomach's a little upset." She shrugged. "Nerves, maybe. I've got a lot on my mind."

"Hmm. You said you'd answer questions?"

"Sure. Might as well. We've got time to kill, and it'll take my mind off . . . other stuff. Ask me whatever you want."

The restaurant was starting to fill up. An elderly woman in a mink stole eyed Carolyn's leg warmers and Steve's bloody concert shirt, then did something haughty with her face. Steve waved at her Queen Elizabeth–style, wrist only, and gave her a big toothy grin. She scurried away. "Hmm. Where to start?" He drummed his fingers on the table. "Can you really talk to Naga? Like, I mean, *really*?"

"I can, yeah. Animal languages are their own specialty, but I get by. My pronunciation isn't as good as Michael's."

"How did you guys learn that?"

"Father figured it out. He took notes."

"Notes on talking to lions?"

"That, yes. Other animals too. Everything that has a language, really."

"That must have taken him a while."

"A hundred years or so for the first couple of species, I think. Less once he got the hang of it." Then, seeing the look on Steve's face, "He's very old, you see. And he stayed busy. Languages are really the least of it." She sighed. "*Really.* The very least of it. Trust me on this."

"Like how old are we talking about?"

"No one's really sure. At least sixty thousand years. Probably a lot more. But the question isn't really meaningful. He spent a lot of his life in the Library. Time is different there."

"I see," Steve said, slowly. "And is that where you're from too? The Library?"

"What? Well . . . yes and no. I was born in . . . Cleveland, I think? Someplace that starts with a *c*, anyway." She gave a small, sad smile. "But . . . yeah. I guess I am from the Library."

"I don't get it."

"I'm not sure I do either, honestly. I mean, I know *what* he did to us, but I really don't have any idea *why*."

"Who?"

"Father."

"Your dad?"

She shook her head. "That's just what we call him. He wasn't my biological father. I'm not sure that would even be possible. No one really knows what he is."

"So . . . what? He's, like, an alien?"

She shrugged. "Maybe? But I don't think so. But I don't think he's human, either. Originally, I mean. The world's a lot different now than it was in the third age. There probably weren't any people when he was born."

" 'Third age'?"

"This age, the age of Father's rule, is the fourth. Before Father, creation was ruled by something else. It was darker then. By all accounts it was a worse time. That's the world Father was born into, the one he conquered."

"I don't—"

She fluttered her hand, as if waving away a distraction. "How Father started doesn't really matter."

"Then what does?" Steve asked, irritated. She made him feel like a child.

He was obscurely pleased when she took this question seriously, wrinkling her brow as she thought about how to answer. "He's smart," she said finally. "That's the key. I think it all flowed from that." She looked at him. "This is just speculation, you understand. I don't really know."

"Welcome to my world."

She frowned.

"Sorry. Go on, please. I'm interested."

She nodded, peered down into her club soda. "OK. This first part I'm fairly sure of. Imagine someone like Isaac Newton, a once-in-history genius. Maybe human, maybe not so much. All that matters about him is that he's really, really smart. That and the fact that he was born into a terrible time, probably worse than you can imagine. Something like hell, except real. It was ruled by a thing called the Emperor."

"With you so far."

"Good. Here's where I start guessing. In the Library there are twelve catalogs—but the *first* one, the white catalog, is medicine. I think that might be significant. Maybe Father started out as whatever passed for a doctor in those days. Father stumbled over something that was very useful for repair—a plant, a potion, whatever. Somehow he figured out how to stretch out his life, to buy himself time. And he used *that* time to learn *more*, live longer. Eventually he was satisfied that he could live as long as he wanted, heal whatever wounds came up. After that . . . he used that time to teach himself other things."

"Like what?"

"Well . . . the second catalog is war. I think that might not be a coincidence, either. Father is crafty. I imagine he was quiet at first, planning, arranging things, gathering his power. How do you guys say? 'Flying under the radar.' Then, eventually, when he was ready"—she tapped the bar with one lacquered fingernail—"he turned his attention to the author of his misery. He understood, I think. The only real escape from hell is to conquer it. He had allies—Nobununga was a key player, and someone named Mithraganhi. They're the only ones who knew for sure what happened, and they aren't talking."

"The three of them killed him? This Emperor guy?"

"Well . . . I doubt Father let him off that easy. But yeah, they usurped him."

"OK. Then what?"

"I don't know. The records are lost. But one way or another, the third age ended. There were other battles after that, betrayals, wars. Enemies rose and fell. The Duke, Q-33 North, others. Eventually Father grew powerful enough that no one could challenge him."

"So where do you come in? Collective 'you,' I mean. You and David and the rest."

She took a sip of her club soda. "Sixty thousand years later, give or take. Twenty-three years ago. It was late summer. I was maybe eight or nine when they . . . well. That was when he adopted us." She considered. "Or maybe 'adopted' isn't the right word. We were more like his apprentices."

"Then what . . ." Steve trailed off. The TV behind the bar was tuned to CNN. During dinner the coverage had centered on the sun's mysterious absence—what was up with that?—but now, evidently, there was Breaking News.

Wolf Blitzer, looking dazed, was talking over some grainy camcorder footage taken from the sidewalk in front of the White House. A section of the wrought-iron fence around the front lawn was broken away. There was a bare, bloody footprint on the sidewalk next to the body— unconscious or dead—of a teenage boy. The camera looked up. In the background, the East Wing of the White House was in an uncontrolled blaze. Talons of fire thirty feet long clawed at the night sky. Wolf Blitzer was saying things like "catastrophic loss of life," and "constitutional order of succession."

"Fuuuuck me," Steve said softly.

The images were grainy, and whoever was holding the camera wasn't doing a very good job of keeping it steady. Even so, Steve could make out a man in the middle distance, silhouetted against the fire. He carried a long stick that flashed yellow when the light caught it right. *And . . . oh. Oh, wow.*

The puffy bit at his midsection could only have been a tutu.

Steve ordered a tequila.

Carolyn followed his gaze. Seeing what was on TV, she nodded. "Are you about done? We'll need to head out soon."

"I guess," Steve said, distracted.

Carolyn got up and disappeared into the ladies' room. Now Wolf Blitzer was doing a live interview with a lawyer type who'd seen the attack on the White House. The lawyer, mildly hysterical, kept running his fingers through his thinning hair and repeating "He killed three guys, man! Three of 'em! Messed 'em alllll up!" Every so often Blitzer would nod, gravely but encouragingly. While they were talking, someone blew up the Capitol Building. Shrapnel from the blast—it might have been an office chair—ripped off the hysterical guy's left arm. The overpressure knocked Wolf Blitzer on his ass. A second later Erin Burnett cut to a recorded interview with a soccer mom in Maryland who had seen something "bigger than an elephant" walking down the side of the interstate.

The bartender refilled Steve's tequila without asking and poured one for himself.

"You ready?" Carolyn said.

"Yeah—I mean no. Or maybe. I guess. Do we have another minute? I just . . ." He nodded at the tequila.

"OK. But hurry."

"Yes, ma'am." He knocked off half the tequila at a gulp. "Did you have something to do with that?"

On TV, the woman who had seen the elephant thing held up her hand. Her eyes rolled back in her head. She was screaming. The skin of her arm was pitch-black, as if it had been dipped in ink, and something was wrong with her fingers—they quivered, not like fingers at all anymore. They looked to Steve like tentacles.

"Not really. Well . . . indirectly. It comes from Barry O'Shea, or maybe one of his people. They're very contagious."

"Who? Contagious? What?"

"She's got a—it's called a reality virus. It's not actually that dangerous, it just looks bad. The tentacles act like, umm, antennas, sort of. They make her receptive to the underthoughts. If she lets it go untreated she could get possessed."

"Possessed? You mean, like, by demons? *That* kind of possessed?"

"What? No." Carolyn laughed. For one horrifying moment Steve thought she might pinch his cheek. "There's no such thing, Steve."

"What, then?"

"Silent Ones. They're pure thought, but they manifest as big lumbering things, sort of silver. They're a relic of the third age. They can't be killed, but the sun's wide-spectrum radiation was deep enough to make them inert. With it gone, Barry's decided it's time to make his move. Does that make sense?"

Steve just looked at her. "No. No, it really doesn't."

"Well . . . don't worry about it. When things settle down I'll sort that part out. Barry is a lightweight." She nodded at the tentacle woman. "Anyway, there's an easy cure."

"An easy cure for having your fingers turn into monster hands?"

"Well . . . easyish. The best thing, obviously, is just don't touch him in the first place."

"Oh, obviously."

"Don't worry so much, Steve. People will adjust."

"Adjust to *what*, exactly? I still don't understand what all this is about."

"It's about the Library," Carolyn said. "Right now the only thing that matters is who takes control of Father's Library."

"Library? Who gives a damn about a library?"

Carolyn rolled her eyes. "Americans."

"What?"

"You've seen a little of what we can do—Lisa, me, David. What did you think?"

Steve swallowed. "Some of it was . . . yeah, it was pretty amazing."

Carolyn's face was bathed in the red light of the bar lamps, but her eyes were dark. "What you've seen is *nothing*, Steve. Parlor tricks. For all intents and purposes, the power of the Library is infinite. Tonight we're going to settle who inherits control of reality."

"What do you mean?"

"Just what I said."

"Carolyn . . . that's just crazy. I know you can do some weird stuff, but—"

She held up her hand. "We can argue later. But right now we need to go."

"Go where, exactly?"

"Garrison Oaks," she said.

"Why would we do that? I just got away from there. It was the exact opposite of fun. And why the hell did you send me in there in the first pl—"

"Later. Now I have to meet David. He'll be done with Erwin soon."

"Erwin? David's with Erwin?"

She nodded. "Erwin was trying for an ambush. If we don't hurry, David will kill him."

"When you say 'meet David,' what exactly do you mean? Are you . . . you're not, like, conspiring with that guy, are you?"

She didn't answer. Try as he would, she would say nothing else.

INTERLUDE IV

✳

SORE, AND IN NEED OF COMFORT

I

Carolyn died about five years after the bonfire of the bull. It happened at the very end of winter, during that six weeks or so when the breeze still blows cold but the forest nights are filled with the yowls of rutting cats. She was sixteen or seventeen then.

Mostly when people are resurrected they sleep for a while, but Carolyn came back to life like a match flaring at midnight. There were hands on her; she was being *touched*. She snapped out, caught hold of someone's hair, pulled herself in to bite.

"Fuck! Carol-aagh!" Jennifer's eyes, inches away, terrified.

"Oh . . ." Carolyn blinked at her for a moment, then let her go. "Sorry."

Jennifer skittered back a few feet, out of grabbing distance. "Dammit, Carolyn!" She put her hand to her heart. "You scared the *shit* out of me! Sheesh!"

"I'm sorry." She made an effort to sound calm, mild. It—whatever *it* was, she couldn't quite remember—wasn't Jennifer's fault.

Jennifer eyed her, suspicious. She didn't look stoned. "It's OK. You shouldn't try to move just yet."

Carolyn nodded. *If she's not high, I must have been pretty bad off.*

"OK, then." She showed Carolyn her empty hands, then patted the air as if soothing an invisible animal. "Friends, right?"

Carolyn nodded again.

Somewhat reassured, Jennifer moved back in and took her pulse. As she did, Carolyn looked around. Her small room, normally immaculate, was a wreck—half the shelves were overturned, with books and scrolls scattered across the floor. Her desk lay on its side. One drawer was jammed halfway open, crooked, pointing skyward. She wrinkled her nose. "What's that smell?"

"Er . . . well. Maybe you, a little bit."

"What do you mean?"

"It happened a couple of days ago. And, you know . . . it's been warming up." Jennifer averted her eyes. "I'm sorry, Carolyn. We all just figured you were studying."

"How long . . . ?"

"Three days, I think. How are your arms?"

"My arms? What do you m— Oh. Right." Her face clouded a little bit. It was coming back to her.

Looking down, she saw faint white scars on her forearms, where she'd been stabbed with the pens. She glanced at the desk. One of the pens—a gunmetal Mont Blanc, her favorite—was still embedded in the wood. In the center of her new scars were little black ink marks. She flexed her hands, her arms. It didn't hurt at all. "I'm fine, I think. Just a little sore."

"Sorry. I'm still not perfect at that part. How's your jaw?"

"My jaw?" Then, remembering, "Oh. Right." She opened her mouth, chewed the empty air for a second, wiggled her jawbone from side to side. "Good. It's fine, really. Thank you, Jennifer. You do good work."

"Yeah, well. I get lots of practice. I'm glad you're OK. You were pretty—" She cut herself off. "I'm glad you're OK." Her work done, Jennifer rooted around in her kit, came up with her silver pipe. "You mind?"

"Go ahead. So . . . I'm confused, Jennifer. What happened?"

Jennifer gave her a professional sort of look. "Do you still not remember it?"

Carolyn furrowed her brow, concentrating. "It's hazy."

"Give it a minute. I'll wait." She set the pipe aside for the moment.

Carolyn looked around the room—her chair was overturned behind the desk. Her bed was still neatly made, but a pot of ink had spilled on the quilt. *Ruined.* One of the books on the floor was open to a page painted with long, broad brush strokes.

That last sparked something. "Oh, wait . . . while I waited on Alicia, I was studying Quoth."

"Studying what?"

"Sorry—Quoth. It's the language of storms. They're great poets, some of them." The open page was a snippet of a decades-old squall from Jupiter, the gloomiest stanza of a larger work. *Now,* she read, *is hell's blackest pit.*

No, Carolyn thought, eyes widening ever so slightly. *That was only part of it. I was* pretending *to study Quoth.* She looked to the bookshelf in the corner, but from this angle it was hidden behind the desk. Faking a casualness she did not feel, she steadied herself against a shelf and stood—or tried to, anyway. She made it far enough to see that the little brown bookshelf in the corner behind her desk was upright and undisturbed. Seeing this, her relief was such that her legs gave way. She collapsed, graceless, back onto the floor. "Dammit!"

Jennifer blinked. Carolyn was usually very mild. "Take it easy. Your heart probably isn't quite up to speed yet. So . . . you remember now?"

"It's coming back to me." Even over the pain there had been his voice, his smile. *Try to scream. Scream for me. If you scream for me, I'll stop. If you scream for me, I'll let you go.*

"Was it David?"

Carolyn didn't trust herself to speak. She looked up at Jennifer, brow knotted, jaw muscles jumping.

"Sorry. Dumb question. What happened?"

"I remember most of it. But not the, you know, the, the end."

"That's normal," Jennifer said. "This was the first time you died, right? No one ever remembers the first time. Next time you'll retain a little more, and so on."

"Oh. I've heard that. Why is it? Do you know?"

"I do, but I shouldn't say. My catalog. Sorry."

Carolyn shook her head. "It's fine."

"Go on," Jennifer said, still gentle. "Tell me what happened."

Carolyn sat silent for a long time, looking into the middle distance.

When she spoke, her tone was perfectly calm, bored even. She might have been talking about lunch. "Does it matter?"

Jennifer raised her eyebrows a little. She put her pipe back in the bag. "Doesn't it?"

Something in her voice set off alarm bells. Carolyn came back to herself. "Sure! I mean, of course it does. I'm, um, very upset. Obviously."

"Do you want to talk about it?"

The actual answer to that was that she'd rather have gone another round with David. *Almost*. But she couldn't say that, couldn't even think it. If Jennifer thought she was . . . whatever . . . it might bring attention on her. She might even say something to Father. "I'd hate to take up too much of your time. I'm sure you've got things to—"

Jennifer reached out and touched her forearm. "I do, but they can wait. It's what friends are for. Anyway, it's sort of my job."

The door to her room was soundproof, but Jennifer had left it open. Up on the main hall, Peter was practicing his drums. The beats echoed strangely, rolling down the metal hall. Carolyn felt them as much as heard them, a low rumble in her temples, her heart. Trying to channel Asha, she gave her best plaintive look. "All right," she said in a small voice. "Just give me a second."

"Of course."

She concentrated and, after a moment, managed to produce a single tear. She let it roll down her left cheek for an inch or two, then brushed it away. *Perfect.*

Jennifer sat down beside her on the floor, an intimate distance. "You mind?"

She did. "No, of course not. So . . . the way it started was David came in with a scroll. He said he wanted my help with a translation." She looked at Jennifer. "But he was naked."

Jennifer gave a dark little nod. Walking around naked wasn't quite the breach of etiquette for the librarians that it would have been for Americans—among other things, the baths were unisex—but it was unusual. When Michael was just back from the ocean he sometimes forgot to dress. People laughed at him for it. *No one laughs at David, though*. And there was really only one reason he might go naked to Carolyn's room.

"What did you do?"

Carolyn looked at her. "I asked him to leave. He did, and that was the end of it."

She had intended this as a kind of joke, but when she said it aloud it sounded bitter, petulant. Jennifer said "sorry" again, but she was eyeing Carolyn with a dispassionate, clinical stare that Carolyn didn't like at all.

Focus. "I started to get nervous when I looked at the scroll. It wasn't anything exotic—just Pelapi, but a little old-timey. 'Verily' this and 'forsooth' that, you know?"

"He needed help with that?"

"No. Of course not. It was an excuse."

"Why'd you let him in?" The dormitory doors had a peephole, and they locked on both sides.

" 'Let' might be a little strong. I was expecting Alicia, so I had left the door cracked. We were supposed to practice Swahili. It's everywhere in the twenty-eighth cen— Hey! That reminds me—you said I was, you know, gone for what? Three days?"

"About that, yeah."

"Alicia didn't show?"

"Nope. She's got called off to the impossible centuries. She's picking up pneumovore teeth or something. Michael was the one who found you."

"Michael's back?"

Jennifer shook her head. "Later. Right now we're talking about you. What happened next?"

Carolyn fought down a nearly insurmountable urge to glance at the small bookshelf in the corner. David had either found what was hidden there, or he had not. She thought not—if he had, she would have woken up in the bull, or more likely not at all. But it was important to focus. This conversation could still be the end of her. *Try to sound hesitant, like you're feeling your way through a dark room. Like you're avoiding something.*

Thinking that, she flashed on the sound her jaw made, cracking under David's grip. *Try to scream. Scream for me.* But the pulse in her neck barely quickened and when she spoke her tone was just right. She had been practicing. The tremor in her index finger was clearly visible, though. *I need to work on that.* "Well . . . I translated the piece for David. It was about the sacking of Megiddo, a couple thousand years ago. The armies of Abla Khan—"

"Who?"

"Abla Khan. It's just another name for Father. Ablakha, Abla Khan, Adam Black?"

"Oh. Sure. Sorry."

"So, they conquered Megiddo. But—and this was the part David wanted me to read—the victory came at a high price. So . . ." Carolyn, not completely faking, squeezed her eyes shut at the memory. "And so . . . seeing that his warriors were downtrodden, sore, and in need of comfort, Abla Khan did say unto them, 'Go into the cities, and take what spoils you may find there. This place is yours now, and all that dwell within it. Use them, man and woman alike, and do with them what you will.'" She opened her eyes. "When I got to that part, David started grinning."

Jennifer winced. "Oh, Carolyn . . ."

"So, then David said what a coincidence it was. Here *he* was, a warrior of Abla Khan. As it happened, he was also downtrodden—another coincidence—and . . ."

"And . . . ?"

"And there I was," she said. "The spoils."

Jennifer gave a small, furious nod.

"And then . . . he sort of reached out and grabbed me." She nodded at her chest.

"Just like that?"

"Yup. Just like that. The weird thing was, he didn't seem cruel about it."

Jennifer, eyebrows raised, looked around the room.

"Well, not at first. He acted like he thought he was being seductive. Like maybe he was doing me a favor, even."

She considered. "I can see that. He does have an awfully high opinion of himself. What did you do?"

"Nothing. I just looked at him."

Jennifer raised her eyebrows again.

"I didn't want to get him, you know, all riled up."

Jennifer gave her a measuring look. "You know, Carolyn, you're pretty self-possessed, for a bookworm. Has anyone ever told you that?"

"No. You're the first." Out in the hall the drums were pounding, pounding.

"Is that when he, you know . . ."

"No. I mean, he tried. But I got in a lucky shot."

"'Lucky shot'?"

"He threw me down on the ground, and I sort of mule-kicked him."

"You kicked *David*."

"A little."

"He didn't, you know, block it or whatever?"

"I caught him off guard. I don't think he was expecting me to fight."

Jennifer boggled at her. "No. Probably not. But Carolyn . . . if you don't mind my asking . . . why?"

"Why what?"

"Wouldn't it have been . . . easier . . . to just sort of go along? I mean, your mandible wasn't just broken, it was *powdered*, about the worst I've ever seen. And he nailed you to—"

"I remember, Jennifer. I was there."

"Sorry. But you see my point?"

Jennifer was right. David was still Father's favorite. He had privileges. It would have been easier to fall back into herself, to go away until he was done. That was what she had done the first time David came naked to her chambers. She would undoubtedly do so again. It wasn't pleasant, but neither was it as bad as, say, her homecoming banquet.

This time, though, simply retreating into herself had not been an option. The angle at which she fell would have put David at eye level with her little corner bookcase. Raping her was one thing. But letting him get a look at her corner bookcase—that she absolutely could not allow.

Jennifer was looking at her much too intently. Carolyn's pulse thrummed in her temples. *If you scream for me, I'll stop.* Up in the hall, Peter's drums were approaching some sort of crescendo. *If you scream for me, I'll let you go.* Now, just as she had provoked David so that he might beat her into some other corner before raping her, she understood that she must not—*must not*—let Jennifer guess why. Thinking fast, Carolyn let a little of her true heart slip out, let it show on her face. "*Why?*"

The beat of the drums rolled down the hall like the pulse of an angry giant.

"*Why?*" she said again, a little louder this time. The best lies have an element of truth at their core. "*Why?* You and David have *met* at some point, have you not?"

"Well, sure, but—"

"Then don't ask me about *why*, Jennifer. *Why* should be fucking obvious to a blind person." Almost shouting now.

"Of course." Jennifer cringed back from her, desperation and helpless misery flashing across her face for a split second before her professional calm reasserted itself. "I'm sorry."

Carolyn could see that she really was, too. She had believed every word. And, coward or no, Jennifer had a kind heart. She only ever meant to help. Carolyn took her voice down to conversational levels, slipped her fury back into its sheath. "It's OK. I'm sorry too. It's been kind of a long day. Long week, whatever."

"Of course. Still friends?"

"Of course." This was true. It was also completely irrelevant. She wondered if Jennifer understood that.

"Good. I'm sorry, Carolyn. I didn't mean to push. But we *do* need to talk. I think you're more upset than you let on."

"I'd like that." She felt like screaming. Instead she gave a wan smile. "But not today, OK?"

"OK. But soon."

"Sure."

Jennifer nodded. Then, with her professional duties discharged, she turned her attention back to her little silver pipe. A moment later she blew out an enormous cone of smoke and made a little "ahh" sound. "I have to say, though, you've got amazing coping skills." She shook her head. "Between us, you aren't the first person David's nailed to a desk. Maybe it's like a fetish or something? He pulled the same thing on Peter last month. Peter at least lived through it, but he's a wreck. If I don't keep him drugged to the eyeballs, he just curls up in the nearest corner and cries."

The bowl of her pipe flared orange as she took another drag. "Not that I'm judging, mind you. I'd be a mess myself."

Carolyn looked up, surprised. She assumed David had come to visit them all at one time or another. "He's never . . . ?"

"Nope. Not me. Not so far, anyway. I'm starting to think he never will."

"Really?" *Interesting.* "Why do you think that is?"

She shrugged. "I'm not sure. It could conceivably be gratitude. There have been times when he would have been in some pretty bad pain if it weren't for me."

"I remember. But . . . gratitude? *David?*"

She sighed. "Yeah. You're right. Probably not. I always try to think the best of people. It's a weakness. It's more likely that he's worried that someday I'll just leave him dead."

Carolyn had been chewing over ways to bring up this very topic. She thought she knew the answer, but she owed it to Jennifer to be sure. "Would you?"

"Would I what?"

"Leave him. Dead."

Jennifer looked up from her pipe. "Well, now. It's funny that you should ask. Something very like that came up just the other day. He and Margaret were having one of their evenings"—she arched an eyebrow significantly—"and I was supposed to come by in the morning and do my thing."

"Heal them?"

"Resurrect them."

"Seriously? Both of them?"

Jennifer nodded. "At least once a month, lately. It's Margaret's idea, I think. It started a couple years ago with broken arms. Since then it's sort of escalated. Once he's done with her, he has a sort of hangman's noose for himself."

"I see."

"Do you? Explain it to me, then." Jennifer sighed. "Anyway, I was standing there looking at them—it was a real mess, half a day's work at least—and it occurred to me how no one ever seems to have any idea how much time has passed when I bring them back. And with Alicia's thing about clocks"—she smashed them if she saw them, Carolyn kept hers in a drawer—"it can be kind of difficult to tell one day from the next around here." Jennifer took another puff. "So I thought about it for a minute, and then I shut the door and went down to get breakfast."

"Wow." Carolyn shook her head, grinning. "A day or two without David, huh?"

Jennifer grinned back. "I didn't think any of you would mind."

"We would have given you a parade. Why didn't you say something?"

Jennifer's expression flickered to darkness. "Well . . . it didn't exactly work out."

"What do you mean?"

"Father came home early," Jennifer said quietly. "That afternoon. He was the one who found them, who brought them back."

Carolyn felt a cold burst of fear on Jennifer's behalf. Just as Carolyn did translations as needed, it was Jennifer's responsibility to resurrect them when they died, either at a preordained time requested by the deceased or, in the case of accident, as soon as possible. Intentionally forsaking your catalog wasn't as bad as sharing it, but it was bad enough. "Oh . . . oh no. What did he do?"

Jennifer looked at her levelly. "He took me up to the bull."

"Oh my God."

"I know. I've never been so scared in my life. He didn't make me get in it or anything, we just went up there. And I got a stern talking-to. Professional responsibility, the patient relies on you, et cetera."

Carolyn goggled at her. "That's *it*?" The bull was probably a little excessive for this, even by Father's standards. But she would have expected something like fifty lashes. Fifty *minimum*. Nothing up to "skinned alive" would have surprised her.

Jennifer nodded. "That's it."

"Any idea why?"

Jennifer shrugged. "He's never been as hard on me as on the rest of you, but for something like this . . . well, I was as surprised as you are."

Carolyn gave her an expectant look.

"I don't actually *know*, but . . . look, this is just between us, OK?"

Carolyn nodded.

"It crossed my mind that if something happened to Father, I might be the only one around who could bring him back."

"What about—"

"Liesel"—one of Father's courtiers—"is getting on in years and, honestly, she was never much good to begin with. Anyway, I've heard rumors that there might be . . . political issues. That was always an uneasy truce. Liesel was never particularly happy with this iteration of reality, is what they say. So far as I know she and I are the only other ones who've studied the white folio." The white folio, medicine, was where the secret of the resurrection was written down.

"Interesting." Carolyn considered. "Have you thought about what you'd do if it came to that?"

"Came to what?"

"If Father were dead," Carolyn said levelly, "and you were the only one left who could bring him back."

Jennifer's eyes went wide. Speaking formally, as if to an audience, she said, "I would resurrect Father, of course."

"Of course," Carolyn said.

Then, whispering, "I—Carolyn, I don't know if you know this, but there are things you don't even want to *think* about. Not around Father, maybe not anywhere. I mean that literally. Not even *think*." She paused, then said, very quietly, "He can *hear*."

"I know," Carolyn said, also whispering. She did, too. *But there's also such a thing as a calculated risk.* She wondered if Jennifer knew about those. Probably not. Gentle, frightened people didn't think much about calculated risks. "He can't be everywhere, always. Can he?"

Jennifer's eyes narrowed. She looked away, then busied herself with the drawstring on her bag. "I don't want to hear any more of this. I mean it, Carolyn. Not now, not ever. I won't say anything about it—I won't even *think* anything about it, if I can help it, but don't ever say anything like that to me again. If you do I'll go straight to Father. Am I understood?"

"You are," she said. The professional part of her mind noticed that

Jennifer had used the phrase 'Am I understood?'—Father's preferred version—rather than the more colloquial 'Understand me?' that the rest of them used among themselves. *Must be spending a lot of time with him*, Carolyn thought. "I won't. And I didn't really mean anything, Jennifer, I just—"

"Yeah. That's fine. No problem, really. We'll pretend it never happened."

Carolyn nodded. It seemed safer not to speak.

Jennifer slipped forceps into her bag and pulled it shut. "OK, look. I need to go. And I imagine you could use some time to yourself."

"Also a bath. But thank you, Jennifer. For everything."

"You really are welcome." Jennifer hesitated. "Look . . . later tonight Rachel and Alicia and I are going to smoke some weed and go up and watch the Milky Way. Just us girls, but Peter made a picnic basket. We'd love to have you come along."

"That's really nice of you, but I can't. I'm a little behind. I've got a test coming up and—"

Jennifer held up her hand.

"What?"

"Forgive me, Carolyn, but that's bullshit. You're not behind in anything. The way you work you could be dead for a year and still be two weeks ahead of schedule. Why don't you come with us? It'll be fun. You still remember fun, right?"

Carolyn gave her another smile, noticeably cooler. "I really can't."

"Yeah." Jennifer drummed her fingers against the door frame. "I wasn't going to bring this up until later, but—"

"I really need to—"

"Just give me a second. OK? I'll be quick."

Carolyn gave a very small nod. She wasn't smiling at all anymore.

"Thank you." Jennifer drew in a breath. "Look . . . part of my catalog is that they teach you how to talk to people. Some people, you want to talk around the edges of a situation. Others, you want to fluff things up, put the best face on it that you can."

"Oh? How interesting."

"But with the strong ones, the best approach is to dispense with that sort of thing. You just lay out the facts. That's what I'm going to do with you."

"I appreciate that. You've always been a good friend, Jennifer. You've always been very—"

Jennifer held up her hand again. "Spare me. I'm being straight with you, Carolyn. Do me the same courtesy."

Carolyn nodded. "All right. If you like. What do you want to tell me?"

"Thank you. Here's what I think: There's a particular species of crazy that people around here are prone to. Margaret has it worse than anyone I've ever heard of. David has it as well. They're both lost causes—I'll try, but unless things change radically, what they have is not something I'm going to be able to fix."

"What's that got to—"

"You're showing signs as well," Jennifer said soberly. "I was going to bring it up anyway, even before this . . . business . . . with David."

"Signs?"

"With this particular species of crazy, you stop trying to make things better. You start trying to maximize the bad. You pretend to like it. Eventually you start working to make everything as bad as possible. It's an avoidance mechanism." Jennifer looked Carolyn directly in the eyes. "It can't actually work. That's why they call it crazy."

"I see," Carolyn said. "That's very interesting. Thank you for that information."

Sighing, Jennifer leaned back against the door frame. "Yeah. OK. Just think about it, all right?"

"I will."

Jennifer opened the door and, blessedly, stepped out into the hall. "Look, if you don't want to come tonight, that's fine. I can't make you. But I think you should. That's my professional opinion, and my opinion as your friend. Also, in the unlikely—but welcome—event that you'd like to talk more about, you know, the other stuff, you know where to find me. Lacking that, best of luck to you and you have my condolences."

They looked at each other for a long moment. Finally, Carolyn said, "Is that all?"

Jennifer rolled her eyes. "Yeah. That's all."

"Thanks again."

"Sure, of course. We're going to meet at the jade stairs around sunset." Carolyn shut the door.

II

When Jennifer was gone, Carolyn went down to the baths. They were communal and unisex, but there was no one there at the moment. She filled one of the tubs with the hottest water and bathed herself. She stood up and dried off.

She took down a clean robe to dress, looked at it, then hung it back up again. She filled the tub a second time. She felt the filth of him on her even still. She rummaged in the closet until she found a very stiff brush and a caustic soap used to remove tar or certain toxins. She scrubbed herself with these until her skin was raw, scrubbed until her skin was *bleeding*. She only stopped when she noticed she was sobbing. Then she composed herself and dried off a second time.

Rachel came in while she was dressing. She gave Carolyn a sympathetic look. "Hey," she said. "How are you holding up?"

"Fine. Why?" She busied herself with putting up her hair.

"I, um . . . you know. I heard." Rachel walked over and put her hand on Carolyn's shoulder. "If you want to come by later, Alicia and I could—"

Carolyn looked down at Rachel's hand. "Thank you," she said, "but I'm fine. Really, it was nothing."

"Um . . . OK. If you say so. But if you change your—"

"You're very kind." Her tone sounded a little bit like David's. Neither of them recognized this consciously, but Rachel let her hand drop.

"OK," Rachel said again.

Carolyn walked back down the hall to her room. On the way out she passed David and Father walking down the hall. They were both covered head to toe in ballistic armor, and sweating.

Father didn't seem to notice her, but David gave her a two-dimple grin. "Hello, Carolyn."

She nodded back at him, expressionless. "Hello, David."

He tipped her a wink.

Carolyn didn't react at all.

In her room she shut the door behind her, and locked it. She didn't waste any more time thinking about David. It was the first time he had killed her, true, but he had hurt her before and she'd survived. This was her world. She had adjusted.

Instead, she cleaned. She was by nature a tidy person, and this business had left her room cluttered. Teeth gritted, she shelved the books first, then turned the desk back over and scraped off the blood. The Mont Blanc he had crucified her with was ruined, but she thought the Montegrappa he used on the other arm would be fine with a new nib. Jaw muscles jumping, knuckles white, she cleaned the pen with a solution of ammonia and water, polished it, and set it back in the coffee cup she used as a holder.

By sunset, around the time Jennifer and Rachel and Alicia were setting off on their picnic, she had the room back in something like good order. Only then did she return to the scrap of paper she had been holding when David came in. When he shut the door behind him, she used it as a bookmark for the text on Quoth. He hadn't noticed.

The bookmark was something she had found three years ago, in a Spanish text. It was a rough draft from a book on various methods of travel. It was not part of her catalog. It had apparently been left in the Spanish text by accident. It described something called the "*alshaq urkun*" which "maketh the light to pass through." It was related to something called the "*alshaq shabboleth*," which "maketh the slow things swifte" in some deep conceptual way. The *alshaq shabboleth* apparently had some side effects that rendered it impractical.

Alshaq urkun, though, was eminently practical. The way *alshaq urkun* worked was by making physical objects transparent to the electromagnetic spectrum—invisible, among other things. When it was invoked on, say, a person, that person might walk about freely and unobserved, no matter who was watching.

It had some drawbacks, too. The worst of them was that the rods and cones of the eyes were also transparent to light—that rendered you completely blind for however long the *alshaq* was invoked. But if you were careful, and if you planned your route in advance, you could get around just fine.

Carolyn picked up the book that was only slightly hidden on the small corner bookshelf, the book whose presence she had concealed from David at such horrific cost. David would have recognized it immediately, of course—it was bound in red leather, as were all the books of his catalog. Carolyn's own catalog was green. The title of the red book was *Mental Warfare vol. III: The Concealment of Thought and Intention*. It was a master-level text. Carolyn had finished it just the night before she died.

She stood in the doorway of her cloister, then performed the ceremony of the *alshaq urkun*. She didn't need to consult the slip of paper, not anymore. Everything she needed was committed to memory. When she was done, the world went dark. Red book in hand, she turned right. There were thirty-seven steps down the hall to the staircase. There were thirteen steps up to the main level of the Library, each of them nine inches high. That brought her to the jade floor. From there, one thousand and eighty-two steps took her to the ruby floor, where all books with red bindings were shelved.

Still counting her steps, she brought the book she had hidden back to the shelf from which it had come—radial eight, case twenty-three, shelf nine. She returned it to the twelfth slot from the right, just where she had found it the week before. She would not need to consult it again. She had studied diligently. She had mastered the concealment of thought and intention. Now it was time to move on to other things.

She took down a different book from shelf two of the same case, slot eight. It would be red as well, she knew, with a cover the color of arterial spray.

Back in her quarters, Carolyn shut the door behind her. She went to her desk, sat down, lit the oil lamp. Even with the blood gone, her desk was scarred with two holes, just under arm's length apart. She considered filling them, then decided against it. She would look at them from time to time. They would help her focus. Then, with a small smile, she opened the red book she had stolen—well, borrowed—from David's catalog.

This was cheating a little bit. She had first happened on the *alshaq urkun* bookmark about three years ago. She had been studying ever since. She started with Jennifer's catalog, then bounced around as her plan began to take shape. The course of study she'd laid out wouldn't have brought her to this volume for another month or two. But it was one she'd been looking forward to very much, and she thought that tonight she deserved a treat. The title and author were printed on the cover in the gold leaf of Western tradition. It was called *The Plotting and Execution of Vengeful Murder* by Adam Black.

She opened it to "Chapter 11: Notes on the Subjugation of the Martially Superior Foe."

She read until late in the night.

It was very comforting.

Chapter 11

Notes on the Subjugation of the Martially Superior Foe

I

"This is far enough," Carolyn said.

Steve rolled to a stop about a quarter mile down the road from the entrance to Garrison Oaks. He didn't bother to pull over onto the shoulder. Carolyn was twitchy, nervous, swaying and rocking in her seat. Steve had never seen her like this. Naga watched from the backseat, fascinated.

It was around nine p.m. Now even the light of the stars was gone. *Is it just cloudy, or did she do something to them, as well?* He realized, dimly, that he was in something like shock.

"Why are we stopping?"

Carolyn pointed. Not far from the subdivision sign a streetlight shone down, a little island of light in the long sea of black. Steve squinted. Three people stood under the light. His vision wasn't good enough to make out faces, but one of them was clearly wearing a tutu. Somewhere in his belly fear squirted, bright and cold.

"Is that David?"

Carolyn pursed her lips, considering, then nodded. "He's bleeding. Erwin must be better than I realized. It's been a long time since anyone made David bleed."

"That's *Erwin* down there?"

She nodded.

"What's he doing here?"

"He's angry. He came to 'fuck a bitch up.' "

"Anybody in particular?"

"The enemy. Me, David, anyone else who's left. He figured out that we'd turn up here eventually. He's very smart."

"But what—"

"Shh!"

Erwin raised the pistol to David's face. David grinned. He leaned forward and put his nose right at the tip of the gun's barrel. Erwin fired. The pistol's slide slammed down on an empty chamber. David backhanded Erwin across the mouth.

"OK," Carolyn said. "Game time."

"What?"

"Later," she said. "Right now I want you to go to the Library. Do you remember which one it is?"

"I do but—you're not going down *there*, are you?" Steve gestured at the streetlamp, David. In the backseat Naga rumbled.

"I am. And you're going to go to the Library. You'll be safe there. I'll be along when I've finished."

"What? Are you crazy? Do you have any idea what that guy can—"

"Steve, you need to listen," Carolyn said. "There isn't much time. I need to go down there, and you can't come."

"You're going there? Alone?"

She nodded.

"I'll go with you," he said. "Maybe I can—"

"Steve, *listen*. I'm not saying this to insult you, but if it came to a fight against David, you would have absolutely no chance of winning. None. It could not happen."

Steve opened his mouth to reply, but then he remembered how David had come to the jailhouse armed only with his spear, how he had filled the corridors of that place with the corpses of armed men. He shut his mouth. Then, after a moment, "Oh-kay. Point taken. And you do?"

"More than just a chance."

"Carolyn, unless you can fight a lot better than you've been letting on—"

"Steve," she said. "Go. Just go. I can do this. You'll be safe inside the *reissak*. No one that matters can get to you there."

"How could you possibly know that?"

"I just do." She hesitated. "A long time ago, there was a . . . sort of homecoming party. A feast. The main course was two deer. That's the *reissak*'s trigger. No one who tasted of their flesh can approach the Library. And that's everyone of consequence. You'll be safe there."

"But—"

"Just *go*, Steve. Everything will be fine if you leave it to me."

They glared at each other. After a long moment, Steve said, "All right. OK. But what do you want me to do if it doesn't work out the way you think? Should I come back, or—"

"No." Her tone was flat. "Don't try anything. I *could* lose. It's possible. It might happen. We'll know one way or the other in a few minutes. If I don't come for you in an hour or so, or if you see David at all, ever—don't try anything. Find a gun and blow your brains out. Or hang yourself. Or jump off a bridge. Anything. David can't do the resurrections, not yet. Probably by the time he learns he will have forgotten about you."

Steve gaped at her.

"I mean that literally," she said. "I am not kidding. It is not a joke. Tell me that you understand."

After a long moment he gave her the barest sliver of a nod. "Sure," he said. "Yeah." He didn't know whether he meant it or not.

She smiled, a little, then blew out a long breath. "But it will not come to that." She spoke calmly, and with great certainty. "I will not allow it." She examined her hands. Steve looked too. Her fingertips were steady, untrembling. "I still love you, Steve. You should know that, too."

"You what?" He paused. " 'Still?' " He trailed off, baffled, completely empty of things to say. After an uncomfortable moment he opened his mouth. "Carolyn, I . . ." dribbled out.

She smiled, a little sadly. "Wait until they're busy with me, then you and Naga sneak in over there." She pointed over her shoulder into darkness. "The fence doesn't go all the way around. You'll be fine."

He followed her finger, saw nothing. "What about the dogs?"

"What? No. They won't be a problem."

They were a pretty damn big problem yesterday, he thought, but bit it back. There was something about her now, something like a hooded cobra, swaying. Instead he said, "How can you be sure? I thought they were your father's—"

"You won't be harmed, Steve. The dogs obey me. They've been mine all along."

Steve stared at her, his expression darkening. *Dresden.* "Carolyn—"

"*Later.*" Her voice was infuriatingly calm.

Steve's eyes narrowed. *Dresden, swarmed by the pack, buried under them, but still fighting as* . . . He felt his anger rising, fought it down.

"Now, I have to go," Carolyn said. "Do you understand what you need to do?"

Steve managed to nod without looking too pissed off.

"I'll explain later," she said. "Really." She studied him, clearly unhappy with what she saw. She frowned, then leaned over and kissed him once, very quickly, on his right cheek. It was over almost before he realized it was happening. Then she sank back in her seat, shut her eyes, let out a long breath. Without a word, she opened the car door and stepped out in front of the headlights. Her shadow stretched out, eclipsing David and Erwin and Margaret.

For just a moment Steve watched, transfixed.

Carolyn was barefoot, and wore the same ridiculous clothes—bicycle shorts, sweater, leg warmers—he had first seen her in, now torn and dirty. There was a streak of dried blood down the side of her thigh. Steve could see himself and Naga framed in the rearview mirror, both of them bloody and taut, the lion peering over Steve's shoulder from the backseat. But at the same time he saw Carolyn walking, saw the way the muscles of her calves flashed in the headlights with each step.

Something in this tableau—he never quite settled on exactly what— put him in mind of Dresden, turning to face the pack of dogs, how every muscle of the lion's anatomy stood out in taut relief, the mute vehicles of his titanic and furious will.

II

David was twirling Erwin's pistol on his fingertip. Erwin knelt on the ground in front of him, trying to stand. David put the gun against Erwin's head and said, "Bang!" He laughed and tossed the pistol into darkness. Margaret sat with the president's severed head in her lap, cooing softly to it. The president's dead lips were moving.

Carolyn couldn't tell what he was trying to say. "Hello, David."

David turned. He was crusted in blood from head to toe, mostly dried. The lace of his tutu was stiff with it. It jutted out like knives. Here and there little bits of meat stuck to his skin. He smelled metallic, with just a hint of rot underneath, or maybe the rot was Margaret. He grinned from ear to ear, as happy as she had ever seen him.

"Looks like you've had quite an evening," Carolyn said.

Margaret tittered.

"Hello, Carolyn," David said. He winked at Margaret and punched Erwin in the face. Erwin sagged to the ground, semiconscious. David turned to face her. "So . . . it was you?"

Carolyn nodded.

"I have to say, I'm more than a little surprised. You're so . . . *mousy.*"

"It's the quiet ones you have to watch out for."

"I'll keep that in mind. Father's dead, isn't he?"

She nodded again.

David's grin widened a little bit. His teeth were strong and brown. "You killed him."

She nodded again.

David threw back his head and laughed, long and loud. "Amazing," he said. "Simply amazing. I'll bet"—he wagged a finger at her—"I'll *bet* someone's been reading outside of her catalog. Hmm? Hmmmm?"

Carolyn smiled, shrugged.

He laughed again. "I hope you were careful. You can get in trouble for that."

"I was."

"How did you kill him, if you don't mind me asking? Father is—was—very good. Even discounting the rest of his skills, I think he may have been the single best hand-to-hand fighter in the world. He told me he was stiffening up a bit, but you couldn't tell it by me. I—*I*—wouldn't have wanted to fight him. Not yet, anyway. Please tell me how you killed him. I am simply dying to know. Scholarly curiosity and all that."

"I used a knife."

"A knife." His tone was incredulous.

She nodded. "I had the element of surprise, of course."

On the asphalt behind David, Erwin stirred, trying to push himself up.

David's brow furrowed under thick, bloody locks. He kicked Erwin, but in a distracted way. He was studying her, trying to decide if she was lying to him. He was a little telepathic, she knew. Not to the same degree that Father had been, but he could see things in the minds of his enemies, especially in the heat of battle. She might have concealed the truth of what she said, might have let him wonder, but she didn't.

"The element of surprise," he said slowly. "Yes. I'd say that you do have that. With a *knife*." He shook his head. "Amazing. For what it's worth, I was leaning towards a knife myself. The simplest weapons are the only chance, against one like Father. Most people wouldn't understand that." He squinted at her, considering. "I may have underestimated you, Carolyn."

Carolyn didn't want him to pursue that line of thought. "Did anyone get out at Mrs. McGillicutty's?"

Erwin was on his knees now, crawling slowly away from them.

"Nope! I'm pretty sure it was just me and Margaret. Those soldiers were good, for Americans. Maybe a mouse could have snuck out. Not much else. Oh—sorry, Carolyn. You and Michael were buddies, weren't you?"

Carolyn felt Margaret's gaze on her, hot and greedy. She was careful to keep emotion from her voice when she spoke. "No," she said. "Not really."

Margaret frowned, disappointed, and turned her attention back to the president's head.

"And I suppose it's your *reissak ayrial* as well?" David's tone was casual, but he wasn't fooling anyone. If the *reissak* was hers, that meant she had worked alone. When she was dead, the Library would stand unguarded. David would find a way in sooner or later. Then, unopposed, he and Margaret would plunder Father's catalogs. The universe would enter a darkness that would make the third age seem like paradise. Out of the corner of her eye Carolyn saw that Erwin had reached the sidewalk.

"Mine, yes."

"I thought so. What was your plan, then? You thought Nobununga and I would do one another in, perhaps?"

"It was a possibility I considered." This was true. She had also rejected it. "But he died earlier than I was expecting."

Erwin, groggy, picked up the empty pistol. He looked at it as if he didn't quite remember what it was.

"So then . . . what? Were those soldiers supposed to do me in? *Americans? Kill me?*" He smiled. "Is that it?"

She shrugged. "Conceivably. There were a lot of them. They had guns. You're not invulnerable, David."

"True enough." David smiled. "Neither are you."

"What if I told you that I have a propos—"

Faster than she could even see, David's hand shot out. Her left cheek exploded with pain. She tasted blood. "—proposal. We could join forces, David. I've always admired you, you know—"

Another slap. More pain, this time on the right side. Margaret giggled.

"—that. Admired your strength." Her heart was like ice. She dropped to her knees, her face inches from his crotch. "I could be yours," she said. "Willingly. I've always wanted that, you know. I often thought about you. In secret. I would have said something, but I'm so very shy."

The cogs of her plan were ticking into final alignment. At first she had rejected this approach out of hand. It was too obviously a ploy. Only after deep study had she considered the idea seriously. Father's texts were adamant about its effectiveness. As illustrated in any number of footnotes, men are almost always 50 to 60 percent dumber in matters involving their crotch. Close proximity enhances the effect. Now, with clinical approval, she saw that something stirred in the depths of David's tutu.

Margaret raised an eyebrow. Erwin staggered into Garrison Oaks, inside the boundary of the *reissak*.

Safe for now.

Carolyn turned all of her attention to David. He looked skeptical, but not disinterested. "Here," she said, "let me show you." She reached out and stroked his leg with the tips of her sharp nails.

David stank of rotting meat and sour sweat. She raised her hand into the fluffs of fabric and probed, gently, until she touched the shaft of his penis. "There," she said, "there." She traced the tips of her fingernails down it to his scrotum and cradled it in her palm. David tilted his head back, shivering with pleasure.

"*There*." She snarled, simultaneously digging in with the long, lacquered nails of her left hand, twisting, and yanking down as hard as she could. She didn't get both of his testicles, but one of them came away in her hand. His training would be up to the task—after what he had suffered in the bull, it would be up to almost anything imaginable—but it would take him a moment to marshal it. She had bought seconds.

David roared. He struck out blindly, trying to backhand her, but Carolyn ducked under it. She was not so quick as he, but she had been practicing this moment every day for ten years. She let go of his crotch. Reflexively, he jumped back a step.

"You nasty bitch," David growled, not without admiration.

Father's notes were clear on this topic as well—there were several ways to incapacitate men instantly, but striking them in the crotch was not one of them. It would take a second or two before the real pain hit.

"Wait," she said slowly, "I'm sorry. Did I do something wrong? I thought you liked it rough." David stared at her with increasing disbelief as she said this . . . but he listened to the whole sentence. It took about four seconds.

By the time she finished speaking, he was near the true depth of his pain. David groaned.

Carolyn, smiling, flicked the blood off her claws. "Oh well. My mistake."

David roared again. He balled his hands into fists and stepped toward her, one hand held protectively over his groin, bent over almost double.

Carolyn rolled over backward, sprang to her feet, and took off running toward the gates. David was faster than anyone . . . usually. *Right now, though, not so much.*

But she couldn't outrun him for long. He would be on her as soon as he had the pain under control. She sprinted toward the entrance to Garrison Oaks. In a dozen steps she was inside the gate . . . and inside the perimeter of the *reissak*. She stopped then, and turned.

Snow was just beginning to accumulate on the ground. The tracks of her bare feet stretched back to where David stood, now bent over double with pain. She was gratified to see a few drops of blood staining the snow below.

David blew out a hot breath, vapor cloud white under the streetlight. He drew himself up to his full height. Margaret handed him his spear and faded back, as from a fire that burned too hot.

David looked down at the footprints in the snow, then out into the shadows. His eyes blazed with murder, ancient and savage, the malevolent glare of a death god's black idol.

"I'm coming for you, Carolyn."

III

With the expression of a man diving into ice water, David waded into the *reissak*. She watched him closely. His face betrayed no pain with the first step, nor the second, nor the third. But on the fourth he grunted—very softly.

Carolyn, still standing alone in the dark, heard his pain and smiled.

"Over here!" she said, cheerful and mocking. She took a single, measured step away from him, closer to the Library. "This way!"

David thudded after her, heavy and relentless.

David would be capable of going much deeper into the *reissak* than any of the others, much deeper than he had thus far chosen to go. She knew he would have tricks for controlling pain, minimizing internal damage. There would be techniques.

Even so, seeing his strength with her own eyes, she was in awe of it, the raw, brute will of him. She had caught him off guard with the testicle shot. Probably he had been toying with her as well. But there was no play in what he did now. The tendons of his neck stood out like cables. Sweat ran off him in a literal stream, trickling down his arms and dribbling off the end of his spear to steam in the snow.

She braced herself for what came next. "Had enough? You really should turn around before it's—aaagh." The cry was startled out of her, as much surprise as pain. He was so very *quick*. She looked down to see the barbed point of his spear sticking out of her left leg and felt real fear. *He drew back, threw, and skewered me* literally *so fast that I couldn't see it.*

Grinning, David yanked the chain. Carolyn's legs failed her. Suddenly she was on her back on the asphalt.

He began reeling her in. The pain was immense. Carolyn alternated between straining against the chain and crab-walking with it to avoid having her back grated off by the road.

"Oh, David, no . . ." she said, injecting a tremble in her voice, knowing that it would excite him further. Inside, though, she was like ice. When she judged the moment was right she reached down and broke off the spear point.

She allowed a single, measured moan to bubble out, then turned over and began crawling away.

"Raah, you *bitch*." David changed spearheads. A moment later she was pierced again, this time through the foot. This pain dwarfed anything she had previously felt, ever, in all her life. As she clawed at the asphalt her fingernails peeled back, and this was like candles measured next to the sun. David yanked her back toward him. She barely noticed.

His hand clamped down on her ankle. His grip was like iron pincers, his fingers thick with calluses. He flipped her onto her back. She scrabbled at the rough asphalt of the road, desperate, clawing at it with her fingertips. Tiny pebbles shredded her shoulder blades. They were so very deep in the *reissak ayrial* that she thought even a few more *inches* would be enough to kill him.

But she could not move. He was too strong.

David was reeling her in. He reached up and took her knee. Small bones creaked in his grip. She knew what he would reach for—*nonononono*—and he did. He dug his index finger into the hole his spear had left in her leg. He pushed.

She felt another scream bubbling up under his hands, just as she had so many times before. She pushed it back down. She kicked at the asphalt with her bare heels, struggling to move deeper into the *reissak*. He tortured her wound for another moment, then reached up to her collarbone. He did something terrible and it snapped, the sound of it muffled by her skin.

She let a scream slip loose—just one. It was necessary, it was the bait she needed to draw him in that one final inch, but it cost her, too, in a way she hadn't expected. There was a note of truth in that scream.

Now his hand was at her throat. He dug his pinkie finger into a pressure point below her jaw while using the rest of his hand to cut off her air. *This is how he murdered me the first time*, she thought. *Auld lang syne.*

Her mind, scrabbling and frantic, flipped through her mental grimoire for anything that might help. She pounded him with her small hands, scratched him, poked at his eyes.

David was implacable. David was a stone.

Now there was a cloud around the edges of her vision. *It didn't work*, she thought. *David is going to win. He's murdering me one final time.* She thought of Steve as he had been at age twelve, tall and lanky, grinning in the summer sun. Behind her eyes, black flowers bloomed.

"This is just the beginning," David whispered. "When I've mastered the other catalogs I'll call you back. We'll do this over and over again. We'll do this every night forever."

Far behind her, out in the night, she heard a soft metallic tap, the sound of the final cog clicking into place. Hearing this she ceased drifting, coalesced, came back to herself.

Now.

Carolyn opened her eyes. Hypoxia occluded her vision almost completely . . . but she saw well enough. She composed herself, stopped struggling. She smiled up at him, reached up and stroked his dimple gently with the remains of one ragged, bloody nail.

David's smile withered at her touch. His voice came to her as from a great distance. "What?" he demanded. "*What?* Stop! *Why are you smiling at me?*"

Her lips moved, soundless.

"What?!" David said, screaming now. "*What is it, you crazy, horrible bitch?!*" The question wasn't rhetorical. As he asked it he took his hands away from her throat.

Carolyn felt the urge to gasp and cough, but mastered it. She sipped a single, cool breath of night air, drew it into her lungs slowly, savoring the first breath of the rest of her life. When she was perfectly ready she spoke.

"And *then* . . ."—she spat, blood spattering on his face in a fine spray—"from the *east* . . ." The words hissed out of her ragged, shattered throat as she took her finger away from his cheek. "Thunder."

David's face exploded.

IV

Time was short now. The bullet had caught David a little bit high of perfect, half an inch or so too far up the cheekbone—a small miscalculation. The left half of his face was mostly gone. She could see his brains. Even taking his training into account, David would die quickly, one or two more heartbeats at most.

But both of his eyes worked, and he still had an ear. Any one of those would have been enough. Carolyn wrapped her hands around the back of his neck and pulled herself up. She examined the gaping hole in his head, reached up with the tip of one finger, and touched him, very gently, in a deep part of his brain. A small spark flashed at her touch. Then, in the second heartbeat, she leaned in close and whispered in David's ear, speaking the word that Father whispered to Mithraganhi so very long ago when he called up the dawn of the fourth age.

For David, hearing this . . .

. . . time . . .

. . . stopped.

Carolyn slumped back onto the asphalt. Her breath puffed white under the streetlamp. She smiled a little, but couldn't bring herself to do much more. *I did it*, she thought. *I really did*. She felt no real triumph, not even relief. She was numb.

It was a pleasant species of numbness, though.

As a side effect of being outside of time, David was now weightless. She pushed him off her with the barest touch. He hung frozen in the night air, bobbing slightly, like a deflating balloon.

Carolyn heard footsteps behind her. "Hello, Erwin." Her voice was very hoarse. She sat up, coughing, and wrapped her arms around her knees. "Can you help me up?"

"Err . . ." Erwin said, speaking through lips that were split and swollen, "I ain't for sure. I'll try." He limped toward her a little quicker. He was holding his left hand over a bleeding hole in his leg. In his right was the HK with which he had shot David. Smoke curled up out of the barrel.

Erwin reached down with one thick hand. Carolyn took it. He lifted her easily.

"What's wrong with him?" He poked David with a finger. He spun easily, a foot or two off the ground.

"Don't do that," she said. "Let me in there for a second, would you?" Erwin looked at her, then shrugged and stepped back.

She stopped David's spinning, then turned him so she could examine the wound. It would certainly have been fatal, even for one such as David. The left side of his head was missing. "Good shot," she said, "almost perfect, really." She flicked her eyes at Erwin. "The angle was a little off, but that was my fault. We were supposed to be at a seven degree angle to you, but it was more like nine. It was tough to focus with that darn spear hole in my leg."

"Yeah," Erwin said slowly. "I 'spect it was. How'd you know I'd—"

"Command Sergeant Major Erwin Charles Leffington, US Army, retired. Born April 8, 1965, late of the Eighty-Second Airborne. Before that, two years in US Army Marksmanship Unit. When was the last time you missed a shot, Erwin?"

"Before tonight, you mean?" David had allowed Erwin to empty the pistol at him before they arrived, for sport. "I don't remember exactly," he said. "It's been a while."

"Don't beat yourself up about it. You couldn't have hit him earlier. No one could. Come over here; let me take a look at that leg." She squatted down to examine the cut in Erwin's thigh. "You're OK. No arterial bleeding. He was going to play with you for a while." She lay back on the street. "I'm sorry about that. I had to wait until you were pretty beaten down. That way he wouldn't consider you a threat."

"'Saright. Don't mind takin' some licks in a good cause." Erwin spat. "And that guy was a real asshole."

"You have no idea." Carolyn closed her eyes, collecting herself. *I did it*, she thought again. *I really, actually did.*

"So . . . what did I miss?" Steve asked. He and Naga were walking down the road from the direction of the Library. "What happened here?"

"*Dammit*, Steve!" Carolyn said. "I told you to wait in the Library. Don't you *ever* listen?"

"You're not the boss of me."

Erwin looked over his shoulder. "Hey, kid. How ya doin'?"

Steve gave him a little wave. "C'mon, don't keep me in suspense. What happened?"

"Well," Erwin said, "basically that asshole there was all strangling her, so I kinda shot him a little. In the face, like."

"Thanks, by the way," Carolyn said.

Steve furrowed his brow, confused. "How'd you manage that? When we rolled up you had just run out of bullets."

"I wondered about that myself," Erwin said. "It was the damnedest thing. So, like, when you guys showed up the big dude just dropped me. I was too punchy to fight. I was gonna fall back to that house over there"—he pointed at the only house on the street with lights on—"and call for backup. In training, they drilled it into us never to leave a weapon on the field—I used to beat the shit out of guys for that—so on the way I grabbed my pistol, even though it was empty. Kind of by reflex, like.

"Then, when I was circling around the streetlight, I happened to look down. And, y'know, fuck me if there wadn't a full magazine right there in front of the sewer. Not the cleanest I've ever seen, but after I wiped it off on my shirt it worked just fine. I couldn't believe it. It was like magic."

"No such thing." Carolyn blew twin columns of smoke out her nostrils.

"Whoa," Steve said. "I bet I know where it came from. Can I see that?" Erwin held up the pistol but didn't hand it over.

"Is that the same gun I took when I went out running?" Steve asked. "The one you gave him earlier?"

"It is, yeah," Carolyn said.

"Then the magazine *you* found must have been the same one *I* dropped when the dogs jumped me."

"Hey, I bet it is!" Carolyn said. She laughed. "Imagine that!"

Both the men were looking at her now. "So . . ." Steve said slowly. "You set this whole thing up? Me running yesterday . . . the dogs . . . so I would drop the magazine, where Erwin could find it? Right then, when David was grabbing you?"

"Yes." Carolyn's eyes blazed out like searchlights in the night. "Yes. I did."

"Why?"

"Well, David was kind of a jerk."

"No, I mean why go to all that trouble? Couldn't you just—"

"There's no 'just.'" She stepped around David's floating body, examining him as she spoke. "Not with one like David. He's too skilled. He was the master of his catalog in all but name. Once I watched him kill a hundred Israeli soldiers—armed men—with that knife of his. That was just an exercise, part of his training. If you didn't take measures to stop it, he could hear your thoughts. There's no one on Earth who could have beaten him in a fair fight. But here, inside the *reissak*—"

"The what?" Erwin said.

"*Reissak ayrial*," Steve chimed in. "It's kind of a perimeter-defense system. It's very advanced!"

Erwin gave him a look.

"Nothing to do with microwaves, though. That part was bullshit."

"You're kind of a smartass, ain't you, kid?"

Steve nodded modestly, scuffing his feet in the dirt like John Wayne talking to the pretty schoolmarm. "Yeah."

"Well, couldn't you have—"

"Sent in the Army, maybe? A shitload of professionals—big, burly fellows, well trained, with a lot of guns? Mmmmaybe—just maybe—I could figure out a way to get someone like Delta Force involved. Surely that would do it?" She made a show of sniffing the air. The breeze still carried a hint of burning oil from the crashed helicopters. "Oh, wait . . ." She laughed again.

"OK," Erwin said. "But how'd you know I'd be—"

"Do you like that job with Homeland Security? Interesting work, I bet. Right up your alley."

"Yeah . . ."

"How'd you end up there?"

"Kind of an accident," Erwin said. "I went out to lunch and—"

"Ran into an old buddy of yours? Someone you knew in high school? Just a chance thing? A real long shot?"

Erwin didn't answer, only looked at her. Understanding dawned in his eyes.

Steve got it too. "Holy friggin' crap."

"I've been working on this for a long time," Carolyn said. "I like to plan. It's something I'm good at. You've seen those guys who do trick shots in pool? Make the cue ball jump, or roll backwards or whatever? This was my trick shot."

Erwin and Steve looked at each other. After a moment, Erwin nodded. "Ah-ite. If you say so, I guess I believe ya. But why's he all floaty like that?"

"That was me too."

"Yeah, I figured," Erwin said. "What I mean is, how?"

"I put him outside of time."

"Come again?"

"I changed some physical constants inside his body. For him, time isn't passing anymore." Her throat felt ragged, torn. She coughed, then spat blood into the snow. "David won't fall because, falling, you see, that's a *process*. But if time doesn't pass, there really can't be a process, as such, can there?"

Erwin chewed on this, then filed it away for later consideration. "Yeah, OK. Why?"

"Why what?"

"Why'd you, uh, do it? He woulda been dead in just a second or two, I figure."

She nodded. "Yes. He would have. That's why."

"I don't follow."

"Have you ever died?"

Erwin gave her a look. "Can't say as I have."

"I have, a couple of times. It's not as bad as you might think. Not nearly bad enough for him."

"But this is?"

"I'm not sure. But *he* thinks it's worse. That's what matters."

"How do you mean?"

"Well, David died a good bit. It was part of his training. Not as much as Margaret, but enough that he was used to it. A few years ago I overheard the two of them talking about it. By then Margaret didn't care. She'd kill herself if dinner was late. But she said that there was one part that still bothered her. Not the pain—they could deal with pain. Any of us could. But she hated the *realization*."

Carolyn paused. "Well, no. That's my word, not hers. How did she put it? She said she still felt it, even now, in her stomach and the soles of her feet. When the wound was struck and no one could save her, her body knew. Margaret's died every way you could think of, but she said that part was the worst thing she knew. And David agreed with her."

"That's where David is now." She smiled. "That moment when he feels it in his stomach and the soles of his feet. *Wazin nyata*—the moment when the last hope dies. He'll be there forever."

At the sight of her smile Steve fell back half a step. Even Erwin flinched a little.

Her instinct was to make her expression neutral. *But why? There's no reason to hide. Not anymore.* She looked down at her hand. Her fingertips no longer trembled.

"He pissed you off too, huh?"

"A bit. Yeah. Got a smoke, Steve?"

"Right before you did . . . whatever . . . before you froze him, you touched him," Erwin said. "Inside the wound, like. Why'd you do that?"

Steve handed her a Marlboro, then lit another for himself.

"You saw that, huh? Yeah, I gave him a little shock. Static electricity, right in the parieto-insular cortex."

"The what?" Steve asked.

"The pain center of his brain," Erwin said.

"Exactly. It wasn't much—barely more than you'd get from touching a doorknob after you'd rubbed your feet across the carpet. But of course you don't *need* much, not when the anatomy is laid out in front of you like that."

"They did experiments," Erwin said. "Cheney's guys, trying to figure out what to do with bin Laden. I heard stories. You give somebody a shock like that, it'd be the sum of—well not just every pain you felt, but every pain you possibly *could* feel. All at once, like."

"Yes."

"And then you froze him? In that moment, exactly?" Steve thought about it for a second, then gave a low whistle. "Why?"

Carolyn remembered how the rain ran warm, remembered the salty, coppery taste of Asha's blood. "Because *waẓin nyata* isn't enough. Not for him. This, though . . . I'm pretty sure that it's the worst thing that ever happened to anyone, anywhere. Ever. I think it's the worst thing that *can* happen, the theoretical upper limit of suffering. Despair and agony," she said. "Absolute. Unending."

"Damn," Erwin said. "That's some fucked-up shit."

"Thanks, Erwin. That means a lot, coming from you." She blew smoke up into the night sky. "I wanted to do it by impaling him on that spear of his, or maybe to nail him to a desk. But I couldn't figure out a way to make that work. This will have to do." She examined David with a surgeon's eye and a malice that had no bottom. "And I think it will. Yes. It's working already."

"What is?"

"Look in his eyes and tell me what you see."

Steve and Erwin leaned in. "They're black," Steve said. "I mean, not like he got bruised. The whites of his eyes are *black*. And . . . are they glowing, a little?"

"Yes." She saw it too. "I thought so, but it could have been the light." Carolyn spun David to face her.

It was very dark out now—no moon, no stars. The snow that fell on her did not melt. Her brow was in shadow, but when she took a drag from her cigarette, twin reflections blazed orange in the dark pools of her eyes.

"Scream." She spoke softly, in Pelapi. "Try to scream. If you scream for me, I'll stop." Smiling now. "If you scream for me, I'll let you go. Going once . . . going twice . . . no?"

V

Now Steve and Erwin were both giving her looks. *Anyway, David can't hear me.* She let her hand drop. When she spoke next she made an effort to sound normal. "Yeah, that's a good, strong connection. I must have timed it just right."

Naga sniffed David, then yowled.

"You fed that lion lately?" Erwin asked.

"She'll be fine." Steve patted Naga on her back. She shoulder-dived against his hip. "She's just a big ol' sweetie. Ain't ya, girl?"

Carolyn smiled and crushed out the Marlboro under her bare foot. "Got another?"

Steve fished out the pack. The two of them lit up. Steve held out the pack to Erwin.

Erwin waved it off. "That shit'll kill ya." He put in a dip instead.

"You're bleeding," Steve said. There was real concern in his voice.

She looked down. Blood was dribbling out of the hole in her thigh—it didn't squirt the way it would have if an artery was nicked, but it was bad enough. "Oh, right. That. Steve, could I get you to run and get something for me?"

"Sure. What do you need?"

"I need to patch my leg up. Erwin's too. Remember that pile of stuff I left for you in the living room of that white house?"

"Yeah, sure."

"There's a big canvas bag tied with twine. Get that, some bandages, and as much water as you can carry. Pressure bandages, if there's any left."

"Will do." Steve took off.

"Erwin, can I have one of your shoelaces?"

"Er . . . yeah. If you want." He took off his Reebok and extracted the lace, then handed it to her. "What do you need it for?"

She tied one end of the lace to David's hairy big toe, and the other to a mailbox. "We've got one more thing to take care of, and I don't want him bobbing off."

CAROLYN WASN'T AS skilled as Jennifer, but their wounds weren't all that bad. She packed the hole in her foot and leg with a gray powder, then poured water on it. As she worked on Erwin, the powder knitted itself into flesh, pink and new.

They found Margaret just outside the gate, still playing with the president's head.

"You killed David," Margaret said. She didn't look up. "How could *you* kill David?"

"Not exactly." Carolyn felt ferocious, triumphant . . . but she was wary as well. It was hard to tell what went on in Margaret's head. "That would have been too good for him. I found something worse."

"Worse than the forgotten lands?"

Carolyn's smile was streaked with blood. "Much."

Margaret looked up, interested for the first time. "Really?" She searched Carolyn's face. "It is *true*. You *did*. You are a horror, then. I did not know." She smiled. "We are sisters." Then, to the head, "David said she might be reading outside her catalog, but I didn't beeee-leeeeeeeve him. She seems so *pink* and *mousy*." She punctuated "pink" and "mousy" by poking the president in his cheeks. The head tried to moan, but it had no air.

Margaret moaned for it, weaving her head back and forth in the night. Then something occurred to her. "Father will be upset." She made the head poke out its bottom lip.

"Father is gone too. I killed him."

"He'll be back. He always comes back."

"Not this time."

Margaret wavered. She spoke softly. "You have *ended* Father? Ended him *forever*?"

Carolyn thought she saw the faintest, tiniest flicker of expression in Margaret's face. Hope, perhaps? She couldn't tell. "Yes. He's gone."

"Forever?"

"Forever."

"Oh." Again that little flicker of expression, hard to read. "I believe you." She looked back down at the head, then back up, as something new occurred to her. "Then you are horror *and* death. Yes?" She looked at Carolyn seriously, waiting for an answer.

Carolyn blinked. "I guess you could put it that way."

"Then I suppose that makes you my mistress." She set the president's head on the ground, stood up, and curtsied. "What would you have of me, madam?"

Carolyn didn't know what she had expected, but this wasn't it. "Only one thing." She looked at Erwin, nodded. Erwin raised his pistol.

"Oh," Margaret said, bored again. "You are sending me home?"

"Yes."

"Hmm." She paused. "May I ask one thing? Madam? A favor, please?"

Carolyn was in a generous mood. She touched Erwin on the shoulder, spoke in English. "Not yet." Then, in Pelapi, to Margaret. "Sure. Why not?"

"Do you remember the way David died? The first time?"

"Yeah. But Margaret, I wouldn't—"

"I would like to go home that way. Through the bull. The way David went."

Carolyn squinted at her, unsure if she had heard right. "Can you say that again?"

"I would like to be roasted in the bull. Father said it would be my final lesson. I believe that I am ready."

"Margaret . . . why would you *possibly* want such a thing?"

"You don't know?" She sounded disappointed.

"No. I really don't."

"David never understood either. I wanted to hear him, you know, but . . . he couldn't get through. Not anymore. Not for a long time. But you and I are sisters, it seems. So perhaps . . ." Margaret frowned at her, searching for words. "I'm very far now. Far from all of you, far from myself. I am in the outer darkness, you see." She blinked, imploring. "I have wandered for so very long. You understand this much?"

Carolyn gave a small nod. "I do."

"I often think of the bull, though. Do you think of the bull?"

"Sometimes."

"You remember how it glowed? How the fire made it orange, under the moon, and David sang?"

Carolyn's mouth was dry. "I remember."

"If someone were to light a fire like that for me . . . I think I might feel it. Even here in the outer darkness, I might feel it. And . . . if it were bright enough, and burned very long . . . perhaps I could follow it back." Margaret, pale and atrocious, aged about thirty, gave a wistful smile. "Back to myself, you see. I might even have a song called out of me. I think there might be one left to call." She looked to Carolyn with the ghost of hope dancing in her eyes. "Just one. That's all I ask. Do you think? Perhaps?"

"Yes," Carolyn said quietly. "Perhaps."

"You'll do it then?"

They looked at each other. Maggots squirmed in Margaret's hair. *When we were children, she had the best toys*, Carolyn thought. *Pretty little dolls. She let me borrow them sometimes*. "Yes. If that's what you want." Then, in English: "Erwin, put the gun away. New plan. Margaret has a last request."

"I ain't shooting her?"

"No. That's not insane enough, apparently."

The muscles at Erwin's temples jumped. "What, then?"

"It's easier to show you. There should be a wheelbarrow in that garage over there. Can you and Steve grab it for me? And some stove lengths, from the wood pile in back? We'll meet you at the top of the hill."

Erwin eyed her. "Ah-ite." He uncocked his pistol and put the safety on. After a moment's hesitation, he held it out to Carolyn, butt first. "Wanna borrow this?"

Margaret boinged up and down on the balls of her feet like a small child at a candy counter.

"Thanks, but I don't think I'll need it."

. . .

THE DEAD ONES polished the bull every few days. Even under the faint light of the distant streetlamp it had a certain glow.

Fifteen minutes later, sweating, Erwin dragged the wheelbarrow up the last of the railroad-tie stairs cut into the bluff. His cart was full of knotty pine, dry and sticky with sap. He set it down next to the bull and wiped sweat from his forehead with the back of his hand. Then, rapping his knuckles against the bronze, "What's this thing?"

"That," Carolyn said, "is the worst barbecue grill in the world."

Margaret hadn't been able to wait. She was lugging logs from the wood pile by hand, her small body bent under the load. She carried them to the bull two at a time and arranged them just-so. Seeing Erwin's mound of pine, she smiled.

"We having a cookout?" Erwin sounded suspicious and . . . something else.

Hearing his voice, Carolyn thought of the diamond pattern of rattlesnake scales, almost but not quite hidden under autumn leaves. She considered sending him away. *He's not David, but he's not nothing, either.* "Not exactly. It's . . . something we do. Sort of a ritual."

Erwin's right hand drifted to his left shoulder, rubbed it. There was, she knew, a number 4 branded there. Everyone in his unit had gotten them in Afghanistan. Erwin would understand about ritual.

Margaret dropped her armload of broken limbs. She flashed Erwin a greedy smile and plucked a split log from his wheelbarrow.

Erwin considered this. "Yeah. OK. Want me to lug summa that wood?"

"Sure. That'd be great."

The four of them settled into a rhythm, Steve and Erwin filling the cart, Erwin pushing and dumping it. Carolyn was supposed to be helping Margaret, but Margaret had some theoretically optimal vision of a wood pile in her mind, and she kept slapping Carolyn's hand away.

After twenty minutes or so, Margaret stepped back and looked at the pile. "This is enough."

"Margaret, are you sure you—"

"Yes. Any higher and it will be over too soon." Margaret took hold of the hatch, but she was a slight woman. The tendons in her neck stood out as she strained to open it, but the most she could manage was a couple of inches. Carolyn walked over to help. Together they raised it past the tipping point. The thick bronze clanged against the bull's back. "Are you sure this is what you want?"

"Oh yes." Her voice was eager.

Carolyn spoke to Erwin in English. "Can you give her a hand up?"

"What?"

"Part of the ritual."

"Uh-huh." Erwin squinted at Carolyn, suspicious, then at Margaret. Margaret nodded, bouncing on the balls of her feet. Erwin knelt and made a sling out of his hands. Margaret lifted one bare, dirty foot, then hesitated. "Here," she said, and held out her Zippo to Carolyn. "For you."

Carolyn didn't want to touch the thing. "It's OK. I've got my own."

"Take it."

"Really, I—"

"Take it. You'll need it sooner or later." Margaret smiled. Her teeth were black. "You're like me now."

Carolyn felt a little squirt of horror at that but squelched it. Just get this over with. She took the lighter with two fingers, touching it as little as possible.

Margaret scrambled into the bull.

"I don't understand," Steve said.

"I don't either. Not really. But this is what she wants."

Margaret's eyes shone wide and white against the black grease inside—excited, but not wanting to hope for too much.

"She wasn't always like this," Carolyn said. "When we were little she . . . she had a really big dollhouse. We'd play, sometimes." She sighed. "Can one of you give me a hand with the hatch?"

"What are you doing?" Erwin asked. But he knew. He was American, not stupid.

"What does it look like? Give me a hand."

"Yeah, um, no. I can't let you do that," Erwin said.

Carolyn sighed, exasperated. *Maybe Steve could help? No. Just push. You can do this.*

"You wanna put her down, that's fine. I'll shoot her myself. But you can't burn her. 'Tain't right to do that to a person." Erwin glared at her. "Smart lady like you oughtta know that."

"I'm with Erwin on this one," Steve said.

Carolyn frowned, tapped her teeth with her fingernail. "If you guys don't want to be involved, that's fine. I don't blame you. Help me with the hatch and I'll meet you by the gate."

"I can't let you do that," Erwin said again.

Carolyn turned to him. She spoke gently, as if explaining something to a small child. "Erwin . . . this isn't a negotiation. There's no 'let.' Are you going to help or not?"

Erwin didn't move.

Carolyn rolled her eyes, then turned back to the bull. She strained against the lid, arms quivering with effort. She didn't quite lift it past the tipping point before her strength failed. The hatch fell back open with a clang, deafeningly loud. The sound rolled out over Garrison Oaks like a gong. Down in the neighborhood, doors began to open. She heard one of the dead ones call out, saying, "Here you dogs! Get out of that trash." But its voice was uneasy.

Behind her, there was a tiny click as Erwin thumbed off the safety of his pistol. "I can't let you do that," he repeated.

She heard a low, bass rumbling. It was still distant, but it was closing fast. "Put down the pistol, Erwin."

"I'm thinking no," Erwin said.

Naga looked up at the sky and roared. Down in the neighborhood the dogs had come out to join the dead ones. At the sound of Naga's voice, a couple of them barked. One of the dead ones called out, "Heeeere kitty-kitty."

All of a sudden the night was very bright, very loud. A low-flying helicopter came around the curve of the ridge line. It had a search light, hot and white. Stubby wings on the side bristled with bombs, missiles, guns.

"What is that?" Carolyn called out, shouting to be heard above the rotors.

"AH 64," Erwin said. "Apache gunship."

A moment later a second helicopter appeared as well. The two of them hovered over the clearing of the bull, searchlights blazing. The air filled with pine straw, dirt, leaves, small twigs. The light was painfully bright.

Margaret peeped out of the bull to see what was happening. She said something, too soft for Carolyn to hear, then lay back down inside.

"What are they doing?" Steve asked.

One of the helicopters had a PA system. "SET DOWN YOUR WEAPONS. SET DOWN YOUR WEAPONS AND STEP AWAY FROM THE DOG."

Naga roared again. Steve patted her shoulder. "She's not a dog!" Naga brushed Steve's waist with her shoulders and swished her tail, grateful. Carolyn smiled. *They really do get on well together.*

"They're looking for me, I 'spect." Erwin set his pistol down and waved at the pilots. Then, yelling over the rotor wash, "That's a M230 chain gun. Thirty-millimeter rounds." He held his fingers apart to illustrate. "I saw a guy get hit in the chest with one of them. All that was left was his legs."

"Tell them to go away," Carolyn said.

"Can't. No radio. They wouldn't lissen, anyway."

"You're sure you want it this way?"

Steve touched Erwin on the shoulder. "Erwin, I think you really ought to—"

Erwin shook his head. "Nothing I can do."

"OK," Carolyn said. "Fine." She turned back toward the neighborhood and spoke quietly, to no one in particular. "*Orlat keh talatti.*"

"*What?*" Steve shouted.

"'Project and defend.'"

VI

At first there was nothing.

Then, from the dark recesses of Garrison Oaks, came the sound of . . . what? *Something is coming*, Steve thought with a shiver. *Some terrible thing.* He heard it even over the helicopters, low at first, but building—the deep scream of nails wrenched from wood, the clatter and tinkle of breaking glass, thick pine cracking to splinters.

The light from the streetlamps was poor, and of course there was no moon. Even so, squinting down the street, he got a distinct sense of motion in the shadows. *Whatever it is, it's big.* He caught a flash of motion and looked over at Erwin. *He sees it too.*

The worry lines around Erwin's eyes were deep and well worn. He turned to the helicopter with the loudspeaker and waved his arms over his head. "G'wan! Get the fuck outta here!"

"Close your eyes," Carolyn said to Steve.

"What?"

The helicopters were ignoring Erwin. He changed to a more complicated hand signal. "Go on before she—"

"Steve. Close your eyes."

But she didn't wait—she stepped behind him and clapped her hand over his eyes. A bare instant later, there was a bright flash, as if a camera the size of a football field had gone off.

"Ah, fuck," Erwin said. "I'm blind."

"It's just temporary," Carolyn said. "It wasn't aimed at you. Give it a few minutes and you'll be fine."

The pitch of the helicopters' rotors began rising, the engines cycling up toward a scream.

"Are they leaving?" Steve asked, too quiet to be heard outside his own head.

"What?" Erwin said.

"IT'S JUST TEMPORARY," Carolyn said.

"WHAT? I CAN'T UNNERSTAND YA. TOO LOUD."

The searchlight that had been on them wavered a bit, then fell away entirely. Blinking, Steve looked up at the Apache. It banked to one side as if it had been called away on some urgent business. Then, neatly and professionally, it pointed its nose down, accelerated—it was surprisingly quick—and crashed into the road a hundred yards or so away. Even at this distance, the heat of the fireball was immense.

"Fuck!" Steve said. "Holy fucking fuck!"

"Ah, shit," Erwin said. "Was that what I think it was?"

A moment later the other helicopter performed a similar move—nose down, a quick acceleration, then a tidy, professional crash. In the light of the fireball Steve recognized the bluff he had jogged around that morning. Suddenly the night was uncomfortably warm. Without the rotor wash, it was once again possible to converse normally.

"I *said*, it's only temporary."

"What's only temporary?" Steve asked.

"Erwin's blindness. It's a vehicle. The signal is bespoke—it only kills hostiles, but it's blinding for everyone."

"Bespoke," Steve said. "What?"

"It means 'tailored,'" Erwin said. "What signal?"

"The light you saw. It's a defense mechanism. It radiates out from the optic nerve and activates the slave neurons."

"What?"

"Slave neurons. They make you suggestible. The light activates them—once they're part of the architecture of thought, a person will do as they're told."

"Like them bank tellers?" Erwin said.

I wouldn't have thought of that, Steve thought. Once he heard it, though, it made perfect sense. *That Erwin's a clever guy.*

"Exactly."

"What were the pilots told to do?" Steve asked.

"An expeditious suicide. Painless if possible, but immediate." Carolyn paused. "If you care, they probably didn't suffer. I'm told the overall experience is quite pleasant."

Steve felt sick. *Slave neurons?* "Jesus, Carolyn. Those guys were just doing their jobs. I mean, they probably had families, little kids and—"

She shrugged. "It was their choice."

"Carolyn, they—"

"That's the risk in working to be a dangerous person," she said. "There's always the chance you'll run into someone who's better at it than you."

Erwin's lips peeled back over his teeth in a flash of raw, simian aggression. Carolyn watched, sphinxlike.

Steve stood between them. *Dangerous people, indeed.* "Hey," he said. "What's that?"

"What?" Erwin said.

"There's something *moving* back there. In the sky. I can see it blotting out the lights from town, but I can't quite make out what it is." He turned to Carolyn. "Is it . . . like, your mother ship? Something like that?"

She ignored him and spoke to Erwin. "Are your eyes any better?"

"A little, yeah," Erwin said. "I don't think she's an alien, kid."

"Good. You should be fine in a few more minutes. Steve, head back down the hill. I'll meet you there in a few minutes."

Steve glanced at the bull, uneasy. "Carolyn, I really don't think you should—"

"Just go, Steve. I know you don't understand, but it's what Margaret wants. I'm going to give her that." Then, softening, "But you won't want to see it. Wait for me, at the bottom of the hill. I'll be along."

"What about Erwin?"

"He'll be fine in an hour or so."

"Where are we going?"

"Home."

VII

"C'mon, Naga." Steve turned his back on Carolyn and Erwin and headed down the stairs. Back on Highway 78 he took a couple of steps toward a burning helicopter, thinking to look for survivors. But even from this distance the heat from the fires was enough to curl the hair on his arms. *No one could have survived that.* He walked a little closer anyway, morbidly fascinated—then he heard a quick series of explosions. Pop! Pop-pop-pop!

Ammunition cooking off. "Ah, shit."

He turned and fled, hunched over, to the Garrison Oaks sign. He took cover with his back to the decorative stone column. He saw a bunch of people milling around in the neighborhood, and some dogs, too. They didn't seem interested in him.

A few minutes later a clanging gong sound rolled down from the top of the hill. *I guess Carolyn figured a way to shut the hatch.* Morbidly curious and suppressing a shiver, he stood and looked back up the hill. There was a new fire up there, smaller than the burning helicopters. Carolyn was walking toward him, silhouetted against its yellow flame.

She was alone.

"What did you do?" Steve said as she walked up. "Did you—"

She shook her head. "It's done. That's all. Come on." She walked past him without breaking stride. It was dark in the neighborhood. After only a few steps she was in shadow.

"What about Erwin?"

"He wouldn't come. He wants to be with his people. Come *on*, Steve."

Steve took a last look at the top of the hill. The third fire was blazing merrily now, a proper bonfire. He thought of Margaret's hand, pale skin against black bronze. He shuddered again. It occurred to him that the burning helicopters would also work very well as a roadblock. *No one's getting through that until morning, at least*, he thought. *It's just the two of us now.*

That was true in a way, but they were not alone. The dead ones were out—dozens of them, maybe hundreds—men, women, and children. They were dressed in decades-old rags—polyester, ancient denim, and paisley. One kid held an Atari joystick. The cord hung limp between his bare, dirty feet. It looked like it had been chewed. He looked up at Steve and said, "It's time for *Transformers*."

"You betcha." Steve jogged up to join Carolyn, grateful for Naga's bulk at his side. Carolyn was untying the shoelace that tethered David to the mailbox. The bubble of blackness that started at his eyes had grown, Steve saw. Now it was over two feet across. It encased his head completely, and a good bit of his chest as well.

"Don't be afraid," Carolyn said, gesturing at the people milling on the street. "They won't hurt us."

"Well, good," Steve said, dubious.

The bonfire behind them was burning merrily now, and it put out a surprising amount of light. The dead ones stood watching it, bathing their faces in its yellow glow. Some of them had tears running down their cheeks. At first he thought they might be mourning—Margaret, maybe? *Was she their Dear Leader, or something?* Then he noticed that many of them were smiling as well. *Maybe it's the kind of crying you see at weddings?* "Hey, Carolyn? Why are these guys so worked-up?"

"It's the fire. Around here fire means something."

"Oh."

There were dogs as well, Steve saw. He even recognized a few of them from before. They didn't seem to remember him, or maybe they just didn't care. They wandered freely among the people, un-petted. There were other animals as well—a fox, something that might have been a bobcat, or maybe a lynx, and—"Holy crap!"

"What?"

"Is that a tiger?"

"It is. Don't worry. He won't hurt you. He's one of the sentinels."

"Hear that? 'Don't worry.'" He and Naga exchanged glances. "What's that thing next to it?"

"It's from the future. Don't *worry*, Steve."

The animals and people and . . . other . . . milled around the street and the lawns. They moved out of the way when they saw Carolyn coming, but some of the dead ones reached out to brush her with their fingertips as she passed. They were speaking as well, muttering to themselves, one word over and over, a constant low murmur in a language he didn't know.

"What do they keep calling you?"

"Sehlani."

"What does it mean?"

"There's no good translation in English. 'Head librarian,' is literally correct, but the connotations are wrong." She made a sour face. "It's what they used to call Father."

"Oh."

And then, finally, they were at 222 Garrison Drive. What was left of it, at any rate. *The Library*, Steve thought. *At long and painful last*. Then, giving it a critical eye, *Whatever it was that came out to "project and defend" really did a number on the place*. The brick front was still standing, but that was about all. The sides and back had caved in on themselves. Behind the false front there was now only rubble.

"That's it?" Steve asked. He was a little disappointed. Even before it had crumbled into itself, the Library must have been a rather unremarkable building—a brick saltbox, four columns and a couple of windows.

Then he looked up. A few hundred yards overhead, the very large, very dark whatever-it-was swooshed by in the night. He felt the wind of its passage on his face. Suddenly he was uneasy again. "We're going in that?"

"Kind of. Not really. That up there is just a projection. The real Library is, um, distant. This doorway is the passage." She walked up the brick steps to the porch and held her hand over the doorknob. "Come on."

"A secret passage?" He rolled his eyes. "I should have known." He walked up the steps, but stopped just short of joining Carolyn and snapped his fingers as something occurred to him. He looked around. "Hey, wait a second . . ."

"What?" Carolyn said.

The porch was completely bare. *Not even a welcome mat?* "Where's that token thing? The one you sent me in here for?"

"That doesn't matter. Not anymore."

"I still want to see what it is. After all that I'm curious."

Carolyn shrugged. She pointed to the shadow at the base of one of the columns. "There."

Steve walked over and squatted down. There, almost invisible in the shadows, he found it. "It's a book?"

She smiled. "Of *course* it's a book."

He picked it up. It was old and tattered, the pages yellow with age and the grime of uncounted readings. The cover was missing, but there was something about it, something familiar . . . "Hey! I recognize this."

"Do you?"

"Yeah! I had a copy when I was a kid. It's about that horse, right? The one that gets taken away to this terrible life. *Dark Beauty*, I think?"

Carolyn turned toward him, the muscles of her calves and thighs flashing in the light of the fires, her face half in shadow. "Something like that."

Steve frowned. "It's funny. I know I read this, but I can't remember the ending."

"Are you coming?"

"Yeah," Steve said. "I guess I am. Should I bring the book?"

"No. Leave it."

"What if it rains, or—"

"Leave it. That book has been through a lot. It's tougher than it looks." She reached out to the doorknob again but stopped just short of touching it. "Are you ready?"

"Um . . . I guess. What's the big deal?"

"It's easier if I just show you." She touched the knob gently with the tips of her fingers, then took a step back.

There was a soft clicking, metallic and well oiled. The sound, perhaps, of brass tumblers aligning in the world's largest lock. The door swung open into darkness. Warm air spilled out, dry as desert wind and heavy with the scent of ancient dust.

Behind him Naga yowled, a feral, alien sound that Steve had never heard from her before.

He turned to steady her, and her fur was high, prickly under his hand. "What's wrong, girl?" But he knew. He felt it too.

"Animals don't like this place. She probably won't come in. Here, give me David."

He handed her the shoelace with David bobbing at the end. "What is . . ." He trailed off, squinting into darkness.

"Come on." Carolyn stepped inside.

Steve blinked. As she crossed the threshold she receded as if she had been shot out of a cannon. "Yeah," Steve said. "Fuck a whole bunch of that."

He turned to go, then froze. Behind him, the dead ones and the animals stood on the lawn, watching. He took a step down. One of the dogs growled, just a little. A quarter mile or so to the east and west on the highway, the Apaches blazed like bonfires. The wind was filled with the scent of burning kerosene, and every few seconds there was a pop or bang as the ammunition kicked off.

Beyond that, approaching sirens wailed. *How long would I last out there? Alone, broke, the most wanted guy in the country? Even if I don't wind up back in jail immediately, where could I go? Africa? Bolivia? The moon?*

From the hill he heard a woman's voice. He couldn't tell whether she was screaming or if it was the beginning of a song.

Steve sighed, then turned back onto the porch. "You up for this?"

Naga looked up at him for a long moment, dubious, then gave her tail a small swish.

They stepped over the threshold together.

Chapter 12

The Library

I

Thinking of how Carolyn had seemed to recede, Steve was expecting . . . something. A yank, a sense of forward motion. Something. But it wasn't like that. He stepped into darkness. A moment later he stood on dry, ancient oak. Carolyn was waiting, hands poised to catch.

"Well, that wasn't so . . ." Then, seeing where he was, he staggered back against the wall behind him. "Jeee-zus *fuck*."

"Yeah," Carolyn said, relaxing a little. "That was pretty much my reaction. At least you didn't faint. A lot of people faint." She steadied herself against a nearby bookcase and set about peeling off her leg warmers.

"What . . . I mean . . . Jesus . . . what is this place?"

"It's Father's Library." Something occurred to her. "Well . . . I suppose . . . it's mine now." She blinked. "Hmm. Mine."

"Library," Steve said, his voice flat and toneless. At his side, Naga yowled. He patted her shoulder. "Yeah, sweetie. Me too." He looked around, gaping. "Jeee-zus *fuck*," he said again, this time with real reverence.

The Library was *vast*.

It was easily the largest structure he had ever been inside, ever heard of, ever *imagined*. Bookshelves stretched across the floor as far as the eye could see. He saw a globe of light high overhead—like, skyscraper high—and a ceiling somewhere beyond that. It was impossible to estimate how far away the ceiling was—thousands of feet? Miles? The space

he stood in was higher than the Superdome, wider than the airport terminal in Atlanta. "You could fly a plane in here," he said. "Maybe not a 737,
but a Cessna—easy. Probably even a Lear."

"Yeah, I guess." Her voice was muffled by cloth.

Steve glanced over and saw that Carolyn was taking off her sweater.
He clapped a hand over his eyes. "What are you *doing*?"

"Getting out of these ridiculous clothes. Want a robe? One size fits
all, and they're clean." Cloth hit the floor with a soft rustle.

"What? No, I'm fine." He peeked, just a little. Carolyn's bicycle shorts
were puddled around her ankles. He turned his back to her and opened
his eyes. A moment later she stepped into view wearing a gray-green
robe of some rough cloth, vaguely monk-like. It suited her better than the
Christmas sweater.

"Are you hungry?" Carolyn said. "I'm starving."

"What?"

"Food," Carolyn said. She rubbed her belly with one hand. "All of a
sudden I'm starving again. Walk with me, OK? I'll show you around."

"Uh . . ." He blinked, remembering the modest house with the crumbling porch. When she had said "hidden," he had thought of an underground bunker, something like a fallout shelter. *But this* . . . "Big. How
can it be so *big*?"

"It's not *that* big. I paced it once. It's only about two miles on an edge,
give or take."

"Edge?"

"Yeah. We're in a pyramid. See?" She poked a finger up.

Following her finger he saw the pyramid's apex, three equilateral triangles meeting at a point impossibly high overhead. "Oh," Steve said. "I
see. But what I meant was"—he did some quick algebra in his head—"a
mile and three quarters is a lot of square footage for this neighborhood.
Aren't you violating the building codes? Or the laws of physics?"

"Building codes, probably. None of the wiring is grounded. But the
laws of physics don't apply in here."

"Whatever the fuck might you be talking about, Carolyn dear?"

"Can you freak out while we walk? Pretty please?" She jiggled the shoelace impatiently. David, now almost completely swallowed by blackness, bobbed at the end of it.

The floor was mostly unfinished wood planks, wide and smooth—acres of them. But he and Carolyn stood on jade, the endpoint of a main access path—road?—running the length of the floor. It was as wide as a three-lane highway, all of it neatly inlaid with jade tile. It glowed faintly underfoot. Carolyn set out down the road, walking quickly, not waiting to see if he would follow.

Steve trotted after her. "What's that?" he asked, pointing. About halfway between him and the far wall something that looked like DNA stretched up to the sky, thin and spindly. It was capped by a jade disk. *Maybe it's a lookout deck? Like on the roof of a skyscraper?* Just over the platform a cloud of lights rotated slowly, bathing the hall with a warm, candle-like glow.

"That's where we're headed."

"Man," he said. "This place is *huge*. Are we, like, still inside the house somehow?"

"No. The house wasn't important. The only thing about it that mattered was the front door. It's one of the places where the Library and normal space overlap. Defensible choke points, you see. Father was very particular about who got to see his work."

"What do you mean, 'his work'?"

Carolyn spread her arms out to the uncounted thousands of bookcases. "His work."

"*One guy* wrote all of this? There are, like, millions of books in here."

"Yeah. Like I said, Father was old. He did a few pages every day, sometimes on one thing, sometimes another. Over time it adds up."

"Wow." Here and there along the jade corridor there were teetering stacks of unshelved books, little trays for scrolls, mini shelves for folios. Naga was sniffing one such now. *Actually . . .* Her look reminded him of the one Petey got when he was about to defile the carpet. He trotted over and patted her on the shoulder. "Don't pee on the magic library, OK, sweetie?"

Carolyn, still walking, called back over her shoulder. "No such thing as magic, Steve."

"If you say so." Steve looked around, then up. He blinked. The sides of the pyramid that were *overhead* had bookshelves as well. *What, are they like nailed to the ceiling or something?* All this was half a mile or more above him, far enough that he could see that their layout made a fractal pattern, complete with little clearings here and there. Squinting, he could make out tiny couches and desks, all of them apparently immune to gravity. Three broad, ruby walkways radiated out from the geometric center of the ceiling. It was like looking down when your flight was coming in for a landing.

A couple of seconds of this gave him vertigo. He reached out to steady himself on the pile of books. He grabbed the top book, an oversize volume bound in purple leather, and set out after Carolyn, who was moving away at a surprising rate. It was too heavy to fully open while he walked, but peeking in he could see that the pages were all handwritten. "So if these aren't magic, what *are* they about?"

"Different things. There are twelve main catalogs." She glanced over. "The violet ones are mathematics—that one's a primer on alternate geometries, I think."

He cracked it open and peeked inside. "It looks medieval. Like one of those, whaddya call them, a book of hours?"

"That one's at least twenty thousand years old. And if the Inquisition caught you with it they would have started heating up the thumbscrews."

"Really?" Very curious now, he stopped at the next tall pile of books and used it as a pedestal for the book. He cracked it open at a random spot. The pages were thick vellum, crammed with neatly inked pictograms arranged in vertical rows like cuneiform, or maybe hieroglyphics. He couldn't read the writing or even guess what language it might be in. A couple of pages later he found a two-page illustration—pale ink, inlaid with gold leaf, hand-drawn and faded with age. It had a weird aesthetic, part technical diagram—neatly ruled planes, measured angles, squiggles that were probably equations—and part battle scene. Interspersed with the lines and parallelograms, an army of long-necked toothy things were clawing their way out of a hole in the sky. The forest below was littered with their corpses. A few survivors—they looked a little like giraffes—cowered before a man in black robes.

The hair on the back of Steve's neck got all prickly. *Her Father's work.*

Beside him, Naga rumbled. She was hunched over, peering into the shadows between the shelves.

Following her gaze, Steve thought he saw a hint of motion, out there in the dark. He patted Naga's neck, as much to reassure himself as to calm her. Her muscles were tense, quivery.

He glanced down the jade corridor. Carolyn hadn't stopped. Now she was half a football field away, the black ball bobbing behind her on its shoelace. "Carolyn?"

She didn't answer.

"Carolyn?" He left the book on the pile and jogged to catch up with her, wiping the fingers that had touched it on his shirt. He caught up with her faster than he would have thought possible. It occurred to him that the jade floor might be helping him along somehow, like one of those slidewalks at an airport. "I think I saw something move back there," he said, panting a little.

"Hmm? Oh. Yeah, you probably did. We have housekeepers. Remember the guy with the lawn mower? Like him. They take care of the menial stuff—dusting and shelving and the like. They try to stay out of sight when real people are around."

"Well, that's creepy as fuck. And what was up with that pict—" He broke off. "Daaaayum." They had come farther than he would have thought possible. Now the DNA spiral was just ahead of them. From here he could see that it was actually a staircase, however enormous. It hung in midair, thousands of feet tall but unsupported, leading to a vast cloud of light overhead. "What is *that?*"

Carolyn pointed at the cloud. "It's the universe. The normal one, I mean. The one you grew up in."

"Like a planetarium, or—"

"No. It's the real deal. The original."

"That's imposs . . ." He trailed off, then sighed. "How? How could a thing like that be?"

"Do you know the word 'superset'?"

"Yes. I don't know. Maybe. Not really." He rubbed his temples. "It sounds vaguely familiar."

She patted his shoulder. "Don't beat yourself up too much. It's a lot to take in, especially at first. It was the same way for me."

"Good of you to say."

"The Library is a separate universe, a superset of the one you grew up in. There's a little bit of overlap, but not much."

"A separate *universe?*"

"Yeah. There are some very dangerous, uh, people, who would do anything at all to get their hands on Father's work. He tried earthly fortresses—towers, keeps, some very advanced defense mechanisms. But anything that can be locked can be unlocked. The stakes are enormous, and there were some close calls. Eventually, he created this place."

"But . . ." He looked up at the cloud of lights overhead. "I mean . . . the universe is, like, big? Right?"

"Yes and no. Size is notional. It has to do with the structure of space. The door we came through was a gateway, but it's also sort of a transition function. You wouldn't be wrong to say that going through the transition makes you bigger."

"I feel the same size."

"Well . . . you also wouldn't really be *right* to say it either. It's sort of mathy."

Steve rolled his eyes or, perhaps, looked to the heavens for strength. "I don't *think* she's being deliberately obtuse. And the words *sound* like English . . ."

"Think of the Library as the wrapper a Big Mac comes in."

"OK. What's the Big Mac?"

"The universe. The other one."

"That's somewhat helpful," Steve said. "Thank you. As long as you're feeling comprehensible, here's another one: What are we going to do up there?"

"I need to hang David." She jiggled the shoelace, and he bobbed, weightless. The black ball had grown as they walked. Now only the bottom half of one foot was still visible, the shoelace tied to his hairy toe.

"Hang him?"

"Yeah. Plus I left some food in a cooler. And there are lawn chairs, and a barbecue grill. I thought we could have a picnic! Do you like picnics?"

"Um . . . sure. Picnics are nice, I guess."

She flashed him a smile and, to his astonishment, giggled a little. Then she started up the stairs. "Food!"

Steve looked up, daunted. Even setting aside both his fear of heights and the fact that the stairs hovered unsupported in thin air, the towering spiral was easily the tallest man-made thing he'd ever seen—three thousand feet, minimum. Probably more. *No railing, either.* The disk at the top looked small enough to hide behind his thumbnail. "You really want to walk all the way up this?"

"Yeah. It's not as bad as it looks." And indeed, in just a few seconds she'd somehow traveled upward fifty feet or more.

"No elevator?"

"No. Father thought they were ugly. I could fly you up, if you like."

He considered this. "I'll pass. Thanks, though."

"Oh, come on! It's good exercise." She bounced on tiptoes a couple of times, flexing her calf muscles. "Keep you fit! And there's steaks!"

Still he hesitated.

Carolyn said something in lion-speak, possibly about lunch. Naga started up the stairs without so much as a glance back.

"Traitor!" Steve called.

"There's also beer," Carolyn said.

"Beer?"

"Beer."

"Yeah," Steve said with a sigh. "OK."

II

It was still a bit of a climb, about the equivalent of five normal flights of stairs, but nothing like the pack-some-sammiches-and-we'll-make-a-weekend-of-it alpine ordeal he had envisioned when looking up from the base. Steve mentioned his thought about airport slidewalks. Carolyn said, "Sort of," then explained—if that was the word—that the jade surfaces changed the way distance worked. Steve said, "Oh." A few steps later he looked down to see that they were over a thousand feet up. Numb now, his only real reaction was to be grateful that there wasn't much of a breeze. Just as his calf muscles were starting to burn, they emerged at the top of the tower.

It was capped by a sort of observation platform, also jade, about a foot thick and about as wide as a football field. Steve was susceptible to vertigo in tall buildings, but this was more like being in an airliner. For some reason, that wasn't as bad. Anyway, it felt rock-solid underfoot. Over in one corner he saw a barbecue grill and half a dozen lawn chairs. His stomach rumbled.

Then he noticed something else.

Nearer the geometric center of the disk the cloud of lights hung low, close enough to reach up and touch. Under that point he saw a small brown lump on the floor. He took a couple of steps toward it, squinting. Carolyn didn't follow—she was looking up at the lights.

"Hey, who's this?" The lump was a young woman—barely more than a child, really—sleeping on the floor, curled in the fetal position. "Another one of your sisters?"

"What?" Carolyn frowned. "No. There shouldn't be anyone here. Move away, Steve." Her tone was chilly again, the way it had been in the car. "That's got to be Mithraganhi."

"Who?"

"Mithraganhi. One of Father's anointed, from the third age. Nobununga's sister, I think. She was the sun, until a couple of hours ago."

"The sun?"

"Yeah. Remember when it got dark out, a couple of hours ago? I changed her back."

"Uh . . . if you say so. What's she doing up here?"

"I don't know. She should have died up there." Carolyn walked around Steve, heading toward the girl. "She must have climbed down somehow."

"From where?"

She pointed up. Steve followed her finger, then froze. He hadn't noticed at first, but this close, the points of light in the cloud overhead weren't really points anymore. He saw now that each of them was itself a tiny swirling spiral, almost but not quite frozen. *Galaxies?* He reached up to touch one and—

"*Poru sinh Ablakha?*" The girl's voice was high, childlike. She was awake now, propped up on her elbows. She was a platinum blonde and pretty, if a trifle smudged. Her eyes were a shade of gray he'd only ever seen on battleships.

Carolyn squatted down next to her, smiling. "You'll be with him soon." She stroked the child's forehead with the back of her right hand. Her left moved to the small of her back and emerged with the obsidian knife.

What the hell? "Carolyn, *no!*"

Carolyn stabbed the girl in the neck, just once, then bounced backward, getting a surprising amount of air. She came down in a three-point stance, knife at the ready, her eyes fixed on the girl.

All three of them froze for a moment. *We're the murder exhibit at a wax museum,* Steve thought, horrified to the point of giggles. Blood squirted from the child's neck in a finger-thick stream—once, then again. It landed on the jade with a splashing sound. Another squirt. A puddle began to collect.

The girl touched her hand to her neck. Her fingers came away red. She showed them to Carolyn. "*Moru panh? Moru panh ka seiter?*"

Carolyn smiled the way a gargoyle might. "*Chah seh Ablakha.*"

The girl slumped. Another squirt of arterial spray, weaker this time.

"*Jesus!*" Steve screamed. "Carolyn, what did you *do?*" He ran for the girl, thinking, perhaps, to hold his hand over the wound, stanch the bleeding somehow. But his course took him near Carolyn. Somehow, passing her, he tripped. He hit the jade floor hard.

"It's all right, Steve."

His front tooth was rough now, newly chipped. He tasted blood. "*All right?* It's not all right! That kid is just a *kid*, Carolyn. What did she ever do to you?" He felt Naga near him, muscular and violent.

Carolyn spoke without emotion. "She's sixty thousand years old, and she's loyal to Father."

"*So. Fucking. What?*" He wasn't quite screaming.

Carolyn blinked. "You have no idea what the stakes are, Steve. You don't understand about Father, how dangerous this is."

"She's just a kid, Carolyn!" Steve scrabbled to his feet and went to the girl. She clutched at his sweatpants with one bloody hand, pleading in a language he didn't know. Her lips were blue.

Steve lifted her hand away, inspected the wound. Her carotid artery gaped open, a lipless mouth. "Hold still," he said. "I'll—"

Carolyn put her hand on his shoulder. "Don't. It'll be over in a minute." She didn't threaten him with the knife.

"Can I . . . would you mind if I just held her hand?" Naga paced between him and Carolyn, guarding him.

"No," Carolyn said. "Too dangerous."

Steve hesitated for a second, then took the girl's hand anyway. He could hear Carolyn's teeth gritting, but she didn't move to stop him. Mithraganhi's hand was small, birdlike in his palm. She looked at him with her gray eyes, pleading.

"I don't know what to do," Steve said to her. "I'm so sorry."

"*Moru panh?*" she said again. Her voice was fading.

"What's she saying?"

"It means 'Why are you doing this?'" Carolyn said.

"I'm so sorry." Steve reached out to her cheek, but she flinched away from his touch. Her eyelids drooped.

Then she was gone.

"There," Carolyn said. "That's done."

Steve shut the girl's eyes, then looked at his hands. They were red. He showed them to Carolyn. "Yeah. I guess so."

Seeing the look on his face, she seemed to return to herself a little bit. Her face fell. "You don't understand," she said again.

"*You got that right.*" He was thinking, *However handy she might be with that knife, I'm a lot bigger than she is.* He was thinking, *We're not that far from the edge.*

Carolyn's expression darkened. Her hand drifted to the small of her back. "Don't."

"Don't what?" His tone was pleasant.

"Just don't. OK? I won't kill you, but I'll hurt you if I have to. I don't want to—I *really* don't want to—but I will." Then, pleading, "Steve . . . let me explain."

"OK," he said. "Fine."

"Mithraganhi might have looked like a child, but she wasn't."

"What, then?"

She rubbed her forehead. "I'm not sure. Not exactly. The records are lost, or maybe destroyed. But she was important. She was one of Father's key lieutenants. If she was still loyal to him—and there's no reason to think anything else—she might have found a way to bring him back."

"OK. All right. Fine. But . . . so what?"

Carolyn boggled at him, laughed a little. "We really are from different worlds, you know that?"

"Yes. Yes, that thought has crossed my mind once or twice as well. Can you maybe try to explain it to me? Small words?"

"Father was . . ." She trailed off, then laughed a little. "You know, I know literally every word ever spoken, but I can't think of a single one that's adequate to your question. Father was Father."

"That's not much help."

"I know." Carolyn held her hand up. "Give me a minute." She pinched her chin for several seconds, then looked up at him. "When one of my brothers was about nine, Father tasked him with convincing a Deep One to accept him as an apprentice."

"Deep One?"

"A giant squid. Sort of."

"Oh."

"Michael tried and tried, but the Deep One wouldn't go for it. Something to do with the Forest God, or maybe he just hated people. Probably that was the real lesson, but we still didn't understand how Father worked. We were young then. My brother tried to explain the situation, but Father wouldn't listen. He said my brother was 'not properly motivated.'" She shuddered.

"You OK?"

"I just—even hearing those words, you know? 'Not properly motivated.' I want to throw up."

"You can stop if you want."

"No. Thanks, but no. You need to understand this." She was looking up at the lights overhead. The iron was back in her voice.

"So . . . what happened?"

"He got a hot poker and burned out Michael's eyes."

"*What?* Jesus! He *blinded* the kid?"

"Yeah. Blinded him. Well—not the way you probably mean. Not permanently."

"How can that—"

"The white catalog, Jennifer's catalog, is medicine. *Exotic* medicine. None of our physical wounds were ever permanent. Father could heal anything. Jennifer was even better."

"That's convenient."

"Well . . . I suppose. Yes. It had its moments. But there are costs, too. *Philosophical* costs."

"Now I really don't understand."

Carolyn knelt at the puddle of the child's blood. Her back was to him, but the blood was still, not yet coagulated, shiny. He could see her face reflected in it. "It was different for us. For you, Americans, if things get bad enough . . . well. You always have an out."

"Suicide?"

"Death."

"But . . . you guys didn't?"

"No. Father burned Michael's eyes out. Every night, over and over. The rest of us had to attend him, had to watch. Each time took about twenty minutes—the first eye was quick, but after that Michael had to. To. To watch. One-eyed, you see. He'd watch as Father, um, Father, you know, heated the poker back up. The next morning Jennifer would grow them both back. Both eyes, you see. And then they'd do it again." The muscles of her back bunched and coiled like thick snakes under her robe as she spoke.

"What happened? How did it end?"

Carolyn snarled. In the puddle of child's blood Steve saw a flash of white teeth, reflected. "Michael became *motivated*." She spat the words out like someone vomiting up rotten food. "After eleven days of this my brother concocted a way to bow the Deep One to his will."

She was trembling. It crossed his mind to go to her, to touch her shoulders and offer comfort, but he didn't quite dare. "That's the worst thing I ever heard of."

"That," Carolyn said, "is Father. He wasn't even really angry. It was routine. Just a discipline thing. Do you see?"

Steve thought about it before he answered. "Yeah. Maybe I do. A little bit, anyway. And this kid, what's her name—Mythronnie?"

"Mithraganhi."

"She's buddies with this guy?"

"Well . . . she *was*."

Steve groaned, feeling sick. He went to the edge of the platform and looked down. "I went up to the top of the World Trade Center once," he said. "This is higher."

"Yes. A lot."

"Let's say I believe you. About the girl."

"Do you?"

"I don't know. Maybe. She looked harmless to me." He shrugged. "But I'm not used to being up this high. Maybe the rules are different up here. Are they?"

"I don't know that there are any rules," Carolyn said. "I won. That's the only rule I'm aware of."

"Why me?" He spoke softly. "Why am I here? I don't understand."

"You're a klutz, Steve. I needed someone to drop the magazine. I couldn't do it myself, couldn't even look at it. David might have seen it, in my mind."

"That's *it*? You expect me to believe that you dragged me into this because I'm *clumsy*? That's why you ruined my *life*?"

"Oh, you're exaggerating."

"EXA—" Steve cut himself off. *Peace of mind is not the absence of conflict, but the ability to cope with it.* That helped a little bit. "You fucking framed me for fucking murder, Carolyn, and then tried to get me eaten alive by wild dogs. Remember?" He patted Naga on the shoulders. "Naga remembers."

Naga shoulder-bumped Steve in solidarity. The two of them glared at Carolyn.

"OK, fine, yes, there is a bit more to it than just that you're clumsy."

"Well. That's progress." He and Naga exchanged a glance. "Do, please, go on. Why me?"

"I'll explain. I really will. But first, I need to hang David." She wiggled the shoelace. Blackness had swallowed him completely, even his last hairy toe.

Steve felt his eyes go wide. The blackness around David had grown noticeably in just the last few minutes. Now, even from five feet away Steve felt the heat. It was like a furnace. He took a half step back. "What's happening to him?"

"Remember how I said he was frozen in time?"

"Uh . . . I guess." The blackness around David had a fluid quality, the surface swirling.

"And do you remember what he was doing when I froze him?"

"Is this a quiz?"

"More like a teaching method. You'll understand better if I pull it out of you. Do you remember?"

"Well . . . yeah, I guess. He was dying, right? And you'd just given him a little zap in the pain center of his brain. You said it was 'the theoretical upper limit of suffering.'" Then, under his breath, "I mean . . . *damn*."

"Exactly. But here's the difference. Suffering—normal suffering—is transient. What we perceive as emotion is just a quick connection between three-dimensional space and one of the higher physical planes—rage, joy, pleasure, whatever. The repercussions can echo for years, but the actual link usually only lasts for a fraction of a second." She gave her gargoyle smile again. "Usually."

"But . . . not this time?"

"Exactly." She jiggled the black sphere. "Time isn't passing inside this. And I got it just right, too. David is connected to pure anguish, and *he can't move on*." She looked at Steve expectantly.

Steve thought about this for a good long while, then gave up. "Um. So what?"

"So," she said, "the potential energy between the planes will continue to be realized. It's like a capacitor with an infinite charge."

"Energy." He looked at David, now completely swallowed by blackness. The ball had grown visibly while they talked, and it was warmer now. "You mean, the black stuff? That's energy?"

"Exactly."

"How big will it get?"

"I'm not sure. A million miles, give or take. That's why we came up here. We need to set him in the heavens, where there's room."

"Come again?"

"By this time tomorrow, David will be our new sun."

III

She reached into the cloud of stars overhead and made a shooing motion with her hand. The lights spun at her touch, not unlike the lazy Susan on the big corner table at a Chinese restaurant. When she had the right spot, she poked up a finger to stop the spinning, and pulled. Space rushed past them, the scale of the things they saw shrinking—first whole galaxies, then clouds, then individual stars, and finally planets. "Recognize that one?"

"Uh . . . Jupiter?" His lips felt numb.

"No, it's Saturn. See the rings?"

"Right. Saturn. That's what I meant."

"It's OK. Now, hush for a second. I need to concentrate."

Steve watched as she took David by the shoelace—only a few inches were still poking out—and pushed him gently through the thin membrane separating the reality Steve had grown up in and the Library. David seemed to shrink as he passed through.

"There we go," she said, and dusted her hands off theatrically. "All done!"

"How long before he's the sun?"

"I'm not sure. At least a couple of hours. I'll come back and fix the orbits later. Can't have the wee little marbles bumping into one another, can we?"

Steve, who was a plumber, spoke through dry lips. "No. I guess not. When does he turn bright and yellow?"

Her face fell, a little. "Well . . . he doesn't."

"What do you mean? He's going to stay like that? All black, like?"

"Yeah. It's a plane-of-anguish thing."

"Where will the light come from?"

She frowned. "There, ah, won't be quite as much. Light, I mean. Plenty of heat—anguish is very hot—and gamma radiation, and all of that, but there's not much for the visible spectrum."

"It's going to be dark *all the time?* Even when the sun's up? Forever?"

"It'll be warm enough," she said defensively. "No one will freeze. And people will adjust."

"*Adjust.*"

She nodded. "You can adjust to almost anything."

Steve looked, but he couldn't find an answer in himself for that.

After a long time, Carolyn spoke again. "Well . . . that brings me to the other reason I brought you up here."

"The food?"

"No. Well, yeah. That too. But the bigger reason is . . . I want to make a gift to you, Steve. I know you don't understand—I'm still getting to that part—but I owe you a great deal. It really wouldn't be an exaggeration to say that I owe you everything. I've thought about this day for a very long time and, I . . . I wanted to say that . . . well, it would make me very happy if I could pay you back in some small way. I brought you up here so that you'd see David's ascension." She watched him, smiling and serious.

"OK. Why?"

"The next time you see the sun rise you'll believe that I mean it when I say that I will give you anything—absolutely *anything*—you can think to ask for."

"You mean like a Maserati, or—"

"Sure, if you like. But more than that." She leaned in close. "I can make you immortal. Invincible. Both, if you like. There are things in the apothecary that will make you smarter than the smartest man who ever lived."

"Uh . . ." The moment dragged out. "Right now I just want some barbecue."

He noticed for the first time that Carolyn was sort of pretty when she laughed.

. . .

"PRETTY GOOD," STEVE said. He licked his fingers. There had been steaks in the cooler, but also some things that looked like a giant scorpion and tasted a bit like pork. Carolyn said it had died out in the Pleistocene era, but it was one of her favorites. Steve didn't ask. It *was* good, though, if a lot of food. Naga ate three of the things by herself, plus two steaks and eight hamburgers. Then she curled up like a housecat and went to sleep. Steve debated giving her his leftovers but decided not to wake her. *Poor kitty. She's had a tough day.*

"Glad you like it," Carolyn said. "Thanks for cooking."

"De nada." Whatever other skills she might possess, it was pretty obvious that Carolyn was a lousy cook. After she'd burned two sets of burgers Steve took over behind the grill. Now he settled back into his lawn chair with a contented sigh. At first he hadn't been crazy about sitting this close to the edge, but with a couple of beers in him he relaxed a little. *It really is a fantastic view.* The universe spun above them, casting a warm glow on the labyrinthine shelves below.

Carolyn fished around in the ice chest and came up with a wine cooler. "Another beer?"

"Yeah, sure. I'll get to it eventually." He took a couple of swallows of Bud Light and burped softly, tasting extinct scorpion meat. "So . . . about this gift. Could you make me be president?"

"Of what?"

"The United States."

"Sure, if you like. I can't imagine why you'd want to be, though."

"Good point. How about Emperor of the Earth?"

"Easy-peasy."

"Hmm." He thought about it for a minute. "Could I be faster than a speeding bullet and leap tall buildings in a single bound? And be able to shoot lasers out of my eyes?"

"Lasers?"

"Well, I think it's technically heat vision. And freeze breath. Could you do freeze breath?"

She nodded. "Sure. It would take me a couple of weeks, but I could put all that together. Is that what you'd like?"

"Uh . . . no. I was kidding."

"Well. OK. You can't help yourself, I get that. Just so that you know *I'm* serious. Absolutely anything at all. When we were kids, sometimes Father would play a game where he'd ask us to make up some impossible thing for him to do. If we stumped him, we got a prize." She looked at him. "No one ever did, though. Not ever. Not *once*."

"Ride a flying alligator through a flying doughnut made of chorizo?"

"Body modification is on the pearl floor, radial three, branch seven. Gravity is radial two, branch three. That covers antigravity as well. Charcuterie is somewhere on turquoise," she said, searching his face with her eyes. "I'd have to look it up."

"Anything." All joking was gone from his voice. "Anything at all."

She nodded.

"That's . . . wow. That's a really nice gift, Carolyn. Thank you." He drained his beer, picked up the next one.

"You're welcome. I'm glad you like it. Are you overwhelmed yet?"

"For days now. Why?"

"If you'd like, I can go into a little more detail. About what's been going on, I mean. Answer your questions, if you have any. Why you . . . and all of that."

Steve cracked his beer, spraying himself with cold foam. "That'd be great. But won't it break you, or something?"

"What?"

"If you stop being really, really confusing all the time. Won't it hurt?"

She held up her second-smallest finger.

"What are you doing?"

"I think it's called 'flipping the bird.' Am I not doing it right?"

"Middle finger."

She adjusted. "Better?"

"Yeah, you got it." He paused, thinking. "OK, I've got one. It seems like you know all about, y'know, the regular world—who's president, how to use a phone, all that—except when you don't. I mean, that first night you were having trouble getting the car door open. How does that work?"

She smiled. "Well . . . sometimes I might have been playacting a little bit—pretending to be more helpless than I really was. In case someone was watching, or whatever. They all think—thought—that I'm very sheltered. I'm not supposed to know much about anything except languages. But there were also some genuine gaps. I figured maybe 'Mr. Cell' was some guy who made the phone you plug into the wall, you know? They didn't have the portable ones when I was a kid." She rolled her eyes. "And I don't think I'll *ever* get you guys' idea of clothes."

"So, you were an actual kid? You're not from outer space?"

"Yeah, um, no. That's ridiculous. Whatever gave you that idea?"

"I dunno. TV, or something. Well . . . are you guys all possessed by demons? Or maybe something magical?"

"Oh God. Shut up before you embarrass yourself."

"I'm sorry," he said, meaning it. "I just . . . Carolyn, I can't begin to imagine something that would explain . . . all this."

"No. Not a demon. And, like I said, there's no such thing as magic."

"What, then?"

"I'm . . . it's like I told you that first night. I wasn't lying. I'm a librarian."

Steve considered this. "I think we're using that word in different ways."

She nodded. "Yeah. Probably."

"When I say librarian, I think . . ."

" 'Tea and cozy mysteries'?"

"Right. Exactly. See? You *do* understand."

"Not really. I like tea well enough, but . . . I don't really know what a 'cozy mystery' is. That's just what you said, the first night, at Warwick Hall. That's what you think of when you say 'librarian.'" She looked at him the way a small animal might look up, hiding in its burrow. "But it wasn't like that," she whispered. "Not at all."

"Yeah," Steve said, leaning back. "I'm starting to get that. But maybe you should tell me what it *was* like. So I won't ask so many dumb questions?"

She hesitated for a long time, looking into the middle distance. But eventually she nodded. "Yeah. Part of me wants to. Really." She opened her mouth, frowned, shut it.

"But . . . ?"

"It's just . . . I always had to hide what I was thinking, planning. I had to hide *everything*, even from myself. Always. Do you understand?" There was a pleading quality to her voice that he'd never heard before.

"I don't think that I do," Steve said softly.

"No. Of course not. How could you?" She nodded to herself one more time. "I don't even know where to start."

"The beginning?"

"All right," she said. She drew in a deep breath, and when she spoke the iron was back in her voice. "The beginning, then. When I was a little girl, about nine or ten years old, I spent a summer living in the forest. This was about a year after Father took us in, just after our parents died. I made friends with two deer, Isha and Asha, they were called, and . . ."

CAROLYN TALKED FOR hours. Steve thought she might have glossed over some stuff—what, exactly, did she mean by "heart coal"?—but she told him a great deal. She told him about David and the bull. She told him how Margaret's madness ate away at her little by little until one day licking tears from the cheeks of dead men was fun. She talked a little about how Michael came to look at indoor things with feral, haunted eyes. Speaking in detached, clinical terms, she told him the things David had done, showed him the ink spots on her forearms where he had nailed her to the desk with her pens.

In the small hours of the morning she came at last to Erwin, who had been her thunder of the east.

"Well," she said, downing the last of her wine, "aren't you going to tell me what an asshole I am?"

Steve shook his head. "No. I'm not. Other people might, but I'm not."

She waited for a beat, then two. "But?"

"But nothing. I'm kind of a shitty, bush-league Buddhist, Carolyn, but one of the first things they tell you is to try to look at other people with compassion. Not 'pity'—that can be sort of a tough distinction to make, at least at first—but compassion. In your case that's not hard. I probably would have shot myself about five minutes after I saw that kid get roasted alive. I literally cannot imagine what that must have been like."

"Peter *did*," Carolyn said softly. "Jennifer too, I think."

"What?"

"Shot themselves. After the bull. Well, Jennifer used poison." She looked up at him, lost. "Father brought them back. Then he punished them—fifty lashes or something. I forget."

"But not you."

"Not me what?"

"You never tried killing yourself? Or running away some other way?"

"No. Never." Carolyn's eyes were like granite, against which soft things might smash and be broken. "My work was still before me, you see."

Right now she isn't acting, Steve realized. *This is what she is when she doesn't have to pretend.* He said "Jesus," very softly. *Roasted the kid alive?* He felt numb.

Carolyn shut her eyes. When she opened them again the shields were back up. "I think it's time for bed."

"No, I didn't—"

"It's OK. I really am tired." Wan smile. "This was a big day for me. And . . . I'm just . . . I don't talk much. I almost never talk about myself. I feel, I don't know . . ."

"Vulnerable?"

Long pause. "Yeah. That."

"I'm sorry."

"Don't be. It isn't your fault. It's just . . . I'm not big on . . . whatever you call it."

"Basic human contact?"

"Whatever. It makes me uncomfortable. But you asked, and I told you, and now you know."

Steve nodded.

"One thing I *am* sorry for, though, is that I put you through so much," she said. "It must have been confusing. Upsetting. I probably could have handled your part of this better."

"Oh? Do you think so? Do you *really?*"

"Steve, I—"

"Just, y'know, for future reference, I probably would have done your little jog for a small fee. Two hundred bucks, maybe? All that stuff with framing me for murder was overkill." He nodded his head a couple of times, wide-eyed and exaggerated. "Yup. Overkill. Big-time."

"OK, sure, but if you hadn't been resurrected, the dead ones would have—"

"Wait. Hold up. If I hadn't been *what?*"

"Um . . . nothing."

"What did you *say*, Carolyn?"

She reached out, almost but not quite touching him. "Steve?"

"Hmm?"

"I'll tell you if you want. But you'd be happier not knowing."

He considered this for a long moment. "Yeah. OK. Coming from you, I'm prepared to accept that." He rubbed his temples. "Anyway, I've got the mother of all consolation prizes."

"Right. Have you got any ideas about what you might want?"

"No. Not really."

"OK. Well, think about it. We'll talk more tomorrow."

"Did you bring, like, sleeping bags or something?"

"What? Oh. No. There are dormitories below the jade floor. I made one up for you, American-style."

"How do you mean?"

"Well . . . I sort of borrowed a penthouse. Out of a hotel, I mean. Have you heard of the Al Murjan? It's supposed to be really nice. C'mon, I'll show you."

IV

"Good night," she said. "I'll be upstairs if you need anything."

"You're not going to bed?"

"Not just yet. I have a couple of things to take care of first."

"Thanks." Steve shut the door with a small measure of relief. The "hall" below the jade floor was like being inside the metal artery of some giant beast. But she was right—the penthouse, wherever she had gotten it, *was* really nice, if perhaps a trifle exotic for his taste. *The couch alone is probably worth more than my apartment.* It was comfy, though—Naga fell asleep on it immediately. Steve made himself a drink and explored a little, then plopped down next to her. Naga stopped snoring, then raised her head and showed him a fang.

He rubbed her between the ears. "Go back to sleep, grumpypants."

All of the writing on the remote was in Arabic, but On buttons aren't hard to figure out. The TV also had a split-screen feature. After a bit of fumbling he set it up to watch CNN, Fox, and Al Jazeera all at once.

David's damnation had progressed, it seemed. Now he was visible to the naked eye. It was still night in Virginia, but in places like Sydney, Beijing, and Fiji crowds of commuters drifted slack-jawed and motionless through city streets, watching the black dawn of this new age. As promised, David was warm enough and about sun-sized. But even at his brightest he was very faint, a dark gray disk against the backdrop of stars.

CNN had a bunch of astrophysicists on teleconference. Anderson Cooper was polling them about why the sun was black all of a sudden. What, pray tell, was up with that? Some guy from Harvard was going on about dark matter, how poorly understood it was.

Steve listened to him for a few minutes, then saluted him with his scotch. "A valiant effort."

He flipped channels for an hour or so, increasingly drunk but too wound-up to sleep. MTV was doing a *Beavis and Butt-Head* revival, complete with videos. There was, of course, endless footage of the fire at the White House, the explosion at the Capitol. There had been a small earthquake in California—nothing to get excited about, really! They had some footage of the black sun filmed from the little cupola thing on the International Space Station, which was pretty. The vice president was governing from a secure, undisclosed location. A couple of Norwegian snowboarders claimed that they saw part of a glacier get up and walk away. That was obviously ridiculous, but before and after photos showed that a big chunk of the glacier in question had indeed gone missing. Also the moon might be just a bit wobbly. Gravitational anomalies, perhaps caused by the solar incident, were suspected—

"Yeah," Steve said. "Fuck this." He went out the double doors of the penthouse, leaving them open in case Naga got restless. "Carolyn?" he called.

The metal hall of the dormitories was rounded, arterial, maybe a hundred yards long. It was very dark.

"Carolyn?"

No answer. He went anyway, padding down the uneven metal in his socks. He was much drunker than he had realized, it seemed, but he found that if he moved at a deliberate pace he didn't stumble too badly. At the far end of the hall oak stairs, rounded and smoothed by the passage of uncounted bare feet, floated in midair. Steve climbed them to stand among the stacks of the Library.

He had worried about how he might find her in that vast space, but it wasn't hard. Carolyn hovered a couple hundred yards above the floor, spinning in place like a figure skater doing a pirouette. Her arms were thrust above her in a *V*. The loose, oversized sleeves of her robe fluttered as she spun. She was shouting at the top of her lungs, babbling in a language Steve didn't recognize, still covered in David's blood, now dry and clotted. Tears streamed down her cheeks. Steve couldn't tell whether she was sobbing or laughing. *Maybe both?* Beneath her, the jade floor glowed. Looking up, Steve saw the universe he knew, hanging suspended in the center of the Library. Carolyn's shadow lay over it like black wings.

Steve watched this for a time. He had come out there meaning to speak with her, to explain to her how bad things were outside, explain her mistake. They would have a laugh, after. But seeing her like this he could think of nothing at all that he might say. Eventually he turned, fled back down the metal hall to the "penthouse," and slammed the door behind him. Naga raised her head at the sound.

He went into the bathroom, slamming that door behind him as well, then bent double over the toilet and threw up—once, twice, again. He spat thick drool into the bowl. Oily sweat beaded his forehead. He thought of Carolyn spinning, cackling, thought of the dispassionate, just-relaying-information tone in which she told of ax murders at dinner, told of children roasted alive.

Seeing her at the bar that first night he had thought, naturally enough, that she was like him. He understood now how wrong that was.

He went back out to the living room. Naga was waiting for him, wide-awake, real concern in her eyes. Steve opened a bottle of water and patted her hindquarters. "It's OK. I'm OK."

But he wasn't. He was beginning to understand, and he wasn't OK. *We're the only ones in here*, he thought. *No help. No one else is coming.* "What are we gonna do, huh? What are we gonna do?"

Naga didn't answer.

Back on CNN Anderson Cooper had gotten around to an old woman with bright-blue eyes. She had the words "Gretl Abendroth" and "Lucasian Professor" written under her head. She was answering Anderson's question, or trying to. Choking with laughter, tears streaming from her eyes, she said that the other professors were fools, said that current theory could never be stretched to include the black sun. She cackled at them, saying, "Admit it," saying, "You don't know any more than I do. Our understanding is a bad joke. It always has been."

Some of the panelists took offense to this. One of them said she sounded like a superstitious peasant. Another said something like "OK, maybe it's *not* dark matter; why didn't she explain it to them if she was so goddamn smart?" Anderson Cooper nodded, concerned.

Abendroth went quiet. Steve, a longtime viewer of talk shows, thought she might be on the verge of tears. But when she spoke she sounded calm enough.

"I think perhaps God is angry."

Steve suddenly wanted very much to buy Dr. Abendroth a drink. In all the world, she was the only other person who really got it. "Well," Steve said, "you're not wrong. But it's worse than that." He cast a shifty, paranoid glance into the shadows. "I think she might be *out of her fucking mind*."

Hearing himself say this, the thought came to him fully formed as from the void: *The vocabulary of such a creature would be different from what I am used to, different from what I know.*

It was in that moment that he first began to understand what he had to do.

Chapter 13

Sing, Sing, Sing!

A little over a month later, Carolyn walked down the stairs from the Library proper to the dormitories. She was lugging a good-sized cardboard box, too big to see over. She probed each step with her toe.

The box held a bowl of popcorn, two bottles of Everclear, and half a carton of Marlboros. Steve had asked for the booze and smokes, but the popcorn was her idea. She didn't hold out much hope that he'd be grateful, but she thought there was a reasonable chance he might at least be civil.

She'd thought of calling down to him for some help, then decided against it. Steve didn't like the stairs. It bothered him that they hung in midair, unsupported. Steve said this "weirded him out."

This wasn't surprising. The list of things that Steve found objectionable was long and growing. It included the Library itself ("How can the furniture hang on the ceiling like that? It's creepy."); the jade floor ("Jade isn't supposed to glow."); the apothecary ("What the hell is *that* thing? I'm out of here."); the armory (David's trophies made him throw up); the Pelapi language ("It sounds like cats fighting"); her robes ("Did you borrow those from Death?" She hadn't.); and, of course, Carolyn herself.

Just ask. He'd tell you aaaaaaaaaaaalllll about it.

"My *robes*?" she muttered, peeping over the top of the box, trying to find her footing. "What's wrong with my *robes*? They're just robes, for gosh sakes."

Carolyn vaguely remembered the way it had been for her at first—the vast spaces of the main hall, the sick, rudderless feeling of having everything she knew snatched away. It was disorienting, sure. *But you'd think that after a month he'd be starting to adjust.*

He hadn't, though. Transporting the penthouse had been a hassle, but now she was glad she had gone to the trouble. Steve seemed determined to set up camp in there.

When she was younger, forming her plans and preparing, she had sometimes daydreamed about the things the two of them would do when they were together—picnics, little vacations, reading together by the fire. Instead, he mostly got drunk and played video games.

Well, not always. Sometimes he and Naga came up to play in the stacks, a cat's game where they took turns hiding in the shadows and pouncing on each other. And today the two of them were just back from a three-day trip to the Serengeti. Steve had invited her to come along, but when she said she was too busy his relief had been obvious.

She thought of Jennifer's voice, soft and pitying: *She has a heart coal.* And, worse, *It never works out the way you would think.*

"Fuck you, Jennifer," Carolyn said. "I'll figure something out. I always do."

The slick metal of the dormitory hall still felt homey underfoot after her months on American carpet and asphalt. Steve, of course, hated that, too.

The polished wood and precise lines of Steve's door looked alien against the hall's organic smoothness. She set the box down and checked her reflection in one of the bottles. She'd had one of the dead ones do her hair. It seemed like a good idea at the time but . . .

Well . . . it's different. The problem, she decided, was that she wasn't really sure what hair was supposed to look like. *It's not bad, right? I mean . . . it's at least tidy.* Well, maybe. But she thought that it also smacked of desperation. *And what are you going to do if this doesn't work out, Carolyn? What then?* "I'll make it work," she said again.

But she didn't sound sure.

She sniffed her armpits—they, at least, were good—then breathed out a stiff breath and arranged her face in something like a smile. Knock-knock.

After a long time Steve opened the door, just a crack. "Hi."

"Hi! Can I come in?"

"Why do you bother asking?" At the side of his neck his carotid artery was pulsing. His sweat smelled like fear. "You could just come in. I couldn't stop you, right? No one could."

"I . . . I wouldn't do that. Not to you." Her heart sank. *Is he really afraid of me?* She shook her head. *Of course not. That's just silly.* She let a little of the misery she felt show in her face.

Steve's expression softened, a little. "Yeah. Well. OK. Come on in."

Stepping inside, she stifled the urge to wrinkle her nose. The room stank of stale smoke and lion piss. She had brought in a kiddie pool and several pallets of Fresh Step, but by the time they convinced Naga to try it, the carpet was a lost cause.

"Have a seat." Steve flopped down.

"Thanks." It was a large sofa, but Carolyn chose to sit close to him. Back in the shadows, Naga studied her with golden hunter's eyes.

"How was Africa?"

"Dark," Steve said. "How did you think it would be?"

"Steve, I—"

He held up a hand. "Sorry. Forget I said anything. Naga had a great time, though. She met up with an aunt of hers. And we ate some wildebeest."

"How was that?"

"Naga loved it. It was a little undercooked for my taste, but it was very, very fresh."

"Wait—they took you *hunting*?"

"Yeah. Actually they insisted."

"*Wow.*"

"What?"

"That's a huge honor, Steve." Michael had lived in the veldt for two years before he was granted an apprenticeship—and that was with the benefit of an introduction from Nobununga. "*Huge.*"

"Yeah? Well, that's nice."

She waited, but he didn't elaborate. Mentally, she shrugged. *Fine.* On the coffee table a three-ring binder lay open, surrounded by overflowing ashtrays. "How's the studying going?"

"I'm making progress." He turned and rumbled to Naga in the language of the hunt: "Thank you for not eating me today."

Naga's voice came from the darkness: "Your affection is not meaningless to me, puny one. I shall devour you another day."

"Not bad," Carolyn said. Steve's accent was thick, but his pronunciation was better than she would have expected. "I think you've got a knack for this. The cat dialects are tricky." She eyed the three-ring binder. He was well past the halfway point. "How soon before you need the next one?"

"Another week or so, I think."

"OK. I'll get started on volume two. You'll like that one. It covers hunting." Michael's texts tended to be about half diagrams, so translating them went relatively quickly. Even so, it was time she couldn't really afford.

"Thanks."

"You're welcome."

Uncomfortable silence.

This time Steve cracked first. "So . . . what's up with the Farrah Fawcett do?"

"What? I—I'm sorry, I don't understand what that means."

Steve traced the air next to her head. "Farrah Fawcett? The chick from the poster? Your hair is . . ." Seeing her expression, he trailed off. "Ah, forget it." He sighed. "You look, um, nice, is all."

She could tell he was lying, but it didn't sound like a cruel lie. "Thank you," she said, which was safe enough. "Would you like some popcorn?" She peeled the Tupperware lid off the bowl and held it out to him.

He looked at her. "*Popcorn?*"

"Sure. Don't you like it?"

"No, it's not that." He hesitated. "I just didn't figure you for a popcorn kind of gal, is all."

"Well . . . it's been a while. My mother used to make it, when I was young. I remember that. I thought you might enjoy something, you know, familiar."

"Yeah, sure."

She set the bowl on the coffee table. He dug out a handful.

"Thanks, it's good."

They munched for a little while.

"Have you thought any more about what we talked about?" Steve affected a casual tone when he said this, but he wasn't fooling anyone.

Mentally, Carolyn rolled her eyes. Steve refused to let go of the idea that David's light might be made yellow somehow. He brought it up every time they were together, at least once. "Steve, even if I wanted to, I couldn't." At this point, she almost *did* want to. *Forsake a revenge that was fifteen years in the making? Sure! Anything to shut him up.* "It's just not technically possible. Why is that so hard for you to accept?"

He gave a knowing smirk, like she was hiding something but he was too clever for her. She felt like throttling him.

"Well, Carolyn, the last sun we had was yellow, and the sky seems to be full of stars that are—"

"The circumstances were different, Steve. David's spirit is crushed, and half his head is missing. Forging a connection to any plane besides anguish is going to be a problem."

"But what if you—"

"*Enough*, Steve." Then, calmer, "It's not going to happen."

They sat silently for a while, munching popcorn and not looking at each other.

It was Naga who broke the silence: "My Lord Hunter? Have you given my question to the dark one?"

"Not yet, sweetie. I'm getting to it. Give me a minute, OK? Remember what we said."

Naga bared her teeth. "Very well."

Carolyn gaped at them.

"What?"

"Did you hear what she *called* you?"

Steve shook his head. "Er . . . no? I mean, I heard it, but I still have a lot of gaps in—"

"She called you 'My Lord Hunter.'"

"Awww," Steve said, skritching Naga's ears. "Thanks, sweetie. That's nice." Then, seeing the look on Carolyn's face, "What?"

"You really don't understand."

He shrugged. "How is this surprising?"

" 'My Lord Hunter' is . . . it's like an honorific. More than an honorific. It's a term of extreme respect. Lions only dust it off for special occasions."

"Oh." He frowned. "So, it's a big deal?"

"Yeah, Steve. It's a big deal. It's the lion equivalent of getting your face carved on Mount Rushmore. And calling a person that . . . wow. I've never heard of such a thing. Never. What did you *do*?"

Steve shifted. "Er. Nothing. Not really." Then, in a small voice, "We just talked."

"About *what*?"

"Stuff."

"Naga, what did he do?"

The lion looked at her. "My Lord Hunter will be the one to save us all. It has been foreseen. He will—"

"Naga!" Steve spoke sharply, cutting her off. "We said I was going to handle this, remember?"

Naga swished her tail, faded back into the shadows.

"Handle what, exactly?" Carolyn's tone was artificially bright.

Steve put down the popcorn bowl. "Have you been watching the news?"

Inwardly, she groaned. The last time they talked she had promised that she would, and she had meant it. But she'd gotten distracted running down a rumor about the Duke, and . . . "I'm sorry. It must have slipped my mind."

Steve's jaw muscles jumped. But all he said was, "It's OK. I know you're busy. Would you mind if we took a look now? I want to show you something."

She forced a small smile. "Sure."

He pressed a button and the screen lit up. "Do you like the television? It's big!" It was, in fact, huge. She had hoped that this would please him—Americans liked garish things, right?—but he didn't seem to care at all.

"Yeah, it's great." He flipped through channels. "Here, this is a good one. Watch this."

The writing at the bottom of the screen said FOOD RIOTS IN OREGON. There was handheld video of the inside of a supermarket. The shelves were bare, and there was blood on the floor. Out in the parking lot, blue lights flashed.

"Had you heard about that?"

"No."

"There was supposed to be a train full of wheat coming in from Kansas, but it never showed up. Hijacked, maybe? No one seems to know how you can lose a whole train."

"I could go look for it if—"

"That's nice of you, but that wasn't really my point."

Carolyn felt Naga's eyes on her, watching from the shadows. "No? What then?"

"It was more about the riot. Those used to be fairly rare, once every ten years or so. Now there are at least a couple every day. And it's getting worse."

"Oh? That's interesting." Long pause. He was looking at her expectantly. "Um, why is that, do you think?"

"Well . . . people are a little on edge. What with everything that's been going on lately—the White House burning down, and the president being missing, and . . . the other stuff."

He didn't mention David, but she knew what he was getting at. She tensed up another notch.

"People are scared," Steve said. "Down in South Carolina there's a preacher who keeps going on about how these are the End Times. They call him Brother Elgin. He reminds me of a rabid possum, but there are a lot of people who take him seriously. He says he's the governor now. Supposedly he's seceded from the union."

"Is that a big deal?"

"Bigish, yeah. The other day there was a firefight between him and the Army. Some tanks shelled the State House. Brother Elgin had a bunch of college kids chained up out front as human shields. A couple hundred people died. They'll probably get it sorted out eventually. But just a few weeks ago everything was . . . y'know. Quiet. Normal."

A few weeks ago? "Oh-ho! So you're blaming *me* for this?"

"Should I?"

"Of course not! People are just overreacting."

"*Overre*—" Steve cut himself off, then drummed his fingers on the end table. "OK. Maybe from your point of view that's true. I know you didn't intend for any of this stuff to happen. I'm guessing you probably didn't even notice. Am I right?"

Carolyn felt a flicker of irritation and squelched it. *At least he's making an effort to be civil.* She sighed. *Plus, it's not like he's wrong.* "Yeah. OK. Some of this is new information. But I've been really busy!"

"Yeah, I know. I get that, I really do. Your Father dying really shook things up. All his old enemies have their knives out for the new kid, right?"

"Exactly. But I have the advantage."

"How so?"

"They will underestimate me," she said, smiling. Seeing this, Steve actually shivered. He tried to hide it, but of course she saw. *He really is afraid of me*, she thought and, oh, knowing that this was true hurt. She wouldn't cry; she never cried.

But it hurt so much.

Hoping for escape, she looked at the television. The writing on one corner of the screen said CNN. Beside that, the words NEUTRONIUM HULL? in larger letters. Above it all, the Library. It tumbled in place like a thrown die, a dark pyramid bigger than anything made by men. It was black outside, of course, but the camera crew had some sort of light-gathering lens that made everything an eerie green. Helicopters danced around the pyramid like fireflies around a beach ball.

"Is that us?" Steve gestured at the TV with a handful of popcorn. "That's the thing that was whooshing by in the sky, the night Erwin shot David? The 'project and defend' thing?"

"Yeah."

"Is it the Library? Like, we're inside?"

She hesitated. "Sort of. It's a four-dimensional projection of a seventeen-dimensional universe. Kind of like a shadow, or the place where the circles overlap in a Venn diagram."

On the television, the camera panned down from the Library to a pretty woman in an overcoat. She stood in front of a roadblock on Highway 78. Carolyn recognized the spot. The sound was off, but Carolyn read her lips. She was saying things like "day thirty-two" and "unusual activity," and "military has not responded." Her teeth were very white. Then, from behind her, stern-faced soldiers came around the tank, waving their arms in "shoo" gestures.

"What's going on?" Steve looked around for the remote.

"The Army is evacuating all the reporter people."

"What? Why?"

"They're going to start bombing us in a few minutes."

Steve stared at her. "You know about that?"

"Sure."

He raised an eyebrow. "You don't want to, like, flee?"

"I thought it would be fun to watch. David used to bomb things sometimes. The lights are kind of pretty." She smiled and held up the bowl. "Plus, popcorn!"

Steve just stared at her.

A moment later she got it. "Oh. They can't hurt us. I promise."

"Umm. Have you heard of something called atomic bombs?"

"I'm familiar with them. They won't try that. Well . . . they talked about it, but I think they decided not to. Erwin and the Chinese guy wanted to, but the president kept saying 'not on American soil.' I'm pretty sure, anyway. I got bored and tuned out."

He boggled at her. "How the *hell* do you know these things?"

"I stole it from David's catalog. When someone is planning to harm me, I can tell." She glanced at Naga. "It feels sort of like an itch, here." She tapped the base of her skull. "When I got the itch, I listened in on them. It should start any minute."

Steve rubbed his temples. "Carolyn . . . even if they don't use nukes, they have these things called bunker busters. And something else, I think it's called a 'daisy cutter'? Something like that. They're huge bombs, almost as big as nukes." He searched her face. "Are you sure that won't—"

"Relax," she said, misunderstanding. "There's nothing to worry about. I promise." She looked out at the wall behind the television. "Actually, it's already started. The stuff on television must have been recorded, or something. Look." She made a gesture and the wall became transparent.

Steve squinted against the glare. "Has the sun come back?"

"No, it's just the explosions. Hang on." She gestured again and the glare dimmed a bit. "That's better."

For as far back as the eye could see, the air was filled with warplanes. Seeing them she thought of flocks of birds, migrating for the winter. A flight of cruise missiles streaked in through the night sky and blossomed against the wall of the Library, orange flowers in the night. "See? Told you it was pretty." She ate a piece of popcorn. "Don't you think?"

"Uh . . . I guess."

Next in the line were three big bombers. The bomb-bay doors were open in their bellies. As they approached they disgorged their cargo. Now she could see them on the television as well as through the wall. Fireballs marched up the side of the pyramid in surprisingly tidy rows. One of them was a direct hit. Carolyn adjusted the brightness again.

Steve walked over and put his hand on the wall. "I can't even feel it. Nothing."

"Of course not." She gestured at the pyramid on the TV. "Like I said, it's a projection. The bombs can't reach where we actually are. Think of it this way—if someone shot your shadow, that wouldn't hurt, right?"

"Hmm." Steve sat back down—farther away from her than he had been—and took a handful of popcorn. "I have a confession to make."

"What's that?"

"I knew they were going to bomb you. Well . . . I knew they were thinking about it."

"Oh? Did you?"

"Yeah. I've been talking to Erwin. And the president—the new one, I mean. Not the head. Plus a couple of others." He held up Mrs. McGillicutty's cell phone.

She waved her hand in the air. "I appreciate you saying something, but it's not a problem."

"You knew, didn't you?"

"Yeah."

"Have you been eavesdropping on me?"

"I'd never do that. Not to you."

"Then how?"

"Different universe, remember? I had to set up a relay before your cell phone would work. Remember how the first couple of times you tried to make a call, nothing happened?"

"Oh." He paused. "You're not mad?"

"Nothing to be mad about."

"I sort of conspired to murder you. That's nothing?"

She shook her head. "Nope. On some level you knew it couldn't work."

"How do you mean?"

She tapped the base of her skull. "No itch."

"Ah." Steve thought to himself for a few seconds. He and Naga exchanged a look. Finally he nodded. "Yeah," he said softly. "OK." Then, to her, "Can I get you a drink? There's something I want to talk to you about."

"Sure." *A drink sounds really good.* "What's on your mind?"

"Well, the first thing is, I wanted to talk to you about that wish."

"You know what you want?" She tried to keep the eagerness out of her voice. *Maybe he's coming around after all!*

"Yeah. I thought of something. You remember me talking about my dog? The cocker spaniel?"

"Er . . ."

"That first night, back at the bar."

"Oh," she lied. "Of course."

"Can you find him? Make sure he's OK? His name is Petey."

"Yeah, sure. I can do that. But Steve, that's nothing. If you have—"

He gave her a very earnest look. "You promise?"

"Sure. I promise. I'm not much good with dogs, but I'll figure something out."

Steve sat back, nodded. "Thank you, Carolyn. I really appreciate that."

He fell silent. After a long pause she pulled at the air, a get-on-with-it gesture. "Steve?"

"Mmm. Sorry. How do I put this?" He pursed his lips. "Look, first, I want to tell you that I thought a lot about what you told me the other night. What happened to you. How you got to be . . . whatever you are."

"I told you, I'm just a libr—"

He held up his hand. "Whatever. Just know, I'm making a real effort to put myself in your place. To understand why you do the things you do. Like, that's all I've really done since then."

There was something in his tone that she didn't like. "Oh? And now you have . . . opinions?"

He ran his fingers through his hair. "In terms of what you did? To David and Margaret? No. I personally try to stay away from stuff like that, the kicking of ass and so forth. On the other hand, no one's ever nailed me to a desk. So, really, who am I to judge?"

Ice cubes clinked in a glass. In her heart, something unclenched. "Thank you."

"But I do have an opinion about something else."

"What's that?"

"About what it did to you."

"What do you mean?"

"Well . . . for instance, most people I know wouldn't get bored and tune out of a conversation where someone was deciding whether or not to drop a nuclear bomb on them. Even if they were pretty sure they'd live through it, they'd be curious to hear how the conversation turned out." He shook his head. "Not you, though. It did not rise to your threshold of interest."

"I'm not sure what you're getting at."

"At first I thought you were fucking crazy. Maybe you are, by whatever standard the doctors have, but now I don't think crazy is the right word."

"What, then?" Her lips felt numb, as if she'd been given some sort of toxin.

"I can't think of a word for it. It's like you're living at a different scale than the rest of us. Normal things—fear, hope, compassion—just don't register with you."

"That's . . . OK. Maybe. There might be something to that." Her tone was guarded. He didn't mean her any harm, she'd know if he did, but there was something there, something . . .

"It has to be that way," he said. "I mean, really. How else could you have survived? But, the thing is, it cuts both ways."

"Steve, you're going to have to spell it out for me."

"Yeah, OK. I'm trying to." He poured half an inch of Everclear into her glass, then filled the rest with orange juice. He emptied the rest of the bottle into a steel stock pot. "Letting it breathe," he said. He walked over and handed her the glass.

She sipped her drink, made a face.

"Don't like it?"

"It's pretty strong." She drank it anyway.

"Yeah." He touched his cup to his lips, then set it aside. "Like I said, I've been watching the news a lot lately. Are you aware that there have been some agricultural problems? With this new sun you put up?"

"What sort of problems?"

"Well . . . most of the plants are dying. Almost all of them, really. Trees, grass, wheat, rice, the Amazon Basin . . . pretty much everything. That has some people a little concerned."

"About plants?" She was honestly confused. Americans were constantly killing one another. Every time you turned around there was another war. "Why would they care about *plants*?"

"The thing is, pretty soon there isn't going to be any food left."

"Oh! Right. Well, that's easy. There are plenty of molds and fungi and whatnot that will grow under the black sun. I've got books. When I get around to it I'll make a translation, and—"

"That's really nice, and I know people will appreciate it. But the problem is getting to be kind of urgent."

She shifted uncomfortably. "I'll see if I can block out some time next week."

"CNN is running a series of special reports on how to get nutritional value from stuff you wouldn't normally think of as food," Steve said. "Making stew out of shoe leather. Recipes for your house pets. Things like that."

"Hmm. Come to think of it, the store *was* out of guacamole."

"Did you notice the price on the Everclear?"

"Not really."

"Seven thousand dollars a bottle is a little higher than usual," he said. "Probably the only reason you could find it at all is that it's as much an industrial chemical as a food product. I don't think anyone except high school kids actually drinks the stuff. They only do it because they don't know any better."

"Now that you mention it, the shelves *did* seem kind of bare."

"I bet." He made a concentrating face. "The other day I saw something on the news that made me think of your deer. Isha and . . ."

"Asha."

"Right. The other week this kid, sixteen or so, got caught poaching deer on a rich guy's estate. That's a capital crime now. They caught him red-handed. Literally. He was sucking the marrow out of a doe's femur bone. His defense was that the deer were going to starve to death anyway, so why shouldn't someone get some nutrition out of them? I kind of saw his point."

Carolyn flashed on a morning she had spent nibbling dew-drenched clover with Asha, watching the spring dawn. This brought a flicker of . . . something . . . but she pushed it down.

Steve was watching her intently.

"What happened?" she asked. Her voice was perfectly normal.

Steve was silent a long moment before he answered, softly. "They hanged the kid anyway. Afterwards there were more riots. Like I said, it's kind of an everyday thing now."

"Oh." She drained her glass.

"Another drink?" His voice was stronger.

"Sure."

He walked back into the kitchen and opened the second bottle. He fixed her drink—a full inch of liquor this time—then poured the rest of that bottle into the stock pot with the first.

"Anyway. There's some other problems besides the famine. Earthquakes are the biggie. There's a new one almost every day. There's not much left of San Francisco. Tokyo is gone. Mexico City isn't far behind. And apparently there's some kind of volcano under Yellowstone that's rumbling. Nothing has really happened with it yet, but the geologists seem worried." He met her eyes. "They say it's got to do with this place."

"The Library?"

"Yeah. Apparently the pyramid thingy over Garrison Oaks is heavy. They say it's got the same mass as the moon, or something? It's shifting tectonic plates around?" He took a sip of her drink before he handed it to her. "You hadn't heard any of this?"

She shook her head.

"Yeah," Steve said. "I figured. Keeping an eye on your Father's enemies, right? And catching up on all these other—what did you call them?"

"Catalogs," she said. "I've been consolidating the catalogs. Strategizing. And laying the groundwork for some contingencies. Just in case."

"Sure," Steve said. "Sure. You're careful. You've got a lot on your mind. That's the world you live in, the world you know."

"Yeah." She ran her fingers through her hair, stressed. "Look, Steve, about the earthquakes and the famine and all that—I'll figure something out. But there's more going on here than you know. Q-33 North is in motion, and I can't find him. If Liesel or maybe Barry O'Shea decided to make a move against me now, it would be bad for—"

"Bad for everyone. All of us. Regular people. I get that too. And these are legitimately large problems. I do not doubt you for even a single second." He drummed his fingers against the marble tabletop. "But it leaves me with a problem of my own."

"What's that?"

"I talked this over with Erwin. And the rest of them too, the president and the Army guys, but Erwin was the only one who seemed to really get it."

"Get what?"

"How I can't get through to you." He held his hands out to her gently, palms up. "I've said it every way I know how, and it's like you don't even hear me. I was talking to Erwin about it and he said it's because we don't have a common vocabulary."

Carolyn's eyes narrowed. "My English is pretty good."

"That's what I said too, but that's not what he meant. He told me about how when he got back from the war, everyone kept telling him to let it go, to find something that made him happy and do that. He said he heard the words, said they even made sense, but he just couldn't relate to them. Then he said there was this kid, this kid he helped somehow. And that was the thing that made him understand it was possible to move on. And after that the words made sense."

"Dashaen," she said. "I remember him."

"So then I started thinking about how you must have had to shut down, inside. You had to be cold, didn't you? To get through things like a little kid getting her head split open with an ax, and people being roasted alive."

Carolyn didn't answer.

"Cold. Yeah." Steve was peering at her again. "But you're not frozen through. Not quite. There's that one little thing left, isn't there? The heart coal. That's it, isn't it? The very last thing."

After a long moment she surrendered the barest possible sliver of a nod.

"I thought so. Yeah. That's going to be the only way anyone can reach you, isn't it? The only possible way for you to . . . wake up. To not be cold anymore."

She didn't answer.

Steve nodded to himself, then smiled.

Something about that smile was different. *What's changed?*

"You never came right out and said, but I think I've guessed what it is. The heart coal, I mean." Still smiling, he stood and walked over to the stock pot.

It took her a moment, but then she got it. *He's at peace,* she realized. *That's what's different about him. It's the first time I've ever seen him look really happy.*

Standing at the counter, still smiling, he picked up the orange juice. "Another drink?"

"No." Her voice was hoarse. "What are you doing?"

"I'm so glad you asked. Thank you for cooperating with my segue. Sure you don't want another drink?"

She shook her head.

"Well, that's OK too." He picked up the stock pot filled with Ever-clear and poured it over his head.

The room filled with the sharp chemical scent of 90 percent pure ethanol. *It would*, Carolyn suddenly understood, *be highly flammable*.

Steve spoke to Naga. "Now, sweetie."

Carolyn, very quick, moved to stop him. Naga, quicker still, moved to block her way.

Steve smiled at her, calm and friendly. "Before I move closer towards my vision of the Buddha, I would respectfully plead that you adopt a stance of compassion towards the small things of this world."

He closed his eyes. Somehow he was holding Margaret's lighter.

Clink. Scratch. Click.

Then, suddenly, all of the great and eternal now was blue flame. Naga held the space between Carolyn and Steve, an impassable frenzy of claw and fang. Carolyn could only watch, helpless, as the flame rendered Steve into blazing tallow, rendered him into black smoke. *Normal men*, she understood for the first time, *burn surprisingly fast*. In less than a minute, he was dead. *Therein, perhaps, we find God's mercy*. Beyond that, the outer darkness.

Alone now, Carolyn felt the regard of Isha and Asha settle cold upon her.

Someone was screaming.

I

Carolyn resurrected Steve, of course. It took a couple of weeks. She was getting the hang of medicine, but burns were tricky. He asked her for two more bottles of Everclear. She said she couldn't find any. A week later she came down and found him dead in the bathtub, razor at his side. She had to tranquilize Naga to get at the body. That one only took a day or so to fix, but she got the blood type wrong—a rookie mistake, but she was upset—and he died of heart failure almost as soon as he came back. She replaced the razors with an electric and brought him back a fourth time, but the next night at dinner he recited his little speech— "adopt a stance of compassion"? what the hell did that even *mean*?— before downing a glass of Liquid-Plumr with his roast.

She had left him dead, after that. She couldn't bear it. Not anymore.

That had been over a month ago. Now she was fully immersed in her studies. One day while she was researching the theoretical framework of reality viruses she happened upon something mis-shelved. There, among the pale violet mathematics, a brown folder. It turned out to be the crafting of the *alshaq shabboleth*.

It changed everything.

In and of itself the *alshaq shabboleth* was of little consequence. It was conceptually related to the technique she had found on the bookmark, the one that enabled her to move through the Library invisibly. Its only advantage over the *alshaq urkun* was that it could be invoked very quickly, with a single word. She had seen it used—once.

"Adoption Day." She spoke softly, but the vast spaces of the Library seemed to seize on her words, amplify them. She looked down at the parchment in her hand.

> *Through my studyes of the one True Speeche which Commandeth Alle, I have wrought the Crafte of alshaq shabboleth, which maketh the slow things swifte.*

She unrolled the scroll another few inches. It was ancient, written before Father came into the height of his power. It concerned itself with minor procedures of only occasional use. She might very well have gone years—millennia—without stumbling across it. Chance? Possibly, but in matters where Father was involved she was very suspicious of chance.

He meant for me to find this.

To the side was a hand-inked illustration of a man outrunning a lightning strike, and another, less faded, of the same man on fire and screaming. Her expression darkened. "*Alshaq shabboleth*," she said, testing the sounds.

> *But approach the alshaq with trembling! It is a dangerous Crafte at the best of times, and though it may be a great friend in time of need, it can also be a grievous Enemy! Only the wise should—*

Next to the pale, ancient ink, the following was scrawled in ballpoint pen:

> *Carolyn,*
> *Onyx-7-5-12-3-3.7*
> —*Father*

It was a catalog designation—Onyx floor, radial seven, branch five, case twelve, shelf three, third from the left. Chapter seven. Blood roared in her ears. Very softly, she whispered, "Father?"

No answer.

Then, with something like a roar, Carolyn pitched the brown folio down the stacks. A dead one holding a feather duster shuffled away in distant, dreamlike terror.

Adoption Day. That was what they'd called it—the day their parents died, the day they stopped being Americans and became librarians, part of Father's world. Before that, Garrison Oaks had been just another subdivision. Before that, as far as anyone knew, Father was just Adam Black, some old guy who lived down the street.

There had been an attack. It was not an especially clever attack, but it was very strong, and executed quickly. It caught him off guard, or at least he let it seem so. She thought it might even have stood a chance of killing him. Not a large chance, perhaps, but a chance. It was this suspicion and what it implied that ultimately gave her the courage to act. Father was not quite omniscient. Sometimes he could be surprised. If he could be surprised, he might possibly be vulnerable.

All that came after sprang from that.

Numb, feeling not quite all there, Carolyn made her way down the main corridor of the jade floor and onto the onyx face of the pyramid. There, moving alone through vast, empty spaces she walked over to the book he specified. It was in the apothecary section, part of Jennifer's catalog. The volume was titled *An Assortment of Useful Elixirs*. Chapter 7 was "The Font of Perfect Memory."

INSTRUCTIONS

Having prepared the liquid as indicated, retreat to a place of solitude. There begin your contemplations. You shall find that the formulation releases in you every smallest memory; it will be as if you are there again in the flesh, experiencing it with fresh eyes.

She took down the book. Then, browsing the nearby shelves, she added a couple of others—one on chemistry, another on lab techniques. She took the stairs down into the apothecary and set about assembling ingredients.

II

C arolyn was not much of a chemist. It took three frustrating days before she learned enough of the basics to even understand what the formula was telling her to do. It was another week, long and almost sleepless, before she completed a batch that tested to the purity she required and didn't kill any mice.

When she was reasonably confident she had it right, she went back to her chambers, ate a huge meal, and slept for twelve solid hours. The next morning—or it might have been evening, it was impossible to tell and, really, who cared?—she went back to her desk in the great hall and sat there for a moment, looking at the small glass vial that contained the fruit of her labors. Gently, careful not to spill, she wiggled the cork out and set it down on her desk blotter. She cut a lemon into quarters and set them next to the cork.

The vial contained about two tablespoons of brown, bitter liquid that smelled like tears. Grimacing, she tossed it back like a shot of liquor, then bit down on one of the lemon quarters to get the taste out of her mouth.

There begin your contemplations.

"Well," she said. "All right."

Adoption Day, she remembered, had been a holiday of some sort. It was one of the turning points of her life, probably *the* turning point, but she hadn't thought much about it in years. *It was at the end of the summer, still hot out during the day, but if you were outdoors at night you could sometimes feel the first breath of winter, blowing down from the north.* School had just started up a week earlier, and she remembered thinking that was silly. Why start school and then give you a vacation just a week later? It was a silly time to have . . .

"Labor Day," she said out loud. *Perfect memory indeed.* An hour ago she couldn't have conjured that name to save her life.

Labor Day, 1977. She would have been about eight years old. She woke up in the bedroom at her parents' house. There was a stuffed animal in bed with her, a green puppet shaped like a frog. *Kermit*, she thought. *His name is Kermit the Frog.* Next to Kermit sat Miss Piggy. She had slept in later than usual because she'd stayed up late the night before and watched *The Waltons* on TV.

In her memory, Carolyn went downstairs. Her mother, a pretty blond woman about the same age that Carolyn was now, was doing something in the kitchen. Mom went to the shelf and took down a box of Frosted Flakes—Carolyn was too short to reach it herself—then turned back to her cooking.

Carolyn no longer had any clear memory of her mother's face. She remembered her only as a series of impressions—laughter, cashmere, hair spray.

Until now. *Hi, Mom,* she thought. *Pleased to meet you.* Alone in the Library, she gave a small smile.

Still, though, she was relieved that the woman's face remained unfamiliar to her. She wasn't sure what she would have done if Mom turned out to be one of the dead ones. She was glad she didn't have to find out. She made an effort to commit her face to memory. *I'm sorry, Mom,* she thought. *This time I won't forget you.*

Back in 1977, when little Carolyn was done with her cereal she and her mother worked at making a big batch of potato salad for the picnic later—boiling the potatoes, chopping things, mixing it all together in a bowl. Just as they were finishing up, her *actual* father came home from the hardware store. He was a handsome man, a few years older than her mother. His hair was graying at the temples. She addressed him not as "Father" but instead as "Dad," which sounded delightfully informal to Carolyn's adult ear. Little Carolyn kissed his cheek. The stubble was rough against her lips. He hadn't showered. He smelled of sweat and, faintly, yesterday's Old Spice.

When the potato salad was ready, Carolyn covered the bowl with Saran Wrap and put it in the "fridge." She helped her mother clean up, then went back to her room to kill a couple of hours. The picnic wouldn't start until noon. Now, a quarter century later, she ached to stay in that kitchen, to be with them again for one last time, but the memory was immutable. Carolyn was a bookish child, even before Father had come into her life. She preferred to spend time in her room reading.

Just before noon, the three of them put on suntan lotion and walked across the street toward the little park behind the houses. "Dad" held out his hand and she took it, weaving her small fingers around his large ones. His palms were rough, she remembered. *He must have worked with his hands. But doing what?* But she hadn't thought about it that day. Now it was gone, gone with his name, the stories he told, any other time they might have spent together.

He smiled down at her distractedly. Remembering this, Carolyn thought, *He has such a kind face.* With that her tears slipped free and rolled unnoticed down her cheeks.

The shortest route to the park took them through the yard of the man they knew as Adam Black. He was on his back deck, wearing shorts, an apron, and a chef's hat. Standing on the concrete slab that served as his back patio was his eccentric barbecue grill, a huge bronze cast in the shape of a bull. Carolyn remembered how this thing had been an object of fascination for her as a small child. One stormy afternoon she had snuck into his yard and lay her tiny hand against its smooth leg, seen her reflection in its shiny belly. Now, smoke drifted from the bull's nostrils.

"Hi, Adam," Dad called out. "Mind if we cut through your yard?"

"Adam" raised a hand in greeting. "Hi yourself!" He spoke in English, suppressing his usual trace of Pelapi accent. "Yeah, come on through."

They stopped on the way to chat for a minute. *This is "being neighborly"* Carolyn thought. Two decades ago Father looked exactly as she last saw him.

"Man, that smells *great*," her dad said. "What you got in there?"

"A little of everything—mostly pork shoulder and lamb at the moment. They should be done in an hour or so. I've been smoking them all night. When the pork is ready I'll probably do a batch of burgers."

"One day would you teach me the recipe? I don't mind telling you, that stuff you made last year was about the best barbecue I've had."

"Sure. Why not? I've been in a teaching mood lately." He poked the meat with a carved wooden fork. "The secret is to start with a hot fire, as hot as you can make. Such a fire will burn away impurities, you see. Plus, there's a ceremonial aspect to it. Fire gives a person something to focus on." He rapped the bull with his knuckles, grinning. "So, yeah. Fire. That's the first step."

"Yeah? That's it?"

"Well, there are some spices for the meat as well—old Persian recipe." This time he let a little Pelapi accent slip in—"reshipeeeeee."

Eight-year-old Carolyn giggled. "You talk funny!"

"Carolyn!" said her dad.

"No, it's OK," said Adam Black. He squatted down to be at eye level with her. She remembered how the giggles drained out of her when she saw his eyes. "No . . ." she said, and buried her face in her dad's leg.

"Don't be scared," Adam Black said, and reached out to brush away her hair. "You're right. Sometimes I *do* talk funny, but most people don't notice. You've got a good ear."

"Thank you." She could tell from his tone that he meant to be comforting, but she was not comforted. Not in the least.

"How *should* I say it, honey?"

Carolyn peeked out from her dad's leg. " 'Recipe.' "

"Reshipeee."

Despite herself, she giggled. "No, 'recipe'!"

The giggle seemed to satisfy him. His face erupted again into that soft smile. "Hey, you guys want to stay and chat with me for a minute? I don't think they're quite set up down in the park. I've got beer in the cooler, and soft drinks for your daughter."

Her dad looked down at the park, where some men were setting up a volleyball net.

"Can I have one, Dad?" She liked Sprite, but usually she wasn't allowed.

Dad considered. "Yeah, sure. Why not? Grab me a beer, too."

Carolyn had brought her book with her. She sat down on a metal lawn chair to read while the grown-ups talked.

"So, can I ask where you got that grill?" Dad asked. "Never seen anything quite like it."

"You know, I honestly don't remember. Somewhere in the Middle East, probably. I used to kick around there when I was a young buck."

"Oh, yeah? Doing what?"

"Soldiering, mostly. Seems like I walked up and down just about every hill in Asia at one time or another."

"Really? Wow. I bet you must have some stories."

"A few." They waited, but he didn't volunteer any of them.

"Is that what you do now? We don't see much of you around here."

He laughed. "No, no. Not for years. Soldiering is a young man's game. Actually, I'm in the process of retiring," the old man said.

"Really? You look kind of young for that."

"Nice of you to say. I'm older than I look, though."

"Retiring from what, if you don't mind my asking?"

"Don't mind a bit. I'm head of a small company. Well, small but influential. We're in the book business, kind of a family thing."

"Cool. How do you like it?"

"It's interesting work. It can be kind of cutthroat, though. A lot of competition. My successor is liable to have a rough go of it, in the first few years anyway."

"Oh, you've got a guy all picked out?"

"I do. Actually, it's a girl. It took me a long while to find the right person. Now it's just a question of getting her trained." Carolyn didn't remember noticing at the time, didn't remember *any* of this, but Adam Black was looking directly at her as he spoke. Something about the look in his eyes stirred her mom's maternal instincts and she put her arm around Carolyn's shoulder. It would be the last time they ever touched.

Now, today, Carolyn sat alone in the heart of the Library with her jaw hanging open. *Successor? Picked out? Surely he can't mean . . .*

"Who's the lucky *gal*?" Carolyn's mom asked, ribbing her husband. Feminist issues were a source of mild friction in the marriage.

"Her name's Carolyn. She's a niece of mine—well, sort of. She's a pretty distant relation, actually. I see a lot of me in her, though."

"Oh?" her father said. "Weird coincidence. That's our daughter's name."

"You don't say." Adam Black rooted around in the grill with a spatula, flipping ribs.

Her father took a swig of his beer. "So what's the training process involve, exactly?"

"Actually, if you don't mind, I'd rather not get into too much detail. Trade secret and all that."

"Oh? Yeah. Sure, no problem, I understand." He obviously didn't.

"I can say, though, that the toughest part about it is going to be getting through it with her heart intact." Seeing the look on Mom's face, he added, "Figuratively, I mean."

"Tough business?"

"Oh yeah. Some of the competition are real monsters."

Her dad interrupted. "Really? What exactly are—"

Adam Black let the interruption slide, but a little iron crept into his voice. "I'm not worried about that, though. She's like me. She'll do whatever's necessary—after I get her attention." He smiled, flipped a burger. His eyes blazed.

Mom gave a nervous smile. Dad, oblivious, sipped at his beer.

"The tricky part will come later—after she's won. When I was young, the war was everything to me." Father's gaze burned into her. "In the service of my will, I emptied myself. It was long and long before I understood what I had lost, and by then it was gone forever." He shrugged. "Perhaps she will be wiser." In the ancient, dusty recesses of her memory, he tipped her a wink. Now, today, Carolyn felt like fainting.

Her mom's eyes narrowed. She hadn't seen the wink, but this last exchange had pushed some mothery needle into the red. "Well," she said, "I guess we better get going."

"But I—" her dad said.

"We don't want to take up too much of Mr. Black's time, dear." Her tone had a distinct chill to it.

"Oh. Um, right." He smiled at Adam Black. "Well, thanks for the beer. You going to come down and join us? Maybe play some volleyball?"

Adam Black smiled. "I'll be along in just a minute. I want to get a good char on this pork first."

Carolyn's parents exchanged a look. "OK," said her dad. "See you later." He took Carolyn by the hand and they set off down the hill.

III

I n those days Garrison Oaks had a common area, a sort of park, in the spot that was the lake today. The houses of the neighborhood ringed it, which gave everyone the illusion of a three-acre backyard. The park was full of people, adults sitting on the picnic benches drinking Coke or Sprite out of green glass bottles or smoking Tareytons. Children swarmed over the swing set and the wooden jungle gym. Adam Black's house stood on the highest hill in the neighborhood, so from there Carolyn, holding her dad's hand, had to pick her way down a moderately steep slope to get to the park. Her father's grip was gentle but not un-tight. At least once he saved her from a fall. When they reached the bottom of the hill she shook his hand off for the last time.

"Look, Dad, there's Steve!" She waved. "Hi, Steve!" Steve was a bit older than her. *He's eleven,* she thought, *or maybe twelve*. He was playing tag with a herd of other kids.

There was David, reaching down to help a younger child who had fallen in the grass. "You OK, Mike?" David said. His voice was kind. At the sound of it the younger boy, who had seemed on the verge of tears, got to his feet and smiled. David smiled back, then tagged him and said, "You're it!" They ran off together, laughing.

Margaret was there as well, she saw. She seemed a bit older than the rest—nine or ten, perhaps? She was jumping her way across a hopscotch grid laid out on the basketball court in yellow chalk. Her pigtails flopped in the sunshine as she hopped. Her skin glowed from the exertion, pink and alive.

"Hi, Carolyn!" said Steve.

Something inside her jumped at the sound of his voice. In those days Steve lived across the street from her. *Our parents were friends. Sometimes we all ate dinner together. I thought he was "cute."* Once, she remembered, she had taken a crayon and written his name and hers together on pink construction paper and then encased the two names with a heart. She never told anyone this.

Her father looked down at her, bemused and perhaps just a tad apprehensive. He waved at Steve. "Hi."

Steve waved back. "Hi, Mr. Sopaski!"

"Daddy, can I go play with Steve?"

"Oh, honey, Steve doesn't want—"

"It's fine, sir," Steve said, and Carolyn's eight-year-old heart soared. "Wanna go over to Scabby Flats and shoot a few?"

"Sure!" Carolyn said.

"Go where?" said her dad.

"The basketball court," she said. "That's just what we call it." She and Steve had made-up names for a bunch of stuff in the neighborhood. The basketball court, paved with a mixture of black asphalt and rough gravel, was Scabby Flats. In her room there was a map, hand-drawn in crayon, with these and other names. The woods at the end of the road were Missing Muttland. The stream in the woods was Cat Splash Creek after an amusing accident. And so on.

"Oh," her dad said. "Right. Well . . . you guys have fun."

They walked together over to the basketball court. Steve bounced a ball as they walked.

"How are you?" she asked, a little apprehensively. She hadn't seen him in months. The day after school ended, Steve's dad had been in a car accident. Mr. Hodgson was in the hospital for a week, and then he died. Steve and his mom had spent the summer with his grandparents in Wisconsin.

"I'm OK. It's good to be back." He bounced the ball on the asphalt. "Good old Scabby Flats."

He didn't sound OK. Carolyn didn't blame him. Having her dad die was about the worst thing she could imagine. When she tried to picture something similar happening to her it felt like a bottomless hole opened up in her mind. "Really?"

"Yeah. I mean, it sucks. But you adjust."

She looked up at him, awed. To Carolyn, eight years old, that one sentence seemed to contain all that might ever be known of courage. "You do?"

He nodded.

"How?"

"You just do. You can adjust to anything if you don't give up." He smiled wanly. "That's what my dad used to say, anyway."

"Oh."

"Hey, do you mind if we talk about something else?"

"Sure." She tried to think of something to say, but anything that might have come was swallowed by the bottomless hole. After a long pause, she said, "Like what?" in a small voice.

Steve chuckled. "What have you been reading?"

Steve was the only kid in the neighborhood who was as bookish as she was. They didn't read much of the same stuff—he liked spaceships and superheroes; she was more into animal stories and Beverly Cleary—but they both enjoyed talking about what they'd read, and every so often there was some overlap. "*A Wrinkle in Time*," she said. "Have you read it?"

"Yeah! It was really good. Did you know there's another one after that?"

"What, like with the same characters?"

"Pretty much, yeah. I'll bring it if you want."

"Thanks!"

"Sure," he said, reaching into his pocket. "But meantime, I brought you this one. I think you'll like it."

She examined the cover. "*Black Beauty*. It's the one about the horse, right?"

"Yeah."

"Is it sad? Margaret said it was sad."

"A little. Well, sort of. At the end—"

"Don't tell me!"

"Sorry." Steve raised the ball to shoot, then froze and cocked his head, listening. "Do you hear that?"

"Hear what? I don't—" She broke off then, because she *did* hear it, a whistling in the sky that grew louder, an approaching sound. She looked up and saw a long, thin, arch-shaped contrail. When she first saw it, it was very high in the sky, but it drew closer as she watched, then closer still.

"I think it's coming towards us," Steve said.

She saw that he was right, and for some reason that made her afraid. She reached out to take his hand and—

. . . everything . . .

. . . stopped . . .

I have wrought the Crafte of alshaq shabboleth, Carolyn thought now, *which maketh the slow things swifte.* To the children it seemed as if the world had frozen in place. She saw her dad talking to Mr. Craig from down the street. Dad's mouth was frozen open, midsentence. Mr. Craig was blowing out a puff of cigarette smoke. It hung in the air, motionless.

The leading point of the contrail was frozen above them. It hovered motionless about a hundred feet over their heads. Well, not quite motionless. As she watched, it moved down an inch or so, then another.

Her young eyes saw what was coming for them. She thought at first it was a space capsule, like the kind she had seen on TV. But as she examined it a bit closer, she realized that wasn't right. It was too small, for one thing, too small to hold a man. And there were no windows. But it was shaped a bit like a space capsule, a plain cone of metal. It had an American flag and some writing on the side. USAF-11807-A1. Below that, hand-painted in bright red, was a smiley face and the words "Hi 'Adam'!"

She remembered thinking, *They sent it for him. It's for Adam Black. But what is it?* She knew now. David explained it to her some years later. "It's called a Pershing missile," he said. "It's a weapon. It holds a lot of things called 'kilotons.' Mostly it's for blowing up cities. The Americans thought it might be strong enough to kill Father."

At the time, though, Carolyn had no idea what she was looking at—fireworks, perhaps?—but, whatever sort of show this was, she thought it was rather pretty. She remembered how a small crack had appeared in the thing hovering over their heads, how it glowed inside as if it were an egg about to hatch something magical.

She looked at Steve. He was saying something, or his lips were moving at any rate, but she could hear nothing. *We were too fast,* she realized now. *The alshaq shabboleth made us too fast for sound.*

The crack grew as she watched. The light inside spilled out like the sunrise breaking over the mountains. It ate away the metal on which the letters USA were written.

Steve clapped his hands over his ears and looked up the hill. A moment later she heard it too. The inside of her head rang with the voice of Adam Black. *No,* Carolyn thought. *He's not Adam Black anymore. He's Father now.*

"Those of you who would live may take shelter behind me," he said, not in the mild and amused old-man tones he had affected for her dad, but in his true voice, the voice that cracked mountains and called light out of darkness. It rolled through the children's minds like thunder.

At the sound of it Carolyn moved instinctively toward Steve for protection. That was when she noticed that something was different. When she moved, the parts of her skin that were exposed to the air felt hot, like the time she had held her hand over the outflow nozzle on a hair dryer and burned her fingers.

Now, today, she understood what was happening. *Friction,* she thought. *Friction with the air.* Under the influence of the *alshaq* their speed was such that even the air burned.

At the time, though, she knew only pain. She and Steve gaped at each other in soundless terror. Fifty meters over their heads a small bright sun was flaring into life.

She cried out to her dad, lips moving soundlessly. She took a step toward him, feeling that strange warmth on her cheeks again as she moved. Her dad was still as a statue, the beer Adam Black had given him held to his mouth.

He was directly under the fireball.

Later, when she learned to make the *alshaq shabboleth* for herself she understood why it worked on her but not him. The effects of the *alshaq* are felt first by the dead, then by the young, and last by the old. Her father was beyond help. Even today she could think of nothing that might have saved him.

She herself was in only slightly less danger, although she didn't realize it yet.

Steve figured it out, though. He shook her shoulder and pointed at the fireball overhead, eyes wide. Then he pointed at Adam Black—Father—waiting for them on the hillside.

Carolyn looked up at the ball of fire in the sky. It was growing. She nodded understanding and she and Steve set out toward the hill.

The real problem became apparent to them immediately. They set out together at a slow jog. She stopped after only two steps with a sound-less cry.

Steve was gritting his teeth, but he did not cry out. He looked up in the sky. She followed his gaze. *If the fire doesn't stop getting bigger, it could swallow us up.*

She could see from his face that Steve understood this as well. His face was very red, and his hair was smoking a little. He looked back at her, eyes wide with fear and pain, then took a half-step forward, moving slow and languorous in air that had turned cruel.

She imitated him. When she moved in this way it was still warm, but not so hot as it had been when she ran, certainly not so hot that she cried out.

On the crest of the hill Father watched this. He said nothing.

Together they inched their way toward the hill. The other children had been affected by the call of *alshaq* in the same way, and were dealing with the same problems. Some of them had frozen with terror, or fallen to their knees weeping. A skinny boy about age eight panicked. *His name is Jimmy*, she remembered. *He's not very bright.* Jimmy took off running toward his mother—actually *running*, not just the light jog she had tried. After a few steps his skin blistered. He screamed, but apparently it didn't occur to him to stop. After three more steps his shirt was in flames. She looked away then.

She and Steve moved as quickly as they could without pain, but that wasn't very fast. They had a lead on the expanding ball of superheated plasma behind them, but it wasn't a large lead.

Some of the others were luckier. David and Michael's impromptu game of tag had carried them to the base of the hill. She thought they would reach safety well before the fireball reached them. She and Steve, on the other hand, had started out directly under the missile. They might arrive quickly enough to take Adam Black up on his promise of safety, but then again they might not.

The ball of light grew quickly, and it was gaining on them. By the time they reached the base of the hill it had touched the ground. There it claimed another victim, a sixteen-year-old girl who had started in a rea-sonably good position but, because of her age, had been a bit late to hear the call of *alshaq*. She was about to become the first person who Carolyn ever saw die. As the light drew near her skin boiled away. Her eyes widened in agony; her mouth opened in a silent scream.

It was this moment that would haunt Carolyn's nightmares in years to come. She notched up her speed a little bit, then a little more, her terror overriding the pain.

Now she was moving almost at a jog, heedless of the burning agony. Her shirt was smoking. She could smell burning hair, but she wasn't sure whether it was her own or Steve's. But the top of the hill was close. *I'm going to make it!*

Then she tripped.

A loose rock slid away beneath her foot. She put her hands out to break her fall and the rock cut her palm. Worse, she lost ground, slipping a few precious inches back down the hill.

Steve had reached the summit. He was safe. He turned, almost smiling, but the smile faded when he saw her. His mouth moved, but she couldn't make out the words. He waved for her to come on. She read his lips saying, *Get up.*

But she couldn't. She had scraped up her hands, her knees. She wanted her mother. She was afraid. Her chin trembled. She remembered thinking, *It's too hard*, remembered thinking, *I give up.*

Seeing this, Steve jumped back down the hill. His face was impossibly bright, lit by the approaching fireball now only five yards or so behind her. He reached where she had fallen with two giant, bouncing steps, grabbed her by the wrist, and yanked her to her feet. As she stood she saw that his hair and shirt had both caught fire, tiny tongues of flame beginning to grow.

Burning, he grabbed her by the waist and lifted her. The fireball was only a few scant feet behind them now. Her shoulder socket stung with the jolt, but she didn't feel the fire; Steve was holding her in his wake. The burn was all on him. The left side of his shirt burned off his skin in a puff . . . but now they were at the top of the hill.

They rushed into the crowd of children a few precious inches ahead of the fireball. They were the faces of her future—David and Margaret,

Michael, Lisa, Peter, Richard, others she didn't know then. They milled around behind Father, mouths wide *O*'s of terror, screaming too fast for sound.

When the ball of energy reached the crest of the hill, Father held out his hand. When the light touched him he winced . . . but he did not burn. David later told her that there were thirty of the "kilotons" in that explosion. He seemed to think this was an impressive number. Probably it was. But when the four-hundred-kiloton blast reached the finger of Adam Black it stopped . . . quivered for a moment . . . then began to shrink.

The receding fireball left a perfectly round crater where the park and most of the houses had been. The edges of the crater glowed red. She traced the arc with her eyes until it came to something she recognized; a mailbox with "*305*" and "*Lafayette*" stenciled in gold. The Lafayettes had been her next-door neighbors. Half their house was still standing, snipped neatly open by the explosion. She could see into the bedroom of Diane Lafayette, who had a Barbie Dream House that Carolyn coveted. Her own house, where she and her mother had made potato salad, had been located a few yards inside the crater.

Only then did she think to look where her parents had been.

When she last saw them they were standing in the park. Now that spot was a hole one hundred feet deep. Molten sand glowed like lava in its depths. Mom and Dad would have been among the first to be swallowed by the fireball. Carolyn understood that she was now an orphan.

Farther out, where the volleyball game had been, other adults lay dead as well, their flesh blasted away, their chromosomes in shreds. She recognized them as well. *The dead ones*.

Father did something and the *alshaq* fell away. Time returned to normal. The children were speaking, it seemed. Their voices rose as if someone had turned up the volume on a silent radio. But she heard only Steve.

"—n't know what you were *thinking*," Steve said. "You can't *ever* give up, Carolyn. You can't quit. Not *ever*."

She looked at him, wide-eyed.

Then, kicking down the first stone of an avalanche, Steve said, "You have to be *strong*."

IV

Adam Black turned to the children and regarded them with eyes that were calm and dark.

"Your parents are dead," he said. Some of them wept. Others looked up at him, dazed and uncomprehending. "Most of you had no other family. In America, this means you would be taken away. You would live in an orphanage. You are too old. You are too ugly. You could not find new homes. No one would love you. No one would want you.

"But this is not America," Adam Black said. "Things are here as they were in the old age. I will take you into my home. I will raise you as I was raised. You will be Pelapi."

"We'll be what?" Carolyn remembered asking.

"Pelapi. It is an old word. There is no single word like it in English. It means 'librarian,' but also 'apprentice,' or perhaps 'student.'"

"Pelapi." She tested the sound of it for the first time. At the time they had thought he was speaking to all of them. Now Carolyn understood he meant only her. Alone in the Library at the other end of her life, she mouthed the words again. "What do you want us to study?"

"We will start with the language. It is called Pelapi as well. All of you will learn that first."

"Why?"

"It is the language that your lessons are written in, for the most part. You can hardly do without it."

"What kind of lessons?" Carolyn asked.

"For you, I think it will be the other languages."

"Like what? French and stuff?"

"Yes. Those and others."

"How many?"

"All of them."

She made a face. "What if I don't want to?"

"It won't matter. I'll make you do it anyway."

She said nothing to that—she was starting to realize that Adam Black frightened her—but she remembered how his words kindled the first, faint flicker of rebellion in her gut. Now, today, that same flame burned high and black over all the mountains and valleys of the Earth.

"And what about me?" David asked.

"You? Hmm." Father squatted down in front of David and felt his forearm. "You seem like a strong little fellow. You remind me of myself at your age. Would you like to learn how to fight?"

David grinned. "Yeah! That'd be cool."

Father spoke again, very quickly, not in English. At the time she could make no sense of what he said. It was only gibberish, quickly forgotten. Today, though, remembering it, she recognized the Pelapi for what it was. *It will be as if you are there again in the flesh,* the instructions on the elixir said, *experiencing it with fresh eyes.*

"You shall be the thing she fears above all others, and conquers," Father said in Pelapi. He touched David gently, with real love. "Your way shall be very hard, very cruel. I must do terrible things to you, that you may become a monster. I am sorry, my son. I had thought you might be my heir, but the strength is not in you. It must be her."

At the time, they all thought David was the biological son of the Craigs, who had been chatting with Carolyn's own parents when the fireball hit. Now, today, Carolyn was thinking, *His son? He did that to his actual* son? Then, on the heels of that but worse, *He did it for me?*

"And me?" Margaret asked.

Father turned to her. "Hello, Margaret."

"How did you know my name?"

"I know lots of things about you. I've been watching you for a long time. Tell me, do you like exploring?"

She shrugged. "I guess."

"Good. There's a very special place I know of. Almost no one knows about it but me. I could send you there. You could learn your way around."

"Is it a fun place to go?"

Father pursed his lips. "More of an adventure, I should say. Would you like that? It would make you very special." Then, at Carolyn, in rapid-fire Pelapi. "When the time comes, Margaret will serve as your final warning."

Carolyn remembered Margaret calling her "Mistress," remembered her saying, *You're like me now* and *We are sisters.* How had those words passed by her so easily? Now the chill of them cut bone-deep.

Father went down the line, speaking to each of the children in turn until he came, finally, to Steve. "What about me?"

"I saw what you did back there," Father said. "You're a very brave boy."

Steve's chest swelled with pride. But when the skin of his chest stretched, he winced. His torso was red, blistered from the fire, even black in spots. He did not cry out.

Father knelt and examined the burns. "Does it hurt?"

"A little." His voice sounded strangled.

Father took a Ziploc bag from the pocket of his jeans. He squeezed a pale green ointment from it and, working very gently, applied it to Steve's chest. Steve flinched at first, drew back from Father's touch—then his eyes went wide and he leaned into it.

When it was done, Father stood and dusted his jeans off. "Is that better?"

"Yeah," Steve said with obvious gratitude. "A lot better. Thanks!"

Father smiled a little. He even patted Steve on the shoulder. Steve didn't wince. "You're welcome. You should heal up OK." Then Father's smile faded. "But I'm afraid I'm going to have to send you away. I can't use you."

"What?" Carolyn and Steve spoke simultaneously.

Father shook his head. "There are only twelve catalogs, and each of them already *has* an apprentice. I'm sorry."

Steve looked at him, not sure whether he was serious or not. Father fluttered his hands in a "shoo" gesture. "Go on. Your aunt Mary will take you in, I think. We'll make it so that your mother died in the car alongside your father. You were badly hurt. You've been in the hospital all this time. You don't remember anything . . . do you?"

"What?" Steve looked confused. "I . . ."

"Just go." Then, in Pelapi: "I must send you into exile, that you may be the coal of her heart. No real thing can be so perfect as memory, and she will need a perfect thing if she is to survive. She will warm herself on the memory of you when there is nothing else, and be sustained."

Rubbing his neck, Steve walked down the road to the entrance to Garrison Oaks. He stopped there, looked back over his shoulder, and waved at Carolyn. She saw real longing in his face.

She waved back.

Then, without saying anything, Steve stepped out of Garrison Oaks and back into America. Carolyn, eight years old, looked up at Father and said, "Couldn't he stay? He's my best friend."

"I'm sorry," Father said. "I truly am so very sorry. It must be exactly this way, and no other." Then, lighting the coal of her heart, "But perhaps you'll see him again someday."

Carolyn, tears streaming down her cheeks, gave a fierce little nod.

When Steve was gone, Father dried her tears. He let those of them who still had houses go back to them, to get toys, or clothes, whatever they liked—but only as much as they could carry in a single trip. The twins returned with a partially burned gym bag full of G.I. Joe dolls. Michael piled his clothes into a red wagon and dragged it down the street.

Carolyn's house had been vaporized, so for her there was nothing to pack. All she had left in the world were the clothes on her back and the copy of *Black Beauty* that Steve had given her. She walked with Father to the back patio.

"I do wish they would hurry," Father said, scanning the street for returning children. "I haven't got all the time in the world. It will be suppertime soon, and I still have to punish President LeMay."

"Punish the president? Why?"

"Well, he's the one who sent the bomb. Don't you think he deserves to be punished for that?"

"Oh. Yes." She thought of her mom and dad. Her lip trembled. "Punish him how?"

"Well, for starters, he's not going to be president anymore."

"You can really do that?"

"Oh, yes. I really can."

"How?"

"Well . . . I'll tell you later. For now let's just say that the past kneels before me."

"That doesn't make any sense."

Father shrugged. "Maybe not. But it's true. Tell me, who do you think I should replace him with? Carter? Morris Udall? Jerry Brown?"

"Which one is nicest? My dad says President LeMay is a mean man."

Father considered this. "Carter, I should think."

"Make him president, then."

"Carter it is. Would you like to watch me change the past?"

Carolyn said that she would. She was about to ask if that was all, if LeMay's only punishment for killing her mom and dad was that he wasn't president anymore, but she never got the chance. *Knowing Father, though, I doubt that was all there was to it.* As she was opening her mouth to ask, David returned, lugging a suitcase almost as big as he was. Father said that he was a strong little fellow. David grinned.

When they were all back, Father led them around to the front porch and opened the door into the Library. The house seemed normal enough from the lawn, but with the door ajar the space inside seemed to loom. It was very dark. "Come in," Father said. "What are you waiting for? It's time to begin your studies."

One by one they filed in—David first, then Margaret, Peter and Richard, Jacob, Emily, Jennifer and Lisa, Michael, Alicia, and Rachel. Carolyn waited until last. Even then she hesitated at the threshold.

"Don't be afraid. It will all be OK, in the end. Come. We'll go in together, shall we?" Father reached down to her, smiling.

Still she hesitated.

"Come along," he said, wagging his hand, a don't-leave-me-hanging gesture. "Come along now."

After a long moment, Carolyn took hold of his fingers, thick and rough. She did so reluctantly, but in the end it was of her own free will. They crossed the threshold together.

"Step down into the darkness with me, child." Just that once, Father looked at her with real love. "I will make of you a God."

Chapter 14

The Second Moon

I

The entrance to the apothecary was on the onyx floor of the Library, between the catalogs of healing and mercy. Carolyn rarely came down that way. That was probably for the best—she'd lost a lot of the dead ones on the night that she projected the Library into normal space, and there wasn't anyone around to do the housework. It had been ten weeks or so since anyone tidied up, and Jennifer's shelves were cobwebby. Carolyn left footprints in the dust as she walked.

She kept a smaller version of Jennifer's medical kit in her chambers, fleshed out to suit her specific needs. Medicine was never going to be her favorite subject, but she'd been chain-smoking Marlboro reds since she was sixteen and it was starting to catch up with her. Jennifer had fixed incipient carcinomas twice, and she'd treated her own emphysema a few weeks back. What she was dealing with today was a bit more serious than cancer, though. She would need extra supplies. "Open."

The floor in front of her fell away, reassembling itself into stairs. Down below, the lamps in the hall lit themselves, lending the bronze walls a particular sort of glow. Seeing this, Carolyn winced. That glow was something she associated with Jennifer. Carolyn was no longer aging at a cellular level, but the choices she made were beginning to carve lines in her face.

The particular line that wincing brought out ran deep.

Jennifer's apothecary was a good-sized hall even by Library standards, ten acres or so. When Carolyn opened the door, a cloud of scent rolled over her—nightshade, ethyl ether, a hint of fried clams, other things. She surrendered a small, nostalgic smile. Once, late at night, she'd gone to Jennifer for an aspirin and found her just *ridiculously* stoned, frying clams over a gas burner. Jennifer had been too high to use verbs, much less track down an aspirin. After a certain amount of unintentional slapstick she managed to communicate that she thought the weed would probably help Carolyn's headache. Carolyn, desperate, had conceded a couple of puffs. To her surprise it *did* help. Also it made the clams taste fantastic. *That was a good night*, she thought. *They weren't all bad. Not all of them.*

The apothecary was a minor labyrinth of exotica. Probably there was some system to it other than "Be confusing," but Carolyn would need the map. Happily, it hung in plain sight, tacked up over Jennifer's desk in the far corner. As she made her way there she traced her fingers across the things lining her path—tiny wooden drawers filled with dried roots, a two-foot bronze sphere engraved with runes of binding, a baby stegosaurus in a tank of liquid. The stegosaurus blinked at her as she passed.

Jennifer's desk was flanked by stacks of notebooks, teetering and, to Carolyn's eye, painfully untidy. Even so, seeing them made her smile a little. Jennifer, like Father, had something of a fetish for office supplies. A Miquelrius spiral notebook lay open on her desk. Carolyn picked it up and blew off the dust, stifling a sneeze.

On the morning that Carolyn consecrated the *reissak*, Jennifer had been working on an anatomical drawing. The notebook was open to a half-finished diagram of something like a millipede with a baby elephant's torso, its musculature laid bare. Carolyn didn't recognize it. *Far future? Distant past?* Shrug. *Who knows.* Whatever *it* was, according to a note in the margin it had "hypertrophied inguinal mammae."

Whatever *that* was.

She set the notebook down, closed it, laid her hand on the cover. "I hope . . ." she began, then faltered. *What, Carolyn? What do you hope, exactly? That wherever Jennifer is now, the clams are good?* Then, suddenly furious: *Keep it to yourself. You don't have the right.*

In addition to her own first-aid supplies, she kept a fairly well-stocked resurrection kit upstairs—she'd given up on bringing Steve back, but every so often the dead ones had an accident. Today she would need other things as well. She un-tacked the map from the wall. Using it as a guide she drifted through the shadows of the apothecary gathering supplies—a Klein bottle half-filled with anaconda blood, the crystalline ash of a rare psychosis, two ounces of powdered arsenide of gallium-67. It took about an hour. When it was done she fled upstairs, not quite crying.

The floor closed behind her with a little whoosh of air. She breathed out a sigh and tilted her head back. High above, the lights of the Milky Way burned down upon her. It was getting up on lunchtime. *Maybe I'll climb up there.* She could spread out a picnic and—

No.

The word for that is "procrastination." Instead she trudged up to the ruby floor, radial seven, row sixteen.

His remains lay where they had fallen.

The wood floor was stained black with the juices of decomposition, but his body was pretty well mummified. Happily, the smell had dissipated. Yesterday, or whenever, she'd stashed a wheelbarrow there containing a keg of distilled water, two gallons of ammonia, enough food for a week or two, and a good-sized baggie of amphetamines. This was probably going to take a while.

The expression on her face when she took off her knapsack was that of a person picking up a burden rather than setting one down. It would be a spectacularly difficult resurrection, even for Jennifer, but Carolyn figured she'd make it work somehow. She always did.

Sighing again, she sat down next to the corpse and began to work.

It took longer than she thought, closer to three weeks. Maybe longer? She lost track of time—she'd been doing that a lot lately—but all the water was gone and she was almost out of amphetamines before she got a heartbeat. After a certain amount of trial and error, three days or so, she got him back to normal brain activity. Not long after that he started snoring.

Her back ached, her knees ached, even her fingers hurt. She fell back the length of half a dozen shelves and put on a plain-looking but spectacularly lethal glove she'd gotten out of David's armory. There she squatted, intending to keep an eye on him until she was certain everything between them was good. Instead she collapsed almost immediately into something between "deep sleep" and "mild coma" on the responsiveness scale. Some time later it penetrated, gradually, that someone was shaking her foot.

"Fuggoff."

Instead, he shook harder. Carolyn, remembering, jerked herself awake and held the gloved hand before her like a shield.

He stopped shaking her foot, then took half a step back and held out a steaming mug. "Hello, Carolyn."

She sniffed. *Coffee?* She eyed him warily for another moment, then lowered the glove.

"Hello, Father."

II

Normally she hated coffee, but someone had hidden her uppers while she was asleep. She took the mug, nodded thanks. "How long have you been awake?"

"Twelve hours or so. How long was I dead?"

She rubbed her eyes. "I'm really not sure. A while. Months."

He nodded. "I thought so."

"How?"

"It doesn't smell too bad. And everything's all dusty."

"Oh." A thought occurred to her. "I'm, uh, sorry about . . . you know."

"Murdering me?"

She nodded.

"Forget it. We both know I had it coming. Nicely done, though. Been a long time since someone snuck up on me like that."

"Really?" In light of Father's big Adoption Day revelation, it had crossed her mind that maybe he had let her kill him.

"Oh yeah. I know what you're thinking, but I didn't. If I'd seen it coming, I'd have shut you down. Shut you down *hard*. Nope. You got me fair and square. And you're so *young*. I wasn't expecting you to make your move for at least another fifty years. A century wouldn't have surprised me." He patted her on the shoulder, gently. "I'm really proud of you, Carolyn. I hope you don't mind me saying."

"Mind?" She thought about it. "No. I don't mind."

"So . . . who's left?"

She shook her head. "Just me."

"Oh."

"You're surprised?"

"A little. I wasn't sure you'd have the heart to . . . well. David and Margaret, sure. They wouldn't have been hard. But the others? Jennifer? *Michael?*"

Michael. Michael had always been kind to her—a rare thing in itself—but there was more to it than that. The first time David murdered her, Michael had been in Australia, but he'd known, somehow. He came back for her. He was the one to find her body. Then, after he fetched Jennifer he ducked back into the woods. At sunset he returned, this time in the company of a wolf pack and a pair of tigers. The lot of them set on David, practicing in the back field. He had to have known this was futile, had to have known that David would hurt him for the attempt, but he did it anyway. "Yeah," she said. "Even Michael. I couldn't leave any loose ends. You understand, right? The stakes were too high."

"It was the correct move. If it makes you feel any better, I arranged things so that you didn't have much choice. Knowing what you knew at the time, leaving anyone alive would have been an unacceptable risk."

"I understand that. But it doesn't help. Not really."

"No. Of course not. So . . . what? You went to Liesel?"

She shook her head. "Americans."

"Ah. Interesting approach."

"It worked well enough."

"And Steve?" Father's tone was gentle.

She didn't answer with words, only grimaced.

"Dead?"

"Yes."

"Some sort of dramatic suicide, I expect?"

She blinked. "How did you know that?"

"It's the way he's wired. His great-great-great—seventeen times great—grandmother was the same way." Father made a dramatic face and pantomimed stabbing himself in the heart. "'Free my people, Ablakha!'" He lolled his head, let his tongue hang out the side of his mouth. "Sound familiar?"

"Close enough."

"How did he do it?"

"Fire, the first time. A couple other things as well."

Father winced. "I'm sorry. That must have been hard for you."

She shrugged. "You adjust."

He nodded. "That we do. I'm still sorry." He paused. "Could you bear a little fatherly advice?"

"You're asking?"

"I am, yes. You're in charge now, Carolyn. If you want me to keep my mouth shut, just say so."

"No . . . no." She straightened. "It's gracious of you to ask, but I'll attend any lesson that Ablakha might care to give. It would be an honor." She bowed her head a little.

Father bowed back, a little deeper than she had. "How did Steve seem, the first time? With the fire? Was there something different about him?"

"Yes."

"What do you think it was?"

"He seemed . . . happy, I think. Happier than I ever saw him. Well . . . maybe not 'happy,' exactly. At peace. It was the only time I ever saw him that way."

Father nodded. "Just so. He meant well, and he was a brave boy. But if you hadn't been around, he would have found something else to martyr himself over." He watched her reaction carefully. "Or, perhaps, he would have died mourning the lack of it."

"You're saying he was born that way?"

"Partly. The potential was there. Some people have an enormous capacity for feeling guilt, deserved or otherwise. The bit with his friend dying cemented it. By the time you caught up with him, there really wasn't much to be done."

"Yes," she said. "That's one of the things I wanted to talk to you about. I've been studying. I think I can—"

"What?" Father said, gently. "Fix it? Make it so the two of you can be together?"

"No! Not like that. I mean, maybe . . . but it's not the point."

"What is the point, then?"

"He was my friend," Carolyn said softly.

"Did you try talking with him?"

She nodded.

"How did that go?"

"He was . . . kind. Compassionate, I think. That was the word he kept using, anyway. But . . ."

"But?"

She sighed. "But compassion was all there was. It wasn't like when we were kids. We didn't connect. There was this huge gap between us. We used the same words, but they meant different things, and . . . and . . . I couldn't figure out how to fix it."

"It's not surprising. The two of you had very different lives." Father's eyes went distant for a moment. "I am sorry, though. I really do know how you feel."

"What should I *do*?"

Father shook his head. "I can't answer that, Carolyn. But the way I see it, you have three options." He held up a finger. "First, you could change the past. Make it so that Steve was Pelapi all along."

"I've been thinking about that."

"And?"

"I don't know. I understand why you raised us—raised me—that way, but . . . there were times . . ."

"It was hard, I know. I'm sorry, Carolyn. It was the only way."

"I understand that, too. But I'm not sure I want to subject Steve to it. I'm not sure I want to subject *anyone* to that." She sighed. "What's the second choice?"

"You could abdicate," Father said. "Change it so that all of you were raised American. You and Steve could grow up together. Quietly. Peacefully."

She turned the notion over in her mind—what *would* happen if she was out of the picture? The Duke would move first, almost certainly. But Barry O'Shea and Liesel couldn't afford to just stand by while the Duke eliminated intelligent life—there wouldn't be anything left for them to eat. They'd pretty much have to ally against him, at least temporarily. She frowned. Either way, it wouldn't be long before people were—

She felt Father's eyes upon her. He was smiling slightly.

"Well . . . what would *you* do? If I abdicated."

Father shrugged. "I'd have to start looking for my successor again. I've looked after this world so long I don't think I could bear to know it was ruined." He flashed a small, ferocious smile. "Call me sentimental."

She blinked. "If you say so. What would it mean in practical terms?"

"Hmmm. I'm not entirely sure, to be honest. It took a long time to isolate your bloodline, and longer still to arrange for the lot of you to be in Garrison Oaks. I'd have to do something like that again." He pursed his lips. "Or I suppose I could start from scratch? Work my way up from base clay? Perhaps I could—well. Never mind. Either way, it would be more complicated this time, and your part of it would be over. All of you, I mean. On Labor Day, 1977, everyone would have a nice picnic and go home sunburned and overfed. A few days after that someone would notice that old Mr. Black has gone missing, and that would be the end of it." He looked at her. "Is that what you want?"

Once or twice, Carolyn had wondered about this. "What would we have been, do you think? Without the Library? Without you?"

"I can tell you exactly. Would you like me to?"

"Please."

"You were quiet," Father said. "A bit mousy. You and Steve were an item through high school. You took each other's virginity after your junior prom, but it didn't last." He shrugged. "Both of you ended up marrying other people. You were friends, though. You stayed in touch until your forties."

"What did I do?"

"For a living?"

She nodded.

"Actually, you were a librarian," Father said. "The American sort."

She snorted laughter. "Seriously?"

Father chuckled too. "Cross my heart. You can't make stuff like that up. You had a nice, quiet life. You worked at the University of Oregon. You were really good at office politics, but there weren't any major challenges. You got a little chubby after the second baby was born, so you took up competing in triathlons."

"What's that?"

"It's a kind of race. You swim for a while, then run, then ride a bicycle."

"Oh."

Father smirked. "Also, you studied French in your spare time."

"Ha! Was I any good?"

"Passable. Your vocabulary and grammar were decent, but your accent was atrocious. You never made it to Paris, though. Thyroid cancer, when you were fifty-nine."

"Oh." She thought about it. "What's option three?"

"You could let him go." He waited a long time, but she didn't answer. Finally, he said, "Well, you think about it. What was the other part?"

"Beg pardon?"

"You said getting a consult on Steve was part of what you wanted to talk to me about. What was the other part?"

"Oh. Right. I guess I understand what you did—training me, I mean—but I still don't understand *why*. And what do you mean when you say you're retiring? Are you, I dunno, getting an RV and going to Boca Raton or something like—"

Father laughed. "Not exactly. You said it's been, what? Six, eight months?"

"Something like that."

"What catalogs have you been focusing on?"

"The priority has been strategy and tactics. Q-33 North is in motion, and there have been some rumblings about the Forest God. He has a priestess that—well. Never mind. It's not your problem anymore."

"Any mathematics?"

"Only peripherally. Why?"

"Are you familiar with the notion of regression completeness?"

She had heard the term somewhere, but couldn't quite call up the meaning. "No."

"It's the idea that however deeply you understand the universe, however many mysteries you solve, there will always be another, deeper mystery behind it."

"Ah."

"You know I didn't create this universe, right? I left my mark on it, and I like to think I made improvements, but I was only working with rules that were in place from the third age. Light was one of my touches, and pleasure."

"We wondered," Carolyn said. "No one was sure. But if not you, who?"

Father shook his head. "I asked that same question, once. If there ever was an answer, it's been lost."

"Oh."

"Whoever it was, though . . . he was a craftsman. I've been studying his work for a long time. I've picked up some tricks"—he waved his hand, a gesture that took in the uncounted acres of books, scrolls, and folios of the Library—"but I'm no closer to understanding the whole picture than I was when I started."

"You think so?"

"I've proven it. This universe is regression complete. I'll never understand the whole thing. No one will. So I'm leaving."

"Leaving?"

"I'm creating my own universe. My place, my rules. That's my retirement."

"Sounds lonely."

Father shook his head. "I have my friends."

"Friends?"

"While you were sleeping I resurrected Nobununga. Mithraganhi as well."

Carolyn remembered Michael, speaking of his master. *You understand that Nobununga is more than just a tiger, yes?* She remembered Nobununga trudging into the *reissak*, his unshakable faith in Father. *He said Father would let no harm come to him. And, as it turned out, he was right.*

"Where are they?" She felt uneasy.

"Waiting for me," Father said, pointing at the jade staircase. "Would you like to see them?"

Carolyn thought of Mithraganhi holding out her small, bloody hand, asking, "*Moru panh ka seiter?*" *Why are you doing this to me?* She shook her head. "Probably not a good idea."

Father nodded. "I understand."

For a moment she imagined the three of them together, Father and Nobununga and Mithraganhi, hanging out, maybe playing volleyball or something. It seemed outside of his nature. But she was coming to understand that Father's nature was, perhaps, something other than what had been presented to her. "May I ask you something?"

"Sure."

"You remember the . . . the day of the bull? David?"

"Of course."

"Why were you smiling?"

Father looked at her for a long moment. "Walk with me, Carolyn." He stood, still lithe, and set out through the shelves.

Carolyn bustled to catch up. "Where are we going?"

"It's not far."

He led her out of the red catalog—David's catalog, the meditations on murder and war—and into the violet stacks. Violet was a small catalog, part of Peter's world. She wasn't even sure what sort of gem the floor was made of. Amethyst? Garnet? Tanzanite? She didn't recall ever setting foot in it before.

Father stopped at a tall dusty shelf filled with titles like *Larousse Gastronomique* and *Le Cordon Bleu at Home* and *The Joy of Cooking*. Carolyn wondered, *What the hell are we doing here?*

Father selected a three-ring binder. It was flimsy and cheap and half-hidden behind a book about Cornish pasties. The cover was stamped with the words "Charlie's Angels." It had a picture of three pretty women printed on it.

He handed the notebook to her. Something caught her eye. In the deep shadows of the Library there was a flicker of motion, a small sound.

"What's this?"

"That," Father said, "is the black folio."

Carolyn looked at him. "Seriously?" Supposedly the black folio contained instructions for altering the past. As such, its power was effectively limitless. Early on, she had spent years looking for this. She had finally concluded it didn't exist.

He nodded. "It was mis-shelved, I'm afraid. Didn't want you stumbling over it before you were ready."

She opened the binder. The pages inside were ancient vellum, and the handwriting on them was not Father's. She blinked. As she watched, the writing changed on the page. A moment later it did so again. When it did so a third time she understood that though the verses set down in the black folio did not change, the language in which they were written did. Every few seconds the ink on the page rearranged itself. First it was Arabic, then Swahili, then the poetry of storms. "Oh my God."

Father nodded. "Mine too, very possibly."

The black folio. "Who wrote this? How old is it?"

"No one knows." Father looked at her levelly. "I took it from the Emperor of the third age. It wasn't his handwriting either."

She closed it. "But what does this have to do with—"

"The reason I was smiling when we put David in the bull was because he begged."

"Oh." Her face fell.

He held up a hand. "I don't mean that the way you think."

She shook her head, confused.

"You understand that he was my son, right? I mean, you were all my children in some sense—you most of all, Carolyn—but David's mother was the only one I had actual sex with."

"Father! Ick."

"Sorry."

"But that . . . I mean . . . I guess I don't understand. Doesn't that just make it worse? What you did to him? The fact that he was your son, I mean."

"It does, yes," Father said, grave. "Much worse. Worse than you know. Worse than you *ever* know, I hope."

"Then why did you smile?"

"Because *he* begged. *You* never did. Not once."

"I might have if you'd tried to put me in that damned thing."

"No. You didn't."

"What? I don't—"

He tapped the black folio. "The past kneels before me, Carolyn."

"I still don't see—" Then she did. "David . . . was supposed to be your heir? In some . . . some other version of the past?"

"Correct."

"But . . . it didn't work out?"

"No."

"Why not?"

"Because David wasn't strong enough," Father said. "The culmination of the training was to conquer a monster. But he never could. I gave him a lot of chances. Too many. Nine times I roasted an innocent child alive so that David would have a monster to kill. Nine different times the monster won. It finally occurred to me that I was training the wrong kid." He shrugged. "So I gave the monster a shot. That day, when David begged, I knew I'd finally figured it out, finally found my heir."

"Nine times?" *The belly of the bull, glowing orange in the black of night.* "*Me?*"

"You never begged," Father said. "Not once. I still can't believe it. You don't remember, of course, but I've ridden that bull a couple of times myself." He shuddered. "Once I even roasted you two times, back to back, so you knew, really *knew*, what you were in for. I wanted to see what you would do. You just *looked* at me." He shook his head. "I still have nightmares."

"What was I like?"

"Like David," he said. "But so much worse. Worse than me, worse than the Emperor . . . worse than anything, anywhere, ever. You were a demon. A devil."

"Hmm."

He waited awhile. "Do you have any more questions?"

"No. I—" It was on the tip of her tongue to thank him, but she didn't. Not much later, she would regret that. "No."

"Then Ablakha decrees that this fourth age of the world is ended. It's all yours now, Carolyn. 'Congratulations' isn't the right word, but I know you'll do well." Father stood, dusted himself off. "And that means it's time for me to go."

Just like that? "Will I see you again?"

He shook his head. "No. Never. There is no return from where we are going."

"Oh."

Father turned and set out walking to the jade staircase, toward Nobununga and Mithraganhi and what came next for such as them.

Carolyn watched him for a few steps. He did not look back. "Wait!" Carolyn said. "There is one more thing."

"What's that?"

"How did you know? That I'd resurrect you?"

"I didn't."

"Then what—"

"I didn't *know*, Carolyn. I had faith in you." Father's eyes twinkled. "You should probably start getting used to that."

She didn't get the joke.

Father sighed. "You're a strong one, Carolyn, but would it kill you to lighten up a little, maybe just every so often?" He snapped his fingers. "Oh! I almost forgot. I left you something."

"What?"

"A surprise."

She was wary of Father's surprises. "A good one?"

He only smiled.

She watched him walk away until she was sure he couldn't hear her. Only then did she whisper, "Good-bye, Father."

She never saw him again.

III

Steve came back to life on the floor of the penthouse. He was accustomed to dying now; he had clear memories of everything up to the very last moments. Now, the apartment was thick with dust. The glass of Liquid-Plumr had partially dried up while he was away, crystallized. It sat where he had left it . . . how long ago? He remembered the flavor of it, metallic but not all *that* unpleasant, remembered also how it had boiled away in his guts. The bottom was crystallized, but there was enough floating at the top for another drink. *It's been waiting for me. Belly up to the bar, pardner!*

For some reason this struck him funny, and he giggled.

"Don't do that."

"What?" He turned to the sound of Carolyn's voice. She was perched on the granite island between the kitchen and living room like a gargoyle, smoking a cigarette.

"Don't giggle like that. You sound like Margaret."

"But I'm all *dusty*. Heh. Hee."

"It's been a while." She tossed him a pack of Marlboros, half full, and Margaret's lighter.

He caught them. "Thanks. Where's Naga?"

"She went home," Carolyn said.

"Back to Africa?"

Carolyn nodded.

"Why?"

"She wanted to be with her people. When, you know, at . . ." She trailed off.

"At the end?"

She nodded.

"Jesus, Carolyn. How bad *is* it out there?"

Carolyn was silent for a time before she answered. "Well, it's not the *end*." Then, softer, "not yet."

Steve nodded. "You haven't changed." He looked at the Liquid-Plumr, and suppressed a shudder. *Here we go again. Maybe this time I could get ahold of some explos—*

"Actually, I have." Then, following his gaze to the Liquid-Plumr, "Here." She held up a pistol. "I'll make it easy for you. Or isn't a gun horrible enough?"

"I suppose I could make it work. Am I getting through to you at all?"

She just looked at him.

Steve sat up, brushed the dust off one of the kitchen chairs, lit his cigarette. "You're getting better at the whole resurrection thing. I'm not even sore this time."

"Thanks."

He squinted at her over his Marlboro. "You do look different. How long did you say it's been?"

"Three or four months, I think. I don't keep track. Different how?"

"I'm not sure. You don't look any older."

She snubbed out her cigarette. "I wouldn't. I don't age. Not anymore. It's a trick of Father's."

"You've got a couple of lines, though." He traced his hand across her cheek.

"Yeah, well. What is it you guys say? 'It's not the years, it's the mileage'?"

Then he saw it. "I know what it is. You don't seem so angry. Well . . . grumpy, maybe. But not like you were."

"How do you mean?"

"It used to be that your eyebrows were all crushed together all the time." He made a face imitating her. "And your jaw muscles kept jumping when you thought no one was looking. Now, less so."

"Hmmm."

"So, what have you been up to?"

"This and that," she said. "Studying, at first. Thinking things over. Then I had a chat with Father."

"Seriously? I thought he was dead."

She shrugged.

"Hmm. Just a chat? Not a fight, or anything?"

"Yeah. It was pretty civil, actually. Why?"

"Well . . . I bet an argument between the two of you would be something to see. Did you ever see that movie where King Kong fought the big dinosaur?"

"I have no idea what you're talking about."

"That's a shame. I'm kind of funny."

Carolyn's brow furrowed . . . but then she relaxed. "Yeah," she said, smiling a little. "You are. I've missed that. And maybe I *am* less angry." She held her hand out for the lighter.

Steve passed it over. "That's good. You need to get stuff out of your system. If you let it fester, it'll eat you up." She was looking at him strangely. "What?"

"You're one to— Nothing."

"So . . . four months, huh?"

"Give or take."

"That's longer than the last time."

"Yeah."

"Why'd you wait?"

"I wasn't going to bring you back at all."

"Are you mad at me?"

She winced. "No. Not mad. I just . . . I didn't think I could bear it if you . . . did, you know, something. Again."

"Oh." Steve considered this. "Well . . . I'm sorry."

"It's OK. I understand why you did it. Or, I think I do, anyway." She walked around the kitchen island and fetched the copy of *Black Beauty* off the counter. "This is for you."

He took it. "This is that, whatchacallit, the token thing? From the porch? Right?"

"It is, yeah. Open it."

He handed it back to her. "I don't have to."

"What? What do you—"

"It's got my name inside the cover, right? Handwritten, in red ink. This isn't *like* the one I had, it *is* the one I had. When I was a kid, I mean. Right?"

"You remember?"

"Sort of. I dreamed about it. After the fire. The first time I, you know . . ."

"You did?"

"Yeah. And again, just now. I dreamed I was reading it in the car, on the day my parents . . . you know, the day of the wreck. Then I was handing it to this little kid I was friends with, a little girl from the neighborhood. I hadn't thought about her in years." He shook his head. "We used to talk about books and stuff. I couldn't remember her name, though." He smiled. "And then I could. You used to be so *blond*."

Carolyn smiled back. "I've changed."

"Yeah. I guess you have. Me too, for that matter. I was wondering why that one house—that one where the beagle was hanging out—looked so familiar. I didn't recognize any of the rest though."

"You wouldn't. There was a fire. Most of it's been rebuilt."

"Oh?" He frowned. "It *seems* like I remember what happened, but . . . it can't be real. *Can't* be. Your Father did something, didn't he? To my mind, my memory."

"He did, yeah."

"So what really happened? Wait! No." He rubbed his temples. "On second thought, don't tell me. Whatever happened, I bet I was a huge asshole in some way."

Carolyn blinked. "No. You weren't an asshole. Not at all. You really couldn't be more wrong."

He looked up, not sure whether to believe her.

Carolyn's expression was gentler than he had ever seen it. "I have a proposal for you, Steve. What if I told you that there was a way to make it all better?"

Steve gave her a sharp look. "What exactly are we talking about?"

"The sun," she said. "The earthquakes. Everything."

"You're going to put what's-her-name back?"

"Not exactly. I really can't do that. Mithraganhi is with Father now."

"Dead, you mean?"

"No. Not dead. They went away. Mithraganhi, Nobununga, Father. We won't see them again."

Steve raised his eyebrows. "What do you mean, 'away'?"

"A new universe, I think. One Father created. One where he makes all the rules."

Steve shook his head. "You guys really are playing at just a completely other level. You know that?"

"Well . . . you might be surprised. I'm really not that different from you. Anyone could have done what I did."

"You know, I really doubt that."

She stood quiet for a long moment, looking down. Then, softly, "It has a price, though. In the service of my will, I have emptied myself."

Steve nodded. "Yeah. I get that, too."

She looked at him. "Do you? Do you really?"

"Yeah. I really do."

Carolyn smiled. "You know, I believe that you do. Thank you." She reached out and touched his cheek. Her fingertips were warm. For some reason this surprised him. "But I will be wiser than that."

"Yeah?"

"Yeah." She let her hand drop. "I'm going to fix it, Steve. I should have listened to you. You were right all along."

He raised an eyebrow. "Oh? You're going to bring the sun back?"

She nodded. "By this time tomorrow it will be just the way it used to be."

"I thought you said it was impossible. That David couldn't—"

"David is gone. I let him die."

"What? When?"

"A couple of hours ago."

"What about your whole revenge thing?"

She shrugged. "I've had enough revenge. I'm done."

"Well . . . yay you, I guess. But if he's not the sun, then how do you—"

She looked at him. "I found another way."

"Wow. That's great, Carolyn. Really. But what about outside? There's a famine, right? People are still starving. And that volcano, and—"

"It's not quite that bad, not yet. And I won't let it get any worse. I spoke with the volcano under Yellowstone and calmed him down. As far as the famine . . . there's a trick I know. A way to make a sort of bread out of clouds. It takes a lot of energy and a little time, but I have both. By the time the sun comes up tomorrow food will be falling down from the sky. All over the world. And I'll do that every couple of days until the crops come back."

"Seriously?"

She nodded.

"And the Library? The earthquakes?"

"The Library is back in hiding. The earthquakes will cease. I've put the moon back in its old orbit—the tides will normalize. Soon."

"Carolyn . . . that's . . . that's fantastic. But *why*?"

"Because of you, Steve. Because of what you did."

"Me? What the hell did *I* do?"

"You were my friend," she said. "That's what. And you were a really, really good one. The best I'll ever have. Not just mine, either."

Carolyn cupped her hands in front of her as if to drink. Mist rose from her palms, coalesced into a sphere. It took a moment for him to recognize it as the Earth, only basketball-sized and seen from below—Antarctica on top, South America below, clouds, oceans. It hovered inches above her palm, turning slowly. Squinting, he saw the tiny contrail of a jet over the Pacific.

"Look, Steve. Right here. Billions of people. They're going to be OK now. As OK as they ever were, anyway. You have my word. I'm going to make it all better. Because of you."

Steve looked. He stretched his hand out to touch, then thought better of it. He looked at Carolyn, still not understanding. Her eyes were shiny.

"You saved them," she said. "Every last one of them. Naga. *Petey*. You saved them all. Just you."

"Really?"

"Yeah."

Steve smiled.

A single tear broke and ran down Carolyn's cheek.

"Carolyn, why are you—"

She took her hands away. Earth hung there, unsupported now, still spinning. Steve watched, fascinated, as the contrail of the jet grew a tiny fraction of an inch.

Saved them? Me? In his mind's eye, just for a moment, he saw Jack stepping out of the shadows into sunlight.

Carolyn stepped around to the side and whispered in his ear, speaking the word that Father whispered to Mithraganhi so very long ago when he called forth the dawn of the fourth age.

For Steve, hearing this . . .

. . . time . . .

. . . stopped.

IV

S teve floated weightless in the kitchen of the penthouse. Carolyn fished a dusty club soda out of the refrigerator and sat down at the kitchen table. She didn't touch her drink, but she smoked cigarettes slowly, one after another. Sometimes she didn't inhale, just let them burn down to a teetering column of ash.

By the time the pack was empty, Steve's head was encased in a sphere of boiling energy—yellow-orange, just like the former sun. His connection to the plane of joy was very strong. If anything, he would burn even brighter than had Mithraganhi. She might have to fold space a little so that he didn't cook Mercury to a cinder.

She untied one of Steve's shoelaces and, using it as a leash, carried him through the great hall, up the stairs to the jade platform under the universe. David's body was there, bloody, under a plastic sheet. His pain was in the past now. Later, she would have the dead ones carry him down. She would find whatever was left of Margaret and wrap them in a single shroud. She would bury them together.

She set Steve in the heavens, then adjusted the orbits to the way things had been, before. She didn't even have to use a calculator. *I'm getting the hang of this.*

She had a great deal to do, but she didn't want to be in the Library anymore. Not today. The bombing had reduced Garrison Oaks to rubble, and it was surrounded by tanks, soldiers, but the Library had other doors, other facades. She chose a farmhouse in Oregon, a quiet place at the far end of a long road.

In this new place she went to the kitchen and made coffee. Unthinking, she picked up the plates and cups, washed them. When that was done she went into the bathroom—it took her a minute to find it—and drew a very hot bath. The tub's backsplash was lime-green tile, and the faucets were stiff with disuse. *It's clean, though.*

A long time later she got out of the tub and dried herself. Steve hadn't dawned yet, and it was a trifle chilly—something like ten below. She didn't know how to turn on the furnace. But looking through the closet she found a pink terrycloth robe hanging there, waiting for her. It was brand-new, with the tags still attached, just her size. It had almost certainly been hanging there since the beginning. She shook her head. *Father.*

On the floor below the robe she found a box containing a pair of overstuffed slippers. The slippers were ridiculous—the stuffed head of some cartoon cat was mounted over the toes, grinning. She examined them, bemused. *Father really* did *have a sense of humor. Who knew?* But silly though they might be, they were also soft and warm.

She put them on, then went and stood at the back window. It looked out over a broad field, white with snow. There was a barn, and a small stream.

She blinked.

On the far side of this field, a man stood, almost hidden in the forest. She blinked again. "That's impossible," she said, remembering the smoking, perforated ruin of Mrs. McGillicutty's house.

Then Father's voice came to her. *"I almost forgot. I left you something."* And another man's voice, hesitant and soft. *"I was with . . . with . . . the small things. Father* said. *Father said to study the ways of the humble and the small."*

And David. *"Maybe a mouse could have snuck out. Not much else."*

She went to the back door, not quite running, and threw it open. "Michael!"

He came to her, flanked on his left by a cougar and his right by three wolves. They stopped just outside the yard. Michael stared at her, wide-eyed, and called her by Father's old title. "Sehlani?"

Carolyn opened her mouth to deny it, then shut it again and, after a long pause, surrendered the smallest possible fraction of a nod.

Michael spoke to the wolves and the cougar, and all of them lay on their backs in the snow, showing her their bellies.

Carolyn stared at him, aghast. "No! Don't! What are you doing? Get up!"

But he wouldn't. He lay on his back, trembling and afraid. He wouldn't meet her eyes.

She plowed through the snow to him, the yellow eyes of her cartoon cat poking up through the crust. She clouted him in the ear—gently. "Get up, Michael. Please get up. It's only me."

Michael stood slowly. "You . . . what you did . . . you . . ."

"I'm so sorry, Michael. I had to. There was no other way. Don't you see?"

He looked at her for a long time, doubtful. He didn't answer.

Desperate, she smiled, then touched his cheek. "It's freezing out. Are you hungry? Any of you? You should all come inside. There might be food, or . . ."

Michael considered this for a moment then, slowly, he smiled back. Seeing this, something in Carolyn unclenched. Michael turned to the wolves. He spoke to them. She didn't quite understand it, but they wagged their tails.

She led them into the house.

It turned out that there *was* food in the refrigerator, lots of it, five roasts of beef and a whole turkey. Michael and the animals ate hugely, then huddled together and went to sleep in front of the bay window in the living room. Carolyn pulled a pillow onto the floor and sat with them.

Then, for the first time in a very long while, the sun rose. Under its orange glow the shadows of Michael and his pack stretched long across the floor.

Seeing the angle of the sunrise, she thought *the American word for this time of year is "April" or, sometimes, "spring."* That was true, but it was also true that in the calendar of the librarians it was the second moon, which is the moon of kindled hope. Carolyn, clean and warm, sat watch over her sleeping friends. The pink cotton of her robe lay soft against her skin. The stuffed heads of the cartoon-cat slippers covered her toes. She sat this way for a time, watching as the new sun began to melt away the gray ice of the long winter.

She was smiling.

So, What Ended Up Happening with Erwin?

The shit that landed Erwin in prison took place in the span of a single sweaty afternoon, but it ended up costing him ten years, minus time off for good behavior. This was just after the air raid on the pyramid, around the time that food was starting to get seriously scarce. There was a trial, but it only lasted about a week. After that he went straight to USP Big Sandy, a federal high-security prison in Kentucky. Erwin was surprised to discover he didn't mind prison.

For starters, the pressure was off. He'd sweated for a week or two before he finally took his hostage, wondering whether it was the right thing to do, worrying about, well, ending up in prison. Now that it was over and the deed was done, he could relax. *Really* relax. For the first time in years, there was nothing left to worry about.

Life in Big Sandy had a regimented quality that sort of reminded him of basic training. He'd made a deal to keep his mouth shut about what he'd actually done in exchange for a relatively lenient sentence. The ten years sounded like a lot, but on the whole it could have been a lot worse. The president assured him they'd find a way to make it "life without parole" in Supermax if he gave them any crap. Jail was surprisingly comfortable. Not a luxury hotel, mind you, but his cell was newish and clean, and he had it to himself. Most everybody had seen the Natanz movie or read the book or whatever, so they knew who he was. In exchange for Erwin dropping an occasional war story, one of the guards, a card-carrying Natanz fanboy named Blakely, made runs to Barnes & Noble. Dashaen, the kid Erwin had taught to fight, was now in his twenties and a successful bond trader. He insisted on paying for the books, and also put a couple hundred into Erwin's commissary account every month. Erwin appreciated everyone going to the trouble. Also it was nice to have some way to pass the time besides jacking off.

A couple of the other prisoners tested him, of course. Erwin understood. They had tested fucking Mike Tyson when he was inside. One guy tried to take his pillowcase, so Erwin knocked out his fillings. A couple of days later the guy's buddy, an Alabama weight lifter, came by to talk it over. Erwin hit the second guy so hard that for a couple of weeks he thought people were reading his thoughts. Actually he was muttering to himself without realizing it. He had brain swelling, or some shit. Erwin felt bad about it, but the big fella had rushed him. Listening to him think out loud *was* sort of comical, though. He got real excited when it was banana-pudding night in the cafeteria and made a lot of mental notes about who to jack off to when everyone was watching TV in the commons area. It cleared up after a couple of weeks, though, and after that everybody was polite to Erwin.

Other than that, it was pretty peaceful. He got to Kentucky just after the sun came back, but for the first couple of weeks all the prisoners were still on food rations. Six hundred calories a day didn't leave you much energy to go starting shit. By the time that bread stuff started falling out of the sky, guards and prisoners alike had more or less concluded that the smartest thing to do with Erwin was let him be.

That suited Erwin fine.

As a new prisoner, he wasn't supposed to get mail for the first two months. But one of the guards knew of him from Afghanistan and another had actually been there at Natanz. They accidentally dropped off letters from Thorpe, Dashaen, other guys he had served with. They didn't know the full story, of course, but their faith in Erwin was absolute.

It was kinda nice.

So he had mail, he had books, he had a place to himself when he wanted it and people to play chess or whatever with when he didn't. Admittedly the food sucked, but whatcha gonna do? On the whole, he was content with his lot in life.

Tonight, though, lights-out snuck up on him. He was reading a new

book he'd been looking forward to—*To the Nines*, the next Stephanie
Plum—and he'd lost track of time. The guard, Blakely, had popped an
eyebrow when Erwin asked him to pick up *that* particular title. Erwin explained that one of the perks of being a Medal of Honor winner was that
he could read whatever the fuck he wanted to. Anyway, fucking Janet
Evanovich was fucking funny as fuck. Blakely, cowed, asked if he could
borrow it when Erwin was done. Erwin said sure.

He'd been planning to hand it over the next day, but he'd gotten a let-
ter from Dashaen today, and he spent half an hour answering that, and
so had ten pages left when it got dark. He gave a moment's thought to
trying to read by the light spilling in through the observation slit in his
door—the book was good, and he'd just put in a fresh chew—then decided against it. Instead, he folded down one of the pages and put the
book on the floor next to his bunk.

As he was setting down the book, someone grabbed his wrist.

Erwin didn't yell, but it was a near thing. He twisted around to peer
over the edge of the bunk. There was just enough light to see that there
was an arm coming up out of the floor.

"Da fuck?"

Erwin pulled hard, twisting, trying to break the hold on his wrist, but
the angle was bad and whoever—whatever—it was, was *strong*. A moment later, the tip of another hand popped up through the floor. With
a motion like someone pulling themselves out of a swimming pool, it
gripped the concrete and pulled.

A woman's head rose up through the concrete. She let go of Erwin's
wrist and, pushing against the concrete, muscled her torso up out of the
floor. She pulled her legs up—*nice legs*, Erwin thought disjointedly—and
stood.

"Hello, Erwin."

He squinted forward, then leaned back with a sigh. "Ah, shit. It's you,
ain't it?"

"Yeah," Carolyn said. "What are you doing in here? It took me forever to track you down."

Erwin thought of mentioning that he might have asked her the same
thing, but decided against it. "Eh," he said, sitting up. "You know how

it is. I kind of roughed a guy up a little bit. Nothing much, just a couple cracked teeth, but"—shrug, spit—"he took offense."

Carolyn furrowed her brow, confused. "I don't see why that's such a big deal. It's part of your shtick, right?"

"This particular guy was the president." Seeing the look on her face, he added, "The new one. Not the head."

"Oh." She thought about this for a couple of seconds. "Why'd you hit him?"

"He kept squirming. I was afraid the gun was gonna go off."

"Gun? Did you kill him?"

"Nah, just the teeth. Plus I held him hostage for, like, three or four hours."

"Oh. What happened then?"

"He caved. I knew he would." Erwin spat in his cup. "Pussy."

"What do you mean, 'caved'?"

"Well," Erwin said, "I was kinda blackmailing him. I told him if he didn't launch a couple of missiles, I was gonna spray his brains over all the nice woodwork. He thought about it for a little while, and then he launched 'em."

"At who?"

"Well . . . you."

"Really? Me? Why?"

Erwin sat up on his bunk and turned to look at her face. His eyes were adjusting to the dark. "That Steve kid told me what he was gonna do if our air raid didn't work. Which, you know, obviously it didn't. I gave it a week after that to see if he could convince you to un-fuck stuff, but no change." Erwin paused. "Did he really go through with it? The Everclear and . . . you know."

"The lighter," Carolyn said. "Yeah. He did."

"Damn." Erwin was quiet for a moment. "Well . . . whether he had or not, it was obvious it didn't work. I couldn't see that we had much else left to try. The president didn't agree, though. He said he was 'exploring other options.' Maybe. But I'm pretty sure he was just worried about getting re-elected." Erwin shrugged. "After a while I got sick of arguing about it."

Carolyn stared at him. "So you blew up Mount Char? You *nuked* it?"

"I blew up what?"

"Come again?"

"You said I blew up . . . 'Mount Char'?"

"Did I?"

"Yeah."

"Huh." She smiled a little.

"Yeah, I'm lost."

"What? Oh. Sorry. When we were kids, me and Steve used to have all these nicknames for things. Secret names, you know, the way kids have. We even drew a map. Scabby Flats and Cat Splash Creek and like that. Mount Char was Father's house."

"Any particular reason?"

"You know, I don't—" She snapped her fingers. "Actually, I *do* remember. Steve told you about Father, right?"

"Some."

"Bear in mind, back then, we thought Father was just a regular guy. You'd see him outside every so often, but he never really socialized. I get it now—boy, do I ever—but at the time it was weird. People would invite old Mr. Black to come hang out, have a beer, but he always said the same thing: 'I'll be along once I get a good char on this pork.' Every time. The grown-ups made fun of him for it. And his house was on top of a pretty steep hill. So to Steve and me, his place was Mount Char. Back before the Library and . . . all the other stuff. When we were just kids and . . . you know . . . everything was OK." Carolyn smiled. To Erwin she looked wistful but not especially unhappy. Then she snapped back to herself. "Well, it made sense at the time. I wonder what made me think of that now. I haven't called it that in ages."

"I dunno," Erwin said, even though he thought he might have a guess.

"And you blew it up? *Nuked* it?"

"Kinda, yeah." Erwin looked at her. "You didn't notice? They was all direct hits. Twenty megatons, total. You could see the mushroom cloud two states away."

"Sorry, no. I must have missed it." She gave him an apologetic look. "I've been really busy."

"'s OK." Erwin's brow wrinkled. "I figured you was here to kill me. Revenge or whatever. But maybe that *ain't* it."

"Kill you? Don't be ridiculous."

"What, then?"

"I'm here to offer you a job, Erwin."

"Come again?"

"You've already been a big help. And there's plenty more to be done."

"Thanks, but I've kinda had my fill of shooting people."

"That's not what I had in mind. Well, maybe not *never*, but it wouldn't be the main point."

"What, then?"

"Odds and ends. Errands. Things I'm not good at."

"Such as?"

"The first thing I had in mind is that I want you to look for a dog."

"A *dog?* There's fucking dogs everywhere."

"No, I mean a particular dog. I really need to find him—I promised— but me and dogs don't get along."

"Oh. Which one?"

"His name's Petey. He's a cocker spaniel."

"I don't know no cocker spaniels named Petey."

"Probably he's also dead."

Long pause. "Are you fucking with me?"

"I would never, ever do that, Erwin."

Then, from the stainless-steel toilet, a man's voice. "Sheee would not. Carolyn like you."

"What the *fuck?*"

"That's my brother. His name is Michael." Then, softly, "His English isn't great, but he's trying. Be patient, OK?"

"Yeah, sure," Erwin whispered back. Then, in a normal voice, "Well, I'll be happy to look around the cell, but if he ain't in here I prolly won't be much help." He jerked a thumb at the cell door. "That's locked, ya know."

"Don't be thick, Erwin. Of course I'll get you out. I'll do that even if you don't take the job—I certainly owe you that much. But there are other benefits as well. I could teach you things."

"Things?"

She nodded. "*Interesting* things. Lots of them, actually. I have a library now."

He chewed this over for a second. "Maybe you'd start by telling me what the fuck you did at that bank? How you made them tellers be so helpful?"

"Sure, if you—"

The man's voice again, rapid-fire blabber in some language Erwin didn't recognize.

"*Cha guay,*" Carolyn said.

"*Aru penh ta*—"

"*Cha* guay," Carolyn said, more firmly this time. The toilet fell silent.

"What was that all about?"

"He says they're coming."

Erwin heard a rumbling out in the hall, a huge noise, like the sound the World Trade Center towers made when they collapsed. Then, screams. Through the window slit, he saw a cloud of gray dust rolling down the hall.

Carolyn grimaced. "Decide now, Erwin. I'll do whatever you like, but I really do need to go. Are you coming?"

Erwin thought about it for about half a second. "Fuck yeah. Sign me up."

"Do you need to bring anything?"

"Nope. Well"—he grabbed the Evanovich—"just this."

Carolyn smiled. "You're going to fit right in. Here, take my hand."

Erwin did. Out in the hall he heard a groan of wrenching steel. "So . . . you said 'they're coming.' Who's 'they'?"

"I'm not completely sure yet. My Father had enemies. Some of them are my enemies too, now. They've begun to move against me."

"Dangerous folks? Dangerous like you, I mean?"

"Some of them, yeah."

"Hmmm."

"Don't worry," Carolyn said. "I have a plan."

Acknowledgments

Over the years I've received help and encouragement from more people than I have room to list. Every single bit of it was appreciated. If you don't see your name here but should, I apologize.

First and foremost, my wife, Heather, is a really, really good first reader. She sees when something isn't working and she's not scared to kick my ass until I see it too. Every writer should be so lucky.

I attended the Taos Toolbox writing workshop in 2011. That experience has been a huge influence on everything I've written since, and I recommend it unreservedly to all aspiring fantasists. I am grateful to all my fellow attendees for their thoughtful and honest feedback on the first couple of chapters. Jim Strickland, Fiona Lehn, and Carole Ann Moleti later went so far as to provide feedback on a full draft. The instructors, Walter Jon Williams and Nancy Kress, are gifted teachers and generous people. Thank you all.

The community of writers—internet and physical—is solid and supportive. I've lost track of the number of times that I've been given lengthy and detailed critiques by people I've never met and probably will never meet. Online resources such as absolutewrite.com and sff.onlinewriting workshop.com have also been especially helpful to me. Check out Jim MacDonald's "Learn Writing with Uncle Jim" thread on absolutewrite .com in particular. There are also a lot of industry professionals out there who volunteer their expertise via blogs, interviews, and whatnot to teach aspiring writers how not to shoot themselves in the foot as badly or as often as they otherwise might.

My buddy Lt. Col. Jason Barnhill, PhD, has read every single one of my unpublished manuscripts over the years. He was polite and supportive even back when I was struggling to make the leap from soul-wrenchingly godawful to merely terrible. Thanks, dude—next time I see you, dinner's on me.

Brett Meyer and Steven Wright read and provided feedback on an early draft of the manuscript. Thanks, guys!

My agent, Caitlin Blasdell, is both a dazzlingly effective professional and also an unfailingly pleasant and gracious person. Years before I was a client, she sent me a really nice this-won't-do-but-try-me-with-your-next-one note that was enormously encouraging at the time and is still much appreciated. She smoothed out the rough edges of this manuscript and generally saved me from myself in a variety of ways. I'm lucky to know her. Thanks, Caitlin!

Last, but most definitely not least, as an aspiring writer I would occasionally daydream about what the process of professional publication would be like. The answer is: it's great. My editor, Julian Pavia, and the other folks I've dealt with at Crown have impressed me in one way or another with every single communication. Thanks, guys—it's been a privilege and a real pleasure.